C000108577

For John

THE BORROWED RING

GINA WILKINS

Harlequin
Mills & Boon

Special
Edition

DID YOU PURCHASE THIS BOOK WITHOUT A COVER?
If you did, you should be aware it is **stolen property** as it was
reported 'unsold and destroyed' by a retailer.
Neither the author nor the publisher has received any payment
for this book.

First Published 2005
First Australian Paperback Edition 2005
ISBN 0 733 56568 9

THE BORROWED RING © 2005 by Gina Wilkins
Philippine Copyright 2005
Australian Copyright 2005
New Zealand Copyright 2005
Except for use in any review, the reproduction or utilisation of this work in
whole or in part in any form by any electronic, mechanical or other means,
now known or hereafter invented, including xerography, photocopying and
recording, or in any information storage or retrieval system, is forbidden
without the permission of the publisher, Harlequin Mills & Boon, Locked Bag
7002, Chatswood D.C. N.S.W., Australia 2067.

All the characters in this book have no existence outside the imagination of
the author, and have no relation whatsoever to anyone bearing the same
name or names. They are not even distantly inspired by any individual
known or unknown to the author, and all the incidents are pure invention.

This book is sold subject to the condition that it shall not, by way of trade or
otherwise, be lent, resold, hired out or otherwise circulated without the prior
consent of the publisher in any form of binding or cover other than that in
which it is published and without a similar condition including this condition
being imposed on the subsequent purchaser.

All rights reserved including the right of reproduction in whole or in part in
any form. This edition is published by arrangement with Harlequin
Enterprises II B.V.

Published by
Harlequin Mills & Boon
3 Gibbes Street
CHATSWOOD NSW 2067
AUSTRALIA

HARLEQUIN MILLS & BOON SPECIAL EDITION and the Rose Device are
trademarks used under license and registered in Australia, New Zealand,
Philippines, United States Patent & Trademark Office and in other countries.

Printed and bound in Australia by
McPherson's Printing Group

GINA WILKINS

is a bestselling and award-winning author who has written more than seventy books for Harlequin Mills and Boon. She credits her successful career in romance to her long, happy marriage and her three "extraordinary" children.

A lifelong resident of central Arkansas, Ms. Wilkins sold her first book to Harlequin in 1987 and has been writing full-time since. She has appeared on the Waldenbooks, B. Dalton and *USA TODAY* bestseller lists. She is a three-time recipient of the Maggie Award for Excellence, sponsored by Georgia Romance Writers, and has won several awards from the reviewers of *Romantic Times*.

You are invited....

It's Jared and Cassie Walker's
twenty-fifth wedding anniversary
and you are cordially invited
to the biggest bash in Texas!

After decades of caring and support
for their friends and family,
we want to honour these two lovebirds.

So come one, come all to celebrate on the
Walker Ranch, Saturday, October 15!

RSVP with Molly and Shane Walker

Chapter One

B.J. Samples. Private investigator extraordinaire.

Almost strutting with pride, she climbed out of her rental car and approached the Missouri farmhouse that lay at the end of a long, wide driveway. Actually *farmhouse* did not do the structure justice. This was practically a mansion. Pillars, dormers, balconies. Fountains and a swimming pool and detached pool house. Landscaping that looked like a photograph from a home-and-garden magazine. There was even a private airstrip behind the house.

Having come from a childhood of poverty and homelessness, Daniel Castillo—now known as Daniel Andreas—had apparently done quite well for himself.

He had not, however, been an easy man to find. She had spent the past week trying to track him down, finally getting a lead that had brought her to this spreading east Missouri farm an hour's drive from St. Louis. It hadn't been effortless, but she had gotten the information. And she couldn't wait to boast about it to her three uncles who owned the private investigation agency that employed her.

Her confident steps slowed as she approached the front door. She had the oddest feeling that she was being watched. She glanced around and saw no one, not even in the many highly polished windows at the front of the house.

Maybe it was just an attack of nerves. After all, she didn't usually do fieldwork. Computer searches were her specialty. The only reason she had been sent on this trip was because it was a low-priority assignment. One that could hardly get her into any trouble.

Maybe it was the place itself that was getting to her. Her hand wasn't quite steady when she reached for the doorbell. Was it any wonder? The only mansion she had ever visited regularly in her middle-class upbringing was her wealthy aunt Michelle's. Yet with Tony and Michelle's four children and assortment of pets, that sprawling estate had always been homey and welcoming.

She glanced down at her olive-green camp shirt and khaki pants. Perhaps she should have dressed more professionally. But it was too late for that now. The front door opened, and a very large, very bald man in a shiny gray jacket, a pale blue shirt and sharply creased jeans growled, "Yes?"

He didn't look like a butler. Nor a farmer, for that matter. He looked more like a bouncer in a low-rent strip joint. Not that she'd ever actually been in a place like that. Drawing herself to her full five feet three inches— still a foot shorter than this man—B.J. tried to speak confidently. "I'm looking for Daniel Andreas. Is he here?"

The man's heavy eyebrows rose toward his shaved pate. "Daniel Andreas?"

Never known as a particularly patient woman, B.J. swallowed a sigh. "That's what I said."

Comprehension seemed to light in his dull brown eyes. "Oh! You made it. I'm sure he'll be pleased. Come in."

She didn't have a clue what he was talking about. "I don't—"

"Daniel!" the man bellowed, practically hauling her inside. He glanced toward the staircase. "Oh, there you are. Look who's here. Your missus."

B.J. glanced in the same direction, then simply stared. She had wondered how Daniel would look in person after thirteen years. Now she knew.

He looked fantastic.

For a moment he stared back at her, no expression at all on his incredibly handsome face. She doubted sincerely that he recognized her. It had been too long, and she was sure she had not made the impression on him back then that he had on her.

Before she could speak, he was coming toward her with swift, graceful movements that were vaguely feline. Just a bit predatory. The smile that lit his face was blinding, but she had a moment to notice that his obsidian eyes were deadly serious before he grabbed her and yanked her toward him. "Darling! I'm so glad you could make it after all."

A moment later his mouth was on hers in a kiss hot enough to melt the soles of her leather sandals.

When the kiss ended, he didn't give her a chance to speak—even if she had been able to, which certainly wasn't guaranteed just then. Gripping her shoulders hard enough to leave fingerprints, he looked at the bald man, who hovered nearby with an oddly sentimental smile on his broad face. "Bernard, would you give us a minute alone? We have some catching up to do."

Bernard? B.J. found herself mentally repeating. Was that really that man's name?

The big man nodded. "You and the missus can use that little parlor just behind you. You won't be disturbed. I'll let you know when we have to go. In the meantime, I'll call the boss and tell him your wife will be joining us, after all."

"Oh, but—"

Daniel's fingers dug more sharply into B.J.'s shoulders, causing her words to end in a gasp. "Yes, do that," he said to the other man.

Bernard was frowning at B.J. "Something wrong, Mrs. Andreas?"

She glanced up at Daniel in bewilderment. The look

he gave her in return had her turning back to Bernard with a strained smile. "I just need to talk to my, er, to Daniel in private for a moment."

The large man's face cleared, his somewhat scary-looking smile returning. "Right this way, ma'am."

He ushered them into an elegantly furnished little parlor and closed the door behind him to leave them alone.

B.J. whirled immediately to face Daniel, making no effort now to hide her outrage. "What the hell was that?"

"Please keep your voice down." He had dropped the smile, and his face was an expressionless mask again as he studied her. "You have no idea how you've complicated everything."

Her jaw almost dropped. *She* had complicated everything? Had she just walked into an expensive madhouse?

Because she needed a moment to collect herself or she would end up shrieking at him, she studied the man who stood in front of her, comparing him to the boy she had once briefly known. He had fascinated her when she was fourteen and he was sixteen. Even then he had been striking looking, with his thick black hair, classic features and lazy-lidded dark eyes.

Some of her cousins had been a little afraid of his flash-point temper, but B.J. never had been. There had been something about him that had drawn her into girlish daydreams and amorous fantasies. He had been her first big crush, and she had never forgotten him.

Now he was a man of almost thirty. Still handsome

but seemingly more comfortable in his skin now. The jeans, T-shirt and boots of his youth had been traded for a dark jacket that must have cost a small fortune, worn over an open-necked white shirt, charcoal slacks and expensive-looking shoes.

He looked rich, powerful and more than just a little dangerous. Still, she refused to let him see that she was at all intimidated.

Lifting her chin, she placed her hands on her slim hips and spoke firmly. "Obviously there has been some mistake. I don't know who you and Bernard were expecting, but you have the wrong person. My name is—"

"Brittany Samples," he cut in coolly. "I recognized you as soon as you walked in."

For the second time since she arrived, he had rendered her speechless. How on earth had he identified her that quickly? It had been more than a dozen years, for crying out loud. The last time he had seen her, she had been a shy fourteen-year-old with braces and no figure at all.

Well, okay, she still didn't have much of a figure. She had long ago given up on naturally growing big breasts or voluptuous hips. But still, she was a grown woman of twenty-seven now. She wore her brown hair layered in a choppy short cut that she'd been told was flattering to her lamentably gamine face and she had applied her makeup in a way that played up her blue eyes.

The fact that she had recognized *him* so easily didn't lessen her surprise. After all, she had been expecting to find him. She had a fairly recent snapshot of him in her wallet. And she had carried a mental picture at the back of her mind for years. She doubted he could say the same about her.

Finally recovering, she stammered slightly when she said, "I, um, really didn't expect you to know me. How did you—"

He made a silencing movement with his right hand. "We don't have time for this now. We've got to figure out how to get you out of this mess you've created without putting either of us in any more danger."

"The mess *I've* created?" she repeated incredulously. And then the rest of his words registered. "Danger?"

Daniel put a hand to the back of his neck and squeezed, his brow creased in concentration. "Maybe we should tell them…"

"The truth?" she suggested when his words faded.

"That's not going to work."

"Look—" She took a step toward him, bringing her close enough to jab a finger of her left hand into his chest. "I don't know what's going on here, but I've had enough. All I came here to do was—"

He caught her hand in his, absently pulling it away from his chest but not releasing her. "Bernard thinks you're my wife. If he has any reason to suspect either of us is not who we've said, he'll kill us. And, by the way, he's not the only armed guard surrounding us. The house is crawling with them—and every one of them answers to him."

She felt her stomach clench. "I don't believe you."

"Believe it, Brittany."

Focusing on that name rather than the fear that was suddenly trying to overtake her, she scowled. "I answer to B.J. Any husband worth his salt would know that."

Ignoring her heavily sarcastic remark, he continued, "We don't have much time, so you must listen. How did you get here?"

"I drove from St. Louis. Why?"

"Your own car or a rental?"

"A rental. I don't—"

He seemed to be concentrating on his own thoughts rather than her attempts to turn the questioning back on him. "Do you have any luggage with you?"

"No, I left it all at my hotel. Daniel—"

He studied her left hand, which he still held. "No rings. Not married?"

"No." She couldn't help noticing the gold band on his left hand. "So where is your real wife?"

"I'll explain later." Reaching inside the collar of his white shirt, he fished out a thin gold chain, which he swiftly unfastened. A moment later he had her left hand in his again. His eyes locked with hers as he slid a ring onto her finger.

Dazed, she looked down at the simple, aged-looking gold ring. "This is a wedding ring," she said stupidly.

A sharp rap on the door barely gave warning of Bernard's abrupt entrance. He caught them still standing close together, seemingly holding hands. "Sorry to interrupt the reunion, but we really have to get under way."

"There has been a problem, Bernard. My wife was just telling me she can't join us." Daniel's voice held a touch of regret as he slipped an arm around her shoulders.

Bernard's heavy face settled into a frown. "What's the problem?"

"Her luggage has been misplaced by the airline. The only garments she has with her are the ones she's wearing." He spoke so smoothly B.J. almost believed him herself.

Bernard scanned her casual camp shirt and khakis, nodding as if something had just been explained to him. "That's not a problem. You can buy everything she needs when we get there. We've got several of those fancy boutiques the ladies like."

After only a momentary pause, Daniel said, "She has some things in her luggage that have sentimental value. She's reluctant to leave without tracking it down."

His frown deepening, Bernard shifted restlessly. Suspiciously. The movement made his ill-fitting jacket gap just enough for B.J. to catch a glimpse of the shoulder holster beneath. "I'm sure the boss can take care of everything. Why don't we get going and I'll make some calls on the way."

B.J. thought she detected the slightest hint of apology in the look Daniel gave her then. "There's really no need to go to that much trouble. You have our home address on your luggage tags, don't you, sweetheart?"

Remembering the chilling sight of Bernard's weapon, B.J. nodded mutely.

"Then I'm sure it will all be sent to our home as soon as it turns up. In any event, there's really nothing all that valuable involved, is there?"

She shook her head, as he clearly expected of her.

Daniel gave her an encouraging smile.

Bernard's face cleared. "That's okay, then. You'll see, Mrs. Andreas. Everything's going to work out just fine."

She wished she could believe that.

Daniel could almost feel months of scheming crashing around his ears. Not to mention that his life was pretty much flashing in front of his eyes. One significant memory from his past had apparently materialized and was now sitting right next to him on Judson Drake's private jet.

She looked pale, he noted. And no wonder. Her head was probably spinning.

He knew his was.

He had thought himself prepared for any eventuality on this trip. He had not been at all prepared for Brittany Jeanne Samples to walk through that door—and directly into his arms.

She hadn't really changed in thirteen years, he mused. Oh, there were definitely signs of maturity. She had worn braces the last time he'd seen her. Now her white teeth were perfectly straight. Her glossy brown hair had fallen almost to her waist back then, and it was now cut into a short, shaggy style that suited her.

Her figure hadn't developed significantly since her

teenage years, but rather than the gawkiness of adolescence, she now moved with the lithe grace of womanhood. And her eyes were still an amazingly rich blue, still framed in ridiculously long, lush lashes.

Some might call her cute or even pretty. However one defined it, her look appealed to him as strongly now as it had when he was sixteen.

He had never expected to see her again—certainly not under these conditions. He hadn't had a chance yet to analyze how he felt about having her here, other than fear for her safety and concern about the plans he had spent so long putting together. Still, at the back of his mind was the uncomfortable awareness that Brittany Jeanne Samples was the only living soul who had ever seen him cry.

Thirteen years ago, she was the only one he knew, other than his foster parents, who hadn't been at all afraid of him. She wasn't afraid now. Quietly furious, yes. Healthily cautious, definitely. But not afraid.

Yet he reached out to pat her hand, giving her a bracing smile. "I know how much you hate flying in these small planes. Are you okay?"

"I'm fine."

"Don't you worry, Mrs. Andreas," Bernard said with a heavy-handed attempt at sympathy. "Mr. Drake hires only the best pilots."

Her strained expression didn't change. "I'm sure he does."

"Can I get you anything? Soda? Bottled water?"

"No, thank you."

Daniel trusted that Bernard would attribute B.J.'s terseness to a fear of flying, as he had intended when he had mentioned it. Bernard wasn't the sharpest pencil in the cup, but he wasn't entirely unobservant either. B.J. was hardly acting like a loving wife on her way to a luxurious resort with her husband.

He was going to have to be on his toes every minute to cover for her. He really hadn't needed this complication.

They were in the air for almost four hours. While Bernard played a video game built into a console in the private jet and Daniel read what appeared to be a book about the Spanish-American War, B.J. simply stared out a side window.

She declined the magazines Bernard offered her and had no interest in watching the television he pointed out to her. She was unable to doze. She spent the time wondering where they were going and why and what to expect when they got there.

Had she made a huge mistake going along with this charade? Should she have made it clear that she was not Daniel's wife? Perhaps treated it as a joke? But he had given her little time for that option and he had looked deadly serious when he'd told her that her very life was in danger.

Seeing the gun tucked beneath Bernard's jacket had seemed to illustrate that warning quite clearly.

Still, was she any safer now, flying toward who knew where for who knew what purpose?

Daniel spoke to her occasionally, using a lovingly so-licitous tone that made her back teeth set. She had to make a real effort to respond in kind, but apparently her acting skills were better than she had thought, since Ber-nard didn't seem to notice anything unusual between them. Maybe because Daniel mentioned several times her supposed fear of flying and commented about how brave she was being, even though he knew she must be anxious.

She hadn't been afraid of flying, but this nightmare trip could definitely leave permanent trauma, she decided.

When they finally landed, it was on another private airstrip. From what B.J. could guess from peering out the window, this strip was a part of a luxurious ocean-side resort. She had seen swimming pools and cabanas, sprawling buildings and cozy cabins. Private beaches. Two golf courses.

Florida? South Carolina? She really had no clue.

Maybe the place would have looked more beautiful to her had she been arriving for a voluntary stay. As it was, the only thought on her mind was wondering how soon she could leave.

"See, Mrs. Andreas?" Bernard asked jovially. "Back on the ground, safe and sound."

She would have liked very much to smack him right in the middle of his condescending smile. Instead she merely nodded.

Once again Daniel spoke for her. "My wife is ex-hausted from so much traveling today. I hope we can be shown to our suite quickly so she can get some rest."

B.J. hoped that suite had a back door she could dash out of as soon as no one was looking. At the very least, she would be on the phone at the first opportunity telling her uncles to get busy rescuing her. Well, she would make that call as soon as she figured out where she was.

Bernard ushered them off the plane. A man stepped forward immediately to greet them. In marked contrast to the beefy and belligerent-looking Bernard, this man was handsome, slender and suave. Yet something about his smile made B.J.'s blood run cold.

His heavily moussed hair was sun-streaked blond, and his eyes were a glittering green. He had a perfect profile, a perfect tan, perfect teeth and a perfect physique. She would have bet hard-earned cash that none of those attributes had been bestowed upon him by nature.

As her cowboy uncle Jared would say, this fellow was so slick she could have slid him through a keyhole.

"Daniel," he said, shaking Daniel's hand. "It's good to see you again. And this—" he turned to B.J. "—must be your lovely wife."

His voice practically coated with pride, Daniel replied, "Yes, this is B.J. Darling, I'd like you to meet Judson Drake, the man I've told you so much about."

Judson Drake. If that was his real name, she would eat her shoe.

She nearly flinched when Drake took her hand, holding it more snugly than necessary. "It's my pleasure to meet you, Mrs. Andreas."

"Mr. Drake," she murmured. As much as it unnerved

her to be called Mrs. Andreas, she didn't encourage him to use her nickname.

"Bernard tells me that you've had a difficult time. I understand that your luggage has been misplaced."

He was still holding her hand. B.J. gave a slight tug, freeing it, before she replied, "Yes. I suggested that I should stay behind…"

"Nonsense." He waved a hand dismissively. "We have everything you could need in our shops here. I'll make arrangements for you to select whatever you like. Just give the shopkeepers your name, and anything you need is yours."

"That's very generous of you, but I can provide for my wife's needs," Daniel said with a hint of bruised pride. "If you'll make arrangements for her to charge her purchases to our suite, that will be sufficient."

Drake eyed Daniel with a speculation B.J. couldn't quite analyze. "Consider it done. I'm sure you're both tired and hungry. Perhaps you would like to take advantage of some of my resort's amenities for the remainder of the day. We can talk business tomorrow, Daniel."

Daniel seemed to give the suggestion some thought, and then he inclined his head. "Thank you. For my wife's sake, I think that would be best."

If he said "my wife" in that smugly possessive tone one more time, B.J. was going to kick him. Hard. And she didn't care who was watching.

"Let me escort you to your suite. Bernard will see that your bags are delivered to you, Daniel."

Tucking her canvas tote bag beneath her arm—and

thinking wistfully of the cell phone tucked inside it—
B.J. allowed herself to be led to the main lodge of the
resort. They passed other people, mostly wealthy-look-
ing and highly maintained couples, but other than smiling genially, Drake did not allow himself to be detained.

He led them through an exquisitely decorated lobby,
merely nodding to the young woman behind the recep-
tion desk. He kept up a congenial-host monologue during a brief elevator ride, listing some of the resort's
many attractions.

Drake stood much closer to B.J. than she thought
necessary; the elevator car was not so small that it re-
quired that proximity. When he escorted them into a
luxurious suite, his hand rested casually at the small of
her back, just above the very slight curve of her hip.

Drake was so vainly assured of his appeal to women
that he seemed to expect her to fall at his feet—even
with her "husband" standing right next to them. She
wondered how he would react if she informed him that
his touch made her want to scrub her skin with bleach.

Telling them he was leaving them to relax, he made
a swift exit, pausing only long enough to remind Daniel that they would schedule a meeting for the next
morning.

The moment the door closed behind him, B.J.
whirled to face Daniel. "If that man touches me one
more time, I'm going to punch his capped teeth in."

Daniel gave her what could only be described as a
wryly warning look before saying, "I'm sure he didn't
mean anything by it, darling. He's just the friendly sort."

She watched in disbelief as he pulled a small electronic device from an inside pocket of his jacket and began to walk around the room with it. Having spent the past eighteen months working for her uncles, she figured out immediately what he was doing. Did he really think the rooms were bugged with listening devices?

Just what had she stumbled into here? What exactly had Daniel gotten involved with since he had left the Walker ranch foster home for at-risk teenage boys?

Chapter Two

Daniel motioned for B.J. to keep talking. She figured if Drake was eavesdropping on her, she was going to make it count. "He creeps me out. Obviously thinks he's God's gift to women—but the joke's on him. He's a slug."

Daniel rolled his eyes. Still speaking in a soothing, placating tone, he said, "Now, sweetheart, you're just tired. It has been a stressful day for you."

He could say that again. And then *again,* for emphasis.

She had told her uncles recently that she wanted more exciting and challenging assignments than the computer searches she had been doing for the past months. She had never imagined that this seemingly innocuous assignment would go so wildly off course.

Speaking of her uncles... "I need to call home."

Daniel returned from the bedroom, tucking his little spy gadget back into his pocket. Something about the way he walked told her all was clear even before he spoke. "We can talk freely now. At least, we can until we leave and return—at which point I'll sweep the rooms again, just to be on the safe side."

"I need to call home," she repeated. "But first... maybe you can tell me what the *hell* is going on?"

Grimacing in response to her renewed anger, he shrugged out of his jacket and tossed it over the back of the prissy white brocade sofa that matched the rest of the delicately fancy furnishings in the overdone room. Overdone in B.J.'s opinion, anyway. She preferred simpler, less ornate surroundings. Her idea of resort decor would have involved wicker and cotton, thick cushions and inviting ottomans.

Without directly responding to her, Daniel moved to the white-painted-and-gilded wet bar built into one corner of the room. He opened a small refrigerator and scanned the contents. "Would you like something to drink? We have sodas, juice and bottled water. Unless you need something harder—and I wouldn't blame you if you did, considering everything."

She started to curtly decline anything, but then she realized she really was thirsty. "I'll have a bottled water."

He carried one around to her, motioning for her to

sit down. She chose a chair that sacrificed comfort for style, perching on the edge of the seat with her water bottle clutched tightly in her hand.

She did not take her eyes away from Daniel's unrevealing face as he sat on the sofa opposite her, sipping soda and looking remarkably relaxed. How could he be so calm about this bizarre situation? And what exactly *was* the situation?

"I'm waiting," she reminded him. "I'd like to know what I'm doing here. Why you let them believe I'm your wife. I want to know what you're involved in—and why you seem so sure I'll be in danger if I tell the truth. Mostly I want to know when I can leave."

He took his time answering, and that only annoyed her more, as he seemed to be weighing his words. Deciding exactly what he could—or wanted—to tell her. "Two or three days," he said finally. "That should be all it will take."

"All it will take to do what? Damn it, Daniel, *talk to me!*"

He studied her face for a long moment, then absolutely floored her by chuckling. What on earth was there to laugh about?

"You've changed. You were so sweet-natured and easy to please. The perfect daughter, straight-A student, never caused any trouble, never said a cross word to anyone—except maybe your older brother and sister."

He remembered all that about her? She had been exactly the way he described her, back when he knew her. It was only within the past three or four years that she had become aware of how tired she was of pleasing everyone but herself. Of living a sheltered, uneventful, unadventurous life that had become increasingly stifling and boring.

She had wished for excitement. She should have remembered that old adage about being careful what one wished for.

"You still haven't answered my questions," she prodded gruffly.

Another brief hesitation and then he said, "I can't tell you much. Only that you've stumbled into a very complicated situation—as I assume you've figured out for yourself."

"Go on."

"Judson Drake thinks I have a wealthy wife back in Texas. He invited me to bring her along on this trip, but I had a convenient excuse to explain her absence. When you showed up at the farm, asking for me by name when no one should have known I was there—and asking with a very obvious Texas twang, by the way—Bernard put two and two together. I admit he isn't the sharpest thorn on the rosebush, but even he can handle that level of mathematics."

"So why didn't you tell him that I'm *not* your wife? As clever as you are," she said, adding an extra helping of sarcasm to her "Texas twang," "you should have been able to come up with some sort of explanation for my arrival. Say, oh, the truth, for example."

"Wouldn't have worked. My background, according to what Drake has been told, is one of upper-middle-class comfort. Private schools, public college, fortuitous marriage to a woman with money. Nowhere in that story is a mention of foster care. The truth about how I know you could have blown everything."

"So the wife is as fictional as your upper-middle-class background?"

His face expressionless again, he nodded.

"Why have you told them these things?"

"I can't go into that right now."

"You expect me to simply accept what you've told me and go along with this charade for the next two or three days?"

"I wish I could say you have the option of saying no. Unfortunately you don't. These are dangerous people, Brittany——"

"B.J."

"Sorry. B.J. These men will not accept a change in my story now. One hint that I've tried to deceive them, and you and I will both quietly disappear. That's how they operate."

"Then why are you here?"

He took a sip of his soda before saying, "There's a great deal of money involved for anyone who is clever enough to get a piece of it."

"Money?" She stared at him with narrowed eyes. "You're doing this for money?"

He shrugged and drained the remainder of his soda.

B.J. set her water aside. She simply didn't know whether she could believe a word he said.

She had thought he might try to tell her he was an

undercover operative for some branch of law enforcement. Would that have been any easier for her to believe? And if so, would it have been because she wanted to think Daniel was on the right side of the law?

"So what you're telling me," she said slowly, "is that you're running some sort of scam on some very dangerous men. And I'm stuck helping you pull it off because I accidentally arrived at the wrong place at the wrong time."

"That pretty well sums it up."

"If I refuse, I might just 'quietly disappear.' And if I agree, I could end up making some big mistake, and then we'll still end up dead."

"You won't make a mistake. All you have to do is remember a few details I'll tell you before we go out again."

"And what do I tell my family when I call them?"

"You can't call them. I don't trust either the land lines or the airwaves here. Either one could be monitored."

She shook her head. "You're going to have to figure out some way to let me call. Unless you want my uncles arriving in the middle of your big plan, of course."

Which didn't sound like such a bad idea to her, actually.

"How would they know where to find you? You didn't have time to call anyone when we left."

"For that matter, I don't know where we are exactly," she admitted. "But I wouldn't be particularly surprised if my uncles track me down within twenty-four hours. You do remember who they are, don't you?"

He frowned. "I'm well aware that your uncle Jared

is a rancher, since I spent nearly a year living with his family."

"And my uncles Tony, Joe and Ryan are private investigators. Very good ones. And very protective of all their family members—even one who is on their payroll. Me."

"You work for the D'Alessandro and Walker agency?"

"So you do remember them."

"Vaguely. It seemed like your family found an excuse nearly every week to have some sort of party at the ranch. I couldn't help but remember a few details about them."

"Then you should also recall that we're an extremely close family." Almost suffocatingly close sometimes, she almost added. "They'll start looking."

"You can send them an e-mail," he said after a moment. "I have a small computer in my luggage. You can use that. Don't keep a copy."

"And what should it say?" she asked.

"That you've decided you need a few days of vacation and they don't need to worry about you. You're twenty-seven years old. You don't have to ask permission to take a few days off, do you?"

He remembered an awful lot about her. Of course, she knew he was twenty-nine, because he was two years older than she, almost to the day.

"It's not something I've done before. Take off on impulse, I mean." Even though she had often wished she could.

"Then it's about time you did, wouldn't you say?"

"Maybe. But this wouldn't exactly be my first choice of vacations."

"Yeah?" Looking more masculine than he should have against the froufrou fabric, he stretched an arm along the back of the sofa. "So what would be your first choice?"

"Well...I don't know. I haven't really thought about slipping off on my own."

His beautifully shaped lips curved into a very slight smile. "Liar."

Okay, so maybe she had indulged in a few daydreams lately about getting away from the usual routines. "I guess I've thought about it once or twice," she muttered.

"To where?"

"Anywhere. I've hardly been out of Texas. I've always wanted to go someplace really different and exotic—like—like Singapore. Or Hong Kong. Or Bali."

And then she shook her head impatiently. "Darn it, you're doing it again. Distracting me from the questions you don't want to answer."

Still wearing that annoyingly inscrutable smile, he merely looked at her.

"Will you at least reassure me that I won't be helping you break the law if I stupidly agree to go along with this ridiculous charade?"

He never changed expression. Nor did he bother to say anything.

She scowled fiercely—not that she figured it would affect him. "So my choices are to cooperate with everything you say even though you won't tell me why or refuse to go along and risk having Bernard make me disappear."

"The options haven't changed since I first outlined them to you."

"Maybe it has taken me this long to make myself believe this is really happening," she grumbled.

"Since I assume you're choosing the option that keeps us both alive, we need to go over a few things."

Though B.J. couldn't help but resent Daniel's assumption that she would make the choice he wanted her to make, she couldn't really argue with him either. She had no wish to face the business end of Bernard's weapon. "I suppose you're right. If I'm to play a part, it would be helpful if I have a script."

A sudden thought occurred to her. "Wait a minute. Did you never mention your wife's name? You introduced me to Creepy Guy as B.J."

"That's not a problem."

Something in his voice struck her as odd, but he was speaking again before she could define it. "There's very little that you have to remember. We've been married for two years. You are a homemaker and community volunteer who leaves all business and financial matters to her husband."

"Oh, gee, thanks for making me such a progressive, modern woman."

He ignored her—something he did entirely too easily, she thought. "Last fall you suffered a miscarriage and you've been somewhat despondent since. You've had even less interest in my business dealings with your money, which means I'm free to speculate with it at my own discretion."

The more he told her, the less enthused she became with her role. A mopey housewife. Terrific. "I suppose I adore the ground you walk on?"

That seemed to fit in with the chauvinistic tale he had concocted.

He looked almost amused by her resigned question. "Of course. I've been the loving and solicitous husband since your loss. Which, of course, makes you less inclined to question my actions away from you."

"So you don't love me?" It felt foolish to ask that of a man who was a virtual stranger—but it was only a charade, after all, she reminded herself.

A tiny shiver slipped down her spine when his dark eyes held hers for a heartbeat before he replied. "I've implied to Drake that I love your money more."

She pulled her gaze from his, glancing down at her hands. "Then I would say you're in sorry shape, considering I don't have any."

"My wife has plenty of money," he corrected her.

The gold ring on her left hand glittered. She touched it with her right forefinger. "You just happened to have a woman's wedding ring on a chain around your neck? Just in case someone stumbled into your story?"

"The ring was my mother's. I've worn it for almost a dozen years."

Despite the utter lack of emotion in his voice, B.J.

felt her throat tighten anyway. She knew enough about
his mother's fate to understand how much this ring must
mean to him. He had carried it with him when he left
the Walker ranch and he had worn it since as a reminder
of—what? His mother's life? The injustice of her death?

"I'll take very good care of it," she assured him.

"Thank you." He stood then, glancing toward the
bedroom. "Feel free to rest a while if you like. I'll make
sure you aren't disturbed."

"Actually…" Rising, she put a hand to her midsec-
tion. "I'm starving. It's been hours since I've had anything to eat."

The smile he gave her then was quick and apparently genuine. "We can't have that. Room service or
restaurant?"

Dragging her gaze from his amazing smile, she
looked ruefully down at her wrinkled and travel-worn
clothing. "Maybe room service would be best."

Following her gaze, he nodded. "What size do you
wear?"

"Size two. Why?"

"Shoe size?"

"Seven. Why are you—?"

"You'll need some clothing."

He picked up a phone from an ornately carved and
gilded writing desk. She listened in astonishment as he
briskly and efficiently ordered a meal and then re-
quested that an assortment of clothing, shoes and lingerie be sent to their suite for his wife's consideration.
Despite what she knew about his impoverished back-

ground, he seemed to have adapted very well to a life of privilege.

Hanging up the phone, he moved toward the bedroom. "I'll set up the computer for you. You can send your e-mail while I unpack."

She followed him into the bedroom. This room, too, was overly formal for her taste. Done in French style, it featured carved woods and lots of chintz and toile on little chairs and benches that looked barely substantial enough to support her weight, much less Daniel's.

Whose idea of a vacation room was this? She couldn't see herself putting her feet up on this furniture or lolling around still damp and sandy from a romp on the beach. Did people who were comfortable in rooms like this even *like* romping on beaches?

Daniel chuckled again in response to her expression. "You don't care for the decor?"

It irked her that he read her so easily when she could never tell what he was thinking. She waved imperiously toward another French writing desk. "Set up the computer. I have an e-mail to write."

He reached for a leather computer case. "By the way," he said casually, "you won't be able to hit send until I've read the message. Sorry, but I have to make sure you stay safe while you're under my protection."

She lifted her chin defiantly. "I'll have you know I've been working for the investigation agency for over a year. I can keep myself safe."

"Since my guess is that you've been working primarily at a desk, doing computer searches and making telephone calls, I doubt that you've learned a great deal of self-defense during your stint at the agency."

Without giving her a chance to challenge his guess, he opened the computer, turned it on, then stepped back from it. "Let me know when you're ready, and I'll enter my code so you can send the e-mail. After I've read it, of course."

"Jerk," she muttered beneath her breath as she sank into the tiny chair in front of the desk.

Again he surprised her by laughing softly. "It's not the first time you've called me that," he reminded her. "I'm sure it won't be the last."

His voice grew more serious then. "But you will leave this resort safely. You have my word on that."

The message had been approved and sent by the time their early dinner arrived. Daniel had read every word carefully, weighing the implications and trying to predict her family's reactions to the e-mail. She had said simply that she had been unable to find Daniel and wanted to take a few days to think about her future. She had sent her love and promised to call soon.

"They all know I've been increasingly dissatisfied with my job lately," she had rather grudgingly admitted. "Sitting at a computer all day wasn't what I had in mind when I talked my uncles into giving me a job."

"Most P.I. work these days comes down to just that," he had observed with a slight shrug. "From what I've heard, anyway."

"So I've discovered."

"So what do you want to do?" he asked, discreetly keying in his computer password while he kept her distracted with conversation.

"I don't know," she answered simply. And rather poignantly. "I only know I haven't found it yet."

Barely twenty minutes later, he studied her across the small round dining table set against one glass wall in the sitting room. Apparently her confusion about the situation she had found herself in—coupled with a whirlwind day of travel—had not affected her appetite. She ate with a heartiness that amused him, considering her reed-slender figure.

He remembered that she had liked to eat when they were teenagers. She'd always been one of the first in line for helpings of the barbecued meats that had been the main fare of so many Walker family gatherings.

They didn't say much during the meal. He figured she was replaying the things he had said to her, trying to make sense of them and prepare herself for the role she'd been forced into assuming.

They had just dipped into their desserts when there was another knock on the door. Motioning for B.J. to continue to eat the strawberry shortcake she seemed to be enjoying so much, Daniel moved to answer.

A striking young woman in a brief red sarong-style sundress and sandals stood in the hallway next to a covered, wheeled garment rack. "Mr. Andreas?"

He couldn't help noticing the masses of sun-streaked blond hair, glossy, full lips, golden-tanned shoulders, high, firm breasts and long, tanned legs. He was only human, after all. "Yes."

Her smile glittered, as did her violet-tinted eyes. Young Elizabeth Taylor eyes, he mused. He had no doubt that tinted contact lenses provided the color, but the result was quite nice. "I'm Heather. From the Beach-front Boutique? I understand your poor wife arrived without her luggage."

"Yes. An unfortunate airline mix-up." He turned toward the small dining area at the other side of the room. "B.J.?"

She was already up and moving toward them. Her short dark hair was mussed, any makeup she had worn earlier had worn off and her slightly oversize camp shirt and khakis emphasized her slender frame.

Many men, perhaps, would have preferred Heather's more obvious feminine charms. Yet Daniel found himself increasingly fascinated by B.J.'s subtle—and completely natural—attractions.

"Heather, this is my wife," he said, helping her roll the bulky garment rack inside. "Darling, I'm sure you'll be glad to have some fresh clothing to change into."

He noticed that Heather was eying B.J. in surprise, as if she had expected her to look different. Heather was accustomed, he imagined, to very wealthy men with sleek, ultragroomed eye-candy wives.

He didn't blame her for that expectation, of course. When he had very briefly considered casting the role of his "wife" for this trip, that was exactly the type of woman he would have selected. Someone who looked rich and pampered and a bit disconnected from the real world.

He had rejected the idea of bringing someone along because he was concerned that the situation would become too complicated. Too distracting.

He'd had no idea, of course, that fate would step in to provide a make-believe wife for him. And that fate's choice would be even more complicated and distracting than anyone else Daniel could possibly have found on his own.

Chapter Three

At Daniel's request, Heather left the clothing for B.J. to examine in private. She promised to return in an hour to collect the rack and invoice the selections.

When Heather departed, Daniel removed the cover from the wheeled rack. He motioned toward the colorful garments hanging from the top bar and neatly folded into clear plastic boxes fitted into the bottom part of the display rack. "There you are. A boutique on wheels, with everything in your size."

Hands on her hips, she looked from the rack to his decidedly smug expression. "You enjoy snapping your fingers and having people jump to please you, don't you?"

His eyebrows lifted, as if he was surprised that she had even to ask. "Of course."

"Just what have you been up to for the past thirteen years, Daniel?"

Displaying that annoyingly selective hearing again, he turned toward the clothing rack and plucked a hanger from the rod. "This would look good on you."

The yellow cotton sundress clipped to the hanger was strapless and short and tailored to fit very snugly. "That's not really my style."

"Yes, but remember, you're playing a new role here. You're wealthy, stylish and accustomed to designer fashions."

"According to your backstory, I'm depressed and too self-absorbed to even notice that you're frittering away my money. Would a person like that really wear skimpy, brightly colored dresses?"

"Ah, but you also adore the husband who treats you like delicate and valuable glass. You would certainly want to dress to please him."

She scowled, wondering if he was always so quick at coming up with counterarguments. Just once she would like to win one of their verbal skirmishes. "I don't like yellow."

"In that case…" He replaced the sundress and pulled out a similar one in deep fuchsia. "Is this better?"

"Maybe I should just select a couple of things for myself," she said, moving toward the rack.

"Since it's important that you present the image Drake is expecting, I feel compelled to assist you in your selections."

"And when did you start talking like that? That isn't

the way you used to talk when I knew you before. Back when you were Daniel Castillo," she couldn't resist adding.

She hadn't been surprised to learn from a reliable source that he was now using his mother's maiden name, but she wanted him to know that this masquerade hadn't erased from her mind the reality of who he had once been.

For just a moment his self-satisfied smile faded. She could almost see a few painful old memories swirl in his dark eyes before he hid again behind the bland mask he donned so easily. "Yes, well, you aren't the only one playing a role."

Changing the subject then, he pulled several garments from the rack, piling them into B.J.'s arms. "These look as though they would work for you. Why don't you take them into the bedroom and let's see how well they fit."

She peered at him over the huge pile of clothing. "You expect a fashion show?"

His faint smile back in place, he dropped onto the sofa and draped an arm over its curvy back. "I think I'd enjoy that."

She was strongly tempted to give him a suggestion he would not enjoy quite so much, but she bit her tongue to hold it back. For one thing, she wasn't one to use such language easily. For another, she had a glum suspicion that Daniel was right.

Given her own tastes in clothing, she would probably never pass for a wealthy socialite. Her poor mother had tried for years to talk her into dressing with more of an eye for fashion than comfort.

She sighed heavily. "When this is over, you are going to owe me big-time for saving your butt."

"Technically you're saving both our butts," he pointed out equably. "But when this is over, I will definitely owe you whatever penalty you choose to make me pay."

"I'm glad you agree. Thinking about that penalty will help me get through this ordeal."

He grimaced slightly, as though well aware of the punishments her imagination could conjure up. "Try on some clothes," he said. "You have less than an hour before Heather will be back."

Turning on one heel, she stamped into the bedroom, which wasn't easy when she could barely see over the pile of clothing she carried. Daniel didn't offer to assist her. He probably knew she would have snarled at him had he tried.

Daniel turned out to be surprisingly difficult to please. While B.J. would have just grabbed the first things that fit, he seemed to have a shrewd eye for what suited her best, rejecting the outfits that hung too loosely on her slender frame or were less than flattering to her skin tone. She was beginning to feel like a mannequin by the time he finally approved a couple of sundresses—including the fuchsia one—several summery capri-pants-and-top sets and one classic black sheath.

"This is too much," she protested. "We aren't going to be here that long."

"You never know," he replied with a shrug. "Be-sides, the clothes look good on you. You should keep them."

"And who's paying for them?" she asked tartly.

"That needn't concern you."

"And yet it does."

"Just try on the bathing suits, B.J."

"No way am I modeling bathing suits for you."

He heaved a long-suffering sigh. "Then pick a cou-ple for yourself. You can't stay at an oceanside resort without a bathing suit or two. And be sure you keep enough nightclothes and lingerie for several days."

She started to snap at him that she was perfectly ca-pable of providing herself with lingerie, but she bit the words back. She just couldn't discuss underwear with Daniel, even if it was in defiance. Besides which, she did need some clean undergarments if she was going to stay here even for just two or three days.

Turning silently, she closed herself in the bedroom to complete her shopping without any further input from Daniel.

Heather had just left with the garment rack later when someone else knocked on the sitting room door. Since the dishes from their meal had already been cleared away, B.J. looked curiously at Daniel. "Now what?"

He shrugged and crossed the room to answer. She found herself thinking that he moved like a man braced for trouble, as if he half expected danger to lurk on the other side of the door.

She couldn't help wondering again just what he had been up to for the past thirteen years. She'd been able to find out very little about him through the usual sources.

He glanced through the peephole, relaxed visibly and opened the door. A moment later he closed the door again and turned back to face her. His arms were filled with a gigantic gift basket covered in cellophane and topped with a glittering golden bow. "It's for you."

"For me?" Frowning, she moved toward him as he set the basket on a table.

Through the clear covering she could see that the basket was filled with beauty products. Body lotions, cleansers, moisturizers, sunscreens. An assortment of cosmetics. Dainty little soaps. Hair products, including a brush and a hand mirror.

She spotted a clear plastic case fitted with a toothbrush, toothpaste, mouthwash, a razor and a pink can of shaving gel. Everything a woman on vacation could possibly need. She had never cared much about brand names, but she suspected that the products in this basket were top-of-the-line.

"Did you order this, too?" she asked Daniel.

He shook his head and pulled a tiny card from a fold in the cellophane. The card bore the gold-embossed name of a resort gift shop. He held it so both could see the words as he read aloud, "'Not that you need any enhancement, but perhaps these things will be of use to you during your stay. Please ask for anything else you need. Judson Drake.'"

B.J. wrinkled her nose. "Eew."

Daniel shook his head. "You're going to have to get

past that tendency to shudder every time you hear his name. He's our host, and I'm trying to very hard to take him for a large amount of money. A little kissing up would definitely be in order."

B.J. shuddered again. "If either of us is expected to kiss Creepy Guy, it had better be you."

Reaching out to run a fingertip across her pouting lower lip, he murmured, "He's not my type."

Her mind flooded suddenly with memories of the kiss with which he had greeted her at the farmhouse— had that really been less than eight hours ago?; it seemed longer—and yet she could still almost feel the warmth of his lips against hers.

Dropping his hand, he glanced at the wrinkled clothes she had donned again after trying on the new outfits. "Why don't you put on one of those new dresses and we'll go out for a drink and to listen to some music. We should let ourselves be seen."

She gave it a moment's thought. She had a choice of going out for a drink or sitting in this suite with him— just the two of them—for the remainder of the evening. "A drink sounds good," she said—perhaps just a bit too hastily.

He flashed her a smile. "I'll freshen up after you change. It won't take me long."

Nodding, she turned toward the bedroom, leaving him gazing out the big window toward the darkening beach beyond. It was definitely a good thing she had chosen to go out, considering the way her hands were shaking merely in response to his lethal smile.

* * *

The sun had set by the time they went out, though the temperature was still pleasantly warm. Feeling as though she were playing dress-up, B.J. wore the fuchsia dress. The garment was a much brighter color than she would have chosen for herself, the bodice too low-cut, the hem too high. While she supposed it was fairly modest compared to some of the outfits she saw when they entered the rather crowded outdoor lounge, she would have been much more comfortable in jeans and a T-shirt.

Because it had seemed almost obligatory with the dress, she had even worn makeup for the evening, forcing herself to open the gift basket Drake had sent to the suite. She'd assured herself she didn't have to like him to take advantage of his generosity—especially since he probably had ulterior motives in making the gesture—but it still felt wrong somehow.

Daniel had told her she looked very nice. As usual, she hadn't been able to read his expression to judge whether he'd really meant the compliment or if he was only being polite. Glancing from beneath her eyelashes at the sleek, beautiful women occupying the candlelit little tables around them in the outdoor lounge, she couldn't help thinking that she must stand out among them like a plain brown sparrow in an exotic aviary.

Daniel, on the other hand, fit in very well with the glamorous crowd. His black hair still slightly damp from his quick shower, he wore a thin white shirt and loose cream-colored slacks that contrasted intriguingly with his dark skin and emphasized his long, lean body.

She noticed how many of the beautiful women—and a few of the beautiful men—turned to stare at Daniel as they crossed the stone floor to a rather isolated empty table. She wondered if it was only paranoia making her think she saw surprise in their eyes that a man like Daniel was with her.

"What's wrong?" he asked as he held her chair for her.

It bugged her that he sensed her moods so easily. "Nothing."

He pulled his chair so close to hers that their knees touched beneath the tiny table. "Appearances," he reminded her when she looked inquiringly at him.

"I'm not sure anything is going to make it appear that I belong at a place like this," she murmured, waving a hand around the lounge, with its smooth stone floor, low rock walls lined with waving palm trees and huge pots of tropical flowers, colorful overhead lanterns and dozens of flickering candles.

In the center of the circular lounge was a small bandstand on which a five-piece ensemble played sultry dance music. A wooden dance floor surrounded the bandstand, making it easily accessible from any table, and several bronzed, toned, bleached and designer-clad couples took advantage of the chance to show off their dancing skills. The place was a far cry from the beer-and-barbecue joints her solidly middle-class family tended to frequent back home in Texas.

Daniel frowned. "Why wouldn't you look as though you belong here?"

She shrugged self-consciously. "I would never be able to afford to stay at a resort like this on my own."

"That doesn't make you inferior to anyone here. Don't mistake money for class, Britt—B.J."

A pretty blonde in a sarong—which seemed to describe nearly every employee at this resort—stopped beside the table. "What would you like?"

"Darling?"

B.J. gave Daniel a look. It would serve him right—not to mention prove her point—if she ordered root beer. "Why don't you order for us, *darling?*"

His smile flashed, giving her just a fleeting glimpse of the shallow dimple in his left cheek. She remembered having a rather obsessive fascination with that elusive dimple when she was fourteen. "Champagne, then—since it's your favorite."

He glanced at the server and ordered a brand B.J. didn't recognize. Probably very expensive.

"Champagne is my favorite drink?" she murmured when the server moved away.

"It seemed to fit in character."

Because it was making her rather nervous to be sitting so close to him, gazing into his dark eyes, she forced herself to look away, turning her attention toward the bandstand. Reflections of the tiny white lights strung above them glittered like stars on the glossy grand piano and gleaming wind instruments.

Beneath the bluesy music she could just hear the

sound of the ocean. The scent of tropical blooms drifted past her on a light breeze. The slow swaying of the dancing couples was almost hypnotic.

The server returned with their champagne. B.J. took an appreciative sip before saying, "One thing I will say about Creepy Guy, he runs a nice place."

Though the corners of Daniel's mouth twitched, he glanced quickly around, silently reminding her that she had to be careful. "It does look nice," he murmured. "On the surface."

Yet another reminder that danger lurked beneath the exotic beauty here. Glancing around, she saw Bernard and another large man sharing a table near the stage. Though the men weren't looking her way, she had little doubt they had been aware of the moment she and Daniel arrived. She shivered.

Daniel slipped an arm around her, his shirt fabric very soft against the skin her dress left bare. "Cold?"

"No." Definitely not cold. Not now, anyway.

"We can speak freely—as long as we keep our voices low." He was practically nuzzling her temple as he spoke, so there was little danger of anyone overhearing him, even from the next table. The table he had selected was partially screened by the drooping fronds of a large potted palm, and she doubted that his selection had been made by accident.

She suspected that Daniel's every action was calculated and deliberate. Including the nuzzling.

"You should try to smile at me occasionally. Pretend to be intensely interested in what I have to say."

"Gaze adoringly into your eyes?" she suggested too sweetly.

He chuckled and brushed a kiss against her cheek. "That would certainly be helpful."

It was only the thought of Bernard sitting nearby and watching them that kept B.J. from jerking away. She was afraid it would take more acting talent than she possessed to pretend that the touch of Daniel's lips against her skin was an everyday occurrence for her. "I'll, uh, see what I can do."

"Relax, B.J. I'm not going to bite you. Yet."

Now he was deliberately trying to rattle her. "You always did have an irritating streak in you."

"You're still under the impression that I was the one who put the little snake in your bag?"

"I'm quite sure you were. I saw you busting a gut laughing when I screamed and threw that bag about twenty yards into the bushes."

His smile was a bit nostalgic. "It was amusing."

"Admit it. You did it."

When he merely looked at her, she frowned, a long-held belief beginning to waver. "It wasn't you?"

He shook his head.

"Then who…?"

Lifting his champagne flute, he murmured into it, "Far be it from me to squeal—but you might have a chat with your cousin Jason when you return home."

She narrowed her eyes, picturing her brilliant and unconventional cousin, Jason D'Alessandro. "Practical jokes aren't Jason's style. Now, if you had blamed my cousins Aaron and Andrew Walker, I might have believed you. The twins were always getting into mischief when they were kids. Heck, they're twenty-one now and they're still always up to something."

"I never figured out how you could keep all that family straight. How many cousins do you have, anyway?"

"My father was an only child with a small extended family. But my mother has five living siblings. Between them, and a brother who died years ago, they have fifteen offspring. Two of my first cousins, Shane and Brynn, have children of their own now."

"Shane's a father?" Because Shane was the son of the couple who had served as Daniel's foster parents, Daniel obviously remembered him well enough to be surprised.

"Yes. He and Kelly married only a couple of years after you left the ranch. They have two daughters—Annie, who's eight, and Lucy, who's four."

"Do they all still live at the ranch?"

She nodded. "Shane added on to his house when Lucy was on the way, but other than that, not much has changed since you were there."

"How are—" He broke off the question, took another sip of his champagne, then set his flute down. "Would you like to dance?"

Apparently he had decided to close that door to his past for now. Was it because he was concerned about being overheard—or was it that he simply didn't like to remember those days?

"I don't dance very well."

"Not a problem. Besides, Bernard and his friend seem to be waiting for us to do something. We shouldn't disappoint them."

She glanced involuntarily toward the table near the stage. Bernard was staring right at them now, making no attempt to pretend otherwise. He nodded when she looked his way and lifted his glass in a salute of sorts.

Though there was nothing at all threatening about his actions, she felt her stomach muscles clench anyway. "Actually I'm getting rather tired."

"Then we'll go back to our suite—after our dance." Daniel stood and held out his left hand to her, the gold band on his finger gleaming in the reflected light from the candle on their table.

In other words, he wasn't giving her a choice. Apparently he considered it important that Bernard see them dancing together. She laid her hand in his and allowed him to lead her to the dance floor.

He had been right—as always—when he'd said that it wouldn't be a problem that she wasn't an experienced dancer. He held her so closely and moved so slowly that all she had to do was sway in place along with him. He didn't have to remind her that they were being watched, but he gave her little choice except to cling to him as if there was no one else in the entire resort.

She felt his lips press against her cheek, and it was purely instinct that made her tilt her head to grant him freer access. It was better, she decided, to simply act without thinking for now. Every time she started wondering what Daniel was up to or why she hadn't made more of an effort to get herself out of this situation, her head started to hurt.

She had a nagging suspicion that she should be more anxious, less willing to cooperate with Daniel's instructions. She was still trying to convince herself that he was on the right side of the law. An undercover cop. A private investigator, maybe. She told herself he had been trying too hard to convince her that he was no better than the men he was here to do business with, which must mean the truth was just the opposite, right?

Or was she still operating under the influence of a girlhood infatuation? Unable to believe the worst of the boy she had never forgotten? The man who could make her pulse race with nothing more than a slight smile? Not to mention the way she was reacting to being held so closely against his long, lean, muscular body.

She had never before allowed her hormones to overcome her common sense—and this was a hell of a time to start.

Her cheek rested against his shoulder now. As the song was winding down, he reached up to tilt her face toward him. Before she could say anything, his mouth was on hers. The kiss effectively ended the dance, since it rendered her completely unable to move her feet.

"Now," he said when he lifted his head several long moments later, "we can go back to our suite."

Blinking dazedly, she realized that other couples were leaving the dance floor. No one seemed to be paying much attention to them, but if anyone had been, they probably saw a couple eager to be alone to continue where the kiss had left off.

As Daniel led her away with one arm holding her snugly against him, she knew that was exactly the impression he had intended to give.

B.J. looked rather pale as they reentered the suite a few minutes later. Motioning for her to remain quiet while he swept for listening devices, Daniel regretted again that she had been put into this position. She was dead on her feet, and no wonder, considering all she had been through that day.

He probably shouldn't have pressured her to go out for drinks and dancing, but he believed it had been a useful outing. It had definitely reinforced his tale that his "wife" was completely absorbed with him, so enthralled by his skillful wooing that she had no interest in anything else that went on around her.

Reassured that no one had been in to bug their suite while they were gone, he turned back to B.J. "You're exhausted. You need some sleep."

Nodding wearily, she took a few steps toward the bedroom, then froze when he moved to follow her. "Um…where are *you* going to sleep? On the sofa?"

Had it only now occurred to her that their charade of marriage included sharing a bedroom?

"It's a king-size bed," he pointed out, waving a hand in that direction. "We can both sleep in it without even bumping into each other during the night."

She looked from him to that big bed and back again. "I don't think so."

Reaching up to squeeze the back of his neck, he spoke with deliberate impatience. "Trust me, Brittany, you are entirely safe with me tonight. We can't risk anyone suspecting that our 'marriage' is anything other than what I've said, so we'll share the bed, but only for sleeping. I plan to crash for a couple of hours and then I have some work to do on my computer before I meet with Drake tomorrow."

B.J. flushed, and it wasn't hard to see that she had interpreted his tone to mean that he had no interest in taking advantage of sharing a bed with her. His use of the name she had answered to as a teenager had probably reinforced the impression that he saw her only as an inconvenient reminder of his past, still just a girl in whom he had no particular romantic interest.

It hadn't been true then and it wasn't now. But he saw no reason to share that with her. Once she recovered from her embarrassment, she should be much more comfortable sharing this suite with him if she was reassured that she didn't have to worry about him making unwelcome passes.

At least, he assumed they would be unwelcome. And if they weren't—well, that created a whole new set of problems.

She lifted her chin in a proud little gesture he knew very well and pushed a hand through her short hair, making it stand in defiant spikes around her heated face. "You can sleep wherever you like. I'm so tired I won't even notice you're in the same suite. And tomorrow, after we've both rested, I expect for you to find a way to get me out of this intolerable charade and back to my life as quickly as possible."

He nodded. "I'll wait in the sitting room until you're in bed. I'll try not to disturb you when I come in or when I get back up."

She nodded curtly and turned toward the bathroom. "By the way," she said over her shoulder, her voice still icy, "I really prefer to answer to B.J."

"I'll try to remember."

"Do that."

The bathroom door closed with a snap that almost made him wince.

Chapter Four

B.J. hadn't expected to sleep, but her body had other plans. Dressed in the most modest pajamas that had been made available to her, she slept heavily enough that she barely roused when Daniel lay down beside her maybe an hour after she turned in and she never knew when he got back up. Though she woke early—just before seven o'clock—he was already gone, only a slight indentation in his pillow as evidence that he was ever there.

It was hard to believe she had just spent an entire night in bed with Daniel Andreas. And slept through it. Whether from stress, exhaustion or both, she had simply gone unconscious.

She took a lengthy shower in the huge, ornately elegant bathroom. Afterward she applied a minimum of makeup, then dressed in one of the new outfits—a pale green sleeveless top with green-and-white-checked capris and green flip-flops. Studying herself in the mirror, she thought glumly that she looked like a soccer mom on her way to a PTA meeting. This was so not her.

Her gaze slid to the reflection of her left hand and the gold ring on her finger. Daniel's mother's ring.

She sank slowly to the edge of the bed, still looking at that ring. A simple gold band, it bore a few scratches that showed its age. It looked like what it was—a treasured memento.

Jarringly different mental images jockeyed for a moment in her mind.

Daniel at sixteen. Thin, dark, intense. Angry. Threadbare clothes, shaggy hair, conversation that consisted mostly of monosyllables and curse words.

Daniel at twenty-nine. Sleek, groomed, cultured. His emotions well hidden behind a blandly congenial social mask. In some ways it was hard to believe it was the same person.

And yet…

She remembered a glimpse of rarely seen dimple. A brief flash of amusement at the memory of a long-ago practical joke.

Perhaps he had changed outwardly, but he was still the boy who had broken down in front of her when he had talked about finding his mother's body. Did he remember that powerful moment as clearly as she did?

She would bet that he did. Maybe that was the reason he occasionally looked at her as though he would rather be anywhere other than with her now.

He entered the room so quietly that she didn't know he was there until he cleared his throat. She had never even heard the outer door open, which didn't reassure her about her safety in this luxurious suite.

As she rose to her feet, it was unexpectedly hard to meet his eyes. She kept remembering the boredom on his face when he had reassured her that he had no intention of making a pass at her during the night. He had all but told her outright that he wasn't attracted to her and that any evidence otherwise was merely an act he put on for the benefit of observers.

Even if he had only been trying to set her at ease about sleeping in the same room with him, it had been a fairly humiliating moment for her. She couldn't help thinking about the beautiful, busty blondes who seemed to have congregated at this resort. Perhaps they were more to Daniel's taste.

Not that she *wanted* to get involved with him, she assured herself hastily. He could be a criminal. At the very least, he was trouble.

"Good morning."

Pride made her force herself to meet his eyes. "Good morning."

"Did you sleep well?"

"Yes, quite well, thank you."

She didn't have to ask the same of him. She knew he hadn't had more than a few hours of sleep, but he looked completely rested. His hair was neatly combed, his cream-colored shirt and tan pants impeccably pressed. Even though she was freshly showered and dressed and wearing more makeup than she usually favored, he still managed to make her feel slightly grubby in contrast to him.

His dark eyes mocked her stilted tone. "You look very nice."

She looked down at her neatly matched clothing. "I look like a sitcom mom. All I need to finish off the look is a string of pearls."

"Or this." He pulled a thin rectangular box from his right pants pocket and extended it toward her.

Rather than taking it, B.J. eyed it suspiciously. "What is that?"

"You won't know until you open it."

"I don't—"

He sighed and opened it himself, revealing a glittering diamond tennis bracelet. Each diamond was set in a circle of hammered gold.

B.J. knew little about jewelry, since she usually wore only a functional watch and a pair of diamond-stud earrings—half a carat each—her parents had given her for her college graduation, but she would estimate this bracelet to hold at least three carats of diamonds.

"You don't expect me to wear that?"

Daniel already had the bracelet out of its box. "I certainly do."

"Why?"

"Because Daniel Andreas was in such a good mood

after a night of romance with his wife that he stopped by the resort's jewelry store and picked up a bauble for her. Since certain people are undoubtedly aware of that purchase already, you should be seen wearing the bracelet. Preferably without a look of revulsion on your face."

"It isn't revulsion. The bracelet is certainly pretty. It just isn't…"

"It isn't you, I know." He caught her right hand in his left and wrapped the bracelet around her wrist. "Is it really necessary for me to remind you again that while you are here, you *aren't* you?"

Looking down at the bracelet he had fastened so easily around her wrist, she frowned. She didn't like the eerie feeling that she was slowly turning into someone else. Sure, she had wanted to make some changes in her life, but this was more drastic than she'd had in mind.

"So what are my orders for today?" she asked in resignation.

Maybe she had deliberately tried to annoy him—maybe because it made her so uncomfortable for him to stand so close to her, sliding diamonds onto her wrist. She should have predicted that he wouldn't be fazed by her sarcasm.

"You're staying at a luxurious oceanside resort. Take advantage of it. Lie by the pool. Walk on the beach. Shop in the boutiques. Spend the day in the spa. Have a massage and facial and manicure and pedicure. Or…" he reached up to brush his fingertips across her choppy hair "…visit one of the salons."

Embarrassed, she pushed his hand away. So she

hadn't had time to make a hair appointment lately. She had resorted to hacking at it occasionally herself, just to keep it out of her eyes. Still, she didn't think it looked all that bad. "Maybe I'll just stay here in the suite and watch the soaps on TV."

"Actually I think it would be best if you go out—at least for a little while. Be seen, flash your bracelet, act as though you're accustomed to being treated like a VIP."

"I thought I was supposed to be all depressed and stuff."

He smiled briefly at her wording but answered seriously. "You have been depressed, but you're responding well to my devoted attentions."

"Dancing and diamonds, for example."

"For example," he agreed.

"And while I'm flitting about the resort, basking in the afterglow of your attentions, what will *you* be doing?"

"I have business to conduct with our host."

"And you aren't going to tell me what that business is?"

He brushed a kiss across her temple. "Nothing for you to worry your pretty little head about."

"I want a divorce," she said in disgust.

That made him laugh and step back. "You'll have an annulment as soon as I can safely arrange it."

"Good."

"You must be hungry. Are you ready for breakfast?"

She shrugged. "I could eat."

He motioned toward the door. "There's a breakfast buffet in the restaurant downstairs. It looked pretty good when I walked past."

She looked wistfully toward the little dining table in their suite, but she suspected Daniel had a reason for wanting to go out. As she had noted before, Daniel seemed to have a reason for everything he did.

Saying the breakfast buffet looked "pretty good" had been an understatement. B.J. had never seen so much food spread in one place—outside a Walker family pot-luck, anyway.

Watching the scantily clad woman in front of her place a single strawberry and a half slice of whole-wheat toast on a tiny plate, B.J. shook her head and reached for a serving spoon. Her own plate was satis-fyingly full when she carried it to their table a few moments later.

She hesitated only briefly when she saw that Daniel was already seated—and that he had been joined by Judson Drake. Her appetite decreasing significantly, she slipped into her chair and set her plate in front of her, giving Drake a perfunctory nod of greeting.

"Good morning, Mrs. Andreas." Drake had risen when she arrived and he took his seat again after she was seated.

"Mr. Drake."

"I hope you're enjoying your stay with us."

"It's a beautiful resort." That, at least, was true.

He glanced at her well-filled plate. "It's always a pleasure to see a woman appreciate our chef's efforts."

She really detested this guy. Even though he was being perfectly congenial, there was just something about him that made her want to punch him. And she had never considered herself a particularly violent woman.

She filled her mouth with Belgian waffle to avoid having to respond to him.

Her movement drew his eyes to the glittering new bracelet on her right wrist. "Very pretty," he said, touching it with his fingertips. "Though not as beautiful as its wearer, of course."

His fingers lingered a bit longer than necessary against her skin. She couldn't get over the nerve of this guy. He seemed so convinced that he could charm his way past the cool reserve she had shown around him. And it didn't seem to deter him in the least that Daniel was sitting only a few feet away.

"Thank you," she said and drew away from him to turn toward Daniel with a brilliant and—she hoped—adoring smile. "My husband gave it to me. He's such a sweet man."

"Sweet," Drake murmured, looking rather quizzically toward Daniel. Apparently the man he knew as Daniel Andreas was anything but "sweet."

Daniel took B.J.'s left hand and lifted it to his lips. "That's me," he murmured against her knuckles. "Just a sweet guy."

His gaze locked with B.J.'s over her hand, and she found herself unable to look away. His eyes were so dark, so reflective that she could almost see herself in them. If she didn't know better, she could almost believe that he very much liked what he saw.

"Well…" Sounding only slightly less affable than before, Drake stood. "I'll leave you lovebirds to your breakfast. Daniel, I'll see you in my office at ten. And by the way—all the times you talked about your lovely Brittany before? You hardly did her justice."

With what B.J. considered an especially oily smile, he nodded and moved on.

"That is the creepiest man I have ever met," B.J. muttered furiously.

"He's just—"

"Wait a minute." She set her fork down with a thump and frowned at Daniel. "He called me Brittany."

"Yes. Well, he doesn't know—"

"He said you talked about me—about Brittany—before we even came here yesterday. Or did I misunderstand?"

Daniel sighed in what sounded like resignation. "You didn't misunderstand. When I mentioned my wife to Drake before, I called her Brittany. Fortunately he seems to accept that I use your nickname when we're together."

"You made up a wife named Brittany?"

He glanced around to make sure no one could overhear them before replying in a low voice. "When I thought of a woman from Texas, the name Brittany just popped into my head. I suppose it was an old memory— besides, it sounds like the name of a woman from Texas with plenty of money."

"Which is why I prefer my initials," she muttered. "My mother gave me a name that's never felt like my own. Still—"

Daniel reached for his coffee mug, his face revealing none of his emotions. "The fact that I coincidentally used your name means nothing, of course. It has simply made it easier for us in the long run."

Taking the hint that he didn't want to talk about it anymore, she forced her attention back to her breakfast. Perhaps it truly meant nothing that he had given her name to his fictional wife. But it was very…interesting that he had done so, she mused.

B.J. went outside later that morning, not so much because Daniel had asked her to but because the maids were impatient to clean the suite and she didn't want to get in their way. She drifted through a few shops, but the merchandise displayed for purchase couldn't hold her attention.

There were quite a few people sitting around the pools, sunning, reading, tapping on laptop computers, but few were actually swimming. The tennis courts were in use, as were many of the machines in the workout facilities, but B.J. had no interest in either activity.

She settled finally for a long walk on the beach. She hadn't visited the ocean many times, and it was a pleasant diversion to stroll on the sand, letting the breeze stroke her skin and listening to the sounds of the surf. She walked slowly, stopping often to examine busy tide pools and interesting shells and to watch in delight as a few dolphins played in the waves some distance from the shore.

When the dolphins disappeared, she turned and began to walk again, farther from the resort. She saw a couple on horseback far ahead of her but passed no one else. Apparently this wasn't a popular swimming or sunning area, since the crowds seemed to have gathered closer to the resort, where umbrellas and cold drinks were at hand for their convenience.

The riders had turned and vanished, presumably taking another path back to the resort stables. Looking ahead, B.J. saw only sand and grass and rocks. If she continued walking, she would surely reach another resort. Some private beach homes, perhaps.

With a little luck—and a few phone calls—she could be back in Dallas by the end of the day, back to her own life. Leaving Daniel behind to somehow explain how his wealthy and gullible "wife" had suddenly disappeared. Her bolting would certainly make his story of domestic bliss look suspicious, and Drake would immediately begin to question everything else Daniel had told him.

If she had been told the truth, Drake would then arrange for Daniel to "quietly disappear." To be killed, in other words.

Her steps slowed and then stopped.

She didn't know what Daniel was doing. Which side of the law he was on. Whether anything he had told her was true. Whether she was endangering herself by staying with him. She didn't even know that he was really in danger himself.

She tried to tell herself it wasn't her problem. He was a grown man. He could take care of himself. For all she knew, it would be a relief to him if she removed herself from his life.

But what if he really was killed if she took off? Even though she would probably never know if her actions could cause such a thing, the uncertainty and guilt would haunt her forever.

She looked down at her left hand. At his mother's ring.

"Damn it." With a huge sigh, she turned on one heel to return to the resort.

Trudging doggedly back the way she had come, she called herself a fool. An idiot. A gullible, reckless moron. A—

"Mrs. Andreas."

Bernard had seemingly appeared from nowhere, materializing in front of her with a suddenness that made her gasp and fall back a step. "Where did you—"

"I'm sorry if I startled you," he said smoothly, his eyes gleaming with an amusement that belied the apology. "I thought you saw me approaching."

Which was a lie. He had known exactly what he was doing. Keeping that awareness to herself, she allowed her hand to flutter around her throat and said with a little laugh, "No, it's my fault. I was daydreaming and I completely lost track of my surroundings."

"You've wandered quite a way from the resort."

"Have I?" Absently fingering the diamond bracelet, she wrinkled her nose. "My husband says I live in my own world half the time. I have a terrible habit of getting lost in thought—and then getting physically lost as a result."

His gaze dropped to the bracelet and his thin lips curled in a cynical smile. "I'm sure you had quite a lot to think about. Are you on your way back to the resort now?"

"Yes. I believe I'll read by the pool this afternoon. The main pool is so lovely, with the waterfalls and tropical flowers. It's almost like being in the islands, don't you think?"

"Er, yeah, I think that's what the boss had in mind when he designed it."

"How clever of him. I must be sure and compliment him when I see him again." She moved past him, then looked inquiringly back over her shoulder. "I'm sorry, I forgot to ask. Were you looking for me for a reason?"

"Oh, uh, no, I—actually I wasn't looking for you at all. Just taking a walk on the beach."

The smile she gave him then was deliberately vague. "It's a lovely day for it. Have a nice stroll."

"Yeah. Thanks. See you around, Mrs. Andreas."

She walked much more quickly than she had earlier, the attractions of the beach no longer claiming her attention.

Bernard had been following her. Had she not decided to return to the resort, would he have allowed her to follow through with her urge to run?

Something told her the answer was no.

Chapter Five

Daniel found B.J. in the suite much later that afternoon, almost dinnertime. She was curled in a chair with a book, which she must have picked up in the gift shop downstairs, but she didn't seem to have read much of it.

He did his habitual electronics sweep and then asked her, "Have you been out?"

"I went for a walk earlier," she answered, tossing the paperback aside. "I couldn't enjoy it for the annoying shadows."

"Shadows?" he repeated, momentarily confused.

"One particular shadow named Bernard."

Daniel frowned. "He followed you?"

"Yes."

"Where?"

"I walked on the beach. I went quite a long way, actually."

Just how far had she intended to go? "And he stopped you?"

B.J. shook her head. "I had already turned back when he spoke to me."

He wasn't sure whether relief or surprise was uppermost in his mind when he asked, "What did he say to you?"

"He merely commented that I'd gone a long way from the resort. I did my best airhead impersonation and told him I'd been daydreaming and walked farther than I intended. And then I came back here. That was pretty much the extent of it. I, um, haven't been in the mood to go back out."

He squeezed the back of his neck. "Bernard won't hurt you as long as he doesn't suspect anything."

She didn't look particularly reassured. "I hate being watched. Especially without being aware of it."

"He was probably just curious about where you were going."

She gave him a seething look. "It was none of his business."

Sinking onto an ottoman near her chair, he clasped his hands loosely between his knees and studied her face. "So you had already turned around? Before you knew Bernard was watching you?"

She glanced down at her hands. "Yes."

"How tempted were you to keep walking?"

That brought her eyes back up to his. "Very."

"What made you change your mind?"

Her scowl told him she wasn't going to directly answer that question. Instead she asked, "Would Bernard have stopped me if I'd kept walking?"

"Yes," he replied simply, and he didn't imagine he needed to tell her that Bernard would have used whatever means necessary to do so.

"Then I guess it's a good thing I turned back, isn't it? Whatever my reasons."

She had tried to speak offhandedly, but the faint quiver in her voice confirmed that she hadn't needed the details.

The certainty that she had returned for his sake roused feelings in him he didn't want to examine too closely at the moment. He hadn't thought to warn her not to try to leave the resort while he was meeting with Drake; he'd thought he'd made it clear before that she wouldn't be allowed to leave. The fact that he hadn't reminded her again and that his carelessness could have gotten her— and perhaps him—killed made his stomach clench.

"I promised I would keep you safe," he reminded her. "But *you* have to be careful, too."

Her chin lifted. "I *have* been careful. And I'm fully capable of keeping myself safe."

"I know that." He reached out to take her hands in his. "You simply don't have experience with men like these, B.J. You can't imagine how dangerous they can be."

"I imagined clearly enough what they would do to you if I suddenly disappeared."

His fingers tightened around hers for a moment, and

then he said gruffly, "I can take care of myself, too. But thank you for caring."

"I'm not sure that I do care about the *man* who got me into this mess. But maybe I still care—a little— about the boy I used to know."

Sometimes her frankness caught him off guard, slipping beneath the thick barriers he had erected around his emotions. It was a trick she had first demonstrated thirteen years ago, when they were both just kids—and it seemed she still possessed the talent.

"That boy doesn't exist any longer," he told her.

She looked at him so intently that he almost squirmed, wondering what she saw. "What happened to him?" she asked finally.

A dozen years worth of images flashed through his mind, and few of them were pleasant ones. "Life happened."

"Daniel, tell me what you've been doing since you left the ranch."

"Surviving." He gave her hands another gentle squeeze, then released her and stood. "We should get ready for dinner. I'll wait out here while you change."

"We have to go out? We can't eat in here?"

Though he would have liked very much to give in to the plea in her eyes, he shook his head regretfully. "I'm afraid we have a dinner engagement."

She winced. "Please tell me we don't have to eat with Creepy Guy."

"I'm afraid we do. I'm sorry, I'll try to get us away early."

B.J. was on her feet and shaking her head, her expression turning mulish. "Tell him I have a headache and can't join you this evening."

"I need you to do this with me, B.J. Please."

For a moment he thought she was going to refuse—and short of carrying her bodily downstairs, there was little he could do to force her to accompany him. But then she sighed and pushed a hand through her hair. "Damn it."

He knew better than to smile at her disgruntled expression. "Is that a yes?"

She jabbed a finger into his chest—hard enough to leave a dent. "Your debt to me is mounting—and be warned, I fully intend to collect."

"I have no doubt that you will."

B.J. wore the little black dress for dinner. Sleeveless and fitted, with a moderately deep V neckline, it looked good on her—but it was the color that seemed to suit her mood best that evening. Just the thought of dining with Creepy Guy Drake made her want to dress in black.

Daniel's charcoal jacket was only a shade lighter than her dress, but his white shirt and light gray pants lightened it up. Studying him as he ran a comb through his glossy dark hair, she decided maybe the evening wouldn't be a total washout as long as she had Daniel to look at.

"You were a pretty teenager," she commented with a tilt of her head, "but you're even better-looking now. I guess that comes in handy for a con man."

She was amused when he dropped the comb. "You say the damnedest things."

She shrugged, rather pleased with herself for rattling him. "Just stating facts."

Turning toward her, he crossed his arms over his chest. "Actually you were a rather gangly child last time I saw you. All braces and legs and elbows."

Now it was her turn to be self-conscious—as he had no doubt intended. "I never claimed to be a beauty," she said gruffly.

"And I never thought you would turn into one." And then he smiled and cradled her face between his hands. "But damned if you didn't anyway."

She felt a flush start somewhere around the hollow of her throat and work its way up to the roots of her hair. "Stop that. We both know I'm not…"

"No. You're the only one who has doubts about your attractiveness." His right thumb moved against her cheek, pausing very close to the corner of her mouth. "As for myself, I've spent the past forty-eight hours trying not to notice how desirable you are. And failing miserably, I might add."

Her heart was suddenly racing, her pulse fluttering so rapidly in her throat that she could hardly speak. But he was simply trying to get back at her for embarrassing him—and he was doing a darned good job of it. "Now you're just being irritating again."

"Actually I'm being lamentably honest." He kissed the end of her nose, then dropped his hands and stepped back. "We'd better go. The sooner we get started, the sooner we can come back to the suite."

And when they did return, B.J. thought, turning rapidly toward the door, she was going to lock herself in the bedroom and leave Daniel to fend for himself.

Drake was already waiting for them in the resort's most formal restaurant. The table to which B.J. and Daniel were escorted was located at one end of the main dining room, slightly elevated and surrounded by a glass-brick half wall that screened but did not completely conceal it. The table overlooked the other diners and was serenaded by a small orchestra that faced that way. The crystal chandelier hanging over Drake's table was slightly more elaborate than all the others.

The overall impression was that of royalty, as though Drake and his guests were somewhat superior to the other diners. B.J. was embarrassed to be taken there.

Drake wasn't alone. He rose to greet his guests, then turned to his companion, a statuesque blonde—of course—with a flawless face and spectacular figure. "Daniel and Brittany Andreas, allow me to introduce Ingrid Jorgensen."

Without glancing at Drake, B.J. smiled politely at the other woman, who looked rather bored. "Please call me B.J."

The woman's very thin eyebrows rose a fraction of an inch. "B.J.?"

"My initials. They seem to suit me better than my first name."

Ingrid seemed to lose interest somewhere in the middle of the brief explanation. Or perhaps she'd had so many facial injections she was unable to express emotion, B.J. mused. And then chided herself for being catty as she allowed Daniel to hold her seat for her.

She wasn't usually the type to be threatened by stunningly beautiful women. Maybe Daniel was right that being in this place had triggered an insecurity response in her.

She couldn't help remembering that moment in the suite when Daniel had held her face in his hands and called her a beauty. Could he really say the same thing now that he saw her side by side with the breathtaking Ingrid?

Drake was seated at one side of the small round table with Ingrid on his left, B.J. on his right and Daniel directly opposite him. He turned to B.J. with one of his genial-host smiles. "I hope you had a pleasant day?"

"Lovely," she replied, letting her return smile show teeth. "I had a nice long walk on the beach." As he undoubtedly knew, she figured, since he had instructed his guard dog Bernard to follow her. "And then I relaxed for several hours with a good book."

He probably knew she'd charged the book to her room, too. Not that she could attest to it being a good book. She hadn't been able to concentrate enough to read more than a few pages.

"I've taken the liberty of ordering our meal in advance," Drake said when several servers arrived with trays of appetizers. "I believe my chef has prepared something for every taste."

Daniel replied, "I'm sure we'll enjoy the meal. We aren't picky eaters, are we, darling?"

B.J. turned a saccharine-sweet smile toward him. "Unless you count your unfortunate lactose intolerance." She turned to add chattily to Ingrid, "Poor dear walks the floor for hours after he eats dairy. Just like my grandfather used to do," she added with a sigh.

Ingrid looked vaguely horrified by the excess of information. Daniel stopped himself from reaching for a cheese cube and plucked a stuffed mushroom from the appetizer tray instead. The look in his eyes promised B.J. retribution, but he took some revenge by saying, "And my wife is deathly allergic to chocolate. Other than that, we'll eat just about anything."

Oh, low blow, she fumed. Especially when Drake patted her hand and said, "I'm glad to know that. I ordered chef's special chocolate lava cake for dessert. I'll have something else brought out for you, B.J. A bowl of fresh fruit, perhaps?"

Repressing a wistful sigh—chocolate lava cake sounded like the one thing that could even slightly salvage this evening—she nodded. "That sounds very nice."

Daniel would pay for that, she promised herself. It didn't even matter that she had fired the first shot.

"Tell us about yourself, B.J.," Drake encouraged during their second course. "Daniel and I have been doing all the talking this evening."

B.J. and Ingrid had eaten quietly, neither paying much attention to the men's discussion of current world events. B.J. was usually an active participant in mealtime conversations, but she had no particular interest in anything Drake had to say. "I'm afraid there's nothing interesting to tell you about myself. Perhaps Ingrid would like to share something with us?"

"Actually," Ingrid said, looking up from her barely touched food with the first sign of animation all evening, "I'm a singer. Well, I work as a runway model now, but I hope to…"

"Your husband has told me you're active in several charities," Drake said to B.J. as if Ingrid had never spoken. Ingrid subsided into silence again when he continued, "I suppose you're on the board of several foundations back in Texas?"

Easily checked on the Internet if she claimed that she was. "I've always been rather phobic about maintaining my privacy. I prefer to make my contributions behind the scenes."

Noting that Daniel gave her a look that approved her answer, she turned back to the sullen Ingrid. "I would like to hear more about your career as a model and a singer. That sounds so glamorous compared to my quiet life. What type of music do you sing?"

Glancing rather defiantly at Drake, Ingrid replied, "I love country music. Like Faith Hill and Shania Twain."

A country singer named Ingrid Jorgensen would certainly be a change, B.J. thought with a stifled smile. "I would love to hear you sing. Will you be performing here at the resort?"

The look Ingrid gave Drake this time was definitely resentful. "No."

"With all the venues available to you?" B.J. glanced at Drake in exaggerated astonishment. "I'm surprised."

Drake looked decidedly displeased, despite his forced smile. "I'm afraid not many of my guests are fans of country music."

"I wouldn't be so certain. Country music is quite popular with a broad range of listeners, I assure you."

"That's what I've been telling him," Ingrid said eagerly. "Just because he doesn't like country music, he thinks no one else does either."

"You must understand that Mrs. Andreas is from Texas, Ingrid. Musical tastes are a bit…different there."

"But appreciation for a beautiful, talented woman is universal," Daniel inserted smoothly, giving Ingrid a smile. "I, too, would enjoy hearing you sing…being from Texas myself."

The reproof was subtle but definitely there. Daniel had just made it clear that he would tolerate no insult— not even an implied one—against his wife.

Whatever the connection or power structure between Daniel and Drake, the latter backed off with a nod. "Of course. Ingrid, perhaps you'll work up a number with the band at the Seaside Lounge for tomorrow evening."

"I'd like that," Ingrid all but purred.

Still smiling with gritted teeth showing, Drake reached for his wineglass, giving B.J. a long look over the rim.

"I think you've made a new friend for life," Daniel commented later. "Ingrid practically kissed your hand when we parted."

Remembering the look in Drake's eyes when he had bade her good-night, B.J. swallowed. "I think I made an enemy, as well. Creepy Guy obviously doesn't like it when women challenge him. He was annoyed enough already that I didn't swoon every time he gave me one of his oily smiles."

The moon was full as they walked on the beach, providing them plenty of illumination. Yet B.J. was unable to read Daniel's expression. "Don't worry about Drake. There's a good chance we'll be out of here by this time tomorrow and you'll never have to see him again."

She wondered if she would ever see Daniel again after they left here. "We're leaving tomorrow?"

"I said there's a good chance. It depends on a couple of developments."

"What sort of developments?"

She didn't really expect him to answer, and he didn't. Instead he shrugged out of his jacket and draped it over her shoulders. "Is that better?"

She hadn't realized she was chilly until she felt the warmth of his jacket on her bare arms. The soft fabric smelled like Daniel, she realized as she drew the jacket more tightly against the cool ocean breeze. The scent was subtle, spicy, somewhat mysterious. A fanciful woman might have believed it carried just a hint of danger.

B.J. was trying very hard not to be fanciful tonight. "Thank you."

The moon hung low in the sky behind him, making his shirt gleam almost ghostly white but throwing his face into deep shadows. "You're welcome."

The walk had been Daniel's suggestion. She suspected he wanted to establish a pattern, making it look as though strolls on the beach were commonplace for her—probably to further weaken any curiosity about her trek that morning.

She doubted that he was deliberately procrastinating about returning to the suite. Despite his joke earlier, Daniel had no reason to be concerned about them being alone for another night.

She was the one who had to fret about fighting an unwelcome attraction. Impulses that could lead her into a world of trouble if she gave into them. An infatuation that had begun rather innocently more than a dozen years ago and was now complicated by wholly adult lust.

Despite his outrageous flirting with her earlier— which, she had no doubt, had been intended as an effective way to distract her from inconvenient questions—she didn't believe for a minute that Daniel worried about losing control of his impulses if they spent too much time alone together. For one thing, she couldn't believe that Daniel ever lost control.

They weren't the only ones out on this beautiful evening, but no one seemed to be paying them any attention. Most of the others were couples wrapped up in each other, staying as far away as possible from anyone else. Yet B.J. had the uncomfortable sensation that she and Daniel were being spied upon anyway. The fact that she couldn't spot the watchers made the suspicion even more unsettling.

Daniel draped an arm loosely around her shoulders, pulling her close enough to walk comfortably beside him yet still allow them to converse in very low voices. She knew better than to read anything personal into his action. She wasn't the only one aware of unseen observers.

"You never told me why you came looking for me in Missouri," he said from out of the blue.

"Sure I did."

"No. I'd have remembered."

She thought back over the past couple of days with him—and realized that he was right. She had never actually gotten around to telling him the reason she had tracked him down. "I guess I've been sort of...distracted."

"Understandable. So...?"

"I came to invite you to a party."

Obviously not what he had expected. He actually stumbled a step in the sand before he repeated, "A party?"

"A surprise twenty-fifth anniversary party for Uncle Jared and Aunt Cassie. It was their daughter Molly's idea. She's trying to gather most of the foster sons who have lived on the ranch during the past twenty-five years. She's located most of them, but you and a couple others pretty much dropped out of sight after you left."

"Frankly I'm surprised you found me."

"It wasn't easy—especially since you've changed your last name. But I remembered that you once told me you were considering switching to your mother's maiden name after you left the ranch." The slight uptilt she added to the end of the comment turned it into a subtle question.

He shrugged against her shoulder. "I created a false identity for Drake using my mother's name, thinking it wouldn't be a problem, since that wasn't the name I used as a boy, in case he checked."

"You used my name, too," she reminded him.

"Um, yeah. As I said, that was an odd coincidence."

"Hmm."

"So—all of this was over a party."

"A *big* party," she felt compelled to add. "Dozens of people will be there."

"And that's just your family."

The dry comment made her giggle. "Well…yeah. But other people, too. Uncle Jared and Aunt Cassie have touched a lot of lives during the past twenty-five years."

"I'm sure they have."

B.J. looked rather fiercely at the waves cresting white-topped in the moonlight. "I, um, thought they changed your life, too. At least, that's what you told me the day you left."

"That was a long time ago," he said after a moment.

"Do you remember what you said to me that day? You told me you were going to make something of yourself and then you would come back to thank the Walkers for all they had done for you."

"Like I said—it was a long time ago. I was just a kid. I barely remember those days—and I would be surprised if they remembered me."

"Of course they remember you, Daniel. You were a

part of their lives for a full year. They still have your photograph displayed with the other foster boys who have stayed with them and they mention you often when reminiscing about the past."

He remained silent.

"They would love to see you again," she ventured.

Without glancing at her, he murmured, "You really think they would be proud to learn that I've become a con man?"

"Is that what you are?"

"It's what you called me earlier," he reminded her.

"Was I right?"

"Oh, yeah. You were right about that."

She chewed on her lower lip, trying to interpret his tone and not his words. "Won't you at least tell me why you're here?"

"I've told you that already. I'm here for the money."

There was a ring of truth in his voice. As far as she knew, he hadn't actually lied to her yet. When she asked a question he didn't want to answer, he simply ignored it. So when he said he was here for the money, she supposed she should believe him.

"That's really it?" she couldn't help asking.

"If you're trying to find justification for my actions, forget it. I keep telling you, I'm not the kid you used to know."

His almost harsh tone contrasted with their still-cozy position. To an onlooker, they could have been murmuring sweet nothings to each other.

B.J. looked up at Daniel with a wistfulness she hoped

he couldn't see. Maybe he had changed, but he was wrong about her not being able to find justification—or at least explanation—for the man he had become. It made sense to her, in a way, that after a childhood of helplessness and deprivation, he would pursue power and wealth as an adult.

He had been angry then that extreme poverty had contributed to his mother's untimely death. He would be determined now not to allow himself to be at anyone's mercy again.

She had hoped, however, that he would seek his fortune through legitimate means. Education, career. Had his options really been so limited after he'd left the ranch—or had he only perceived them to be?

"Jared and Cassie wouldn't care what you've done since you left. They would still love to see you."

Perhaps there was just a note of wistfulness in Daniel's voice when he replied, "I closed the door on my past a long time ago. I would rather not reopen it."

And yet, when he had needed a name for a fictitious wife from Texas, he had chosen a name from that past. Maybe that door wasn't closed as tightly as he wanted her to believe.

Though they had been walking very slowly, they'd gone some distance from the resort buildings. B.J. could barely hear the strains of the music from the outdoor lounge. Daniel paused to look at the moonlight-frosted ocean. "It's nice out here, isn't it?"

Brushing a breeze-tossed strand of hair away from her eyes, B.J. nodded. "Very different from Dallas."

"Not quite as exotic as the places you've daydreamed about."

She let that comment go without a response. It was hard to define how she felt about being here. The beauty of the scenery was undeniable, as were the attractions of the luxury resort. Had she not been so constantly aware of those hidden watchers and so continuously worried about her inappropriate responses to Daniel, she could be enjoying her stay here much more than she might have expected, considering her initial response to the place.

He turned to face her, draping both arms over her shoulders and clasping his hands loosely behind her head. "I would like to know exactly how you found me, but perhaps we should concentrate on our roles again for a while. It would seem very odd if a doting husband didn't stop even once to kiss his wife during a romantic moonlight stroll."

She cleared her throat. "Maybe his wife is the sort who prefers to do her kissing in a less public place."

Smiling, he brushed his lips along her cheek. "Maybe she's so wrapped up in her husband that she doesn't even notice if anyone else is around."

As corny as that sounded, B.J. had little trouble believing it could be possible. Standing this close to Daniel, with his arms around her and his eyes locked with hers, she was having a hard time believing they weren't the only two people on the planet.

"A bit full of yourself, aren't you?" she managed to tease lightly.

He chuckled, his breath warm against her temple. "Just playing a part, darlin'."

He didn't have to keep reminding her of that, she assured herself. She wasn't likely to take his attentions seriously.

If there was one thing she didn't need, it was to fall in love with a self-admitted con man.

Daniel kissed her cheek again and then the corner of her mouth. And then his lips settled firmly on hers.

They were simply playing their parts, B.J. reminded herself as she slid her arms around Daniel's waist. Putting on an act, she thought as she tilted her head and parted her lips to cooperate with the kiss. Yet when he tightened his arms around her and deepened the kiss with a thrust of his tongue, she forgot about performing for any audience except him.

Regardless of his motivation, there was no doubt that Daniel Andreas was one hell of a kisser.

The initial embrace lasted for a long time, as did the kiss that followed. And the slow, deep, mesmerizing one after that. She was plastered against him now, and it was impossible not to notice that he was at least partially aroused.

Proving only that he was a man, she reminded herself when she finally drew her head back to end the kiss. No one could help responding to kisses like those.

She was very close to melting into a puddle in the sand herself.

Daniel's voice was rather hoarse when he said, "I think it's time to go in."

He caught her hand when she would have drawn out of touching distance. Reminded that the performance wasn't quite over for the evening, she slowed her steps and tried to appear besotted with him as they made their way back to their room.

The problem was, it was entirely too easy to pull that look off. And she was becoming increasingly concerned that—on her part, at least—it wasn't all an act.

Chapter Six

Three in the morning, and Daniel was lying in the dark in the suite's sitting room. Alone. B.J. had turned in soon after they'd returned from their walk, but he had told her he had some paperwork to look over first.

Even after he had procrastinated as long as possible with the paperwork and turned off the lights in the sitting room, he hadn't been able to make himself go into the bedroom. Instead he sprawled on the uncomfortable sofa, his sock-clad feet hanging over one end, eyes wide open as he stared at the ceiling.

After those kisses on the beach—kisses that had begun for the benefit of anyone who might be watching but had swiftly evolved into much more—he hadn't trusted himself to join B.J. in the bed.

He had told her there was a good chance they would be leaving tomorrow. In actuality, the odds were only about fifty-fifty that he could wrap his business up that quickly. Still, he was going to do everything he could to get this over with as quickly as possible.

Drake and his men were dangerous—but it was beginning to feel as though Brittany Jeanne Samples posed the real threat to the life Daniel had created for himself.

Too restless to wait in the suite for Daniel the next morning, B.J. donned a black two-piece bathing suit and a floral-on-black pareu, deciding it was time to try out the pool.

She hadn't actually seen Daniel since he had sent her off to bed alone the night before. She'd found a note from him when she'd woken. It lay on the pillow Daniel hadn't used last night.

"Darling," he had written neatly, "I'll be in meetings most of the morning. I hope you'll be able to entertain yourself until I rejoin you."

She suspected that it was as much mischief as role-playing that had made him add, "I'll carry the memory of last night with me until I have you in my arms again. Your Daniel."

Oh, puhleeze, she had thought with a roll of her eyes. Was Daniel's idea of marital bliss really so smarmy or was this his attempt at a private joke?

Either way, she had tucked his note into her tote bag rather than tossing it into the trash, and she didn't want to spend much time examining her motives for hanging on to it.

It was while she was stashing the note away that she realized both her cell phone and her wallet were missing from the bag. Since B.J. had arrived at the resort, she hadn't needed them—so there was no telling how long they had been gone. Everything else was still in place, but no amount of digging through her usual clutter produced either of those items.

It occurred to her that there was now nothing in the bag to indicate that she was anyone other than who she had said. Daniel's wife. Anyone snooping through her things might wonder at the absence of a wallet, but they wouldn't find anything to disprove her cover story.

Maybe she should have considered that someone from outside had been through her bag already and had taken her possessions. But for some reason she had no doubt that Daniel was the pilferer. He had been so thorough in making sure she went along with this charade; he wouldn't neglect hiding any evidence that they were pulling off a scam.

Knowing she would be wasting her time searching the suite for her things, she picked up her paperback and headed out of the suite.

Even knowing Drake had designed it himself, she couldn't help but admire the pool. It was so beautiful, with its surrounding tropical plants, the natural-looking waterfalls, the curving lines of the pool itself.

She selected an umbrella-shaded poolside chair, ordered a glass of orange juice from a server who seemed to appear out of nowhere, then leaned back and opened the book she had purchased yesterday. Fifteen minutes later she closed it again. She was too restless to read. Her body ached for…something. It seemed safest to define it as exercise.

She slipped into the pool, which was still unoccupied this early in the morning. The pleasantly warm water closed around her like a lover's arms. Because the analogy made that vague ache inside her intensify, she began to swim, counting laps until she couldn't complete another one.

She most definitely burned off energy during her vigorous swim, but nothing else had changed. Her mind was still filled with thoughts of Daniel as she boosted herself out of the pool.

Water streaming off her, she reached for the towel she had left beside the pool. She swiped the towel over her hair and face and turned toward her chair—then stopped.

A man sat in the chair next to the one in which she had been trying to read earlier. He was young—probably close to her own age—and sandy-haired, with friendly blue eyes and a pleasant smile. The skin on his nose was peeling from a sunburn, and his cheeks were unnaturally pink.

He couldn't look more innocent, but still she wondered if he was yet another employee of Drake's. Had he been watching her for a reason?

"Good morning," she said evenly, reaching for her pareu.

"Got yourself a workout this morning, didn't you?"

"I suppose so." She wrapped the fabric around her and knotted it at her left hip.

"I just came from a run on the beach," he confided. "I'm a morning person myself. But my wife, well, she doesn't think any vacation day really begins before noon. Sleeping in is a rare treat for her."

Something about the way he had said "my wife" made her smile and sink into her chair. "Honeymoon?"

"Yeah. How could you tell?"

She shrugged. "Newlywed vibes."

He laughed sheepishly. "My wife—um, Natalie— says I'm a compulsive talker. If you would rather be alone—"

"No. I was just out here killing time while my, er, husband is in a meeting."

"Are you on your honeymoon, too?"

"No, we've been married for a couple of years," she said, automatically falling back on the details Daniel had drilled into her. "We're combining a vacation with a business trip."

"Great place, isn't it? They've been treating us like royalty. Maybe you're used to that sort of thing? For Natalie and me it's a real novelty. We saved for more than a year for this honeymoon."

B.J. wanted to tell him that it was new for her, too, but that wouldn't have fit the background Daniel had created for her. "It is a lovely resort."

"My name is Kurt, by the way. Kurt McGuire. We're from Tulsa."

"I'm B.J. Sam—um, Andreas. From Dallas."

"Yeah? Neighboring states. Makes us sort of neighbors, too, I guess."

There was some distance between Dallas and Tulsa, but if he wanted to claim her as a neighbor, what the heck. "Sure."

"I'm an attorney—well, I just passed the bar, but I've got a job lined up in my uncle's firm. My wife's a third-year medical student, which is why we only get five days for a honeymoon, because she has to do rotations this summer. What do you and your husband do?"

The guy certainly was a talker. She wondered cynically how long it would take the practice of law to drain the open friendliness right out of him.

It suddenly occurred to her that Daniel hadn't actually told her what his job was supposed to be. "My husband is in investments," she hazarded. "I keep myself busy with volunteer work," she added, dutifully—if reluctantly—staying in character.

"Do you have any children?"

This was her cue to look sad, she remembered. Oddly enough, as her mind filled with images of little dark-haired, dark-eyed replicas of Daniel, it wasn't that hard to pull it off. "No, we haven't been so fortunate yet."

Perhaps she was a better actress than she had thought. Kurt reached out to pat her bare knee. The gesture was more brotherly than presumptuous. "I'm sure everything will work out for you."

She couldn't help smiling in response to his earnest

expression. He seemed like a genuinely nice man. "Thank you. And by the way, congratulations on your marriage and on passing the bar."

Someone cleared his throat rather forcefully behind them. Both B.J. and Kurt looked around to find Daniel approaching them, his dark brows drawn downward between hard obsidian eyes.

B.J. had thought before that there were times when Daniel could look rather dangerous. This was one of those times.

Kurt quickly pulled his hand back to his own knee. "I have a feeling that this is your husband."

"Yes, it is." B.J. smiled at Daniel, pushing inconvenient memories of last night's kisses to the back of her mind. "Daniel, this is my new friend, Kurt McGuire. Kurt, my husband, Daniel Andreas."

Daniel swept the other man with a hard look that traveled slowly from sunburned cheeks to the hand that had just rested on B.J.'s knee. A slight nod was the only greeting he offered.

Kurt cleared his throat and stood. "Nice to meet you, Daniel. I was just, uh—"

"Patting my wife's leg?" Daniel supplied silkily when Kurt faltered for a moment.

"Daniel." B.J. gave him a warning look as she stood.

"You know, I bet *my* wife is awake now. I'd better go see if she's ready for breakfast." Giving B.J. a quick, careful smile, Kurt hurried away.

Planting her hands on her hips, B.J. stared at Daniel. "That was incredibly rude."

"The guy needs a lesson in keeping his hands to himself."

"And you think it's your place to give him that lesson?"

"If I find his hand on your leg again, you're damned straight I'll give him that lesson."

She made a choked sound of sheer disbelief. "Might I remind you that we are not really—"

"I know you were just being friendly to the guy," Daniel interrupted quickly, giving her a look of warning. "He's the one I don't trust, not you."

"He's a nice, chatty man on his honeymoon who was simply waiting for his bride to wake up. And you were very rude to him."

She turned to snatch up her book from the chair, intending to stalk back to their suite. Daniel caught her arm and turned her around to face him. "You're probably right. I really shouldn't blame the guy for being drawn to you. The way you look this morning, he probably couldn't help himself."

B.J. rolled her eyes. Since her dripping hair was still plastered against her head, she wore no makeup and the modest black bikini only emphasized her lack of curves, she found it hard to take his outrageous flattery serious.

"Yes, well, surprisingly enough, I think it was more boredom than uncontrollable lust for my extraordinary body that made a newlywed man so friendly. So—are you through with your meetings today?"

He hesitated a moment—as if he would have liked to argue more about her conversation with Kurt—but then he shook his head. "No, I have to go back in. I just wanted to tell you that Drake urges you to feel free to make use of the spa or salons this morning. I can't join you for lunch, but Drake has arranged for you and me to have a picnic dinner on an island he owns offshore. He says it's a beautiful spot, and only the most privileged of his guests are invited to make use of it."

"I, um—" She glanced around to make sure no one was nearby, then lowered her voice to little more than a whisper. "I thought we were leaving today?"

"I said there's a chance we'd be able to leave today," he reminded her. "It's looking doubtful now. In the meantime, we're still playing along. So I'll meet you at the marina at five o'clock."

It wasn't a question. He expected her to meet him. Since she had agreed to cooperate, she merely nodded. "I'll be there."

Hands on her shoulders, he pulled her toward him and planted a long, hard kiss on her lips.

"I'll see you at five," he said when he finally released her.

He walked away before she could recover her voice sufficiently to answer him.

Staring after him, she ran her fingertips slowly across her still-tingling lips. If she hadn't known better, she would have almost believed Daniel really had been jealous.

Had he not chosen a life of crime—or whatever it was he was involved with—Daniel could have had an impressive career as an actor.

* * *

Almost an hour after he'd left B.J. at the pool, Daniel could still picture her sitting in that chair, smiling at the man with his hand on her bare, damp knee. She had obviously just come out of the pool. Droplets of water had glistened on her skin, and her face was still rosy from exertion. She had looked young, fresh, natural. Desirable.

Knowing that B.J.'s confidence was rather shaky when it came to her own sex appeal, he wasn't surprised that she hadn't even suspected Kurt McGuire was coming on to her. Maybe she'd been right that time—though even a blissful newlywed had probably noticed just how good B.J. had looked in that black bathing suit that had fit her slender figure like a cat's fur.

He had certainly noticed, Daniel thought with a scowl. Seeing her looking like that and smiling cozily at another man had hit him like a blow directly to the chest.

It was the first time in his adult life that Daniel had been struck by a full-blown case of totally male possessiveness. Not to mention sheer jealousy at having B.J. smiling at anyone but himself.

"Daniel?" Drake spoke rather curtly from the table behind him. "You still with us?"

The question had several meanings, but Daniel answered only the most obvious one when he turned and nodded. "Yeah. Just admiring the scenery."

"You'll have time for that later. Let's stick to business now, all right?"

Good suggestion. Daniel needed to stick to business when it came to B.J., too.

On her own for lunch, B.J. considered ordering room service. But it was such a beautiful day—and the truth was, she was tired of sitting in the suite by herself.

She went to the outdoor café instead, finding a cozy table with a beautiful ocean view. A solicitous waiter took her order for a salad made of mixed greens and grilled salmon, which was delivered to her very quickly, accompanied by whole-grain bread with whipped honey-butter spread.

Sipping iced mint tea, she told herself that she could enjoy this lovely meal without missing Daniel one bit. It wasn't as if she had grown so quickly accustomed to his company, she assured herself. They'd only been together a couple of days, and their interactions had been more for the benefit of others than for themselves.

She really didn't even know him now, since he'd been playing a part—even with her—ever since she'd found him in Missouri. After tomorrow she doubted that she would ever see him again, since he had shown little interest in revisiting his past.

Which didn't mean she wouldn't think of him. Often. Unfortunately he fascinated her as much now as he ever had.

"Good afternoon, Brittany."

She glanced up from her salad with a frown in response to the name. "It's B.J.," she said automatically, only then identifying the speaker. "Hello, Ingrid."

"B.J." The blonde motioned toward the empty chair at the other side of the table. "Are you expecting someone?"

"No. My husband is in meetings until this afternoon. Would you like to join me?"

Looking pleased, Ingrid nodded and eagerly pulled out the other chair. "Guess what I've been doing this morning."

Though B.J. was surprised by the other woman's chatty manner, she played along. "Practicing your singing?"

"Yes. The band in the lounge helped me work up a set—three songs. I'm going back to practice again after their lunch break, just to make sure everything will be perfect tonight."

"I'm sure you'll be wonderful," B.J. said, though she was sure of no such thing. For all she knew, Ingrid had a voice like a frog.

Drake certainly hadn't seemed enthused about giving her a gig in the lounge, but that could well have nothing to do with her talent. More likely, he preferred his women to stay quietly by his side, looking pretty and warming his bed without drawing too much attention to themselves.

"I'm a little nervous," Ingrid confided, accepting a glass of iced mint tea from a server with a smile of thanks.

"That's understandable. Aren't you going to order lunch?"

Though she looked a bit wistfully at the basket of

bread, Ingrid shook her head. "I never eat before I perform. I just came here for a glass of tea."

She didn't look as though she ate much, period. B.J. was naturally slim herself, but she could tell when a woman stayed thin by depriving herself as Ingrid, with her natural curves, apparently did.

Giving the bread basket a little push, she said casually, "At least have a little bread. You need something to give you the energy for a dynamite performance tonight."

"Maybe just a bite." Ingrid plucked a slice from the well-filled basket and then, apparently deciding it wouldn't hurt to embellish it a bit, spread a thin layer of honey butter on top.

Watching in satisfaction, B.J. distracted her by asking, "You said you're nervous about your performance tonight. Is this your first time to perform in public?"

"Oh, no. I've been in lots of beauty pageants, and singing was always my talent. I was first runner-up in the Miss Minnesota pageant two years ago. I should have won, but the winner founded some sort of charity for underprivileged kids and the judges made a big deal out of her, like she was Mother Teresa or somebody.

"Anyway," she added, shaking off a scowl, "I'm nervous because it's been a while since I've sung with a real band and everything. And I know Judson didn't really want me to sing here, so I want to do an especially good job and make him realize he was wrong about my talent."

"Have you and Mr. Drake been seeing each other long?"

"Oh, we aren't really seeing each other, if you know what I mean. We met at a big party a few months ago, and I've been sort of staying with him since.

"He told me he would help me with my career," she added with a renewed flash of bitterness. "So far all he's done is line up a couple of modeling gigs to keep me busy when he's off traveling. Probably has other women everywhere he goes—and he probably makes big promises to them, too."

B.J. noted that Ingrid seemed more annoyed by the lack of career opportunities than the fact that Drake was seeing other women. "Have another slice of bread."

Ingrid took another slice without seeming to notice what she was doing. "Your husband is really good-looking. Nice, too. He's always been real polite to me, without ever getting weird about it, you know?"

Since B.J. couldn't say the same about Drake, she merely smiled.

"How long have you been married?"

"Two years."

"No kids?"

"No." B.J. made an effort to look sad again. "I had a miscarriage last fall. We're still trying, but no luck yet."

"Oh. Sorry."

"It's okay." B.J. was particularly uncomfortable with this part of the story she had been instructed to give.

"I'm sure you'll have a kid soon," Ingrid offered encouragingly. "And I bet it's fun trying, right? After all, you're married to a hunk, and he's obviously crazy about you."

Rather amused by Ingrid's awkward effort to make her feel better—something the other woman obviously didn't have much experience with—B.J. smiled. "He is a hunk, isn't he?"

Looking relieved that the possibility of an emotional scene had passed, Ingrid nodded eagerly. "He's gorgeous. Judson's good-looking and all, but if Daniel wasn't married, let me tell you—I'd make a play for him in a minute. A couple of the other girls already have, because a gold ring doesn't mean squat to them unless they're wearing it. But Daniel, he keeps them all at a distance. I could see why when I watched the two of you together last night. You're, like, a perfect couple."

"You, um, think so?"

"Oh, yeah. I mean, I'm not ready to settle down and have kids myself—I really want to have a fabulous singing career first—but if I was, I'd want something like you've got with Daniel. He's good-looking and rich and powerful and he treats you like a queen. Every woman's dream, right?"

"I...I suppose so." Being treated like a queen had never been B.J.'s dream, but she supposed the wife Daniel had created for this fantasy would like that sort of thing.

Ingrid looked in both directions before leaning slightly toward B.J. and saying in a low voice, "I guess it doesn't bother you too bad that Daniel's mixed up with Judson, huh? I mean, I know they're going to make a lot of money, but I just hope it doesn't all go sour on them."

And just what the hell was she supposed to say in response to that? "I, um—"

"I know, I know. We're not supposed to talk about the men's business. Judson's made that real clear, and I guess your Daniel has, too. But, jeez, you can't hang around them very long without figuring out they're up to something shady. I even heard Daniel tell Judson that they've got to be real careful the feds don't catch on to whatever they're scheming before the big payoff comes through. Doesn't it make you mad when they act like we're too stupid to figure things out?"

"Yes," B.J. said slowly, setting down her fork and folding her hands on the table. She had suddenly lost her appetite. "Yes, it does."

"Oh, well, I guess everything will work out. Judson said he's never been caught at anything yet and neither has your Daniel. Neither of them are Boy Scouts, but I never was interested in Boy Scouts anyway, you know? I like men with money and power."

She patted the diamond pendant hanging around her neck, then reached out to touch the bracelet on B.J.'s wrist. "You know what I mean, right? I just wish Judson would use some of that influence to help me get a recording contract."

B.J. sipped her iced tea to avoid having to respond, since she wouldn't have had a clue what to say anyway.

Ingrid's face lit up. "Hey, I have an idea."

B.J. couldn't help thinking rather cattily that it must be

a novel experience for her, but then she told herself to stop being snide. Ingrid was obviously trying to be friendly.

It was likely that she didn't have a lot of experience making friends with other women. Yet B.J. had defended her last night, cornering Drake into giving Ingrid a chance to sing, and that might have been something Ingrid wasn't accustomed to coming from another woman.

"What's your idea?" She was almost afraid to ask.

"Why don't you come listen to me practice after lunch? You can tell me how I sound."

"Oh, I don't know much about music. I—"

"Please," Ingrid said quietly. "I'd feel better if someone gave me an honest opinion. No one who works for Judson would dare say anything negative. I think you'll be honest.

"And besides," she added with a smile, "you're from Texas. You know country music."

B.J. didn't have the heart to refuse, even though she actually preferred rock to country. It wasn't as if she had anything better to do, anyway. "I can come for a little while," she agreed. "I have to go back to my suite at three or so to get ready to meet Daniel, but I'm open until then."

"Great." Ingrid was so pleased, she reached for another slice of bread.

Chapter Seven

As Daniel had instructed—or to be more precise, as he had ordered—B.J. appeared at the marina at exactly five o'clock. She had considered being ten or fifteen minutes late, just to make a statement, but then decided that would be petty and childish.

She was above that sort of thing, she assured herself loftily. But if Daniel got all bossy and snappy with her again, she was going to chew off a large piece of his hide, to use an old Texas expression.

She had changed into red capri pants and a sleeveless white cotton shirt with red piping at the armholes and V neckline. A thin red cardigan was knotted loosely around her shoulders, in case the temperature dropped as the late-May evening advanced. Red-and-white-checked flip-flops completed the look, so that she was gazing at a coordinated stranger in the mirror again when she finished dressing.

Sunglasses and her paperback—both for when the sun was still out—were the only other things she packed into her canvas tote, since she didn't know what else she might need for this picnic outing. Especially since willpower wasn't something she could stuff into a bag, she thought ruefully, once again remembering last night's kisses on the beach.

She was dismayed to see Bernard waiting at the boat slip with Daniel. Was she going to be forced to endure a picnic with Bernard? If so, she could feel an imaginary migraine coming on, which she would use as an excuse to cut the outing short. Actually, after spending any time at all with Bernard, she doubted she would have to fake a headache.

Bernard was dressed in his usual uniform. Jeans, a blue T-shirt and a loose white linen jacket that made him look a bit like a refrigerator. Even though the look was twenty years out of style, the white jacket did a decent job of hiding the shoulder holster he undoubtedly wore beneath it. The sleeves were pushed up as a concession to the warmth of the afternoon, but she doubted he would remove the jacket within sight of any of the guests.

Having changed at some point during the afternoon into a loose white shirt and khaki slacks with espadrilles, Daniel stepped forward to greet her with a smile and an outstretched hand. "Punctual, as always," he said, brushing a kiss against her cheek.

She merely gave him a look. Maybe he had forgotten that little scene beside the pool earlier, but she wanted him to know that she had not.

"Afternoon, Mrs. Andreas."

She nodded. "Bernard."

"Mr. Drake went all out to make sure you'll have a nice picnic. Chef's packed a real special meal for you."

"How thoughtful." B.J. allowed Daniel to help her onto the sleek cruiser, where she settled on a deep-cushioned seat. Daniel sat beside her, and Bernard took the controls, nodding to a brown-skinned teenager who stood by to assist them in casting off.

The cruise took half an hour, and B.J. had to admit the time passed pleasantly. Daniel stretched his long legs out comfortably, one of his arms slung casually behind her. She enjoyed being on the water. Unconcerned about her tossing hair, she held on to her sunglasses and turned her face into the brisk, salty breeze.

The island was as pretty as a calendar page. Bernard docked the boat at a pier marked with bold signs marked Private Property: No Trespassing.

Beyond a stretch of clean, inviting beach, a picnic pavilion had been nestled into the landscaping. Covered by a picturesque thatched roof, the shelter had three open sides that could be closed off from weather by roll-down awnings. Kitchen facilities had been built into the back wall—an enormous grill, a sink and preparation and serving counters, beneath which were cabinets presumably holding supplies. Two doors marked with male and female silhouettes indicated restrooms at either end of the wall.

The stone floor looked recently swept, so apparently the pavilion received regular maintenance, perhaps daily. Two large teak picnic tables and several teak lounge chairs provided seating for more than a dozen people. Tiki torches surrounded the shelter to provide illumination for evening parties, and party lights were strung inside the pavilion ceiling.

"There's electricity?" B.J. asked in surprise.

"By way of large generators, back behind the shelter," Bernard explained. "They aren't on right now, since you and Mr. Andreas won't be needing electricity for your picnic. The restrooms have skylights that will provide all the illumination you need for daytime use."

Setting an enormous hamper on one of the tables, he then handed Daniel a key on a large yellow holder. "This opens all the cabinets and the restroom doors. We keep them locked because sometimes trespassers make use of the island despite the signs, but we send patrols out enough to keep it from being a big problem. You'll find seat cushions and anything else you might need in the cabinets. Make yourselves comfortable while you're here."

Daniel set a covered plastic box of picnic supplies on the table next to the hamper. "Will you be joining us for dinner?"

B.J. was relieved when Bernard shook his bald head.

"I'll be back to collect you later. Mr. Drake wants you to have a relaxing meal—just the two of you."

B.J. was relieved that Bernard was leaving, but the thought of being alone on Drake's island with Daniel didn't make her overly comfortable, either. Especially after the kisses they had shared the last time they were alone on a beach together.

Watching the cruiser disappear into the distance, B.J. turned back to Daniel with a forced smile. "How do you suppose Drake ended up with this island?"

Daniel shrugged. "Who knows? He claimed he often hosts parties here for celebrities wanting to get away from the paparazzi. Other times—like today—he has guests come over just to spend a day relaxing and enjoying a few hours away from cell phones and computers. During the height of tourist season, he said the island is reserved nearly every day. It's even a popular wedding site."

Looking around at the trees and birds and flowers and beach, B.J. had no doubt that Drake's island had a steady stream of visitors who longed to get away from ringing phones and beeping computers.

Because that subject seemed to have been exhausted, she moved toward the picnic hamper. "Let's see what's in this thing. I'm starving."

Daniel chuckled, though she thought he sounded distracted. "You're always hungry."

"Pretty much. I'm lucky I have the Walker metabolism. The Samples family tend to be somewhat stockier. My brother takes after that side. There's no fat on him because he's totally into sports and running, but he's more broad-shouldered and squarely built than the Walkers." Not that Daniel cared about any of this information, of course. She was just babbling nervously.

Yet he proved that he had been paying attention by asking, "And what about your sister? Seems like I remember her being pretty slender."

"Dawne has the kind of figure that makes men walk into walls," B.J. replied matter-of-factly. "I guess she got the best of the Walkers and the Samples."

"As did you."

She hadn't been fishing for a compliment. Opening the picnic hamper, she began to dig busily inside, changing the subject again. "Wow. This thing is packed."

Daniel had been standing rather stiffly, staring at the water in the direction in which Bernard had disappeared. He seemed to give himself a mental shake and turned then to assist her. "Hang on. I'll get the seat cushions out of the storage cabinets."

She watched as he placed brightly colored cushions on the picnic benches and lounge chairs. A bit more digging produced a pile of straw mats, two of which Daniel arranged at opposite sides of the table.

Having watched him with a frown, B.J. asked, "Daniel, what's wrong? You've been acting oddly ever since Bernard left."

"Sorry. Guess I'm just distracted."

"You aren't still angry that I talked with Kurt earlier,

are you?" Because if he was, she intended to make it clear that—

But Daniel was shaking his head, answering in a firm voice, "I was never angry about that. I just want you to be careful who you talk to while you're here, that's all. You never know who's working with Drake."

There was still something off in his expression. Cocking her head, B.J. studied his face. "How did your meetings go today?"

He shrugged ruefully. "Not well."

So that explained it. She reached into the insulated, ice-pack-lined hamper and began to pull out covered dishes, thinking maybe he would open up more during the meal. Maybe he would finally tell her more about what he was involved with now that they were completely alone.

"This," she said a few minutes later, "is not what I would call a picnic. I don't think I've ever had such fancy food from a picnic basket."

Perhaps remembering that B.J. enjoyed seafood, Drake had provided a virtual feast for them. Cold cracked crab, huge prawns marinated with lemon and spices, potato salad niçoise, marinated asparagus spears. An assortment of cheeses and crackers and thinly sliced cold meats, with fresh fruits and delicate pastries for dessert. Nothing chocolate, she noted with a sigh.

Daniel looked up from his plate—a real china plate rather than the paper plates that made up her typical picnics back in Texas. "Drake takes great pleasure in showing off. This spread is meant to demonstrate for us that he is accustomed to the best of everything—for himself *and* his guests."

"So where did he get his money?" B.J. asked, though she doubted she would get a straight answer. "Did he inherit it?"

"Hardly. Judson Drake is what you would call a self-made man. Including his name, by the way."

"I had already guessed that. There's nothing about the guy that rings true to me."

Daniel shrugged and popped a bite of crab into his mouth. "Yes, well…"

She glared across the table at him. "I'm fully aware that he's not the only one creating an entire persona out of thin air."

Daniel smiled and lifted his glass to her before taking a sip of the expensive wine Drake had provided with the meal.

She shook her head in bemusement. "This whole situation is just bizarre."

"You have no idea how much," Daniel muttered, draining his glass.

"Tell me what you've done since I left the ranch," Daniel urged a few moments later, resting his forearms on the table to study her face. "Did you go to college? Have you always worked for your uncles?"

She didn't even pretend to herself that he was all that interested in her life. More likely, he was trying to keep her talking about herself as a means of preventing further questions about him. But since she knew how stubborn he could be about not answering anything he didn't want to answer, she figured she might as well let him lead the conversation. For now, anyway.

"I went to college. The University of Texas. I majored in accounting—like my father and my brother."

"You didn't care for accounting?"

"No. I worked in my father's office for a year, then had to quit before I went slowly insane. So I tried retail, working in a department store. That lasted six months. Since then I've worked in various computer-oriented jobs, and went to work for my uncles just over a year ago. Supposedly they were going to train me in the business, but mostly they've taken advantage of my computer skills. Tracking you down was the first field assignment they've given me."

Daniel looked somewhat stunned. "You found me that easily and it was your first assignment?"

"I didn't say it was easy," she corrected, though she took some satisfaction from the chagrined look in his eyes. "I was about to give up when I stumbled across someone who thought he had seen you with Drake and directed me toward the farmhouse."

"Who? And what led you to St. Louis in the first place? That isn't where I live."

"I know. You move around a lot. Three weeks ago, you sent your aunt Maria a birthday card postmarked St. Louis. She showed it to me. She also gave me a snapshot of you. If you looked through my wallet when you lifted it, you must have seen the photograph. She said she took it herself last time you visited her—about three years ago."

"I didn't rifle through your belongings," he said a bit defensively. "I simply put them away for safekeeping. And you went to see my aunt?"

"Yes. She's your only living relative, so I thought you might contact her occasionally. It seems you do more than that. She told me you've been sending her money in increasing amounts every month since you left her home when you turned eighteen."

Daniel looked uncomfortable. "I've tried to help her out a little."

"According to her, it's been more than a little. She told me that if it hadn't been for you, she'd have ended up in a state-run home a long time ago."

Scowling now, Daniel wadded up his linen napkin and tossed it onto the table. "Sounds like you had quite a chat with her."

And he didn't like it….

"I wasn't trying to pump her for information. If you'll remember, my only objective was to invite you to a party. She said you were in St. Louis. I tracked down the zip code, showed your picture at every hotel in that area and I had just about given up when someone mentioned having seen you with Drake. One tip led to another and now here we are."

"Here we are," Daniel repeated in a mutter. "It's a miracle you didn't set off all kinds of alarms within Drake's circles. Apparently you never wandered onto his radar screen during your search."

"You were lucky, I guess. And lucky that Bernard immediately assumed I was your wife and didn't ask a lot of questions."

"And lucky that you kept your head and didn't blow everything by blurting out that I wasn't your husband."

"You didn't give me much chance to do so. I don't think I've ever seen anyone move as quickly as you did when you recognized me."

Daniel smiled wryly. "When your life is at stake, you don't waste a lot of time considering options."

B.J. selected a cherry tart from the assortment of pastries. "Your aunt is very fond of you. And proud of you. She told me you're a very successful businessman. She didn't know what type of business you're in, but she thinks it has something to do with computers."

Looking out toward the water, Daniel continued to scowl.

B.J. swallowed the last bite of the tart and reached for her wineglass. "It really bothers you that I went to see her, doesn't it?"

"It bothers me that you tracked her down so easily—and me," he admitted. "Perhaps I was being arrogant in thinking she would be safe even if Drake figured out that the background I gave him was phony."

"There was no reason for you to worry about her. Her last name is different from yours—either of yours. There's nothing at all to connect her with you."

"And yet you did."

"I had the old records from the ranch," she reminded

him. "Molly got hold of them and found your aunt's name and number as your next of kin."

"An invitation to a party hardly seems justification for a wholesale invasion of my privacy."

"You're absolutely right."

He seemed surprised that she had conceded so quickly, and without any effort to defend her actions.

"I'm sorry," she added. "I didn't consider the possibility that you would have good reasons for not wanting to be found. I was focusing on proving myself to my uncles, and Molly is sort of obsessed with her plans for her parents' surprise party. Neither of us gave enough thought to your right to be left alone. We thought you'd want to be included in the party. It certainly never occurred to me—to either of us—that finding you could actually put your life in danger."

"You had no way of knowing that, of course," he acknowledged.

"That's no excuse. We should have realized that if you wanted to maintain a connection with our family, you'd have at least called once during the past dozen years."

He looked at her then. "Did you think about me after I left?"

This time she was the one who glanced away. "Of course I did. I considered you a friend."

More than a friend, of course. She'd had a desperate crush on him—but there was no need to mention that just now.

"I thought of you sometimes, as well," he murmured.

"I remembered the way you always told me I didn't have to be trapped in my past. That I could do anything I wanted with my future."

"I'm sure several people told you that. I know Uncle Jared and Aunt Cassie must have."

"They did," he admitted. "But when you said it, for some reason, I believed it."

B.J. toyed with the napkin in her lap, pleating the fabric tightly. "I was just a kid. I'm surprised you took anything I said seriously."

"I took everything you said seriously."

"So what happened after you left? How did you get from there to…here?"

For just a few moments, he had been open to her. Now suddenly he was closed off again. "I told you I was going to make something of myself."

"And what have you become?"

After only a brief hesitation he replied offhandedly, "A prosperous man. Or at least, I'm headed that way."

She continued to look steadily at him, searching his expression for meanings behind the words. "Having a lot of money is your idea of amounting to something?"

"Of course. Maybe money can't buy happiness, but it can sure provide everything a man needs to keep himself comfortable during the pursuit."

"Funny. It was just two days ago that you cautioned me not to confuse wealth with character and class."

A little muscle flickered at the corner of his eye. "I said that?"

"You did. You were trying to set me at ease when I

said I felt out of place among all the rich people at the resort."

"Yes, well, I never said *I* felt out of place there. Or that I was someone who wanted to be admired for my character, as I'm sure you do. Living in luxury, having anything I want with a quick phone call—that's who I aspire to be."

"You are so full of crap."

Her cross comment startled a quizzical laugh out of him. "I beg your pardon?"

"I don't know why you're here exactly, but I think there's a lot more to it than simple greed. Maybe you want the money to take care of your aunt. Maybe you hate Drake for some reason and want to take him down. Or maybe you just enjoy the challenge of out-conning a con man. But it isn't just the desire for wealth that motivates you."

He seemed momentarily disconcerted, but then he reached for the wine bottle, breaking the visual contact between them. "Would you like some more of this?"

"No, thank you." She stood and moved out of the shelter, walking slowly down to the beach. Shells and driftwood were scattered on the sand, begging to be explored. She carried a few crackers with her, tossing them to hovering, squawking seagulls.

She laughed when they grew bold enough to practically snatch the bites from her fingertips. "Shameless beggars."

"Remember the day we fed the Canada geese that lived in the ponds on your uncle's ranch? The geese were so aggressive, they almost knocked us to our knees to take the bread from our hands."

She hadn't realized Daniel had moved to stand behind her until he spoke. "I remember," she said, turning to face him. "We laughed so hard I got hiccups."

"It was the first time I had laughed like that in months," he murmured. "Since the day I found my mother, actually."

It was also the day he had cried. She could still remember the moment his laughter had turned to tears. He had been appalled by the dampness on his cheeks, perhaps expecting her to react with discomfort. Or worse, pity.

Instead she had somehow instinctively understood that he had needed to release the emotions locked inside him for so long. Emotions that had been triggered by their laughter. And even though she had been very young, only fourteen, she had held his hand and told him matter-of-factly that she understood the need to cry sometimes. She did so herself every once in a while— and she hadn't been through nearly what Daniel had.

He hadn't shed more than a few tears. He had wiped them away with the backs of his hands, leaving dirty streaks on his brown cheeks. Without his asking, she had assured him that no one would ever hear from her that he wasn't quite as tough as he wanted everyone to believe.

He had caught her arm when she'd started to turn away from him. The kiss he had given her then had been brief, awkward, unexpected. She had suspected ever since that it had been intended as a distraction of sorts.

He had wanted to leave her with the memory of her first kiss rather than his momentary weakness.

She remembered both. Vividly.

Dusting cracker crumbs off her hands, she turned to face him now. "Is the money really so important to you? It's not really too late to walk away from this, is it?"

"My business here is very important to me," he answered curtly. "And it's much too late to walk away. I'm only sorry you got tangled up in it."

Her throat was tight when she turned away again. "So am I."

Chapter Eight

Tearing his gaze away from B.J., who sat in one of the teak lounge chairs with the paperback she had pulled out of her tote bag, Daniel glanced at his watch for the dozenth time in the past hour.

It was just after seven o'clock. Bernard should have returned for them by now.

He glanced at B.J. again. Even though there was still enough light to see the pages, she was looking at the book so fiercely that he suspected she was having to work hard to concentrate on her reading. She hadn't said much of anything to him since their talk on the beach, when she had told him she was sorry she'd gotten mixed up with him.

That had stung a little, though he didn't blame her at all for feeling that way.

She was making him remember things he had tried very hard to forget. Making him regret choices he had made during the years that had passed since that innocent kiss at the Walker ranch. And that was really starting to tick him off.

Maybe it was just the silence between them that was getting to him now. It wasn't normal for B.J. to be so quiet for so long. Combined with Bernard's tardiness—and the odd feeling he'd had ever since Bernard left them there—B.J.'s pouting was making him cranky.

She was annoyed because he wouldn't tell her more about his dealings with Drake. He knew it wouldn't appease her to tell her that he was trying to protect her by involving her as little as possible.

He sat in the lounge chair beside her. "Good book?"

Holding her place with one finger, she closed the covers. "Not bad."

"Would you like a snack or something? There were cookies and pastries left over, you know."

"I'm not hungry right now, thanks."

"A miracle in itself."

She gave a perfunctory smile in response to his teasing, then glanced toward the water. "When is Bernard supposed to return?"

Was she so bored with his company that she was even looking forward to seeing Bernard again? "Anytime now."

"I guess leaving the resort today is definitely out."

"I'm afraid so."

Another night in the suite with her. He wondered impassively if he would survive it with his sanity intact. Last night had been hard enough, knowing that she was sleeping so close.

He was clinging to his willpower by his fingertips where B.J. was concerned, but he had no intention of letting go. His memories of her were too special to risk hurting her now. And he *would* hurt her if he allowed her to start romanticizing him or the attraction between them. No matter what justification she tried to attribute to his actions, he was not a man for her to admire.

The problem was, when she looked at him now, she still saw the boy he used to be. And when she treated him that way, it was unexpectedly tempting to pretend that he hadn't long ago changed into someone she probably wouldn't like very much at all.

"I hope Bernard doesn't take much longer."

"Had enough of my company?" he asked lightly.

"It's just that I promised Ingrid we would catch her show in the lounge tonight."

His eyebrows rose. "You promised that at dinner last night?"

"No. I had lunch with her today and afterward I sat in on her rehearsal session with the lounge band."

He was genuinely surprised, since his few encounters with the cool, beautiful Ingrid had made him doubt that she had much interest in befriending other women. "How did that come about?"

B.J. shrugged. "We ended up in the same place at the

same time for lunch. One thing led to another. She wanted a friendly face at her rehearsal, since Creepy Guy has done such a good job of sabotaging her self-confidence."

"How was she?"

"She's not bad, actually. With a little training, and if someone advises her not to try so hard to emulate other singers' styles, she could be quite good."

"Good enough for a recording contract?"

"I don't know," she admitted. "I'm no expert on that sort of thing. But I think she has as much talent as several of the singers who've had moderately successful careers. And she certainly has the looks."

"So you actually like her?"

He watched as her nose wrinkled just a little. Just enough to make his mouth go dry. "I don't *dislike* her," she explained earnestly. "I just don't have much in common with her."

"No kidding."

"So maybe she's a bit…avaricious. She still deserves better than Creepy Guy and the insultingly condescending way he treats her. I hope she does make good in music so she can get away from him."

"Don't kid yourself, B.J. Ingrid is with Drake because she wants to be, not because she has to be. Whatever she might feel about him personally, she likes the perks that come with sleeping with him. But if it makes you feel any better, she's history after this weekend. Drake has hinted to me that he's become bored with her."

B.J. frowned, and he added, "I'm sure he plans to give her a generous parting gift. That's his usual style."

"At least she'll have the chance to perform tonight. Maybe that will lead to something better for her."

Daniel glanced at his watch again. "What time does she go on?"

"Nine o'clock. I'd feel bad if we had to miss it, since I promised her I'd be there."

He found her loyalty to a woman she'd only just met and didn't even particularly like rather touching—and typical of her. He hoped B.J.'s innate faith in other people—himself, for example—didn't get her heart broken someday.

"We should have time to change and make it to the lounge to hear her. If Bernard gets here soon," he added with another glance at the water.

"It seems odd that he'd be late, considering how Drake takes such pride in everything running so smoothly at his resort."

"Yes, well, Drake's not so happy with me right now. He probably told Bernard to take his sweet time coming back for us."

"Why isn't Drake happy with you?"

"He asked to sleep with my wife tonight. When I told him no, he became annoyed."

B.J.'s eyes rounded comically. "He did *what?*"

"Of course, if you're interested, I could always tell him I changed my mind."

The paperback hit him squarely in the chest. "You jerk. You made that up just to rattle me."

He grinned, pleased to see the reluctant amusement in her eyes. "I told you you'd call me that again."

"Now I'm convinced again that it was you who put the snake in my bag."

Still smiling, he set the book aside. "Nope. I laughed my butt off, but I didn't do it."

"Mmm." She looked at him as though she were still reserving judgment on his guilt.

He wanted to kiss her. The urge was suddenly so strong he could almost taste her already.

Perhaps something of his thoughts appeared in his expression. B.J.'s smile slowly faded as she studied his face.

"Stop it," she said almost fiercely.

"I'm not doing anything."

"You're giving me that look. The one you use when you're putting on an act for Drake and his men."

His annoyance that she thought he was acting at the moment goaded him into speaking more candidly than he should have. "I'm not pretending to be attracted to you, if that's what you mean."

Her cheeks warmed, but her scowl only deepened. "If this is your way of distracting me from questioning you about your dealings with Drake, don't bother. I've decided I don't even want to know now."

She was irritating him more with every accusation. "Do you really find it so hard to believe that I find you attractive?"

"Let's just say I doubt I'm your usual type."

He had to admit, if only to himself, that she was right about that. His "usual type" would be someone who was worldly, sophisticated and who would expect

nothing more from him than a few hours of companionship. Someone more like Ingrid, to be honest, though
he'd had trouble noticing Ingrid's charms when B.J. had
been nearby.

But actually his general boredom with his "usual
type" had resulted in increasingly lengthy stretches of
celibacy during the past couple of years. It had just
seemed easier to focus on business rather than to pursue one meaningless encounter after another.

As for anything more meaningful—well, he hadn't
been willing to risk that. From his experience, loving
someone was just too painful. He doubted that B.J.
would understand, despite the uncanny insight she
sometimes displayed about him.

Because he had no intention of being the one who
broke her vulnerable, trusting heart, he abruptly stood
and began to pace restlessly around the shelter, watching the water for any sign of Bernard. It wasn't dark yet,
but the shadows were definitely growing longer and
deeper. Would Drake actually go as far as leaving them
here overnight to make his point?

Oh, yeah. And they should probably consider themselves fortunate if that was the extent of the lesson.

Still sitting in the lounge chair, B.J. watched Daniel
openly as he prowled through the shelter like a caged
cat. Several times he checked his watch and once he
pulled his cell phone out of his pants pocket. His low
growl of frustration told her that he wasn't getting
a signal.

When he seemed to become too confined by the stone floor, he stepped down onto the sand and began to pace the beach, sidestepping the rock-lined fire pit off to one side of the pavilion.

The more time she spent with him, the more he confused her. At one moment he seemed so familiar to her, so much like the Daniel she had known before. And then, almost at the blink of an eye, he changed, becoming an enigmatic stranger.

A stranger who claimed to be attracted to her.

She tried to observe him objectively. He stood framed against the deepening blue sky, his thick, black hair rumpled around his face. His white shirt, which contrasted so appealingly with his brown skin, was plastered to his chest by the stiff breeze from the ocean.

Studying the ridges of bone and muscle outlined by the thin fabric, she felt her pulse rate increase. So much for objectivity.

She had never denied to herself that she was attracted to him. From the moment she'd seen him standing on the staircase at the farmhouse—hell, from the time she'd been fourteen years old—his effect on her had been powerful.

She found it hard to believe he could feel the same way about her. And yet she hadn't forgotten the heat generated by the kisses that had passed between them. It hadn't all been an act, on either of their parts.

As improbable as it seemed, there was a bond between them. One that had been formed a long time ago. The question now was, what were they going to do about it?

She doubted that he was interested in—or was used to—anything more than a brief fling. Scratching an itch. Satisfying his curiosity. Some other cliché that translated to no-strings sex.

And really what more could she expect? She certainly had no intention of playing Ingrid to his Drake. Waiting patiently for his attention, content to enjoy his money without questioning where it came from. No way.

The sky was growing darker, and it was now quite dim within the shadow of the pavilion. Bernard was definitely taking his time coming back for them. She was going to have to hurry now to shower and change before Ingrid's show.

Another fifteen minutes of silence passed before Daniel turned on the beach and headed back toward her. Something in his expression brought her to her feet. "What?"

"I think you should be prepared for the possibility that we'll be spending the night here."

His voice was steady and uninflected, but she didn't for a moment suspect that he was teasing. He was completely serious.

"Should I be worried?" she asked, trying to speak as matter-of-factly as he had.

"No. We'll be safe here. And I'm sure Bernard will show up early tomorrow with an elaborate story about how we were 'accidentally' stranded here."

"Do you have any idea why we're being, um, accidentally stranded here?"

He nodded grimly. "It's a message, of course. I haven't been cooperating with Drake today, and he's giving me a little illustration of how easily he could make us disappear."

"You aren't cooperating?"

She had tried to disguise her sudden surge of hope, but Daniel must have caught it. He shook his head. "I'm not pulling out of the deal. I'm just jerking him around to get a better cut for myself—and he knows it."

Disappointed, she asked, "So this is his way of retaliating?"

He glanced at his watch and then at the setting sun. "I believe it is. I had a bad feeling about this picnic from the beginning."

"*Now* you tell me."

"I'm sorry, B.J. I didn't really think he'd pull a stunt like this with you involved. But I'm sure he figures that bringing you into it makes his warning even more ominous for me."

"Men and their posturing," she grumbled with a scowl.

"The hell of it is, he was absolutely right. Doing this to you is much more effective than anything he could have used to threaten me."

"You said we aren't in any danger."

"No. We'll be fine here. Not particularly comfortable, but safe."

"We'll miss Ingrid's performance."

"That's probably just a side benefit to Drake. He was ticked with you and her both for backing him into that corner."

"Have I mentioned that I can't stand that guy?"

"I wouldn't call him my favorite pal either."

"Then why don't you cut your losses and get away from the creep? We can leave as soon as we get back tomorrow—whenever that might be."

Daniel sighed gustily and pushed a hand through his hair. "It's too late for that."

"No, it's not." She took a step closer to him, speaking with an urgency that seemed to grip her by the heart. "You can come back to Texas with me. My uncles can help you with Drake if he becomes a problem. Talk to Jared. I'm sure he'll be able to…well—"

"Reform me?" Daniel supplied ironically. And then he shook his head. "The thing is, I don't want to be re-formed, B.J."

"But—"

"Look." His voice was rough now. "Don't mistake me for the confused kid I used to be. I'm not looking for a foster home now or a mentor. I'm making my own life—and I don't need anyone giving me guidance in how to do it."

Including her. The unspoken addition seemed to hang in the air between them.

Wrapping her arms around herself, she turned away from him. "Fine. If you would rather model yourself after Judson Drake than Jared Walker, you have every right to do so."

"*Damn it,* B.J." He seemed to want to say more, but he bit off whatever it might have been and turned abruptly toward the storage cabinets at the back of the shelter. "I saw some lighters in one of the cabinets. I'll see if I can get the torches burning before it gets dark."

He had sounded oddly insulted by her comment, she thought speculatively, watching him stalk across the rough stone floor. But he shouldn't hold his breath waiting for her to apologize.

She thought the world of her uncle, a former Navy man turned rancher whose tough, work-weathered exterior hid a heart as big as the Texas sky. Though he had always provided for his family—and made time for the troubled boys who had drifted through his life—Jared would never have access to the kind of money or social status that Drake commanded. But when it came to character, Drake wasn't worthy of wiping the dust from her uncle's boots.

It broke her heart to think that Daniel had been more impressed by Drake's flashy posturing than Jared's quiet, steady decency.

Daniel hadn't become the man she had hoped to find. And she realized sadly that she'd brought entirely too many adolescent fantasies along with her on this search.

The torchlights flickered brightly, casting a golden glow through the pavilion and into the immediate surrounding area. Daniel had lit them all, as well as the logs that had been stacked in the fire pit, providing enough light that B.J. probably could have read again, had she been able to concentrate on the story.

Standing outside the pavilion, she could see stars

gleaming in the black-velvet sky and the white crests of waves lapping against the sand. It was a blatantly romantic setting. There was certainly nothing outwardly threatening about the situation. Which made the underlying message all the more insidious.

"We have plenty more food, if you want a snack," Daniel said, stepping out of the shelter to join her. "Cookies and pastries or fruit and cheese and crackers. There are more cold sodas and bottled waters, too."

She started to refuse and then she changed her mind. It wasn't as if there was much else to do. She might as well have a cookie.

"You know, I really love chocolate for a late-evening snack," she said with a regretful sigh after swallowing a bit of crispy almond cookie. "That was truly malicious of you to tell Creepy Guy I'm allergic to chocolate."

"You started it with that big tale about me being lactose intolerant," he retorted. "Just like your grandfather," he added in a mutter.

She couldn't help laughing at the memory of his expression when she'd said that—not to mention the looks Drake and Ingrid had given her. "Sorry, but I thought I deserve to get in one low blow, considering everything."

"You deserve a lot more than that. Especially now that I've gotten you stranded here for a night. I wouldn't blame you if you found a coconut and knocked me upside the head with it."

His rueful tone made her smile again. She was glad they weren't still verbally sniping at each other. Since they were here for the duration of the night, the time would pass much more pleasantly if they got along—which meant she should butt out of his business, she advised herself. After all, she was the one who had stumbled into his life and put both him and his mysterious plans at risk.

Once this night was over and she had returned to her life in Dallas, she would put the old daydreams behind her and write Daniel off as a lost cause, she promised herself. She doubted she would ever see him again. He could try to buy himself happiness, and she would try to find her own through other means—her work, for example. Her family.

And maybe instead of being disappointed with what Daniel had become, she would take some pleasure in remembering a few exciting, if risky, days with the dashing boy of her girlhood dreams.

Chapter Nine

By nine-thirty it seemed quite clear that Bernard wouldn't be returning for them that night. "I guess you were right," B.J. said after checking her watch. "We're here for the night. And we've missed Ingrid's show. I hope it went well for her."

Daniel looked up from the playing cards in his hand. They had unearthed a wooden box from one cabinet earlier, discovering that it held playing cards, poker chips, a set of dominoes, checkers and chess pieces and a backgammon board. Daniel figured the games were to entertain guests during the frequent but usually quite brief autumn showers that kept the vegetation so lush and green.

B.J. had pounced rather eagerly on the games, probably relieved that they had something to occupy them to make the time they spent together less awkward.

"You're still worrying about missing Ingrid's performance?"

"Well...I did promise. And I hate to think there were no friendly faces in the audience for her."

Daniel laid his cards in front of him and rested his elbows on the table, studying her over his loosely clasped hands. "I'm glad to know the nice girl I remembered has turned into an equally nice woman."

He'd meant it as a simple compliment. He didn't expect B.J. to set her cards down with a scowl and push herself abruptly to her feet. "I'm thirsty again. Do you want anything?"

"No, I'm okay." He watched moodily as she opened the cooler and drew out a half bottle of water she had opened earlier.

Why had it bothered her so badly that he'd commented about how well she'd turned out? Was it because she wasn't able to say the same thing about him?

If you would rather model yourself after Judson Drake than Jared Walker, you have every right to do so.

Beneath the table his hands drew into fists on his knees. She didn't understand, of course. She couldn't possibly understand, having come from such a drastically different background.

He continued to watch her as she walked to the fire pit. She had donned her cardigan as a shield against the cooler night air. She sat on the sand with her arms wrapped around her upraised knees, the water bottle untouched on the sand beside her. Her somber expression was illuminated by the leaping flames.

Damn, but she was beautiful. Funny how he hadn't seen that at the beginning, thinking then that she was merely pretty. Cute. The more time he spent with her, the more he appreciated the genuine beauty of her—both inward and outward.

Yet she was openly disappointed with the man he had become. She saw him as more closely resembling Judson Drake than Jared Walker, the uncle she revered.

The hell of it was, he couldn't entirely disagree with her.

Sitting by a campfire had always made her rather melancholy. Now she found herself swamped with nostalgia, thinking of the campfires at the Walker ranch. Muted laughter and the steady rumble of adult conversation. Children's eager chattering. Camp songs. Roasted marshmallows drawn blackened and melting from the flames.

Her brother and sister and parents, aunts, uncles and cousins. Family. As often as she had felt suffocated by the sheer number of them, she found herself missing them all now.

Was her mother worrying about her? Layla Walker Samples was a notorious worrier, especially when it came to her three kids—all of whom had occasionally given her cause for concern. Layla would be wondering what was going on now, since it was so uncharacteristic for B.J. to just take off on her own.

B.J. wouldn't be at all surprised if her uncles were

looking for her despite the explanatory e-mail she had sent home.

She wished she could talk to her mother now. Or even better, her father. The dependable, pragmatic accountant was the one person B.J. could always count on for calm, rational, objective advice.

"Are you cold?" Daniel asked as he knelt beside her.

Her chin resting on her up-drawn knees, B.J. did not look away from the flames. "No."

"You aren't nervous about being here tonight?"

"No, of course not. I've camped out plenty of times before."

Sensing that he was still looking at her in concern, she lifted her head to look at him. "I'm fine, Daniel. I guess I was just a little homesick for a minute there."

He glanced from her face to the fire. "Remembering the campfires at the ranch?"

It was odd to hear him put her thoughts into words, as if he'd had a glimpse into her memories. "Yes."

"I remember them, too. I enjoyed them, as much as I enjoyed anything during that time."

"You always sat on the outer edges, as far away from everyone else as Jared would allow. You never joined in the songs or the storytelling."

"I didn't know how. Cozy family gatherings were a new experience for me."

"You were so angry. It seemed like you were always scowling."

"I *was* angry," he agreed. "But you never seemed to worry that I would take it out on you."

"No."

"Why not?"

She hesitated a moment, then answered candidly, "Because of the way you treated Molly. She was only eleven and going through that pesky, chattery stage, but even though I could tell she got on your nerves sometimes, you never snapped at her."

He looked surprised. "She was just a kid. A little spoiled, maybe, but she always meant well. I remember going to fairly elaborate lengths to avoid her when I wasn't in the mood for her babbling—which was fairly often—but I could never really be angry with her."

"No one ever could. That hasn't changed, by the way."

"I could never figure out why Jared and Cassie took in problem foster boys when they had a little girl in their house. They were taking a pretty big chance with that, weren't they?"

B.J. shrugged. "More than a few people expressed concern about that during the years Molly was growing up. But really she had Jared and Shane watching every move she made, and Cassie always nearby. No boy had the nerve to even try anything under those circumstances. Even when she passed sixteen and turned into a real beauty, she never had a problem with the foster boys. She complained that she was probably the most closely guarded teenager in Texas."

Daniel chuckled. "I suppose she was. I always knew Shane would take my head off if I even looked cross-eyed at his baby sister—and that was assuming Jared didn't pound me into dust first. Hell, by the time I left, *I* was watching out for her like a big brother."

"She was very fond of you, you know. They all were. Molly cried after you left."

"From what I understand, she cried every time one of the foster boys left."

"Well…yeah," B.J. admitted. "But she did miss you. We…they all did."

If he noticed the slight stammer, he ignored it. Instead he tossed another stick into the fire pit. The wood began to burn with a pop and a crackle. Only thing missing was a snap, B.J. mused, propping her chin on her knees again.

"So…you want to play another game? Checkers? Chess?"

"No, thanks." She continued to gaze solemnly into the fire. "I think I'll just sit here for a while."

She felt his gaze on her, but she didn't look away from the flames. After a moment Daniel stood, brushing sand off his pants. "I'll start squaring away the pavilion. Find us a place to sleep. No, don't get up. I can handle it."

She relaxed again, deciding not to argue with him. She let her mind drift again, and though she made a conscious effort to avoid dwelling on old memories and fantasies, those thoughts weren't so easy to dispel.

Daniel rigged makeshift beds by laying out chair cushions on the picnic tables. A flashlight unearthed from one of the cupboards gave B.J. enough light to make use of the now-dark ladies' room.

After helping B.J. onto one of the tables, Daniel extinguished most of the torches, threw another couple of logs in the fire pit, then climbed onto the other table. "Not particularly comfortable, is it?"

B.J. lay on her side, cradling her head on one arm. "It's not too bad."

On the other table, Daniel lay facing her, mimicking her position. Shadows cloaked him so that she couldn't really see his face, nor did she imagine he could see hers any better. "Are you too chilly?"

"A light blanket would feel pretty good, but my cardigan should be warm enough."

"Sorry there's no blanket. You'd think with all the other stuff Drake stocks in those cupboards, he'd at least have one or two."

"I'll be okay."

"Let me know if you need anything during the night."

"Thanks." She closed her eyes, trying to will herself to sleep. It wasn't going to be easy, what with the hard table, the cool air, the sounds of the ocean and the night-calling birds. Not to mention Daniel lying so close to her.

Apparently she managed to doze. She woke with a start when she realized that she was no longer alone on the narrow table. "What—"

"You were shivering," Daniel murmured, wrapping an arm around her. "I don't have a blanket, but I can offer body heat."

She *was* cold, she realized groggily. She had drawn into a tight ball on the cushions and she was shivering. Daniel's warmth against her back felt good, but still—

"I don't think this is a very good idea."

"We're just going to sleep," he assured her, nestling her more snugly against him. "We've slept together before. Our first night here, remember?"

Yes, but that had been in a bed. A bed so large they'd slept the entire night without even brushing against each other.

"Go to sleep, B.J. Tomorrow is soon enough to start fretting again."

It seemed easier to do as he suggested than to argue. Enjoying the warmth wrapped around her, she let herself sink into oblivion again.

It wasn't quite dawn the next time she awoke. The sky was just beginning to lighten to charcoal rather than the inky black of midnight. And she and Daniel were nestled more snugly than two pages in a closed book.

Holding her breath, she lay very still, trying to decide if he was asleep. His breathing was deep and even, each slow exhale brushing against the back of her neck like a teasing caress.

Through her clothing she felt the warmth radiating from his body. A body she could feel in some detail. Biceps, pecs, abs—the man was definitely well-developed from waist up.

As for waist down—

His thighs were solid against the backs of hers. And the bulge against her hip was substantial.

"Are you awake?" His voice was a low rumble in her ear.

Oh, yeah. She was suddenly wide awake. "Uh-huh," was all she managed to say.

"Cold?"

Hardly. "Uh-uh."

"Did you get any sleep?"

"Some. You?"

"Couple hours. I guess a hard picnic table can be pretty comfortable, huh?"

She moistened her lips. "Apparently."

Without thinking, she shifted her weight. The movement pressed her more snugly against his groin, a wholly unpremeditated result.

"Then again," Daniel said, his voice suddenly hoarse, "maybe it's not so comfortable, after all."

She moved instinctively to shift into a less intimate position. Unfortunately Daniel moved at the same time, and they ended up more entangled than before.

B.J. froze before she could get into even more trouble. There was just enough light for her to see Daniel's rather pained expression. She knew she must look mortified.

"Maybe we should just get up," she said in exasperation.

His sudden crooked smile flashed, and even in the faint light she could see the wickedness in it. He didn't have to say a word.

She forced herself to frown at him, trying to speak evenly despite the rapid beating of her heart. "Behave yourself."

"I know I should," he murmured reflectively. But he didn't move.

B.J. felt her throat tighten. "Um…Daniel?"

"Yeah. I'm going to move now." But instead he brushed a strand of hair away from her face and remained where he was, looming over her, bodies touching from chest to ankles. Touching intimately enough that she could tell he was becoming more aroused by the moment.

She put a hand on his chest. Probably to push him away. At least, so she tried to tell herself. Instead her fingers curled into his shirt, slowly kneading the warm skin beneath the thin fabric.

Oh, he was strong. Solid. A man one could lean on. Curl into.

But not one she could completely trust, she reminded herself in an attempt to quell the desire rising inside her.

It didn't work. When Daniel lowered his head, she lifted hers to meet him.

Their previous kisses had begun with an audience in mind. Though the embraces had threatened to spin out of control nearly every time, there had always been the awareness of onlookers, the reality of the roles they were playing to keep them reined in.

There was no audience this time, no reason to perform. And nothing to stop them except willpower—which, B.J. conceded, wasn't going to be enough.

She had been fantasizing about this man, this moment, for almost half her life.

Resting his weight on one elbow, he cupped her face between his hands, tilting her head to provide him unrestricted access to her mouth. He spent a long time exploring her lips, nibbling at them, tasting them, tracing them with the tip of his tongue. And then parting them so that he could delve more deeply.

His tongue swept the inside of her mouth, tangled with hers, then taunted with slow, rhythmic thrusts that made her hips move instinctively in tempo. Murmuring something that might have been an attempt to soothe her, he slid a hand down her stomach. His fingers spread across her abdomen, resting so close to that aching place between her legs that she moaned helplessly into his mouth.

Entreaty turning to demand, she speared her hands into his luxuriously thick hair and kissed him with a renewed fervor. She sensed his control slipping away from him. Heard it in the ragged edges of his increasingly rapid breathing. Felt it in the hammering of his heart against her ribs. Her own was beating so hard and so fast that she knew he could feel it, too.

His fingers moved an inch lower, and she arched in response, one knee rising to cradle him more intimately between her thighs. There was no pretending now that either of them was in control. No way for either of them to deny the need that was driving them.

"B.J.," he muttered against her throat.

She was so very glad he hadn't called her Brittany. That he wanted the woman she had become. Sliding her hands beneath his shirt, she stroked the warm, supple skin of his back and kissed him again. Only this time it was slow, not fevered. Deliberate, not impetuous.

She didn't think she could make the invitation more clear.

He froze for just a moment against her. Just long enough for her to sense the battle taking place inside him. Hunger warred with common sense—and she was so deeply relieved when need won out. When his head lowered again to her throat, there was no mistaking the new purpose in his actions.

He kissed a path from her jaw to her ear, took a tiny, arousing nip of her earlobe, then dipped his tongue into the hollow behind it. More kisses led downward to the deep V of her blouse, toward the rise of her breasts, which were already heaving with the breaths she struggled to drag into her lungs. Her attention was divided between the journey he was taking with his mouth and the movement of his fingers against her tummy, her thighs and—finally—against the so-sensitive area between them.

She jerked spasmodically in reaction, gasping his name. Once again his mouth returned to hers, attempting to calm her but succeeding only in making her want more.

"Don't stop," she said when he lifted his head, breaking the kiss.

His gaze bore into hers, his dark eyes glittering in the pale gray light of predawn. "Be sure," he said roughly. "I won't apologize later."

"I won't ask you to," she said and moved deliberately against the hard bulge at her hip. The involuntary grunt of reaction she drew from him filled her with a satisfying sense of feminine power, giving her the courage to move again.

Whatever thin hold he'd had over his control seemed

to snap then. The man she had thought incapable of acting without careful deliberation proved that he could be as blindly driven by passion as any other mere mortal.

His hands were all over her, drawing away her clothes and the unsteadiness in them thrilled her. His movements were jerky, primal, unpremeditated—yet so innately skillful they took her straight to the edge of sanity.

They plunged over that edge together, filling the shadows in the quiet pavilion with cries of exhilaration. And maybe just a touch of anxiety—on both their parts—at what might come after the landing.

The sky had lightened to a pearly gray-blue by the time B.J. recovered enough to think coherently. Blinking dazedly, she took mental stock of her situation.

Both only half-clothed, she and Daniel lay still sprawled together on the cushion-padded picnic table. Her head rested on his shoulder and her fingers were curled into a death grip on his partially opened shirt. His heart was still beating loudly beneath her ear, but the rate was gradually slowing to normal. His breathing was almost steady now, as was her own.

Yet she knew that some things would never return to the way they had been before. Her heart, for example.

"We didn't use protection," Daniel said, and there was just a hint of disbelief in his voice, as though he was stunned that the realization had only just occurred to him.

Hoping that meant he wasn't usually so careless, B.J. reassured him, "It's okay. I'm on the Pill."

She saw no need to add that she took the Pill more for cramp relief than an active social life.

She felt his shoulders relax just a fraction and sensed his relief that the repercussions of their lovemaking would only be emotional ones. "I'm not apologizing…"

"Good. I don't want you to," she said rather fiercely.

"…but," he continued, ignoring her interjection, "I hope you won't have any regrets later."

"I knew what I was doing. I won't regret it," she managed to say evenly, hoping she was telling the truth. Knowing it was true now, at least.

He muttered something that sounded like, "I hope *I* won't," but before she could ask him to repeat it—or explain—he was moving. Shifting his weight from beneath her, he rolled to his feet, reaching for scattered articles of clothing.

"I'll be right back," he said without looking at her and disappeared into the men's room.

A bit disoriented by how abruptly he had abandoned her, B.J. sat up and ran a shaking hand through her wildly tumbled hair. She hadn't expected a declaration of undying devotion, or even flowery, romantic sweet nothings, but a "Wow, that was great," would have been nice. A couple more kisses, maybe.

Closing herself into the ladies' room with her wrinkled clothes and her tattered pride, she reminded herself that she had promised there would be no regrets. She hadn't been lying—she couldn't regret something that had been so exciting and spectacular, so close to the fantasies she had never expected to experience.

Which wasn't to say there wouldn't be moments of wistfulness that the inevitable conclusion couldn't have been different for them.

A boat arrived for them just after daybreak. It wasn't Bernard at the helm this time, but a young man who seemed braced for unpleasantness when they approached him.

"My name is Greg. Mr. Drake asked me to convey his most sincere apologies for your inconvenience," he recited quickly, before Daniel or B.J. had a chance to speak. "There was a mix-up in communications, and it was believed that a boat had been sent for you last night. It was only this morning that anyone realized you were still on the island. We sincerely hope there was no harm done during the hours you spent here."

Glaring at the young man, Daniel considered knocking him on his butt—just for the satisfaction of punching someone. It would make a nice demonstration for B.J. that he didn't take Drake's threatening gestures lightly, especially when they involved her. But taking his anger out on someone who'd had nothing to do with stranding them here would accomplish nothing.

He would vent his temper toward those who deserved it, he decided, turning away. But not before he saw the quick relief cross Greg's face; he must have read the violent impulse in Daniel's eyes.

Making sure B.J. was settled comfortably on the launch, he took a seat across from her rather than beside her. He didn't quite trust himself to sit close to her yet.

This trip would pass all too quickly, and then it would be time again for them to resume their roles as devoted spouses. It would take him that long to get his impassive mask firmly back into place, his long-buried emotions safely hidden away again.

No harm done? Greg had no idea just how much damage those hours on the island had caused. Emotional barriers that had taken years to build and fortify were now deeply cracked, and there was no telling how long it would take him to repair them.

Daniel was afraid they would never be quite as safe and impenetrable as they had been before.

Chapter Ten

The Daniel Andreas who stepped off the boat at the resort marina was not the same man who had made passionate love to B.J. such a short time before. This man was hard, tensed, jaw set and eyes snapping with temper.

Dangerous.

He had said very little to her since they'd emerged from the pavilion restrooms. He had given her a few terse instructions about how to behave when they returned to the resort—basically, she was to appear bewildered and confused. But there had been no personal conversation at all. No discussion about what had passed between them.

From the way Daniel was acting now, they might as well have spent the entire night on separate islands.

Bernard stepped forward to greet them at the marina. He wore his usual summer-weight boxy jacket with a T-shirt and pressed jeans, and even though it was very early, his bald head was already shiny with perspiration.

He greeted them with an expression of patently false sincerity. "I'm so sorry you were accidentally stranded. There was a mix-up about who was supposed to—"

Daniel's fist connected with Bernard's jaw, rocking the bigger man's head back and cutting off the sentence midword. Even as B.J. gasped in shock at the speed of the strike, another jacketed man appeared seemingly out of nowhere, moving toward Daniel with deadly purpose.

She threw herself at Daniel, catching his arm and tugging him away from Bernard. "Daniel Andreas! Have you lost your mind?"

"That," Daniel said without looking away from Bernard, "was for the discomfort my wife suffered during the night."

"For heaven's sake, Daniel, that wasn't necessary." B.J. was playing her role with a note of desperation now. "You heard Bernard say it was all a misunderstanding."

The deep flush of temper slowly receded from Bernard's face as he glanced at B.J. Jerking his chin to send the newcomer on his way, he wiped at his lower lip with the back of one hand, smearing a tiny trickle of blood.

Playing rapidly on her advantage, she spoke again.

"I must apologize for my husband, Bernard. He tends to be overprotective when it comes to me."

"There's no need for you to apologize, Mrs. Andreas. A man must protect his most valuable asset, isn't that right, Daniel?"

Daniel's arm twitched again, as if he was strongly tempted to hit Bernard again. B.J. held on tightly, her heart in her throat.

"I want to talk to Drake," Daniel growled. "Now."

"I'm sorry, Mr. Drake is away from the resort this morning. I'm sure he'll want to meet with you as soon as he returns."

"That's just as well," B.J. said firmly. "It will give my husband a chance to get his temper under control."

She tried to inject wifely exasperation into her tone, calling on memories of her mother's voice when she was annoyed with her husband of more than thirty years.

Bernard motioned toward the walkway that led back to their suite. "I'm sure you'd like to rest and freshen up. Coffee and brunch will be sent to your suite as soon as you let the staff know you're ready."

"Thank you," B.J. said, keeping a firm grip on Daniel's arm. "We would like to go to our suite for a while. Come along, Daniel."

She was almost surprised when he complied without further resistance.

B.J. was prepared by now for Daniel to sweep the rooms for listening devices when they returned, and he did so swiftly. Only then did he return to where she waited in the sitting room.

"You played that scene with Bernard perfectly," he surprised her by saying. "Exactly the way I hoped you would."

"Who was playing?" she demanded, planting her fists on her hips to stare at him. "I thought he was going to pound you into the sand. And then order that other guy to shoot you to finish you off. Did you *see* the look on Bernard's face when you hit him? He was furious."

With a rueful look on his face, Daniel flexed his right hand. "The guy's got a jaw made of granite. I thought I'd crushed my knuckles."

"Then why did you hit him?"

He shrugged. "I can't afford to be seen as weak in front of these guys. They know *I* know we were stranded there deliberately. I couldn't let it pass without striking back."

"This whole situation just gets more ridiculous by the minute," she muttered, turning away in disgust. "I swear men have a broken chromosome or something that makes them act like idiots."

"You won't hear any argument from me," he replied with an undertone of amusement. "But since that's the equipment that was issued to me, I've got to make the most of it if I want to win the game."

"Let me guess. The one who dies with the most toys wins?"

"Close. The one who stays alive longest with the most toys wins."

"And the one who gets killed trying to collect those toys?" she asked in little more than a whisper.

"That guy should have stayed on the bench."

Moistening her lips, she looked over her shoulder at him. "And what about the people who get in the way?"

After only a slight hesitation he answered, "Usually, even despite the player's best intentions, they get run over."

Having carried the strained metaphor as far as she could take it, B.J. turned abruptly toward the bedroom. "I'm going to take a shower."

He made no move to detain her.

Ten minutes later she stood with her eyes closed and her face turned into the warm water cascading from the brass-plated shower head. The shower soothed her skin and relaxed her tight muscles, but it couldn't wash away the memories of the previous night that would probably haunt her for the rest of her life. Nor could it dilute the fear that something terrible would happen to Daniel if he continued on his present course—whatever that was.

When Daniel's big hands closed gently on her shoulders, she gasped, nearly inhaling a mouthful of water. She had forgotten how very silently he could move. How unpredictably he could behave. And when those hands slid around to gently cup her small, wet breasts, she moaned and went liquid in his arms.

"It occurred to me," he murmured against the back of her neck, "that I never told you how special this morning was for me."

She leaned back against him. "No, you didn't."

"It was—" he turned her in his arms and gazed down into her eyes with a tender smile "—spectacular."

She couldn't stay annoyed with him when he spoke in that particular tone. When he looked at her in that particular way. She wrapped her arms around his neck and lifted her mouth to his.

Hands slid avidly over wet, slick skin, pausing often to explore and caress. B.J. wrapped her leg around his, locking them together, savoring the roughness of his hair against her smooth skin, the bulge of muscle in his calf. The position pressed them together from chest to knees, and she reveled in the differences between them. The way they fit so perfectly together.

She had been self-conscious at first, worried that Daniel would be disappointed with her lack of voluptuous curves. Yet the appreciation on his face when he looked at her, when he touched her, when he slid down to explore her sleek body with his mouth, reassured her that her slender form appealed to him.

The water was beginning to cool, but B.J.'s temperature was rising. She wouldn't have been at all surprised to see steam rising from her skin.

She speared her hands into his wet hair, her back arching when he pressed openmouthed kisses on her thighs. "Daniel?"

He rose to his feet and reached behind her to turn off the water. "Last time we hurried a bit," he murmured. "Now we're going to take our time."

She didn't know why he had changed again from cool and distant to warm and passionate. She could hardly keep up with his mood swings, never really knew when he was playing a role and when he was being himself. If ever. If she had any sense, she would be pushing him away, protecting herself from falling even harder for him than she already had.

Apparently she had no sense at all when it came to Daniel.

Barely taking time to towel off, they fell onto the bed they had shared so platonically before. Despite what Daniel had said in the shower, B.J. expected things to progress rapidly from that point.

Instead he slowed down, taking a leisurely journey of nibbling kisses from her throat to her toes and then back again. He cupped her face between his hands and kissed her mouth, her eyelids, the tip of her nose. But still he didn't hurry.

When she could stand it no longer, when she began to wonder if he was ever going to satisfy the ravenous hunger inside her, she rolled fiercely onto him and took matters into her own hands. So to speak.

Soon it was Daniel who was groaning. Demanding. And B.J. was the one who taunted and teased, giving only so much before drawing back and leaving him aching for more.

His skin glistened with sweat when he finally snapped, when the control that was so much a part of him deserted him. She marveled at the wildness in his eyes when he flipped her beneath him, and then the wildness took charge of her own mind, depriving her of coherent thought.

* * *

B.J. had barely recovered her breath when someone knocked on the door to the sitting room. She opened her eyes just as Daniel pushed himself upright.

"That will be our brunch," he said, straightening his disordered hair with a sweep of his hand. "I'll get it."

Their lovemaking had left her drowsy and lethargic, but the mention of food reenergized her. She sat up, the sheet falling to her waist. "Great, I'm hungry."

Daniel chuckled roughly and leaned over to kiss her, one hand brushing her bare breast in the process. His expression when he drew away made it clear that the intimate contact had not been accidental. "Why does that not surprise me?"

He wrapped himself in a thick terry bathrobe and headed for the other room. Pulling her own robe around her, B.J. took only a minute to ruffle her tumbled, mostly dry hair into place before following him, hoping there would be Belgian waffles on the brunch tray.

But it wasn't room service standing just inside the door in the sitting room. It was Judson Drake.

B.J. froze. Drake's cool eyes swept her from head to toe, and she knew she must look as though she had just crawled out of bed. Since Daniel looked the same way, it must have been obvious what they'd been doing before Drake arrived. She felt her cheeks flame.

The scene worked perfectly into the false stories Daniel had woven about them, of course. Yet surely he couldn't have predicted Drake would find them this way. She didn't want to believe there was anything pre-meditated in the way Daniel had made love to her.

"Mrs. Andreas." Drake's voice held a faint note of mockery that set her teeth on edge. "I just stopped by to express my deepest apologies at the incompetence of my staff in leaving you stranded on the island all night. I understand your husband was justifiably infuriated on your behalf earlier. Fortunately his temper seems to have been…soothed since his encounter with Bernard."

Because she didn't quite trust herself to respond without ruining everything, B.J. merely crossed her arms over her chest and nodded.

"My wife is hungry and she needs time to recuper-ate from our ordeal," Daniel said bluntly. "If you'll ex-cuse us…"

"Of course. As a matter of fact, here's your food now." Drake moved out of the way to allow a uniformed server to push in a fully loaded tray. "Please let me know if there is anything at all I can do to make it up to you, Mrs. Andreas. And, Daniel, I trust you'll be able to meet with me this afternoon while your wife rests?"

"It would serve you right if I caught the first shuttle out of this place," Daniel growled, making B.J.'s heart jump with a foolish optimism.

Drake's left eyebrow rose. "That would be unfortu-nate," he murmured, "for both of us."

Daniel allowed another couple of moments to pass in silence and then he nodded shortly. "I'll see you later. But right now I'd like to attend to my wife."

"Most certainly." Drake took a step toward B.J., obviously intending to take her hand or rest a hand on her shoulder or some other meaningless gesture of sincerity. She and Daniel moved at the same moment—she took a step back from Drake just as Daniel stepped between them.

"I'll see you later," Daniel repeated to Drake.

The other man paused, his eyes narrowing in temper, but then he nodded. "Mrs. Andreas," he said and gave her a stiff little bow before taking his leave. The bellman left immediately afterward.

"I'm not sure I'm hungry now," B.J. said with a shudder.

Daniel was already uncovering fragrant dishes. "Belgian waffles," he said enticingly. "With fresh berries and bacon. Or you might prefer an omelet. Or maybe…"

She sighed gustily. "Okay, maybe I can eat," she muttered, her stomach giving a soft rumble of concurrence. "But that guy still creeps me out."

Saying nothing, Daniel poured steaming coffee into two china cups and waved her into her seat at the table.

They ate for a few minutes in silence. The food was delicious, but B.J. had to make an effort to appreciate it. "Why do you always treat me like a not-very-bright child in front of Creepy Guy?"

Daniel shrugged. "Sorry. It fits our cover story."

"What woman would really appreciate being treated that way?"

"You'd be surprised," he answered drily. "Some

women want nothing more than to be petted and pampered."

"I can't see you being interested in a woman like that."

"No. I wouldn't be."

"Just as I wouldn't be interested in one of those men who needs constant ego stroking and kowtowing by the women in his life. I bet Drake's like that."

"Definitely." Daniel took a sip of his coffee, then asked casually, "So what type of man are you looking for?"

"I'm not looking," she answered tartly. "But if I do meet someone who interests me, it will be a man who treats me as an equal. Who values my intelligence and my opinions. Who wouldn't want to change me into some Hollywood ideal of the perfect woman."

"Any man who doesn't value you exactly the way you are isn't worth your attention."

She looked up from her food in response to the quiet comment. But before she could say anything, Daniel was talking again, abruptly changing the subject. "I'll be meeting with Drake for several hours this afternoon. It might be best if you stay in the suite to, um, recover from your ordeal."

"Oh, give me a break. Even the wimpy woman you made up for Drake's benefit would hardly have to take to her bed for an entire day just because she'd had to spend a night outdoors."

"Still, I'd feel better if you stay away from Bernard and Drake's other employees today. At least when I'm not around."

Her head rose sharply. Even though he'd spoken lightly, there was something in his voice that made her pulse jump. "Is there some reason I should be concerned?"

"I just don't like the possibility that you could be used as leverage against me," he admitted. "Leaving us on that island was a warning. The next one won't be so subtle."

"Will there be a next one?"

"Not if I play my part shrewdly. But I'd like you to keep the doors locked, anyway. Put out the Do Not Disturb sign and take a few hours to rest, watch television, read. Even though I realize you aren't so delicate to be harmed by a night of camping out, you're probably tired anyway. It wouldn't hurt you to spend a lazy afternoon."

She didn't like the thought of being ordered to stay in her room, but she wasn't thrilled about the possibility of crossing Bernard's path either. It wasn't as if there was anything she particularly wanted to do outside the suite.

"The sooner I can conclude my meetings with Drake, the sooner we can go home," Daniel added.

He probably thought that was further incentive for her to cooperate. And though she knew it should be, she found herself dreading the conclusion to this adventure.

As much as she detested Drake, as worried as she was about what Daniel was involved in, as concerned as they both were about the not-so-hidden dangers lurking here at the resort, as much as she missed her family, she wasn't looking forward to saying goodbye to Daniel again. This time it would be for good—unless he came to her aunt and uncle's party, an unlikely scenario.

No matter how hard she had tried to resist, she was falling in love with him. Which only served to prove that she was an idiot to fall for a man she didn't even know.

B.J. had never been one to enjoy an afternoon with absolutely nothing to do. Especially when she felt confined by decisions that were not her own.

Flipping discontentedly through the stranger's clothes in her closet, she dressed in the only outfit that seemed to suit her mood. Her own. The green camp shirt and khaki slacks had been laundered and pressed, and she donned them almost defiantly. The momentary surge of rebellion faded as she began to pace restlessly through the empty suite.

She couldn't nap and she had no interest in reading or watching television just then. She wished she knew what was going on in those meetings Daniel had been conducting with Drake for the past three days. It seemed clear that he was setting Drake up for something, but what? A bust? A scam?

It stunned her to think that she had made love twice to the man and she didn't even know whether he was a cop or a criminal.

Wouldn't he have already told her if he was a cop?

Someone tapped on the door. B.J. approached it cautiously, remembering Daniel's warning. She checked the peephole, then frowned. Now this was someone she hadn't expected at all.

"Ingrid?" She opened the door and looked questioningly at the woman on the other side. "This is a surprise."

Looking as fashion-doll perfect as ever in a body-hugging white strapless sundress, Ingrid reached out to clutch B.J.'s shoulder. "Are you all right?"

"Yes, I'm fine, thank you."

"I heard about what happened to you. I can't believe Bernard was so stupid that he left you on the island all night."

"He thought someone else had picked us up," B.J. quoted dutifully.

Ingrid made a scornful sound. "The man is as dumb as a rock. I heard your husband punched him right in the mouth. I wish I had seen that."

"Drake told you that?" B.J. asked in surprise. She hadn't thought Drake was in the habit of sharing gossip with Ingrid.

"Um…no. Someone else told me. Someone who saw it."

The only other person who had witnessed the blow had been the handsome young man who had piloted the boat that collected them from the island. Noting Ingrid's evasive expression, B.J. drew her own conclusions. But all she said was, "I'm sorry I missed your performance last night."

"It wasn't your fault. Though I've got to admit I was pretty ticked off when you weren't there last night. I thought you'd blown me off after you heard my rehearsal."

"No way. I was looking forward to it. How did it go?"

"Pretty good, I think," Ingrid admitted with an uncharacteristic lack of hyperbole. "People said some really nice things when I was finished."

"I'm sure you were great. I wish I'd heard you."

"You're nice, you know?" Ingrid smiled, and for a moment B.J. caught a glimpse of how the pretty young Midwesterner might have looked before she'd gotten swept into a world of glamour and jaded wealth.

And then that moment of innocence was gone.

"You want to get out of here?" Ingrid asked, waving a perfectly manicured hand to indicate the suite. Diamonds glittered at her wrist and on her fingers with the movement. "Let's find something to do. Something expensive that we can charge to Judson, since his incompetent staff disappointed both of us last night."

Thinking of Daniel's instructions to stay in the suite, B.J. hesitated, "Oh, I…"

"Come on," Ingrid urged. "It will be fun. You don't want to just sit around all day waiting for your husband, do you?"

B.J. shook her head with a sudden rush of recklessness. "No, that isn't what I want to do at all. Let's go."

."Great. Oh, and don't worry about your clothes," Ingrid added with a glance at the camp shirt and khakis. "You look fine."

Not even that rather oblivious insult could change B.J.'s mind. Slinging her tote bag over her shoulder, she stepped out of the suite with Ingrid and locked the door behind her.

Chapter Eleven

B.J. and Ingrid spent the entire afternoon being pampered and prettified in the spa and salon. B.J. would have expected to hate every minute of a session like that, being touched and rubbed and fussed over by strangers, but it wasn't so bad.

By the time she and Ingrid parted outside the spa, her skin was soft and glowing, her hair lay in silky layers around her face and her limbs felt fluid and limber. Glancing at her polished fingernails and toenails, she decided she could see herself doing this again—just not anytime soon.

"I'll see you around," Ingrid said, turning in the opposite direction as they left the spa. "It's been fun."

And then she hesitated and said over her shoulder, "It really *has* been fun, B.J. I don't hang out with other women very often, you know?"

"It was nice," B.J. agreed with a smile. She was more accustomed to spending time with women than Ingrid and she couldn't really see Ingrid fitting into her casual circle of friends, but the afternoon had passed quite pleasantly overall. Much better than sitting in the suite all afternoon worrying and waiting for Daniel to return.

In fact, she thought as her steps slowed, she wasn't quite ready yet to go back to the suite. She wasn't eager to face Daniel again with the awareness that she was falling in love with him hanging between them.

She turned abruptly and headed for the beach, avoiding the more populated areas to stroll slowly along a more deserted patch of damp sand. Daniel would probably be annoyed with her for going out by herself like this, but she didn't intend to go far. She simply needed a few minutes alone to fortify herself before seeing him again.

She walked to the edge of the water, letting the waves lap at her toes, unconcerned about her sandals. The breeze blew her freshly trimmed hair around her face. It felt unusually soft and had a light, flowery scent, thanks to whatever products had been used on her. She wondered if Daniel would notice the difference.

And then she grimaced as the thought crossed her mind. She had never been prone to primping for any man, and this was a lousy time to start.

What was she doing, anyway? How could she possibly explain the last four days to anyone else?

That she had allowed herself to be swept into an insane farce of a marriage, that she was helping a man pull off a scam of some sort that he hadn't even bothered to explain for her, that she was falling in love with that man despite having serious doubts about his motives and his moral fiber?

That she was having a no-strings affair with that man—something that was completely out of character for her? That she was fully prepared to make love with him again right now, knowing he wouldn't offer promises or even an assurance that he cared about her—for now or for the future?

Her parents would be certain that she was headed for disaster. Her sister would think she had lost her mind. Her friends would swear she'd been hypnotized into behavior that was completely alien to her. And maybe they would all be right.

But here she was. And she had no intention of leaving until Daniel sent her away.

Brittany Jeanne Samples had changed at some point between climbing out of her rental car outside that Missouri farmhouse and being swept straight into Daniel Andreas's arms. And she sincerely doubted that she would ever be the same again. She only hoped she would somehow find a way to be content with her old life again once she returned to it.

A shell half buried in the sand caught her eye. She bent to pick it up, swishing it a couple of times in the water to clean it.

The shell was a perfectly formed spiral only a couple of inches long, a creamy tan on the outside and soft, gleaming pink inside. Something about it appealed to her. She slipped it into her pocket, intending to take it home as a memento.

Not that she would need any souvenirs to remind her of every minute she had spent with Daniel at this resort. On the contrary, she was afraid that those memories would haunt her for the rest of her life.

"There's a charge for that, you know."

She closed her eyes and stifled a groan before she turned to face Judson Drake. As much as she hated to admit it, she really should have listened to Daniel and gone straight back to the suite.

"B.J.?" Daniel expected to see her sitting in the chair with her book or maybe sprawled in one of the lounge chairs on the balcony, since she seemed to love the ocean air.

It took him only a couple of minutes to determine that she wasn't anywhere in the suite. "Damn it."

It hadn't occurred to him that she would go out despite his request that she stay inside. She had been so cooperative so far, despite her misgivings, that he had taken for granted that she would continue to do as he asked while they were here.

Remembering the spark of defiance in her eyes, he told himself he should have known better.

B.J. was no one's puppet, he reminded himself. She had gone along with him so far because he'd convinced her that it was for her own good, but that didn't mean she would continue to blindly accept everything he said.

He remembered the last time she had wandered off on her own, when she had been followed down the beach by Bernard. Fortunately she hadn't done anything that time to put herself—or Daniel's cover story—in jeopardy. His stomach clenched at the possibility that she might be more reckless this time.

He tried to tell himself it was the plan he was most worried about, but he knew even as he threw open the door and headed purposefully out of the suite that his concerns were all for B.J.

Drake lounged on the beach behind B.J. with his arms crossed over his chest, his feet planted firmly in the sand. He was giving her one of those smiles he probably practiced in front of a mirror—and maybe some women would be dazzled by its shiny whiteness. B.J.'s reaction was to want to turn and run.

It was pride as much as responsibility that kept her where she was. "I beg your pardon?"

"I said there's a charge for taking my shells."

She didn't want to ask what the charge would be. His smile had just enough leer to it to make her wary. "Perhaps you can bill it to our suite."

He chuckled, the sound so fake it grated on her nerves. "We'll just consider it my gift to you. You can think of me when you admire it."

She was in no mood to banter with him. "I take it your meetings with my husband are over for today.

He'll be looking for me. I should get back to the suite."

Drake didn't move out of her way. "I'm sure he knows you're safe at my resort."

"Funny, I wasn't feeling so safe at one o'clock this morning." The cool remark was a lie, of course. She had felt perfectly safe with Daniel. But she had a role to play—and maybe if she annoyed Drake enough, he'd get out of her way.

"Ah." Drake wasn't notably affected. "You're still annoyed with me about being left on the island. I can't say I blame you for that. It must have been distressing for you to realize that no one was coming for you."

"Yes, it was."

"You must have been terrified."

She lifted her eyebrows. "Inconvenienced, perhaps. A bit nervous. But hardly terrified. After all, I had my husband with me."

"Ah, yes. The overprotective Daniel."

She nodded.

"Your husband is an interesting man. A bit of a hot-head."

"He takes good care of me." It was the reply Drake would have expected of her.

"Mmm." He reached out to run a fingertip down her arm. "You're a woman a man would be proud to take care of."

Oh, gag. She managed not to flinch away from his touch, but she could only hope he didn't see the revulsion in her eyes.

Because she knew for a fact that Drake's tastes ran to busty blondes, she didn't take him seriously. Either he was simply in the habit of hitting on every woman who crossed his path or there was something specific he wanted to find out from her. Something about Daniel, maybe.

"I'm about to make your husband a very wealthy man, you know."

Perhaps he wanted to impress her. Make her feel indebted to him. Instead she merely looked bored. "I leave business matters up to Daniel."

"Not impressed, hmm? Wouldn't you like to be dripping with diamonds, B.J.?"

"I have all the diamonds I want. And money to buy more if I choose," she added, keeping her so-called fortune in mind. "If Daniel wants the satisfaction of making more money on his own, then I fully support him in his efforts."

"You aren't into flash, are you? Simple clothes, tasteful jewelry, a plain gold wedding ring. I'd have bought you something much more spectacular if I'd married you. Just to show everyone how proud I was to have you for my bride."

B.J. instinctively rubbed her thumb over the wedding band on her ring finger. "This ring has deep sentimental value for my husband and for me. It's all I want. Now if you'll excuse me, I'd better—"

Drake stroked her arm again. "You're very loyal to your husband. Perhaps rather foolishly so."

She bit her lip and remained silent.

He took a step closer to her, making her balance her weight on both feet in preparation, should he make it necessary for her to strike out or run. "I don't suppose there would be any point in asking if you'd like to have dinner with me sometime. In Paris, perhaps."

"My wife and I would be delighted to join you in Paris for dinner sometime." Daniel's voice was as smooth as glass as he stepped from behind Drake to slide an arm around B.J.'s shoulders and draw her away from the other man. "Wouldn't we, darling?"

She looked up at him in relief. "I'd have to check my calendar, of course."

Daniel smiled and pressed a light kiss on her nose. "My wife and her social calendar," he said indulgently. "That's only one of the little things I love about her."

Drake's smile was decidedly forced now. "Daniel. Nice to see you. Will you be joining me for dinner this evening?"

B.J. held her breath until Daniel shook his head. His arm tightened around her, and his voice had dropped half an octave when he replied, "Thank you, but B.J. and I have plans for this evening. It's an anniversary for us, and we'd like to commemorate it privately."

"This is your wedding anniversary?" Drake asked somewhat skeptically.

"No." Daniel gazed into B.J.'s eyes, giving her a very private smile. "It's another sort. One we like to celebrate in our own way."

She felt her cheeks go red, which probably only strengthened the act Daniel was putting on for Drake's benefit. Something about the way Daniel was looking at made her knees soften. It wasn't hard to fill in the blanks of the "special anniversary" he was making up for them.

Apparently Drake had filled in a few blanks of his own. Looking as though he had bitten into something sour, he nodded. "Then I'll see you first thing tomorrow to sign the papers. This time tomorrow you'll have something to celebrate again."

"Tomorrow?" B.J. spun to face Daniel as soon as Drake left them alone. "We're going to have to stay another night?"

"Just one more," he replied, studying her flushed face. "I promise."

"That's what you told me yesterday."

"I got us out of having dinner with Creepy Guy," he said hopefully.

She refused to smile. "By implying that we're going to spend the evening in bed?"

"Sorry. It was the first excuse that occurred to me." He didn't look at all sorry.

"Do you know how worried my family must be about me? I've never in my life taken this much time away without telling anyone where I am."

"So maybe now they'll see you as all grown-up, rather than the baby sister. They'll treat you with more respect."

"You spin everything to suit your purposes, don't you?"

"Isn't that what a good con man always does?"

The humor in his voice had turned dark, and it brought a lump to her throat rather than making her smile. "Apparently."

He lifted a hand to her hair, brushing his fingers across the newly trimmed edges. "You got your hair cut."

"Yes."

"Looks good. And you're wearing pink polish on your fingers and your toes."

She should have known he would notice everything. Her toes curled self-consciously in her sandals. "Ingrid and I spent a couple of hours at the spa this afternoon. It was my way of making up to her for missing her performance last night."

"You look very nice." Still holding her in one arm, he turned to sniff appreciatively at her softly scented hair. "Smell good, too."

"Aren't you going to chew me out for leaving the suite after you advised me not to?"

"There was no harm in going to the spa. As for walking on the beach alone—" he shrugged against her "—judging by the look on your face when I found you with Drake, I think my point was made without me having to say I told you so."

She sighed. "I suppose you're right. I was *so* glad to see you."

He turned her to face him. "Show me."

Was this another performance? Did Daniel think Drake was still lurking around, watching them? Bernard, maybe?

Aware of those possible onlookers, she lifted her

face to his. She was still vaguely annoyed with him, still worried about the outcome of all this role-playing…but she couldn't seem to miss any opportunity to kiss him.

The scent that had been sprayed on B.J. smelled sultry and expensive, and Daniel liked it on her. But then, he was turned on by the scent of plain soap on her soft, supple skin, he had to admit. Everything about her appealed to him, and it had nothing to do with any artifice slathered on from a jar.

Even after everything she had gone through because of him, she still kissed him with a sweetness and eagerness that nearly brought him to his knees.

She fit so perfectly into his arms. Felt so very right against him.

A surge of possessiveness coursed through him, making his hold on her tighten and his mouth move more roughly over hers. He could still see Drake standing next to her, putting his sleazy hands on her, bringing a look of wariness to her eyes.

His first impulse had been violent. Murderous. Only the realization that he would have been putting B.J. in even more danger had given him the strength to push the anger back and use his brains instead of his fists.

He lifted his head, gasping for breath. If he were to have his way, they would make love right now, right here on the sand. They would let the surf wash over them, as in that old movie, and forget about Drake and the past and the future and anything but each other.

Because it was the middle of the afternoon and there

was a chance that someone could stroll by at any minute, he forced himself to take a few deep breaths. "Let's go back to the suite."

Her blue eyes were darker than usual, the expression in them hard to read when she gazed up at him. They were pressed too closely together for her to be unaware of how badly he wanted her. She knew exactly why he was in a hurry to get back to the suite.

He could offer her nothing except a few hours of pleasure. And he knew full well it wasn't her usual style to settle for that.

She deserved so much more.

And then she smiled up at him and took his hand. "All right."

He found himself oddly unable to speak, his throat suddenly so tight he almost choked. He turned with her toward the path that led to their suite. Their bed.

"Wait."

B.J. stopped and reached into her pocket. He watched as she pulled out a little shell and threw it into the water. And then she turned back to him and took his hand again. "Now I'm ready."

He didn't know what had just happened, but as she slipped an arm around his waist and matched her steps to his, he found he couldn't really care.

Maybe he would remember to ask her later.

"Daniel?"

He stirred against her, his face cloaked in the early-evening shadows that darkened the bedroom. His voice sounded groggy. Utterly sated. "Hmm?"

She squirmed onto her right side and rested her weight on her arm, touching his face with her left hand. "You need a shave."

He chuckled lazily. "That's what you wanted to tell me?"

"No. Just a momentary distraction." There were so many distracting things about Daniel, especially when he was lying naked in the tangled sheets, his chest still glistening with dampness from their exertion.

"Mmm." He seemed to be getting distracted again himself, as his right hand slid up her rib cage toward her breast.

"Wait. I want to ask you something."

What might have been a slight grimace crossed his face, but his tone was light when he said, "Just as well. I'm not sure I've got the energy for anything else. At the moment, anyway."

"You're scared to death of what I'm going to ask you, aren't you?" she asked in exasperation.

"Not scared. Just…cautious."

It would serve him right if she asked something she knew he wouldn't want to answer—like exactly what was going on between him and Drake. Instead she said simply, "When are we going to eat? I'm starving."

He lay very still for a moment and then he laughed. His laughter was deep, rich, pleasant—and it made her chest ache because she had heard the sound so very rarely. She knew she would always treasure the echo of it.

* * *

They dined under the stars at a table for two set far enough away from the other diners that it was obvious they wanted to be alone. They sat with their heads close together, enjoying the food and wine, sharing bites, grinning foolishly at each other.

They didn't talk much—there wasn't much they could say within the parameters of safe topics Daniel had set for them—but B.J. enjoyed every minute of the meal anyway. She knew Daniel was acting out the story he'd told Drake earlier about them celebrating a private "special anniversary," but she didn't care. The night was magical.

She'd worn one of the pretty sundresses. The diamond bracelet glittered on her wrist and the borrowed gold ring gleamed on her left hand.

Daniel wore a summer-weight jacket and a tie, and he looked like any woman's daydream of the perfect dinner companion. When he held her hand across the table, his own wedding band reflected the multicolored party lights strung above them.

It was so easy to pretend it was all real. So tempting to lose herself in the fantasy, even though she knew it was foolish. Even though she had no doubt she would be devastated when it ended.

They moved to the dance floor when they'd finished their meals. The band obliged their mood by playing blatantly romantic music that allowed them to sway together, arms entangled, his cheek pressed to her hair.

It was the kind of evening that B.J. had experienced

only in books and romantic movies before. The kind she had never really expected to experience herself.

As Daniel's lips brushed the side of her face and his hands slid down her back to rest intimately at her hips, she knew she would remember every moment of this evening for the rest of her life. She only hoped she could recall only the pleasure and not the inevitable pain.

Whatever the outcome, she thought as he pressed a kiss at the corner of her mouth, she could never regret this night. For just a few hours she had been someone different, someone sophisticated and interesting. A woman in love with a fascinating, extraordinary man. A woman who was wanted by that same uncommon man in return.

The music ended and they moved a couple of inches apart to politely applaud. Someone said her name from nearby, and B.J. glanced around to see Kurt McGuire from Tulsa standing a few feet away, his arm around a pretty, slightly plump redhead.

She smiled and nodded to them, then turned back to Daniel, who was frowning at Kurt in a way that had the other man turning hastily away again. "Stop that. You're intimidating him."

"Good. I intended to."

She sighed and shook her head. "You're incorrigible."

"Hmm." He wrapped his arms around her and drew her close to him again, seemingly oblivious to anyone who might be looking on—but then, B.J. knew better. "Come back to the suite and I'll show you incorrigible."

Her eyebrows rose as she slipped her arms around his neck. "I thought you were all out of energy?"

His smile was downright piratical. "I seem to have recovered."

Feeling the hard ridge against her thigh, she blinked in astonishment. "I guess you have."

His smile faded. "Come back to the suite, B.J. We have a few more hours together. Let's make the most of them."

Her heart twisted at the candid reminder that their time was running out—but like Daniel, she was reluctant to waste another minute.

She took his hand and let him lead her off the dance floor.

"There's only one thing I want you to promise me," she whispered as Daniel lowered her to the bed.

Though his lips were already at her throat, she felt him stiffen—and it hurt that he seemed to have braced himself for whatever she was going to ask. "What?"

"Just tell me this isn't casual for you. Even if it's only for tonight."

"B.J." He cupped her face in his hands and stared almost fiercely into her eyes. "It isn't casual. It would be so much easier if it were."

There was no mistaking the truth in his eyes. He was a good actor, but surely no one could be *that* good.

"That's all I wanted to know," she murmured and pulled him down into her arms.

For now.

Chapter Twelve

B.J. should have been sleepy, but she found herself wide-awake an hour after they returned to the suite. They'd made love, and though it was hard to believe it could keep getting better, somehow it did. Something told her a lifetime of lovemaking with Daniel would never grow old—

But that was something she would never know, she told herself glumly.

Which reminded her… "Daniel?"

"Are you hungry *again?*" he asked in feigned dismay.

She chuckled obligingly, then grew serious again. "Those papers Drake said you were signing tomorrow? That's what you've been working toward this week?"

She could see his face well enough in the shadows to watch his relaxed expression go hard and guarded. A little part of her heart broke at this latest demonstration that the closeness between them ended at the bedroom door.

"Yes," he said without further elaboration.

"And then what?"

"I move on. Fairly quickly."

Taking his money and running from Drake? "Where will you go?"

"Somewhere a long way from Drake. By this time tomorrow he's going to be…displeased with me. He'll have figured out that he's taken for a very expensive ride."

She moistened her suddenly dry lips with the tip of her tongue. "And what about me?"

"You'll be safe. I have a plan to get you away as I leave."

Focusing very hard on her questions rather than her pain, she looked at her hand where it rested on his chest. The borrowed gold band on her finger was just visible in the shadows, but she felt its weight as her hand pressed against his steadily beating heart. "Will *you* be safe?"

His silence was an ominous reply in itself.

"Will I ever see you again?" Though she spoke in a whisper, she knew he heard her.

The fact that he didn't answer broke what remained of her heart.

"What did you expect, B.J.?" he asked roughly after a long, painful few moments. "I've told you what I am. What kind of life I live. There's no place for you in it."

It was amazing how a heart that was already broken could still shatter further.

Fool, she told herself angrily, blinking away tears. *You knew this was coming.*

Which didn't make it hurt any less.

Keeping her face averted from him, she tossed off the sheets and reached for her robe. "I think I'll take a shower. I feel a little…grubby."

He made a move as if to detain her, made a sound that might have been the beginning of her name. But then he went still. "Save some hot water for me," was all he said.

Maybe he was feeling grubby, too.

Her legs were somewhat rubbery when she stood, but she thought she could make it to the shower. Just.

Closing the bathroom door behind her, she crossed the spacious granite floor and reached into the glass-enclosed shower stall to turn on the water. She didn't step in immediately, taking a moment to bury her face in her hands and get her emotions under control—at least, as much as possible just then. She refused to allow herself to fall apart in front of Daniel, no matter what might happen between them next.

She would save her tears for after they said goodbye.

Daniel looked at the closed bathroom door for a long time, and then he shoved himself from the rumpled bed and began to pace in long, furious strides. He would have liked to have thrown something, smashed something fragile and expensive against the elegant walls of this oppressively lavish suite, but that would have brought B.J. running to find out what was going on. And he wanted a few minutes away from her.

Damn it, he didn't need this. Hadn't asked for this. He'd been operating just fine on his own, without anyone special in his life. A man with no past, no future, only a grim determination to achieve his goals and move on victorious to the next challenge.

B.J. made him feel too much. Want too much. Regret too many of the decisions he had made during the past few years.

She was so good. So kindhearted. She should never have been tainted by her association with him. She deserved a hell of a lot more than he could ever offer her. He wouldn't invite any woman into the darkness of his life—especially B.J., who belonged irrevocably in the light.

He had to send her back to Texas, back to the family who loved her and protected her, the parents and siblings and aunts and uncles and cousins who would all want more for her than the likes of him. He had never belonged in that circle, never been more than a generously welcomed outsider. He had known that the first time he'd seen her among them. He had known it the first time he had kissed her. And he had known it the first time he'd told her goodbye—a parting he had always believed would be permanent.

He wished it had been permanent. It would have been so much safer for her…and God knew it would have been a lot less painful for him.

Throwing on a robe, he reached into his bag and

drew out a cell phone. The shower was still running, so he figured he had a few minutes of privacy.

It was time that he did something productive with those stolen minutes, before everything he had worked so hard for fell apart around him.

Drawing a deep breath, B.J. dropped her hands and reached for the tie on her robe, intending to step into the now-steaming shower. Only then did she realize that she had forgotten her nightgown.

She sighed again. For some reason, she found herself reluctant to dress in front of Daniel. She would rather emerge from the bathroom with her dignity intact—and herself fully clothed.

Leaving the shower running—Daniel could worry about his own hot water—she stepped into the bedroom, finding it empty and the door to the sitting room ajar. She frowned when she heard the low rumble of Daniel's voice from the other room.

Who was he talking to? Surely Drake hadn't come by even after Daniel had made it clear they didn't want to be disturbed tonight.

She didn't want to be seen by whoever it was, but she was too curious not to at least take a peek. Keeping to one side of the doorway, she moved closer, trying to see into the other room.

Daniel was alone, it turned out. He had his back to her and he was talking into a cell phone. Something about his tone told her he didn't want to be overheard—which, of course, only made her listen harder.

"I want her out of here tomorrow," he said, sounding as if he would tolerate no argument. "First thing."

B.J. bit her lower lip, realizing that he must be talking about her. She leaned closer to the doorway.

"No, I don't care about the details, just get her out of here before she ruins everything. The longer she stays, the more chance there is she's going to make a wrong move. We're too close to the payoff to risk that."

It didn't sound as if he was worried about her as much as his mysterious plan. Which made her irrationally indignant.

How could he act as if she was such a liability? Hadn't she cooperated with everything he had asked? Hadn't she gone beyond what should have been expected of her to convince Drake and the others that she was exactly who Daniel had said she was?

"Yeah, she's asking questions. But I've managed to distract her. For now."

She scowled. He had certainly kept her distracted. It devastated her to think that their lovemaking had been his way of keeping her too occupied to ask questions. He has assured her it wasn't casual—but maybe they defined the term in drastically different ways.

"Look, just take care of her, okay? I'm trusting you to handle this."

Take care of her. There were several ways to interpret that, B.J. thought as she hurried silently back to the bathroom, closed the door without a sound, then ducked into the steamy shower.

Considering the hardness of Daniel's voice and the

harshness of his words, some people might be frightened at this point. At the very least, concerned for their safety.

Perhaps it was just further evidence of B.J.'s idiocy where Daniel was concerned that she had no fear of him at all. Maybe she couldn't trust him with her heart, but she trusted him with her life. He had promised she would leave this resort safely, and she believed him.

Some people might consider her less than intelligent to place her faith in the word of an admitted con man. Or accuse her of once again confusing the past with the present.

All she could say in reply was that she believed instinctively that neither the Daniel she had known then nor the man she knew now would do anything to harm her physically. Nor would he allow anyone else to do so.

She wasn't romanticizing him, she promised herself. She didn't try to delude herself that any of his actions here were noble or selfless. He had told her he was here for the money, and she believed him. But she could never be afraid of him.

"B.J.? You okay in there?"

Realizing that the shower had been running for quite a long time, she hastily shut it off, scooping wet hair away from her face. "I'll be right out."

Daniel woke her with a soft kiss pressed against her lips. Blinking groggily, she realized that it was barely daylight outside, with hardly enough light to filter through the sheer draperies. She didn't remember finally drifting off to sleep.

She could just see his face when she peered up at him. She noted immediately that he was fully dressed, sitting on the side of the bed, gazing down at her.

"What is it? Where are you going?"

"I have to go out. There's something I need to tell you first."

She was suddenly completely awake. The phone call she had overheard the night before came back to her now, giving her a sick certainty that what he needed to say was goodbye.

"This is it, isn't it?"

He didn't seem surprised by her question. She'd like to think he looked a bit saddened by it. "Yes."

She swallowed and asked simply, "What do you want me to do?"

He touched her face. "That's all you're going to ask?"

"Would you answer me if I asked more?"

His mouth quirked in what might have been an attempt at a smile. "Probably not."

"That's what I thought."

He leaned over to kiss her again. "Thank you for making it easier."

"You still owe me," she whispered.

He rested his forehead against hers for a moment. "I know."

And then he straightened, speaking more briskly. "I've got to go. Someone will be here soon—someone who'll take you to safety. I want you to go straight back to Dallas the minute you get the chance. Promise me that."

"I promise."

She saw his shoulders relax and knew that she had just set his mind at ease. Apparently he trusted her word as much as she trusted his.

He would never have to know how much that promise had cost her. How much she wanted to beg him to let her stay with him.

It was partly because she was afraid she would put him in danger if she remained that she agreed to leave. And partly because she couldn't bear it if he told her that he wasn't even tempted to ask her to stay.

Holding the sheets to her chest, she rose on one elbow to watch him walk toward the bedroom doorway. Already she saw him taking on the tough, hardened persona of the man Judson Drake knew as Daniel Andreas. It was something in the way he walked, the way he carried himself.

"Daniel?"

He paused in the doorway, looking over his shoulder, impatience in his eyes. But his voice was still indulgent when he asked, "What is it?"

"I just want you to know I'm in love with you."

She had the minor satisfaction of seeing his impressive control slip then and knowing she had done something few people ever could. She had caught Daniel Andreas completely off guard. "B.J., I—"

"Go play your power games, Daniel," she said

gently. "I'm not asking you for anything. I just needed to say it one time out loud."

He'd gotten his expression back under control now. His white-knuckle grip on the doorjamb was the only sign that he was still reeling from her admission. "Take care of yourself, B.J."

"You do the same."

He drew a deep, painful-sounding breath. "I always have," he said. And then he was gone.

Hearing the sitting room door close behind him, B.J. finally gave in to the tears she had refused to shed in front of him.

Though they were wrinkled from wearing them a few hours the day before, B.J. donned her own clothes again. Nothing went into her tote bag except the things she had brought with her; she wanted nothing that came from Drake's resort.

It was so quiet in the rooms with Daniel gone. It felt oddly as though they were already unoccupied, despite the clothes that hung in the closets and the other personal items scattered around.

She could almost hear the echo of her declaration of love hanging in the still air.

It still amazed her that she had found the courage to say those words to Daniel. Because she hadn't expected to hear them in return, it hadn't hurt—at least, not too badly—that he'd left without commenting on them.

She wasn't sorry that she had told him. Daniel hadn't been given nearly enough love in his lifetime. Just once she had wanted him to know that sometimes love came as a gift, without any expectations or encumbrances. And even if he didn't feel it in return, maybe it would mean something to him someday that she had found him worthy of her love.

Someone knocked at the door just as she was finishing buttoning her shirt. Daniel certainly hadn't given her much warning, she thought with a pang in her heart.

Carrying her tote bag with her, she crossed the sitting room and opened the door. A stocky-looking man in the resort service uniform stood on the other side. Not exactly what she'd been expecting. "Yes?"

"Mrs. Andreas?"

She nodded. Staying in character until the end, she thought ironically.

"Your husband asked me to come for you. He and Mr. Drake would like for you to join them for breakfast."

She frowned, confused. Daniel hadn't said anything about breakfast. But he had said someone would be coming for her. Maybe this was a cover story, in case anyone was watching her or something. "I, um—"

The man held the door open more widely. "They're expecting you," he prodded.

She glanced over her shoulder, saying a brief goodbye to the overly fussy suite—and to the man with whom she had shared it. "All right. I'm ready."

She took great pride in the fact that her voice was steady despite the flood of emotions pouring through her.

Her escort smiled as he closed the door behind them.

Something about that smile sent an odd feeling shooting through her, but she told herself she was being paranoid. She trusted Daniel, she reminded herself. He wouldn't send anyone for her who posed any threat to her.

Holding her head high, she allowed the uniformed man to lead her down the hallway.

Daniel was having a great deal of trouble concentrating on what he was supposed to be doing. Though Drake was droning on about something or other that should be of interest, Daniel heard an entirely different voice instead. Entirely different words.

I just want you to know I'm in love with you.

His fists clenched beneath the table. What on earth could make her think he deserved a gift like that?

It wouldn't last, of course. It wasn't real. She'd been affected by the romance of the evening before, dazzled by their lovemaking.

Maybe it was transference or one of those other psychological phenomena that supposedly happened when someone found herself swept into a bizarre situation and had only one ally to turn to. Or maybe it was just the memory of a troubled young boy who no longer existed and a restless young girl who had felt stifled by the expectations of her huge, loving family.

She would come to her senses as soon as she was safely back in her real life. It wasn't love. But for just a little while it had felt an awful lot like it.

"You're drifting again, Daniel. Having trouble paying attention this morning?"

Drake looked sleazier than usual when Daniel glanced across the table. Maybe it was just the contrast to the purity of the images in his mind. "Go on. I'm listening."

Drake tented his fingers and studied Daniel coolly over them. "You know, I've always paid attention to my instincts. They've kept me out of more trouble than you can imagine over the years."

Daniel lifted an eyebrow. "I'm sure they have." He had great respect for Drake's instincts himself, which was why he had been so careful around him.

"Yes, well, lately I've been getting a few signals from you that have bothered me. So I've taken steps to make sure that I have your full cooperation as we conclude our business."

The small hairs on the back of Daniel's neck seemed to stand suddenly on end. "What are you talking about?"

"I've been watching you with your wife during the past few days. It's been…an enlightening experience for me."

Every muscle in his body going tense, Daniel remained silent, staring at the other man with narrowed eyes.

Drake's smile had turned rather pitying. "You misled me about her, you know."

Oh, hell. "In what way?"

"You implied that you married her for her money. That you've been humoring her so she wouldn't ask many questions about your dealings with her holdings."

Daniel forced himself to shrug carelessly, relieved that Drake was still buying the marriage charade. "That's the truth, basically. I keep her happy and she asks nothing more of me."

"But it's not entirely the truth. You didn't add that you're in love with your wife."

Daniel snorted—and the incredulous reaction wasn't entirely feigned. "Get real, Drake."

"Oh, I am real. I'm not the sort of man to develop special feelings for any particular woman, of course, but I like to consider myself a shrewd judge of other men's weaknesses. Brittany is your weakness. You wouldn't do anything to put her at risk."

B.J. was safe, Daniel reminded himself. He had seen to that. Which didn't mean he had to like the way this jerk was talking about her. "I have no intention of putting my wife at risk. Now if we could get back to—"

"She wasn't what I expected, you know. I would have thought you'd be more attracted to someone like Ingrid. Beautiful. Built. Sophisticated. I didn't think you would have fallen for someone who looks barely old enough to be out of school, with no figure to speak of and too much naiveté to be particularly interesting."

Daniel's fists tightened at the dismissive—and so very inadequate—summary of B.J.'s charms. "Yes, well, there's no accounting for taste," he managed to say lightly. "Especially when there's enough money involved."

"Mmm. I found your devotion to your bride heartwarming. And quite useful. It never occurred to me before that she could be a very handy tool for me to insure that you would give me no problems during our…negotiations."

Daniel grunted impatiently. "My wife has nothing to do with our business. And I've given you no reason to distrust me. You don't need to convince me to cooperate—I've been doing so all along. So let's get on with it."

"But you see, I'm the type of man who takes advantage of every fortuitous development when it comes to business," Drake murmured. "The trait has been very useful to me in the past. And I think you should know that I've arranged a little insurance so that you won't try to pull off anything foolish as we conclude our dealings. I'm sure you had no such scheme in mind, but just in case…"

"What the hell are you talking about, Drake?"

"Your wife, of course. Don't worry, she's perfectly safe. And she'll remain that way as long as you continue to cooperate. Once I've been assured that everything is proceeding as planned, you will be reunited with her."

Daniel started to rise. "What have you done?"

"You'll want to sit back down, Mr. Andreas," Bernard advised from his usual position at the back of Drake's conference room. His hand was already inside his jacket.

A squarely built man with cold eyes and a hard smile tapped on the door and entered the room just then. "Everything's secured, Mr. Drake."

"Thank you, Paul." Drake looked at Daniel with an unmistakable look of self-satisfaction. "Paul has taken your wife to a safe location. At least, safe for now. So…with that out of the way, shall we proceed?"

A surge of hatred coursed through Daniel with enough force to leave him momentarily speechless. Hatred for Drake, who had dared to threaten B.J. And for himself, for putting her in this position in the first place.

He had been so careless. So arrogant. So insufferably certain that he had taken every step to keep her safe, even as he had used her as ruthlessly as Drake was doing now. She had made a handy accomplice in his cover—and she had played her part so convincingly that Drake had bought it even more convincingly than Daniel had predicted he would.

He should have foreseen what Drake would do if a convenient innocent crossed his path.

"Damn you, Drake, what have you done with her?" he demanded in a roar, surging out of his chair with a reckless disregard for Bernard and his ever-present weapon. *"Where is my wife?"*

It took both Bernard and the newcomer to wrestle Daniel back into his chair.

Drake simply looked on with cool amusement. He ended the struggle with a few well-selected words. "I said she would be safe as long as you cooperate, Daniel. I would hardly call this cooperation."

Daniel went still in the chair.

"Much better," Drake assured him, nodding to his employees to release him. They did so but remained poised close by.

Drake reached for the file in front of him again, as

though they were still engaged in business as usual. "Shall we get back to it? And by the way, Daniel, you would really be wasting your breath to try to convince me again that you aren't in love with B.J. It's really very touching, isn't it, Bernard?"

Bernard laughed.

Chapter Thirteen

"Stupid. Stupid, stupid, *stupid!*" With each muttered word, B.J. hit herself in the forehead. The last time she hit hard enough to make her ears ring a little, but she didn't care. She had never been angrier with herself.

She couldn't believe she had just blithely walked into a trap. Hadn't even considered the possibility that she should be on her guard. Daniel had told her he was sending someone for her, and she had just naively followed the first guy who'd come along.

The man she'd assumed had been sent by Daniel had instead locked her in a storage room. According to her watch almost half an hour had passed since, though it felt like much longer.

Glaring at the cases of toilet paper, facial tissues and paper towels stacked around her, she kicked the locked door. The only thing that accomplished was to hurt her big toe, which was left unprotected by her sandals. Cursing herself again, she hobbled furiously around the roughly eight-by-eight room, trying to come up with a plan for escape.

Since she couldn't figure out any way to break through a solidly bolted door with a roll of toilet paper, she sank to the floor and rested her forehead on her up-drawn knees. She didn't know why she was here. The man who had pushed her inside and locked the door behind her hadn't stayed around long enough to answer any questions.

She couldn't help remembering the things she had overheard Daniel saying into his cell phone the night before. He had told someone to get her out of the way—and he'd added that he didn't really care about the details.

Was this his idea of keeping her safe? Out of the way?

If so, why hadn't he just locked her in the suite? Or told her not to leave. After her encounter with Drake on the beach yesterday, he must have known she wouldn't be in any hurry to go out by herself again.

No. There was something else going on here. She really didn't think the man who had locked her in this room had been working with Daniel at all. She would be willing to bet everything that he was one of Drake's men.

Which meant that Daniel didn't know where she

was. He would be worried about her—and that meant he couldn't concentrate on whatever he was doing with Drake. Which, she thought with a sinking feeling, was probably the whole point.

Drake must have figured out—or at least suspected—that Daniel wasn't being entirely up front with him in their shady dealings. Was grabbing her his way of ensuring Daniel's cooperation? If so, they had done a good job of convincing everyone they were really married.

And *she,* B.J. thought with a groan, must have done a very good job of making everyone believe she wasn't very bright. That she would simply walk into a storage closet if someone told her to.

"Stupid, *stupid!*"

She wouldn't entirely blame herself. Daniel should have told her who to expect. Given her some sort of password or something. He knew Drake better than she did; he should have expected an underhanded move like this from Creepy Guy.

But she was the one who had gotten herself locked in a closet, she thought with another low groan.

The door rattled, and B.J. jumped to her feet, braced for trouble. She'd had some lessons in self-defense; she would fight if she had to.

"B.J." Ingrid peeked cautiously into the room. "Are you in here?"

B.J. rushed toward the door. "Ingrid? Yes! I'm here."

Ingrid stepped inside the storeroom, leaving the door ajar behind her. "I thought it was really weird when I saw Paul leading you into the back hallways of the building. I started following—because I'm just nosy sometimes, but I had this feeling I needed to know what was going on. Then when Paul pushed you in here and locked the door, I ducked out of sight and waited for him to go away. I'm sorry, but it took me a while to find a key to let you out."

"Oh, Ingrid, thank you." She spontaneously hugged her.

"I couldn't believe what he did," Ingrid said indignantly. "I know Judson was behind it. I'm sure he was flexing his muscles around your husband. Judson gets off on power, you know—and if he thought he could get something more from Daniel by snatching you, he wouldn't even hesitate."

B.J. would have liked to ask why Ingrid would sleep with the man when she knew so many bad things about him, but that was really none of her business. Maybe Ingrid would demand better for herself from now on— at least, B.J. hoped so. In the meantime, she needed to find a way to let Daniel know she was all right.

"I must find my husband," she said, moving toward the door. It occurred to her that it grew easier all the time to refer to him that way.

Ingrid caught her arm. "Wait."

Impatiently B.J. tried to shake her off. "But I have to—"

"B.J., something's going on out there. I saw some things when I was looking for a key."

"What did you see?"

Ingrid spoke in an urgent whisper. "I think there's been a raid or something. Cops, you know? I saw Bernard in handcuffs, being shoved into a big, dark car. I'm—I'm really sorry, B.J., but I think Judson and Daniel are in trouble."

B.J.'s head was starting to pound. "We need to go find out what's going on."

"Oh, I, uh—"

Seeing the trepidation in Ingrid's expression, B.J. sighed. "Okay. I'll go see what's going on. You go back to your room and pack. If Drake's been arrested, you'll probably want to leave the resort rather quickly. I assume you have someplace to go?"

"Oh, sure. I've got a nice apartment in L.A."

B.J. wouldn't ask how Ingrid afforded a nice place in Los Angeles. "Fine. Make a good life for yourself, Ingrid. And thank you again for letting me out."

"Yeah, sure. I owed you, you know? Maybe we'll see each other again sometime?"

"Maybe we will." With a quick smile, B.J. turned and hurried down the hallway that led past a laundry room—the same hallway through which she had obligingly followed Paul earlier.

It was an indication of how meticulously Drake's employees had been trained that there was little pandemonium at the resort even through the boss had been led away in handcuffs. B.J. heard people talking about the scandal as soon as she reached the lobby of the main lodge, but the staff seemed to be carrying on with their responsibilities, if only because they didn't know what else to do.

She headed for the front desk, intending to ask if anyone knew anything about Daniel. A hand on her shoulder stopped her in her tracks.

It took her a moment to recognize the dark-haired young man who stood behind her. And then she remembered. "You're Greg, right? From the boat."

He nodded, looking relieved. "I have a message for you. From Daniel."

B.J. clutched his arm. "Daniel? Where is he? Is he okay?"

"Hang on just a minute." Greg flipped open a cell phone, pressed a button and held it to his ear. "I've got her," he said a moment later. "She looks fine."

B.J.'s fingers tightened on his sleeve. "Is that Daniel? Can I talk to him?"

He shook his head. "Yeah, I'll tell her," he said into the phone.

B.J. stared numbly at him as he closed the phone and slipped it into his pocket. "Where is he?"

"He had to leave," Greg replied. "I've been instructed to make sure you get on a plane back to Texas."

"I don't understand. Daniel *left?*" Just like that? Without a goodbye or anything?

"Well, he's gone now. He was waiting to make sure you were safe."

Across the lobby, two men wearing dark suits and carrying walkie-talkies entered an elevator and disappeared. A search of the premises? Were they looking for Daniel?

"I don't know what's going on," she said and she knew she sounded bewildered.

Greg patted her arm, his expression sympathetic. "I'm just glad you're okay. I was delayed on my way to collect you this morning and by the time I arrived at the suite you were gone. I was searching the grounds for you when the feds arrived and things got sort of chaotic around here. I ran into Ingrid on the way to her suite. She told me you were safe. I contacted Daniel immediately. I've got to tell you, he just about went crazy when we didn't know where you were."

B.J. bit her lip, keeping her reaction to herself.

"Anyway, he wanted me to tell you that he's sorry Drake tried to put you in the middle. Daniel's really angry with himself for not anticipating that."

"Just what's your connection to Daniel, anyway?" She was getting irritable enough to picture him as a dummy sitting on Daniel's knee and spouting Daniel's words, but it would just take too much energy to be that snide with him at the moment. The ups and downs of the morning had drained all the fight out of her. For now.

Greg shrugged. "He asked me to do him a couple of favors and he promised me a few in return."

Obviously Greg wasn't going to be any more informative than Daniel had been. Still, she tried. "Where is he?"

"In all the uproar, he managed to slip away just as the feds arrived."

"And what would have happened to him if he had stayed?" she demanded, staring fiercely into Greg's unrevealing dark eyes.

He only shrugged.

"You know how to call him. Will you call him now? I want to talk to him."

"He wouldn't answer," Greg said, his voice gentle now, a note of sympathy in it that made her shoulders straighten. "Now that he knows you're safe, he's probably turned off the phone."

She wouldn't ask anything else of him, she vowed. If there was one thing she did not need, it was this guy's pity.

"Fine," she said shortly. "I want to go home now."

Greg nodded. "It will be safe to go back up to your suite now, if you'd like to pack. Daniel told me to be sure you take everything with you."

All the clothes Daniel—or someone—had provided for her during her stay here. She shook her head. "There's nothing in the suite that I want."

"You're sure?"

"Positive."

"Oh, that reminds me." He reached into his pocket and drew out two items that he pressed into her hand. "These are yours, I think."

She glanced at her wallet and her cell phone, then stuffed them into her tote. Now she was leaving with everything she'd brought with her, she thought. Everything except her heart.

Greg waved a hand toward the exits. "Okay, let's see about getting you on your way—"

"B.J.? Are you okay?"

The sound of her name made her turn to face the man who crossed the lobby toward her looking both worried and relieved. A tall, slender man in his early fifties, his dark hair was lightly frosted with gray, and his left eyebrow was neatly bisected by an old, thin white scar.

Had she not been clinging so very tightly to the tattered remains of her pride, she might well have burst into tears at the sight of him. As it was, she walked into his arms and rested her cheek tightly against his reassuringly solid chest. "Uncle Ryan."

"Do you know how worried we've been about you? Your mother's about ready to call out the National Guard."

"How did you find me? No, never mind. I don't care. And I'm not even really surprised. I'm just glad to see you."

Her mother's brother tilted her face up to his, studying her with concerned eyes. "You're all right?"

"I'm fine," she assured him. Physically, it was the truth. Emotionally...well, she would be fine, she promised herself. Eventually.

"What's going on here, anyway?"

B.J. looked over her shoulder, wondering if Greg would be more willing to answer questions for her uncle than he had been for her. But he hadn't waited around to be questioned by either one of them. He was no longer standing where he had been only moments before, nor anywhere else in the lobby, as far as she could see.

"I'll tell you what I know on the way home," she said

to her uncle, drawing away from him. "Let's just get out of here now, okay?"

"Have you got everything you're taking with you?"

She hugged her tote more tightly against her. "There's nothing left for me here," she murmured and turned toward the exit.

Apparently sensing that B.J. wasn't in the mood to talk, Ryan didn't push her for answers or conversation during the long flight back to Dallas. He had arrived in the private jet that belonged to D'Alessandro and Walker Investigations, so they had plenty of room to stretch out and be comfortable.

B.J. stared out the window, watching the ground passing beneath them, wondering if they had flown over Daniel.

Shouldn't she be feeling more like herself now, as they drew ever closer to home? She had on her own clothes, sat with the uncle who had known her since she was barely more than a toddler, was headed back to the extensive family who knew her and loved her.

So why did she still feel so very different from the woman who had left Dallas only a few short weeks ago?

"B.J.?"

She glanced toward her uncle, who sat watching her from the other side of the plane. "Yes?"

"Is that something you want your mother to see you wearing before you have a chance to explain what you've been up to?"

She didn't know what he meant at first. Following

the direction of his nod, she glanced down at her hands. She flushed when she realized she had been pensively spinning the gold band on her left ring finger.

How could she have forgotten Daniel's ring? Or the diamond bracelet on her right wrist? She stared at them, feeling her own identity slipping away again, leaving her confused about who exactly she had become.

"I—it's a long story," she said, her right hand closing over the ring to hide it from her uncle's view—and her own, as well.

"I figured it would be. We've got some time, if you want to talk."

How could she possibly explain how she had gotten so thoroughly swept up in Daniel's crazy charade that she was now having trouble remembering which parts had been real and which only make-believe?

Instead she asked, "What did you find out about Daniel Andreas?"

"Not much," Ryan admitted. "There's very little documentation about him for the past ten years."

"Is there any chance he's a federal agent?"

"Maybe. If so, he works undercover."

"But he could just be a con man."

"That's another possibility."

"Can you find out?"

"I still have a few strings to pull with the feds. But if he is undercover, neither he nor his superiors will appreciate us asking questions about him. And if they're looking for him, they're going to want to know what we know about him."

Which could lead someone straight to his aunt, whom he worried so much about protecting, B.J. thought, chewing on her lower lip.

She lifted her eyes to meet her uncle's. "Don't do anything yet," she said. "And I would appreciate it if you didn't mention this," she added, sliding the ring off her finger.

"If that's what you want."

"Thank you."

Her hand felt oddly bare when she slipped the ring into her wallet for safety. Only then did she notice that the snapshot of Daniel that she had carried in her wallet was missing. He must have taken it when he'd retrieved her things.

He hadn't even left her a photograph of himself, she thought with a clench in her heart. She knew he hadn't intended to leave his mother's ring with her.

It was only because so much had been going on around them that both of them had forgotten that ring. Maybe it had been wishful thinking on her part, she thought with a slight wince, but Daniel had more likely simply forgotten to take it back from her.

That was an oversight she intended to correct as soon as possible.

Chapter Fourteen

Maybe she was still jumpy from being spirited away to a luxury resort, stranded overnight on an island, locked in a storage closet and made love to by a dashing con man. Perhaps that explained why, almost two weeks after her return to Dallas, B.J. nearly jumped out of her shoes when someone knocked on the door of her apartment.

It was Saturday afternoon and she wasn't expecting anyone. She stuffed the gold band she had been holding into one pocket of her jeans and moved across the living room to check the peephole in her front door.

She didn't know who she had been expecting to

see—at least, not that she would admit—but she didn't know if she was more pleased or dismayed to see her mother's face in the distorted view of the peephole.

"Mom," she said, opening the door with a determinedly bright smile. "What are you doing here?"

"I suppose I should have called." Layla Walker Samples stepped over the threshold. "But I had a feeling you would be here."

Knowing her mother's pleasantly casual expression was as deceptive as her own smile, B.J. kissed the offered soft cheek and waved a hand toward the sofa. "Sit down. What can I get for you? Tea? Coffee? As you can see, I've been drinking a soda."

"Nothing right now, thank you. Sit next to me a moment, Brittany."

Her mother was the only person who had been allowed to call her that since B.J. announced on her sixteenth birthday that she preferred to use her initials. B.J. settled warily on one end of the couch, wondering what was coming next.

Layla reached out to take her hands. "When are you going to tell me what happened to you while you were away? I know it's still haunting you. You haven't been yourself since you got back."

Not herself. That was exactly the way B.J. had felt since she'd returned.

"You've been so distracted. You've lost weight—and you didn't have any to lose. I don't think I've seen you smile—not *really* smile—since you came home."

The obviously unsuccessful attempt at a smile that

B.J. had been wearing faded. Why bother when there was no fooling her mother?

"I know you were looking for Daniel Castillo," Layla continued. "Molly told me she asked you to find him to invite him to the big surprise party she's planning for Jared and Cassie. Did you find him?"

"I didn't exactly find Daniel Castillo."

"Is that why you've been upset? Because you feel like you failed in your assignment? You know Tony and Ryan and Joe will teach you more about being an investigator, if that's still what you're determined to do."

"I found Daniel, Mom."

Layla frowned in confusion. "But you said—"

"I said I didn't find Daniel Castillo. He uses the name Andreas now."

"I see. So you did find him. You talked to him."

"Yes."

"What's he like now? I remember him very well, you know. Of all the boys Jared and Cassie took in, I worried most about him. He was so angry. So defiant. Not that I blamed him, poor thing, after he lost his mother in such a terrible way. But I was concerned that you were so drawn to him. I knew you had a crush on him, of course."

"And you made sure I didn't spend much time alone with him."

"That's true," Layla admitted. "I figured you were a good influence on him—but I couldn't help worrying that he would be a bad influence on *you*."

Because that seemed so ironic in light of all that

happened after she found Daniel in Missouri, B.J. moistened her lips and stared at her hands.

"What's he like now?"

How was she to answer that? "Different," she said finally. "A little hard to describe."

"Did he turn out well? Is he a good man?"

Again B.J. was hard-pressed to answer. She settled for the reply that felt right to her. "He's a good man."

"Is he married?"

The gold band felt heavy in her pocket. "No."

"Is he coming to the party in October?"

"I don't think so."

"Molly will be disappointed."

"I know." B.J. reached for the half-empty glass of soda sitting on a coaster on the coffee table. She needed something to do to keep her hands occupied and to give her an excuse not to look into her mother's eyes as she evaded questions she wasn't yet prepared to answer.

Layla sighed lightly. "I tried to warn Molly not to get her hopes too high. All those troubled boys—there's no way for her to know what they've been up to since she saw them last. Some of them could very well have gone into lives of crime, for all we know."

B.J. choked on a sip of soda. She hastily set her glass on the table.

"Honey? Are you okay?"

"I'm fine, Mom. Thanks," she managed to reply.

"Anyway, I couldn't say much to Molly. Because after all, I didn't listen when people tried to discourage me from looking for my siblings all those years ago.

Since we were separated so young and raised in different foster homes and adoptive families, there was no telling how everyone ended up. But I had to follow my heart—and look how much joy my family has brought to my life during the past twenty-five years."

B.J. had heard the story dozens of times, of course. Layla and her six siblings had been split up after their mother died when Jared, the eldest, was only eleven and Lindsey not even a year old. Just over twenty-five years ago, B.J.'s aunt Michelle had hired private investigator Tony D'Alessandro to locate her biological siblings. Layla, who had already been searching, was the first to be found.

Eventually they had all been reunited, except for a brother who had died in his late teens, leaving behind a daughter. That daughter, Brynn, was now another beloved member of the extensive Walker family—as well as the equally numerous D'Alessandro clan, since she had married Tony's younger brother Joe.

Layla shook her head. "Molly's bound and determined to find out for herself what became of all those foster boys she grew up with, and I'm certainly not going to discourage her. Are you sure there's no chance Daniel will come to the party?"

"I don't know. But I really doubt it."

"Is that why you've been so unhappy since you came home? Because you feel like you let Molly down?"

B.J. should have known her mother wouldn't be deterred for long from trying to find out what was bothering her. "I'm fine, Mom. Really."

"Another life crisis?" Layla asked in resignation. "Have you decided private investigation isn't the career you want either?"

"I'm just…trying to make some difficult decisions." It wasn't that she didn't intend ever to tell her mother what had happened with Daniel; it was just that she wanted to do so after she herself knew how the story ended.

There was no need to worry Layla unnecessarily— and she *would* worry if she knew her daughter was tempted to pursue a man who might be a criminal. A man who had given no indication he even wanted to be found again.

Layla searched her face. "You aren't ready to talk about those decisions?"

"Not yet."

Her mother sighed and patted her knee. "You were always one who had to work everything out in your own mind before you turned to anyone else for advice. Just know that I'm here whenever you're ready to talk, all right?"

"I do know, Mom." She felt very blessed to realize that she had that constant, unwavering support base. It was a safety net that had been denied Daniel at much too young an age.

Layla rose to her feet, patting her thick hair, which was now more gray than brown. "I have an appointment at my beauty salon this afternoon, so I'll leave you to brood in peace. Call if you need me, okay?"

"I will."

"And eat something. You're too thin."

B.J. smiled. "I'll order a pizza."

Layla sighed heavily. "At least order veggies on it."

"It's a deal."

They hugged goodbye at the door. "Follow your heart, B.J.—it won't lead you wrong," Layla said as she stepped outside.

Follow your heart. The words seemed to echo in the apartment after B.J. closed the door.

It was not particularly deep or original advice, but it was an adage Layla had adhered to faithfully in her own lifetime. From marrying her college sweetheart to finding her long-lost siblings, Layla had followed her heart into a comfortable, happy maturity. If she had any regrets about any of the decisions she had made along the way, no one would ever guess for her almost always cheerful demeanor.

Follow your heart.

She pulled Daniel's ring from her jeans pocket and rubbed one fingertip across its smooth surface. On an impulse, she slid it onto her left ring finger, marveling as always at how perfectly it fit her.

Daniel would be wanting this back, she told herself. Of course, she could give it to his aunt, but she really wanted to hand it to him in person.

He still owed her a debt—and it was time for her to collect.

The tea was brewed strong enough to be more bitter than soothing, but B.J. drank it with a smile. "This is delicious."

Maria Sanchez smiled back at her. "It's nice to have company. Especially a friend of Daniel's."

"I'm trying to find him again," B.J. confessed. "I hoped you could give me a new lead."

"Daniel doesn't stay in one place for very long at a time," Maria said regretfully. "And he doesn't visit me often enough. The boy needs a permanent home."

"Do you know where he is now, Mrs. Sanchez?"

The old woman eyed her with still-shrewd dark eyes. "You want to invite him to another party?"

"No. I have something that belongs to him and I would like to return it personally." B.J. held out her hand, revealing the gold band resting on her palm.

Maria stared at the band. "My sister's ring."

"Yes."

"Where did you get it? Daniel never lets it out of his sight."

"He...let me borrow it. Now I need to give it back."

Setting down her teacup, Maria studied her so intently that B.J. almost squirmed in her seat. "You know about Daniel's mother."

B.J. nodded. "I know she was killed when a couple of junkies broke into her home to rob her."

"She was trying to raise her son alone after Daniel's father was killed in a bar fight. Anita had little formal education and she had some health problems that she never took the time to address properly. She didn't have much money, and the housing complex where she was forced to live was poorly maintained and overrun by drug dealers. The place was torn down years ago.

"Anyway, my sister planned to move as soon as she could, but she was killed before she could get away. Daniel found her when he came home from school."

"It must have been a nightmare for him." And even that, B.J. knew, was an understatement.

"The killers took an old television set, a pair of gold earrings that Daniel's father had given my sister and ten dollars in cash," Maria said bitterly. "They probably would have taken the wedding band she always wore, but it was very tight on her finger and they must have been in a hurry to get away."

B.J.'s hand tightened spasmodically around the ring that meant so much to Daniel.

"I wanted to take Daniel, but I was battling breast cancer at the time," Maria added. "There was no one else. He was so angry and rebellious that I worried about him getting into serious trouble. He was placed in two foster homes that didn't work out for him before he was sent to your uncle's ranch."

"My uncle has a special bond with angry teenage boys," B.J. said. "Probably because he was one himself."

"I saw the difference in Daniel as soon as he came home to me when I was able to care for him. He was still very quiet but respectful and focused on his studies. He lived with me until he completed high school and he has been taking care of me ever since."

"And do you know what he's been doing during those years?" B.J. asked quietly.

"He tells me he works with computers. I think he

tells me this so I won't worry about him," Maria added, once again displaying the astuteness that must have made it difficult for Daniel to deceive her.

"Do you know how to reach him now?"

"I have his cell phone number for emergency use only. He calls me from it twice a week."

B.J. gazed steadily at the older woman. "I know it's asking a lot, but will you give me that number?"

She could use the number to trace where the calls had come from, perhaps. After all, she had a few strings to pull, if necessary, she told herself, picturing her uncle Ryan's face.

Maria considered her question for a moment and then she smiled. "When you came to me last time telling me about the party, I helped you partly because I thought it would be nice for Daniel to visit the ranch again and thank the people who had been so good to him."

B.J. was curious about her wording. "What was the other reason?"

"I recognized you from a photograph Daniel keeps in his possession. It's almost as precious to him, I think, as his mother's ring."

B.J. was stunned. "A—a photograph? Of me?"

Maria nodded her gray head. "You are a young girl, standing next to Daniel. There are horses in the background, and you are smiling at him. Even in that old photograph, I could see that you were very fond of him."

B.J. actually remembered Cassie taking that snapshot during a Fourth of July party at the ranch. Cassie had taken dozens of pictures that day, and B.J. had seen them all. She hadn't realized Daniel had carried one of them with him when he left.

"My Daniel is a good man, B.J., but he is too much alone. He needs a home. A family. I sent you to him before because I think he has always cared about you. And from the way you have spoken of him today, I think you care about him, too."

B.J. didn't bother to deny it. "Yes. Very much."

Maria smiled. "Then go find him. And you may tell him I sent you to him."

Sighing, B.J. looked at the ring again. "It isn't going to be easy. Daniel has his emotions locked away so tightly, I'm not sure he knows how to let them out now."

"Then teach him. The things that matter most in life aren't the ones that come most easily, B.J."

Gazing into the eyes of the woman whose wisdom had come through years of hard experience, B.J. was amazed that Maria could still sound so hopeful and optimistic. She had a feeling that Maria would get along very well with her mother.

Daniel's steps dragged as he trudged through an alley toward the ratty Chicago apartment building in which he had lived for the past two and a half weeks. The heavy biker boots contributed in part to his sluggish movements, but not as much as the weariness that permeated all the way through to his bones.

His face itched. He scratched absently at the thick

stubble that darkened his cheeks and chin. His hair felt long against the back of his neck and heavy with the gel he'd applied liberally to it. The stained T-shirt and ragged jeans he wore didn't fit very well and they weren't overly comfortable.

He couldn't help thinking of the impeccably tailored suits and casual clothing made of the finest fabrics that he'd worn at the resort last month. Few people who had seen him then would recognize him now as the same man. Which was exactly the point, of course.

As he turned a corner into a second alley, this one even darker and smellier than the last, he tried to push thoughts of the resort to the back of his mind. There were some memories that were just too painful to dwell on. That half hour when he hadn't known where B.J. was or whether she was safe was one of those memories.

Had she had any idea of how worried he had been? How frantically he had searched for her as soon as he had managed to slip out of Drake's office during the pandemonium of the raid? How relieved he had been when he'd heard she was safe?

Maybe she'd thought he hadn't cared. After all, he'd cut out immediately, hadn't even tried to contact her to tell her personally how sorry he was that Drake had dared to threaten her.

Could she possibly know that she hadn't been out of his thoughts for more than a few minutes at a time since he'd left her, even when he had done his best to think of *anything* else?

I just want you to know I'm in love with you.

He doubted that she would say those words so trust-ingly to him now, a month after he'd abandoned her at the resort. After she had returned to the family that had no trouble showing her just how much she meant to them. The family who would protect her from danger rather than leading her into it.

It hadn't really been love, he told himself, as he did every time he heard those words in his memory. Not on her part, anyway. As for himself...

He wasn't afraid of much. But even the thought of letting himself love someone—B.J., specifically—made him break out into a cold sweat.

He winced as he reached the end of the alley. His lower back ached from a well-placed kick in the kid-neys earlier that day. He'd let himself be blindsided—and he hadn't even been thinking about B.J. at the time.

Maybe he was getting too old for the life he'd been leading. He sure felt like it now.

A rustle of sound from his left was the only warning he had before someone slammed into him from behind.

Daniel staggered and almost went down, but he re-gained his footing at the last moment. He started to turn to fight, but someone else caught him from the other side, slamming a fist into his jaw with enough force that Daniel saw stars for a moment.

Another fist hit him in the stomach. Doubling over, he drew a deep, painfully ragged breath and came up fighting, using his fists and heavy boots to put up a de-fense against the two thugs who had jumped him.

Daniel saw the gleam of a knife just in time to throw himself to one side, avoiding the wild slash. He used his momentum to slam his booted foot into the guy's shin. The attacker yelped and reeled backward. Unfortunately, he didn't drop the knife.

Keeping one eye on that blade, Daniel slammed his elbow into the solar plexus of the other assailant, following that with a hard kick to the side of the knee. While that man hobbled and cursed, Daniel kicked upward toward the arm of the man holding the knife, who dodged and thrust wildly in response.

Daniel felt the slash of pain on his forearm, the hot rush of blood, but he stayed focused on the fight. He didn't allow himself to be distracted even when he heard a yell and the sound of running feet headed their way.

"It's a girl," the guy with the knife sneered before swinging at Daniel again. "Take care of her, Mike."

Cursing beneath his breath, Daniel dodged and kicked out again. Great. Some woman was trying to be a hero, and now he was going to have to protect her, too, when he had his hands full fighting off the two men who had caught him so off guard—and this time because he *had* been thinking about B.J.

The knife wielder thrust with a sudden, forceful move. Daniel caught the man's wrist from below in his left hand, then brought the outside of his right fist down solidly on top of the guy's arm. There was a satisfying crack of bone and a howl of pain.

Daniel finished the guy off with a hard kick to the kneecap, eliciting another rather high-pitched shriek, and then he threw him aside. Scooping up the knife, he turned to help whoever had foolishly run to his rescue.

He lifted his eyebrows in surprise when he saw a slender woman in blue jeans and a bright pink T-shirt bent over the man who lay on his stomach beneath her, his arm twisted behind his back, his neck immobilized beneath her sneakered right foot.

Even as Daniel watched, she exerted pressure on the guy's neck and arm at the same time, causing him to grunt and squirm. "You're breaking my freakin' arm!" he groaned, sounding both alarmed and chagrined.

"I'm going to break your freakin' neck if you move again," the woman advised him.

Recognition slammed through Daniel with the force of another blow. "B.J."

She glanced at him without releasing her hold on the man she held down. "Got something to tie him up with?"

Still stunned, he automatically removed his leather belt and strapped the man's wrists tightly behind his back. The other man was still nursing his injured arm, his leg twisted ominously beneath him.

"You broke my arm," he said accusingly when Daniel reached for him. His voice was thickened by the blood that ran from his nose. "And you've done something to my knee."

"Consider yourself lucky I didn't fillet you with your own knife." A bit over the top, maybe, but he couldn't let B.J. sound tougher than he did.

Confident that both his assailants were immobilized,

he whipped his cell phone out of his pocket and made a quick call.

He waited only until he heard sirens very close by before turning to B.J., who had been standing quietly nearby, keeping a watchful eye on the sullen men they had subdued. "Let's get out of here."

She lifted her eyebrows. "Before the police arrive?"

"They'll be here in less than a minute. These two aren't in any shape to get away before that."

"But don't we need to—"

He settled the argument by the simple measure of taking her arm and giving a slight tug. "Let's go."

It was hard to believe this was the same man she had been with less than a month earlier. B.J. studied Daniel appraisingly. At the resort he had been tailored, groomed, styled and immaculate. This man was un-shaven, grubby, disheveled and dripping blood on the dirty carpet of the dingy apartment to which he had led her.

The only thing the two images had in common was that they both looked dangerous. Yet she was no more afraid of this one than she had been of the other.

"You should probably do something about that arm," she advised him, keeping all emotion out of her voice— which wasn't easy. "You're bleeding all over your new tattoos."

He glanced down at his bloody ink-embellished arm and scowled. "They're fake."

"I figured. But the blood is real."

"It'll keep. What are you doing here?"

She looked at her slightly raw right fist. She'd known better than to use her knuckles in a fight. "Saving your butt again, apparently."

That made his scowl deepen. "I didn't need your help."

"Against two men and a knife? The odds weren't exactly in your favor."

"They were amateurs. I could have handled them."

"Maybe. But I wasn't going to stand by and watch."

"You shouldn't have been there at all. How the hell did you find me again?"

She sighed and shook her head. "I'm sorry, Daniel, but I can't talk to you while you're standing there bleeding. Since I don't suppose you'd be willing to see a doctor, is there any chance you have a first-aid kit?"

He hesitated a minute, then turned on one heel and disappeared into the bathroom. B.J. took a minute to look around the apartment. It was only one room, with a kitchenette against one wall and a sitting room/sleeping room taking up the rest of the space. There was no dining area; she supposed Daniel ate off the rickety coffee table that sat in front of a tattered sleeper sofa.

All in all, it was a far cry from the luxury suite in which they had stayed at Drake's resort.

Looking just like a man one would expect to find in a place like this, Daniel returned then, carrying a small plastic case. He tossed it on the coffee table.

"Just slap a bandage on it, if you must," he said grudgingly. "Then I want some answers."

"Sit down. I'm getting a washcloth. I'm not putting a bandage on a dirty wound."

His sigh was a gusty, impatient exhale. Ignoring him, she walked into the bathroom, pulled a threadbare white washcloth from a cabinet and held it under the faucet. Carrying the dripping cloth, a matching towel and a bar of soap back into the other room, she noted that he sat on the couch, as she had suggested.

His face was just a bit pale beneath the beard and the grime. Apparently he was feeling the injury more than he allowed himself to let on. Stubborn man.

Perching beside him, she cleaned the wound as best as she could with soap and alcohol pads—smearing a tattoo of a coiled rattlesnake in the process. Keeping her opinion of that professional-looking artwork to herself, she focused on applying antibiotic ointment to the slice in his bicep, then covering it carefully with gauze and tape.

Daniel remained still during the process, his expression unrevealing. If she was hurting him, she couldn't tell. If he was affected in any way by her touch, she couldn't detect that either.

She hoped her own face was equally inscrutable. Because sitting next to him, treating the ugly wound on his arm, touching him was definitely affecting *her*.

Chapter Fifteen

Daniel wasn't sure if the burning in his arm was due more to his injury or the feel of B.J.'s hands on his skin. It was something he had never thought he would feel again, and his reaction was so intense it bordered right on the edge of pain.

He still couldn't believe she was here. Couldn't believe she had tracked him down again. Was he so easy to find? If so, it was definitely time for him to get into a new line of work.

"There," she said, eyeing her handiwork in satisfaction. "Maybe your arm won't fall off now."

"That's comforting."

Without replying, she stuffed the first-aid supplies

back in the case and snapped it shut. "You'll probably want to take alcohol to the rest of that tattoo. Looks kind of silly to have half a snake on your arm."

He suddenly felt rather foolish in his tough street disguise. Even when she had been dressed in clothes that were not her own, pretending to be someone she wasn't, B.J. was completely herself. Daniel didn't know who the hell he was these days.

He glanced sideways at her face, noting that her hair was still mussed from the fight, she wore little if any makeup and there was a smudge on her nose. She was every bit as beautiful to him then as she had ever been in her expensive resort clothes.

So much for a whole month of trying to get over her.

"Damn it, B.J. why are you here?" Even he heard the deep weariness in his voice.

She dropped the defensiveness, her expression going somber. "I needed to return something to you."

She reached into her pocket and then held out her left hand. Daniel stared at the gold band on her palm.

Rather than taking it from her, he clasped his hands between his knees. Ever since he'd left the resort, he had been aware of the ring's absence. After all, he had worn it around his neck for more than a dozen years. But whenever he'd thought of the ring during the past month, he hadn't pictured it hanging on a chain around his neck. He had seen it on B.J.'s delicate hand.

That thought drew his eyes to her nervously clenched right hand, with its reddened knuckles. Evidence of the way she had thrown herself into a fight between him and two other men, one of whom had wielded a knife.

Maybe not so delicate, after all, he thought with a humorless twitch at the corner of his mouth. But infinitely precious to him.

"When did you learn martial arts?"

His incongruous question seemed to take her aback. She lowered the hand that was holding his ring and eyed him quizzically. "I dated a tae kwon do instructor in college. I got as high as brown belt before we broke up."

"Why didn't you mention it at the resort?"

"It never came up."

"You didn't try to use it when Drake's man shoved you into a closet?" He had heard from Greg, through Ingrid, where B.J. had been stashed.

That brought her chin up, her eyes snapping indignantly. "I thought he was the person you had sent. And I was…thinking about something else."

Daniel turned sideways on the couch and covered her hands with his, the gold ring folded out of sight in her palm. "B.J., why did you come here? You could have sent the ring to my aunt."

She drew a deep breath. "You said you owed me a favor. You told me to name my price. I'm here to collect."

Daniel swallowed hard. He had a feeling this debt was going to be higher than he had expected to pay.

B.J. watched the wariness cross Daniel's face. His fingers tightened momentarily around hers. "What is it you want?" he asked somewhat roughly.

Keeping her gaze steady on his, she reminded herself of the way he had looked when he had recognized her in that alley. For one brief, unguarded moment, she had seen true emotion in his eyes—and she hoped desperately that she hadn't misread him.

"I'll tell you that in a minute. First, I want to ask you something."

"What?"

"Why did those men attack you?"

He wasn't expecting that. "I think it was retribution. I sort of messed up a deal they were putting together," he said after a moment.

"A drug deal?"

He fell back on a particularly irritating habit he had developed the last time they'd been together. He didn't answer.

She sighed. "I just wanted to see if you would be honest with me this time. I know you're a fed. I know you work undercover. I know you were setting Drake up for the bust last month and that he thought you were buying into his drug cartel with your 'rich wife's' money."

Daniel's eyes were narrowed now, his mouth set in a display of irritation. "Anything else you want to tell me about myself?" he asked too politely, releasing her hands and crossing his arms over his chest in a gesture that she interpreted as self-protective.

"Why didn't you tell me what you are before? Why did you lead me to believe you were a con man?"

"I didn't say that. You did," he reminded her.

"Yet you didn't correct me. Why?"

"I thought you would be safer if you didn't know everything."

"That's not the reason. Not entirely, anyway."

He glared at her, his temper mounting visibly. "I didn't want you romanticizing what I do. I'm no movie hero. I chose this career because the money's pretty good, I get bored easily in more routine jobs and I'm sort of a danger junkie. Not for any more noble reason."

"Okay, I get the picture. You're a tough-guy cop."

His scowl only deepened. "I just didn't want you to confuse the boy I was with the man I am now."

"Because, of course, I'm too stupid to know the difference." This time she was the one who spoke with exaggerated civility.

He grunted impatiently. "I didn't say that."

"It was sort of a given from the way you said it."

"Look, I know you're not stupid. It's just—"

"You knew I had a big crush on you when we were kids."

"Maybe. And then you—"

"I told you I was in love with you at the resort."

His throat worked with a hard swallow. "Yeah. That, too."

"And you thought I had confused the two of you. Boy and man, I mean."

"Well—"

She couldn't help smiling at him, though she knew it was shaky. "I know you're not the same person you were thirteen years ago, Daniel. Neither am I. We've both had full lives since we parted back then. But there's still a connection between us, I think."

Maybe the direction the conversation was veering into worried him. He abruptly changed the subject. "How *did* you find me this time? And how did you learn what I do? Your uncles?"

"I found you because I talked to your aunt again. Even though she doesn't know exactly what to do, she has her suspicions. She was able to give me enough information to track you."

"Damn it."

"If it makes you feel any better, no one else has ever contacted her about you," she told him. "I really like her, Daniel. She's a very shrewd woman."

He merely scowled.

"As for what you do—well, I figured that out for myself. It took me a while and a little digging, but mostly I just knew you had to be working on the right side of the law. The Daniel I knew wouldn't work with drug dealers when drugs had already cost him so much."

He looked broodingly at her. "I told you not to romanticize me."

"I can't help it, a little," she murmured. "I admire what you do—no matter what reasons you claim might motivate you. I appreciate how good you've been to your aunt. And I'm impressed by the way you've gotten to where you are pretty much on your own."

He started to speak, but she didn't give him a chance.

"That doesn't mean I think you're perfect," she told him firmly. "You can still be a jerk sometimes. Bossy and arrogant. Leaving me that way at the resort was really rotten of you. So was letting me wonder for so long whether you were as bad as Drake. Making decisions for me based on your assumption that I'm too dumb to make them for myself. That *really* makes me mad."

"I never said you were dumb." He was beginning to sound defensive now.

"And I don't like the way you refuse to talk to me about what you're thinking and feeling, leaving me to try to guess and risk making a fool of myself. I don't like it when you—"

"So your point is?" he interrupted.

"My point is, I know exactly who you are. The man. The cop. The jerk."

"Would you quit calling me that?"

Her mouth twitched. "Starting to bug you?"

She was immeasurably relieved to see what might have been a mere hint of answering humor in his dark eyes. "Yeah."

"So maybe I can be a little jerky sometimes myself."

"Maybe so." Growing somber again, he looked down. "I want you to know that I'm not brushing off your feelings. You have to know you're very special to me, too. But—"

"But?" she prodded when he fell silent.

"You deserve better," he said in a rush. "You deserve someone who knows how to build a real home. A real family. Someone who isn't prone to dragging you into danger."

"Daniel—"

This time he was the one determined to have his say. "I haven't lived in the same place for more than a few months since I left my aunt's house when I was eighteen. I've never had what you would call a serious relationship. I change my identity so often, I don't even know who I am half the time. I could just as easily have been using a fake name as my own when you found me in Missouri. I've been answering to Jonas Lopez for the past three weeks."

She lifted her right hand to his beard-shadowed face. "I know."

"Don't look at me like that," he said roughly.

"I'm sorry. I don't seem to have any control over the way I look at you."

"You aren't listening to a word I say, are you?"

"I'm listening to *every* word you say," she countered quietly. "And it breaks my heart that you think so little of yourself."

He started to rebut that, but she slid her hand from his cheek to cover his mouth. "We've never really talked about that day beside the pond years ago. Maybe we should talk about it now."

It didn't surprise her that he was shaking his head even before she finished the sentence.

"You told me that day that you blamed yourself for not protecting your mother," she continued quickly, before he could turn away. "You thought you should have been able to somehow prevent what happened to her. You said you were afraid to care about anyone else because you were afraid something bad would happen to them."

His face was hot, his eyes haunted as she recounted that conversation he must have found so painful then. So mortifying now. "I was a kid and still hurting over finding her. I said things to you that I hadn't been able to say to anyone else."

"I know. And I'm really not confusing you again with that troubled boy, Daniel. But I want to make sure *you* aren't confusing the past and present either. That you aren't still afraid to take the risk of loving anyone because of that misguided guilt over your mother's death. You worry about your aunt being associated with you and hardly ever visit her. As for me—I don't need to be protected. Nothing is going to happen to me for loving you."

"How can you say that after everything that has happened to you because of me?" he said through clenched teeth, catching her right hand and holding it so tightly she almost winced. He turned her hand palm down to reveal her reddened knuckles. "What about this?"

Glancing down at the bruised skin, she wrinkled her nose. "My fault. I knew better than to punch with my knuckles."

"It wasn't your fault. *Nothing* has been your fault. It's all been because of me."

"I have to admit I've never been bored around you," she said.

"This isn't a joke, B.J. You could have been hurt. Or—"

"But I wasn't," she said, turning her hand to grip his. "Because I can take care of myself."

"I couldn't take it if anything happened to you." His voice sounded strained, as if he were forcing the words out through a tight throat.

Hope knotted inside her own throat, threatening to choke her. "Maybe this is a good time for me to collect on that debt."

He pushed an unsteady hand through his overlong hair. "What do you want?"

"One completely honest answer," she whispered.

Looking as though he would rather she had demanded a kidney, he pushed away from her and rose to his feet. "I'm not playing games with you."

Staying where she was, she gazed up at him. "Good. I'm very serious. You said you owed me—and that's all I want from you. Just one answer."

He sighed. "Fine. Get it over with."

Not very encouraging, she thought, studying his set shoulders and braced feet. Maybe he thought she would lose her nerve if he was forbidding enough.

He should have known her better.

Clinging to the memory of the expression in his eyes when he had said he couldn't take it if she were hurt, she drew a deep breath and blurted, "Do you love me?"

She thought at first that he wasn't going to answer, despite his agreement. He kept his back half-turned to her when he finally said, "Yes."

No elaboration. No qualification. And no encouragement, she couldn't help noting. He had given her exactly what she'd asked for and nothing more.

Still, it gave her more reason to hope....

"Will you give us a chance?"

"It wouldn't work," he said, his voice so low she had to strain to hear him. "I'm no good at that sort of thing. I travel too much. And I know how hard it is to be married to someone in my line of work, never knowing from one day to the next whether you're going to be a widow."

"That would be difficult for me," she admitted. "But I could learn to deal with it if you're committed to your job. I would never ask you to leave it for my sake."

"It's all I know how to do. I'm not fooling myself that I make that big a difference in a world where three more scumbags pop up whenever we put one behind bars. But at least I can say I tried to make things a little better, one bust at a time."

"Like Uncle Jared and his foster boys—helping a few out of the many who are in trouble. I hope you can forgive me for saying you were more like Judson Drake than Jared Walker. That was a low blow—and so very wrong."

He shook his head forcefully. "I'll never be the man Jared is. Some of the things I've done..."

"Daniel." She rose then, moving to face him fully. "Didn't you listen to any of our family history while you were with us? When Jared's siblings finally located him, he was in jail. He was a drifter who had been arrested for an armed robbery he didn't commit, leaving his young son alone on the streets until Cassie found him and helped him clear Jared's name.

"Despite the way the rest of the family pretty much idolizes him, Jared is the first to deny that he's anyone's hero. He calls himself a simple cowboy with a knack for taming horses and teenage boys. A man with flaws and emotional baggage from being raised by an alcoholic father and a mother who died much too young— not to mention spending the rest of his youth in foster homes and his early adulthood trying to find a place for himself. Now he's chosen to try to make a difference in the world, a little at a time. Don't tell me you aren't like him, Daniel. I know better."

He looked stunned, though he was still shaking his head. "Don't—"

"I'm not confusing you with him. I haven't been looking specifically for a man like Jared, though I've always admired him, so it isn't surprising I would fall for someone who reminds me of him in some ways. I'm in love with *you*, Daniel Andreas or Castillo or Lopez or Smith— whatever you call yourself, whatever you do for a living. And I won't stop loving you even if you send me away again. I'll just spend the rest of my life missing you."

"You deserve better."

"You're right. I do," she replied steadily. "And you deserve better than what you've had, too. You deserve a real home. Someone who loves you for exactly who you are rather than the roles you've played for so long. A chance to forgive yourself for things you had no control over. So what are you going to do about it?"

He heaved a long, weary-sounding sigh that might have signaled surrender. "How do you feel about answering to Mrs. Andreas again? I'd rather not go back to Castillo, since I left that part of my life behind a long time ago."

She should have been expecting something like that, considering that Daniel had a habit of giving her no warning before doing something that knocked the breath completely out of her. After taking a moment to steady herself, she replied, "I could get used to it."

"Because if you prefer Smith…"

She shook her head and gave him a tremulous smile. "Andreas is fine."

His tone turned suddenly fierce. "Be sure," he said. "Because I'm sure as hell not going to apologize this time, either, if you change your mind later."

Her smile deepened at the reminder of the first time he had made love to her. "I won't change my mind. And I won't need an apology, because I have no doubt that we can make this work. I love you, Daniel."

She saw the courage it took for him to look her in the eyes and reply, "I love you, too. God help you."

And then he held out his arms to her.

They took their time from that point. Daniel insisted on shaving and showering, getting rid of the last signs of the unkempt "Jonas Lopez." Insisting that he needed help showering—just to make sure he didn't reopen the slice in his arm—B.J. joined him.

The hot water didn't last long, but the heat they generated between them more than made up for it.

Afterward they made love on the sleeper sofa, barely taking time to throw aside the cushions and unfold the bed first. Daniel seemed genuinely embarrassed at first by the grubbiness of the apartment, but she convinced him rather quickly that she didn't care where they were as long as they were together.

Together, they proved almost immediately that the surroundings didn't matter. Whether in a luxury suite or on a picnic table or between the sheets of a tattered bed, they found paradise whenever they were together. And paradise was even sweeter this time because they both knew it wouldn't be the last time they visited there.

B.J. was still wondering whether she would ever breathe normally again when Daniel spoke, his voice still a bit hoarse. "About that tae kwon do instructor…"

She was surprised into a giggle. "What about him?"

"Could he have kicked my ass?"

Daniel would have pounded Tommy into the ground, but B.J. saw no point in inflating his ego any more than she already had for one day. Still smiling, she murmured, "Let's just say I've always had a thing for tough guys."

"Does that mean…?"

She rolled over onto his chest, propping her chin on her hands. "Anyone ever tell you that you've got the prettiest eyes?"

"You're trying to change the subject."

"Yes. But they *are* pretty."

Daniel sighed and shook his head, silently acknowledging that she wouldn't answer any more questions about the ex-boyfriend.

"So—think I can find a job in Dallas? Maybe the police department is hiring."

She was a bit surprised by the new topic, but she answered easily enough. "I'm sure one of my uncles can pull a few strings with the Dallas PD—but are you sure that's what you want to do? Give up what you're doing now to settle into one place?"

He shrugged, but she knew he wasn't taking her question lightly. "Part of the reason I was so good at this job is because I had no real ties to anyone, no place I had to be, no one to worry about me if I suddenly disappeared. I made arrangements for Aunt Maria to be taken care of if anything happened to me, but I also made sure there was nothing else connecting her to me. Things are different now. As Drake pointed out, you've become my weakness."

She frowned, uncertain if that was a good thing.

"It isn't a criticism," he assured her, reading her expression. "It feels pretty good to know someone would care if I didn't make it home."

"You're underestimating the way your aunt feels about you. She loves you very much. And she would care deeply if you didn't make it home."

"Then that's another reason for me to settle down in one place and take a job that's a little more secure. I could see her. And being the wife of a cop isn't a picnic, but it's better than what I can offer you now."

"I'll take it," she said promptly. "Happily. But be sure, Daniel. I won't apologize if you change your mind later."

He flashed a grin in response to her quoting him. "I won't expect you to."

B.J. rested her head on his chest, contentment flooding through her. And then she suddenly groaned and lifted her head again. "Uh-oh. I think you're going to have to come up with one more cover story."

His eyebrows rose quizzically. "What?"

"Jared and Cassie aren't supposed to find out about the surprise party being planned for October. They don't know Molly sent me looking for you. Since I have no intention of waiting nearly four months to bring you back into the family, we've got to make up a story about how we ran into each other again completely by accident."

"How about we tell them that I kidnapped you and had my wicked way with you until you agreed to marry me?"

She grinned but shook her head. "They would never believe that."

He touched her cheek. "Then maybe we should tell them that I've been in love with you since I was sixteen and I finally had the good sense to do something about it."

"I like that," she murmured, shaken by the ring of truth in his deep voice. "Maybe we'll come up with a variation of it."

He caught the back of her neck in one hand and pulled her down for a long, deep kiss. Wrapping her arms around him, B.J. decided it didn't really matter what they told anyone else.

They had always been meant to be together. One way or another, they would have found each other again. This time it was forever.

* * * * *

For their invaluable assistance in my research, thanks to
Scott Salman of the Boston Fire Department, Joel Schwartz
of the Dorchester Bay Economic Development Corp.
and most of all, Stephen Hardy of the
Merrimack Romantic Development Corp.

KRISTIN
HARDY

WHERE
THERE'S
SMOKE

**Harlequin
Mills ❀ Boon**

*Special
Edition*

DID YOU PURCHASE THIS BOOK WITHOUT A COVER?
If you did, you should be aware it is **stolen property** as it was
reported 'unsold and destroyed' by a retailer.
Neither the author nor the publisher has received any payment
for this book.

First Published 2005
First Australian Paperback Edition 2005
ISBN 0 733 56568 9

WHERE THERE'S SMOKE © 2005 by Chez Hardy LLC
Philippine Copyright 2005
Australian Copyright 2005
New Zealand Copyright 2005
Except for use in any review, the reproduction or utilisation of this work in
whole or in part in any form by any electronic, mechanical or other means,
now known or hereafter invented, including xerography, photocopying and
recording, or in any information storage or retrieval system, is forbidden
without the permission of the publisher, Harlequin Mills & Boon, Locked Bag
7002, Chatswood D.C. N.S.W., Australia 2067.

All the characters in this book have no existence outside the imagination of
the author, and have no relation whatsoever to anyone bearing the same
name or names. They are not even distantly inspired by any individual
known or unknown to the author, and all the incidents are pure invention.

This book is sold subject to the condition that it shall not, by way of trade or
otherwise, be lent, resold, hired out or otherwise circulated without the prior
consent of the publisher in any form of binding or cover other than that in
which it is published and without a similar condition including this condition
being imposed on the subsequent purchaser.

All rights reserved including the right of reproduction in whole or in part in
any form. This edition is published by arrangement with Harlequin
Enterprises II B.V.

Published by
Harlequin Mills & Boon
3 Gibbes Street
CHATSWOOD NSW 2067
AUSTRALIA

HARLEQUIN MILLS & BOON SPECIAL EDITION and the Rose Device are
trademarks used under license and registered in Australia, New Zealand,
Philippines, United States Patent & Trademark Office and in other countries.

Printed and bound in Australia by
McPherson's Printing Group

KRISTIN HARDY

has always wanted to write, starting her first novel while still in grade school. Although she became a laser engineer by training, she never gave up her dream of being an author. In 2002, her first completed manuscript, *My Sexiest Mistake*, debuted in Harlequin's Blaze line; it was subsequently made into a movie by the Oxygen network. The author of nine books to date, Kristin lives in New Hampshire with her husband and collaborator.

Dear Reader,

The publication of *Where There's Smoke* is a dream come true for me. About twenty years ago (when I was two, of course) I picked up a Harlequin Special Edition novel at the store and I got the bug to write a romance. Fast forward through several false starts and *long* hiatuses from writing. Even though I never finished a book, I always knew that one day I'd make my living as a romance novelist. Then in September 2001, I finally typed "The End" on a story and sold it to Harlequin's newly launched Blaze line.

My heart has always been with Special Edition, though. When Gail Chasan bought the HOLIDAY HEARTS trilogy I couldn't have been more thrilled. I have so many stories to tell, so I hope that this is a journey we can go on together as I continue to write for both lines.

I'd love to hear what you think of my first effort, so please drop me a line at kristin@kristinhardy.com. Stop by my Web site at www.kristinhardy.com for contests, details on upcoming books, recipes and more.

Happy holidays.

Kristin Hardy

Chapter One

It was beyond him how so much paperwork could stack up in such a short time. Nick Trask stared balefully at the forms piled up on his desk and sighed. He'd joined the fire department to battle fires, not to generate his own personal fire hazard.

When people asked him why he loved firefighting, he usually shrugged and said it was rewarding. It was true, that much of it, but there was more he didn't say. He didn't tell them of the fierce pleasure of firefighting, the euphoria of saving a life or the way the adrenaline blasted through him as he risked everything against the ravening beast of the flames.

Those were the moments that made it all worthwhile. Those were the times that made up for days like this one, he thought, raking an impatient hand through his cropped hair. It had been crazy from the get-go. They'd hardly had time to go over the morning announcements at the start of shift when the bells had sounded for a house fire in a triple-decker just blocks away. Climbing to the roof to ventilate the blaze, hands full with a chainsaw, Bruce Jackson had found out the twenty-foot ladder had a bad rung. The hard way. All things considered, it was a lucky thing he'd only fallen eight feet—if you could call a broken collarbone lucky.

And the day had just gone downhill from there.

Accident reports, damaged property reports, defective equipment reports…Nick was tempted to put a lump of coal underneath them and see if he could make a diamond. It wouldn't have been so bad if it hadn't been for the rescue call, the inspections and the car fire. Not to mention the medical aid calls. Three of them. Even after spending every moment in between calls filling out forms and cursing the department for not having it all online, he was only a little over half done, and everything had to be shipshape by the time they made the shift change.

Nick shook his head and glanced at the books he'd optimistically spread out, hoping to study for the promotional exam. His chances of getting any time to look at them this shift were about as good as his chances of winning Powerball.

"Yo, cap, give me a hand for a minute?" The question was shouted up from the garage area below, rising above the sounds of rock music on the radio. If he craned his neck, Nick could see out the open door of his office and through the stair railing to the long, gleaming red shapes of the fire engine and ladder truck, massive yet oddly sleek under the fluorescent lights of the cavernous garage. Something of the boy in him smiled then, something of the man felt a swelling pride, underlain by a breath of challenge, a taste of danger.

Firefighting was his life. It touched the essence of him in a way nothing else ever had.

Feet thumped up the stairs. "El capitan?" A burly, middle-aged firefighter with a blunt-featured face leaned into the office. From behind him came the sound of U2 singing about a beautiful day.

Nick put down his pen. "Still stuck on these reports, O'Hanlan, sorry."

"Remember the other day when you were asking me why I didn't want to take the exam to move up? 'Nuff said. You officer types, you gotta love paperwork. Me, I'm an action guy."

A corner of Nick's mouth quirked as he looked at O'Hanlan's florid face. "An action guy, huh?"

"Every minute of every day."

"No wonder your wife looks scared. Look, I've got to keep working on this pile if I'm going to get through it by shift change, so if someone else can help you, go for it."

"No problem. I understand. Some people are born bureaucrats. But if your hand starts getting tired and you want to be reminded what the apparatus looks like…"

Nick stopped and considered, tapping forms-in-triplicate with his pen and eyeing the door where O'Hanlan beckoned.

"Were you ever in sales, O'Hanlan?"

"Just pointing out your options." He tipped his head in the direction of the apparatus floor, wagging his eyebrows.

It *was* Nick's duty as captain to take care of any problems, and God knew he could use a break from the endless writing. Nick grinned and tossed down his pen. "All right, you got me."

"Cap." Todd Beaulieu, compact and dark-haired, met them on the stairs, a slip of paper in his hand. "I just found this note by the phone. Looks like you got a call sometime yesterday."

"Yesterday?"

"I guess the other shift forgot to tell you." Beaulieu squinted at the paper. "Jeez, O'Hanlan, this writing looks as bad as yours."

"Hey, I've won awards for my handwriting, I'll have you know," O'Hanlan protested.

"Probably for cryptography," Beaulieu shot back.

Nick reached out for the message. "Eq tes tom?" he asked squinting at the scribbles. "Anybody want to guess?"

O'Hanlan considered. "Abusing a cat?"

"Leave your personal life out of this," Beaulieu told him.

Nick struggled for a moment to make sense of the hasty scrawl. "Looks like someone's doing something tomorrow. Which means today. I guess we'll find out eventually." He shrugged and turned to the stairs. "What did you break this time, O'Hanlan?"

Down on the garage floor, Nick and O'Hanlan threaded their way around the pumper to the ladder truck. The music on the radio segued into a no-nonsense woman's voice reading the morning news.

"In Dorchester, Councilman Donald Ayre, running for re-election next month, spoke again about his new safety plan for Boston firefighters."

"We can't have fire safety in Boston until our firefighters are safe," Ayre said self-importantly. "That's my mission, and that's why I'm looking for reelection."

O'Hanlan rolled his eyes at the sound bite. "Looks like old Hot Ayre is at it again," he said, climbing on top of the ladder truck. "Funny, the last time he got yapping about firefighters it was an election year, too."

"And the time before that, I think," Nick said, following him. "'Course, he doesn't talk about how he pushed for department budget cuts once the voting was over, does he?"

"He's probably shy about his accomplishments," O'Hanlan guessed. "Besides, if the equipment was good enough for our great-grandfathers, it's good enough for us, right?"

"Sure. Just ask Jackson." Nick's lip curled. "Twenty bucks says that inside of two weeks we've got our illustrious councilman in a photo op with some high-tech gizmo the department will buy one of for tests and never use."

"C'mon, how's he supposed to enjoy the budget cuts unless he cleans out the miscellaneous fund, too? Cut him some slack."

"I'd like to cut him something." Nick shook his head in disgust. "If we don't give them something to yap about on the campaign trail, we don't exist for those guys."

"Cushy life, though. Think about it: nice, soft chair in the City Council meetings, free parking anywhere in town. Free lunches, too." O'Hanlan's eyes brightened. "Maybe I should go into politics."

Nick looked him up and down. "I'm not sure you could handle any more lunches, O'Hanlan."

"That?" O'Hanlan slapped his comfortable belly. "That's muscle, sonny boy, and don't you forget it."

"I'll work on it. So what's the problem that you had to drag me all the way down here for, anyway?"

O'Hanlan bent down to the giant aerial ladder that lay folded up in sections on top of the truck. "The ladder felt sticky at that last fire. She didn't open up like she should have. I took a look and this bolt right here is loose and partly sheared." He pulled at the ladder and the bolt rattled in its hole. "I think it'll be okay if we just switch it, but with these mitts of mine I can't get at it."

Nick glanced at it briefly, then at his watch. "Why don't I write it up for repair?"

"Because"—O'Hanlan made a futile attempt to reach the back of the bolt—"you write it up, the motor squad'll take a month to get to it and a month to fix it. Or we'll get stuck working with one of those Civil War relics they keep around."

"I'd think an action guy would want the challenge."

"I have to save my valuable strength for firefighting, not for pushing the truck to the scene." O'Hanlan's voice was aggrieved. "Here I'm trying to save you some writing and you're not even appreciating it, ya bureaucrat."

"That's the trouble with you, O'Hanlan, always thinking of others first." Nick squatted down to get a better view. "Give me a wrench."

Sloane Hillyard strode down the sidewalk toward Firehouse 67, narrowing her eyes against the glare of the October sun, wishing she'd remembered her sunglasses. A group of teenaged boys hanging out on the corner turned to watch her pass.

"Yo, baby, what you in such a hurry for?" the boldest of them called. "Y'oughta stop and be more sociable." He trailed after her a few steps, while his buddies nudged one another and laughed. "C'mon, baby, stop. I'll show you God."

Sloane ignored him and kept going. An angry tangle of graffiti covered the walls of the building she passed. Here where the southern Boston neighborhoods of North Dorchester and Roxbury came together, even the sidewalk looked hard used. Sloane genuinely didn't notice. She wasn't concerned with young boys or with her surroundings. She was only concerned with the men in the firehouse ahead.

Her stomach tightened.

When she stepped through the doorway, she would start the final phase of five years of intense—some might say obsessive—effort. Five years to design equipment that would help ensure no firefighter, anywhere, would be lost in a blaze. Five years to help ensure that no more men would be devoured by the gaping maw of the flames.

The main doors of the station were open as she walked up.

She slowed as she reached the dark crack in the concrete that marked the threshold. It had been a long time since she'd set foot in a firehouse. She'd thought she was ready for it.

She'd been wrong.

Just do it, she told herself grimly, fighting to ignore the quick twist of anxiety. She was so close to achieving her goal, so close. This was no time to let the past take over the future.

Taking a deep breath, she crossed the line and passed into the fluorescent cool of the garage. A compact, dark-haired man with a boyish face stacked air canisters against the wall. A young firefighter in a Red Sox cap swept the floor around the trucks. The sweeping came to an abrupt halt as he glanced up, hastily setting the broom aside and wiping off his hands as Sloane approached. "Can I help you?"

The click of her heels rang in the cavernous garage. "Hello." She smiled, wondering if he could have been a day past nineteen. "I'm looking for Nick Trask."

The boy was blushing, trying to act cool. "The captain? I think he's up in his office. I'll go get him."

The dark-haired firefighter turned before they took two steps. "Yo, Red! She looking for Trask?"

Sloane froze, her chest suddenly constricted.

"He's not up in his office. He's with O'Hanlan." The man pointed toward the ladder truck at the far side of the garage. "Over there."

"Thanks, Beaulieu." The boy smiled shyly. "My mistake." He looked at Sloane more closely. "Are you okay?"

Sloane forced herself to breathe. "I'm fine, thanks." She saw it now, bright auburn hair curling around the edges of his ball cap. "I knew someone else called Red once."

"My name's Jim Sorensen," he said ruefully, taking his hat

off and scrubbing it through his wavy brush. "But you know how it goes. They took one look at my hair and that was that."

"I know how it goes," she agreed.

"Okay, I've got hold of the nut if you can get the bolt through," Nick muttered, jaw set in concentration. "Let's give it a push and get the holes lined up." They leaned on the ladder together and the metal creaked as it moved.

"Let me get my hand in there. It's just about…ah!" O'Hanlan cursed to the ceiling as he barked his knuckles on unforgiving metal. "I signed up to be a firefighter, not a damn mechanic."

"You were the one who was dead against calling in the motor squad," Nick reminded him. "Come on, action guy, repeat *power steering* to yourself three times and let's try it again."

"Power steering, power steering, there's no place like home, there's no place like home," O'Hanlan's voice rose an octave. "There's no place—" Abruptly he gave a low whistle. "Well, well, well. Looks like I should have volunteered for clean-up detail."

Without turning, Nick knew it was a woman. Her voice floated over to them, low, slightly rough, a smoky contralto that belonged in the bedroom and made him tighten before he ever looked at her. When he did, the first thing he saw was her hair. She had it pulled back and looped up in a clip, but not bound into submission. It was thick, nearly down to her waist, he'd guess, and flamed a deep, splendid red. The face…the face went with the voice, decidedly, recklessly sensual. Slavic cheekbones, challenging eyes, a mouth that made him wonder how it would feel on his skin. Her narrow, forest-green suit played up the sleek curves of her body enough to make his imagination temporarily run rampant.

There was more, something about the lift to her shoulders, the cool self-assurance in her stance that intrigued and enticed him.

"Look at Red." O'Hanlan chuckled. "He's falling all over himself, poor kid." He turned back around. "Hey, Nick?"

He'd been staring, Nick realized, shaking himself loose. "And you, of course, are a master of self-control." He gave O'Hanlan a derisive look before bending back to the ladder. "C'mon, let's finish this."

"I'm a happily married man," O'Hanlan reminded him, grunting as he leaned on the ladder and threaded the bolt in place. "And Leanne would skin me alive if she caught me looking at another woman." O'Hanlan peeked over his shoulder at the approaching redhead. "Which is why I do it here."

Nick squeezed his hand in between ladder struts to work a nut onto the bolt. "Stick to fighting fires," he advised, manipulating the wrench expertly. "It's safer."

"Hello? Excuse me?" The words echoed up from beside the truck. "I'm looking for Nick Trask."

At close range her voice whispered over his skin and into his bones, mesmerizing, arousing. He leaned across the top of the ladder until their eyes locked. Up close, she was all the glimpse had promised and more. "I'm Nick Trask. Give me a minute, I'll be right with you."

"A minute?" O'Hanlan grinned. "Take over for me here and I'll be down there in thirty seconds."

"Easy, big fella." Nick passed the wrench to O'Hanlan and patted him on the shoulder. "Skinned alive, remember? Save your strength for Leanne."

She'd always been a sucker for men in uniform, Sloane thought, watching the lean, stripped-down lines of his body as he swung down from the ladder truck. That was all it was. Of course, he filled the uniform as though it had been designed for him. Off limits, she reminded herself. She didn't do firefighters. He neared and Sloane's pulse skittered unevenly, then steadied.

"Nick Trask," he said, wiping his hands on a rag.

Dark, Sloane thought, and dangerous. His looks hit her with the slamming impact of a hundred-mile-an-hour collision. Black hair, tanned, almost swarthy skin and eyes darker than jet combined on a face that simultaneously compelled and alarmed. It was a face that was not so much conventionally handsome as it was filled with the essential character of the man.

Her guard was up in a heartbeat.

"Sloane Hillyard, Exler Corporation." She reached out her hand when he drew near. "Councilman Ayre's office asked me to stop by." She wasn't sure what she found more disconcerting, the almost imperceptible chill that swept over his face as she spoke, or the flush of heat that assaulted her at the touch of his hand. Nerves, she told herself. She was just on edge over being in a firehouse again. "Nice to meet you, Captain Trask."

"And you." There was a cursory politeness in his voice but no warmth. This close to him Sloane could see that his eyes weren't black. They were deep gray, the color of darkest smoke, the color of a stormy sky at dusk. "What can I do for you and the councilman?"

Focus, Sloane reminded herself. "I'm here for our meeting."

"Our meeting?"

"I called to confirm yesterday."

"I didn't get any…" He checked himself and pulled a pink slip of paper covered in illegible script from his pocket. "Ah. This must be you. Sorry, but I didn't get this until about five minutes ago and it's been a really hectic day, so if—"

"That's all right," she cut in smoothly. "I'll only need a few minutes of your time. We need to talk about the gear."

"The gear?" He put his hands on his hips and gave a nod. "Ayre doesn't waste time, I'll give him that."

Sloane didn't need to know the reason for the sarcasm to understand that she was at least a partial target. Irritation pricked at her. "We need to talk about scheduling, plan the testing," she continued, not about to be derailed. "Councilman Ayre's office—"

"Yeah, I know, Councilman Ayre's office." Nick cut her off, glancing at the number of men with sudden, pressing business in the immediate vicinity. "Look, let's go to my office and you can tell me what Ayre's up to this time."

He didn't offer it as a choice, but in the clipped tone of command. "Yes sir," Sloane muttered, following him up the stairs. Perhaps the man could put out fires, but graciousness was clearly not his strong suit.

Nor, she thought a moment later, was neatness.

"Right through there. Have a seat."

Sloane stood in the doorway of his tiny office and threw a glance of disbelief at the jumble of paperwork and books everywhere. "Which stack of paper did you have in mind for me to sit on, Captain Trask?" Her tone was deceptively sweet, as was her face. The sarcasm lurked only in her gaze, which warned him not to push too hard, not to presume too much.

Nick shifted a pile of books to the floor. "There." The telephone jangled for attention and he answered it impatiently. "House sixty-seven, Trask. Oh yeah, right. Giancoli says the brakes on the pumper are down." He slid into his chair, instantly absorbed, leaving Sloane standing in the middle of the room.

Setting down her briefcase, she took the opportunity to look around. Photographs covered the walls: smiling fire-

fighters in front of shining engines, men crowded together at
the kitchen table, competing in the Firefighters' Olympics. A
newspaper clipping showed grim men in helmets and turnouts,
lines of exhaustion etched into their soot-streaked faces as
they carried stretchers out of a smoke-filled building. Hillview
Convalescent Home Burns but the Fire Claims No Victims,
the caption read. The men in the picture were from Ladder 67.

Sloane glanced further along and her interest sharpened.
Stacked haphazardly atop the filing cabinet were a pair of pla-
ques, the top one an award of valor presented to one Nick
Trask for action above and beyond the call of duty. Impressed
in spite of herself, Sloane glanced over to where he sat at his
desk, absorbed in his call.

She'd been wrong when she'd thought his face held more
character than perfection. Clearly, the sharp slashes of his
cheekbones, the compelling shape of his mouth translated into
above-average looks. It was simply that the force of his per-
sonality was so strong that it overwhelmed the handsomeness,
carried it past simple good looks to a more dangerous realm,
giving him the ability to hypnotize, the power to obsess.

The sudden flicker of warning ran through her to the pit of
her stomach. In defense, she moved to stare out the window.
Outside, a dog barked and boys shouted as they threw a football in the street. Inside, a subtle tension filled the air.

Nick shifted in his chair impatiently. "Yeah, okay. Let me
know when it'll go. Great, talk to you later." He hung up the
phone, turning to where Sloane stood. Perhaps it was a trick
of the light, but for just an instant her hair blazed the exact
color of flame. For just an instant, he watched without speaking. He shook his head and forced his mind to business just
as she turned from the window.

"All finished?"

"Yes. Sorry about the wait." Because he was still having a hard time concentrating, Nick plunged in without preamble. "So, Ms. Hillyard, what has the councilman's office promised that we would do for you?"

His tone was more brusque than he'd intended. It made Sloane's mouth tighten and she took her time coming back to her chair. "I believe the councilman's office is taking a sincere interest in your safety, as I think you'll see. Now, I made an appointment through the city weeks ago," she said frostily. "I assumed you'd be ready to discuss this."

Nick silently cursed the man who'd taken the garbled message, then cursed the fact that it had been uncovered so late that he'd had no time to sort it out. And he added Ayre, just on principle. No matter how gorgeous she was, whatever the woman was selling, it was going to take time he didn't have. "Yes, well," he said, summoning his patience for what looked to be a long siege, "why don't you start at the beginning?"

Sloane took a deep breath. "I work for the Exler Corporation," she said, a little too carefully. "I've developed a system called the Orienteer. It's designed to locate firefighters in burning buildings."

"How?"

"It's got a microprocessor that combines global-positioning-system input with a database of building plans to locate anyone, anywhere. You want to find your team members in a burning building, you can. If they need to track their way out, it will lead them. No one will die the way they did in the Hartford packing-house fire ever again." Her voice caught, so briefly he couldn't be sure he hadn't imagined it. "We've gone through the preliminary lab qualification and breakdowns. The last step is testing in a real-life situation with firefighters."

"No way." Nick was shaking his head before she finished. "My guys aren't guinea pigs."

"I beg your pardon?"

"Not a chance." Nick knew how this went, oh, he knew it. Put on the dog for the politicians, invest precious departmental resources and when the photo ops and the elections were done, so was the funding. That was bad enough, but put his men at risk for that photo op? That was where he drew the line.

"You can't just refuse."

"First of all, it's totally impractical." That was the part that really burned him about operators like Ayre. It couldn't be something reasonable or useful. No—some babelicious Girl Scout turned up with her science project and Ayre saw only the headlines, not the lives at risk.

"Impractical?" Sloane's eyes flashed. "How can you say that when you don't know the first thing about it?"

"Where are you going to get all the blueprints?"

"We've *already* gotten them from the planning commission. The microprocessors for the test units are being loaded up with plans for every building in Boston and Cambridge."

He snorted. "Do you actually think those are up-to-date in a city like this? You really want to bank someone's life on that?"

"We're confirming layouts as we're entering them."

"Checking up on every structure? You'll never get it done," he said dismissively. "You want to be useful, get me a couple more thermal cameras, build me a better breathing mask. Something proven. Something practical."

Sloane flushed. "The equipment *is* practical. And proven. It's been completely lab tested, it just hasn't been used in a fire situation before. Both the department and Councilman Ayre's office are behind this."

"I'm sure they are. The chief and Ayre grew up on the same block."

She gave him a level stare. "What's that supposed to mean?"

He sighed. It really wasn't her fault. "Look, I'm sure you've got the best of intentions, but you don't know how the game goes around here."

"But I'm sure you'll tell me."

She looked, he thought, strung tight as a piano wire. It didn't make her any less gorgeous. "Ayre starts with the fire-safety shtick every election cycle. It gets him press, photos in front of shiny red trucks. It's all about exposure and it's nothing he'll support with funding. Trust me on that, I've been through it before." He shook his head in frustration. "Ayre just wants to make headlines. You're the tool he chose to do it with."

"What is with you? I'm talking about equipment that can help you and you're talking about conspiracies."

He bristled. "No, I'm talking politics."

"And I'm talking about saving lives," she retorted. "You've got problems with Ayre? Then vote against him next month. I don't care. All that matters to me is getting this equipment qualified."

"And you're dreaming if you think they're actually going to buy this gadget."

"It's not a gadget," she said hotly. "It's a very sophisticated system."

"A very…" He shook his head like a dog throwing off water. "Do you understand anything at all about firefighting?"

Her eyes burned for a moment; it took her a visible effort to tamp her reaction down. "Of course I do. I consulted with firefighters in Cambridge when I was designing the equipment."

"Great. Take it to them to test."

"We're not taking it to them. We've taken it to the city of

Boston and the city says you. This isn't some project of the week. This testing is critical and trust me, it is going to get done. Bill Grant in the fire chief's office wants your company to do the testing. Ayre wants it. I want it. You're way down the list, Captain Trask."

Nick didn't even attempt to quell the bright flare of anger. "That's where you're wrong. You may think that because you had a couple of nice visits downtown that you can come in here and do whatever you want." He rose, stalking toward her until she was forced to tilt her head to hold his gaze. "But this is my firehouse and I don't care what Ayre wants, I don't care what it is Grant wants and I certainly don't care what you want. I am not going to put my guys at risk so Ayre can take pictures of the two of you testing out a video game."

Sloane paled for an instant, then shot to her feet, two spots of color burning high on her cheekbones. "This equipment is going to get qualified, no matter what it takes. I don't give a damn if I'm a tool or a pawn or whatever the hell you think I am if it means that I save one person's life, just one." Her voice rose in fury. "And you are not going to stand in my way."

They faced each other, inches apart, crackling with tension. Something kinetic surged through the air between them then, something elemental that had nothing to do with firefighting and everything to do with heat.

Sloane moved away first, because she had to, because she felt the shudder of weakness in the wall of anger surrounding her. "Where's your telephone?" she demanded. "You don't want to do this, Captain Trask? I'll save you the trouble. Forget about wasting your time, testing with you would be a waste of my time." She crossed to his desk and snatched up the telephone receiver. "Where's the number for the fire chief's office?"

He studied her a moment, his brows drawn together in a frown of concentration. Then he plucked the receiver from her hand. "I'll dial it for you." He punched in the numbers rapidly and waited. "Bill Grant please. Yes, I'll hold." He handed the receiver back without a word.

Sloane waited, listening to Nick stalk out into the hallway. There was a click on the line, then a voice. "Bill Grant here."

"Hi Bill, it's Sloane Hillyard."

"Sloane, good to talk to you." The words were ever so slightly shaded with relief. "You have perfect timing. I was just trying to reach you."

"Well, you've got me now. What do you need?"

"Can you hold off contacting Ladder 67 for a day? We had a little paperwork snafu here and the memo that should have gone to them is still sitting here in my office. Give me a day to get everything set up with them and we can go ahead."

Sloane glanced out toward the hall and found her gaze pinned to Nick Trask's. He was yards away, but she felt a clutch on her chest as sure as a physical contact. The breath of a shiver that passed up her spine was composed partly of anxiety, partly of feelings she was afraid to identify. She tore her eyes away and turned back to the desk. "Too late, Bill. I'm calling you from the firehouse."

"Oh." He paused for a moment and Sloane heard the rapid, nervous tap of a finger against the phone, maybe, or the desk. "Um, is everything okay?"

"Not exactly. In fact, after talking with Captain Trask, I think it would be best for me to work with a different company."

"Let's not be hasty, Sloane. Nick Trask's one of the best men we've got." Now she heard all four fingers begin to drum the desktop in sequence. "If there's any hitch here, it's my fault. Why don't you let me talk to him and see what the problem is?"

The problem, thought Sloane, was that she didn't want to be anywhere near Nick Trask, certainly not for a period of weeks. "All right." She turned to Nick. "It's for you."

Sloane walked out into the hall where she could finally breathe. The testing couldn't be interrupted. Everything depended on getting the gear qualified. Everything.

After a moment, she looked around. To her left was the stairway that ran down to the apparatus floor. To her right, the hall ended in a T, with the dormitory on one side and probably a kitchen and rec room on the other. Without even trying she could picture the latter—worn, comfortable furniture, a TV and VCR, probably some back issues of *Fire Engineering* magazine tossed down on a table. Before she could block it, the image of a lanky, boyish-faced redhead sprawled on a firehouse couch came to her with painful clarity. Oh Mitch, she thought and grief and loss surged in for a blinding instant.

"Ms. Hillyard," Nick's voice called to her. "Grant wants to talk with you again."

She responded automatically, entering the office, reaching for the phone. "Yes?"

"Hi, Sloane," Grant answered cheerily. "I just wanted to apologize for the mixup over there. I've discussed the situation with Nick and he'll be happy to work with you on this project." Sloane glanced over to where Nick stood, staring at her again. Oh, she could see how happy he was about the project. "It's up to you, of course," Grant continued, "but it's really best. It could take quite a while to get another company lined up."

Sloane bit back a protest. Grant had her neatly cornered. The testing had to be finished in two months, when production was scheduled to begin. There could be no delays and he knew it. Sloane sighed. "All right. Let's stick with the plan."

"Wonderful." She could hear the satisfaction in Grant's

voice. "If you have any more hitches with the testing, just give me a ring and I'll take care of things, okay?"

"Sure. Anything else?"

"Actually, yes. Can you put Nick back on?"

The clamor of the alarm bells shattered the quiet of the firehouse. Sloane couldn't prevent herself from jumping.

Nick was galvanized into action instantly. "Tell him I'll call him back," he barked over his shoulder, sprinting for the fire pole in the dormitory.

"He's got…"

"I know, an explosion at the oil-tank farm. It just came in here. Sloane, thanks very much." Grant's voice was hurried as he said goodbye.

The previous atmosphere of calm had been replaced by one of controlled urgency, the air charged with tension. Even as Sloane rushed down the stairs, most of the men were on the apparatus floor pulling on turnouts, grabbing waiting helmets and gloves. A stocky firefighter turned away from the enormous district map that covered one wall and climbed into the cab of Ladder 67. "I got it, cap. Let's fly."

Sloane hurried to get clear as the last of the men vaulted aboard the gleaming apparatus. Already the motors throbbed, the station door was peeled back. She slipped outside as the ladder truck and the pumper hit the street, lights flashing and sirens shrieking.

The firefighters were on their way.

Chapter Two

If he ever won the lottery, Nick thought, he'd hire people to shop for him. Not just certain kinds of shopping—pretty much anything that involved cash registers and standing in line. Certainly anything with narrow aisles and those shiny chrome racks crammed so close together that he was perpetually bumping them with his shoulders.

"Can I help you?"

A teenaged sales clerk popped up at his elbow. The fixed, Mouseketeer smile on her face scared him a little. On the other hand, having to spend more than two more minutes in the boutique scared him more.

He looked at the piles of silky scarves and fancy handbags. "I need a birthday gift for my mother."

"Well, you've come to the right place. How about something to add a little color to her winter wardrobe?" she asked, holding up a sheer band of fabric with a twisting pattern of burgundy and gold.

The dark red brought Sloane Hillyard to mind. Not that he needed a prompt. She'd been in his thoughts since she'd come to the station two days before. Granted, she had a face that was hard to forget, but if it had only been that, he could have dismissed her as a high-tech huckster. What had made her linger with him was the way she'd looked at the end. There had been that instant that she'd paled. And the words, so impassioned she'd practically vibrated with them: *If I save one life, just one life…*

There was something driving her, that much was obvious. He couldn't help but admire her for it. There was a "Why" there and it was enough to make him wonder about the project. Of course, if his mind returned to the generous sweep of her mouth, the fire of her hair, the heat that had flashed between them in his office, he was only human, right?

Forget about the project, it was enough to make him wonder about her. And wonder where the testing might take them.

"Do you see any scarves your mother might like?"

The clerk's voice broke into his thoughts and Nick brought his focus back to the task at hand. There was plenty to think about there, too. "My mother's not much of a scarf person," he answered. At least not scarves that were more for looks than for warmth. On the other hand, why not? He'd come in with the vague idea that he wanted to get her something different, something other than a new plant or a sweater from L.L. Bean.

Something that would surprise her, maybe put the spark back in her eye, the spark that had been missing since his father had died the previous spring.

Somehow, though, a scarf didn't quite seem likely to do it.

"How about something to pamper her?" The sales clerk

was twinkling at him, he noticed uneasily. "We have some nice bath sets with body gels and lotions."

"Not sure I want to go there. How about something else?"

"A watch?" She led him from the small gift section over to the glass display cases.

"I don't think so." A watch would be unnecessary at the Trask family farm; there, you simply rose before dawn with the shrieking alarm clock and worked until long after dark. He looked at the velvet-lined cases filled with rings and bracelets of gleaming metal. Shiny and cold and all so unlike Molly Trask. He'd never actually seen her wear jewelry anyway, except for the plain band of gold his father had given her. The band of gold she still wore. "Do you have anything else?"

"Well, we've got—"

"Hold on." A warm, soft gleam caught his eye. "What's that?"

"Oh, good choice." The clerk's eyes brightened, this time in a decidedly mercenary fashion as she led him over to the far end of the case. "That's our Vintage Collection, made by a local designer out of antique and rose gold. She does some really lovely pieces."

For those prices they ought to be, Nick thought, but there was a simple grace to the necklace that had first caught his eye. "How about that one?"

She beamed. "Perfect. It's a charm necklace. The artist has made a whole collection of birthstone charms that go with it."

Perfect, indeed. "That's it," he decided, reaching back for his wallet. "Let's see…give me a charm each for October, May, January, September and December." One for her, his father, his two brothers and himself. A reminder of family around her neck all the time. She'd like that, he thought. You needed family around when times were tough.

And sudden guilt nipped at him with tiny, sharp teeth.

He hadn't left Vermont to hurt anyone. He'd left because it was the only way he could breathe. As much as he'd loved his family, he'd needed more than anything to find his own way. He'd always assumed they'd be there when he went back.

He'd never expected his father to die so young.

And yet, in its own way, firefighting was his way of honoring his father's legacy. For as long as Nick could remember growing up, Adam Trask would drop anything he was doing at the sound of the town siren and rush to join the other volunteer firefighters to beat back flames.

Nick remembered the day the siren had sounded when they'd been at the farm supply store: the exhilarating drive to the firehouse, the purposeful rush of the men as they'd leapt into the fire engine. Instructions to Nick to stay put had held only as long as it had taken the pumper to leave, then he'd jogged out into the street and down toward the scent of smoke. The mixed terror and pride of watching his father plunge into the burning building was still as fresh in memory as it had been that day. Seeing him hurry out, soot-streaked, with a young girl clutching at his neck, had filled Nick with a kind of baffled awe.

Somehow, Nick thought as he signed the charge slip for the clerk, staying on the Trask farm to make maple syrup had never even come close.

He walked outside, fishing in the pocket of his bomber jacket for his cell phone, flipping it open to punch up a number.

The line clicked. "Gabe Trask."

"You owe me two hundred bucks," Nick told his younger brother as he crossed the pavement to his Jeep.

"You don't say. You late on your car payment again?"

"Nope. You said we'd split Mom's present. That's splitting it."

There was a short silence. "I left you with responsibility of picking Mom's present?"

"Yep."

"What was I thinking?"

Nick unlocked his door and got in. "How to come out smelling like a rose with zero effort?"

"Hey, I want a shopping mall, I've got either an hour drive over to Stowe or two hours down to Concord."

"You're breaking my heart, here." Nick hooked his phone up to the hands-free cord. "Listen, I just shopped voluntarily, thanks to you."

"Now who's whining?"

"Me." Nick turned the key and the Jeep roared to life.

"So what did we buy for her?"

"A necklace." There was a short silence. "Gabe, you there?"

"Oh, yeah. Sorry, I just fell asleep from boredom for a minute there. Tell me you got something a little more original than a gold chain."

"Have some faith, will you? It's a charm necklace made out of antique gold."

"Hence, the price," Gabe said dryly.

Nick checked behind him and backed out of the parking space. "It made me think of her," he said simply. "She can wear it all the time under her clothes and it's got a charm for everyone in the family."

"That's not bad," Gabe admitted. "Let me guess. A woman helped you pick it out, right?"

An image of Sloane's face flashed into Nick's head. "Nope, not unless you count the clerk who took my money."

"Gee, my brother's evolving in the big city. So are you going to bring it up for the party?"

"I can't make it to the party," Nick said, stifling another

stab of guilt. "I've got one more week until the promotional exam. I've got to spend every minute studying that I can."

Gabe cleared his throat. "Jacob's not going to be happy."

"Now there's a surprise." There was a lot that didn't make their elder brother happy these days and most of it centered around Nick. "I've put a year into this exam. I can't drop the ball at the last minute. I'll overnight you the present and you can take it to her. She'll understand."

"I'm sure."

"Look, I'm sorry Dad died, but I can't quit my job and move home." The words were out before Nick could stop them.

"And I didn't ask you to," Gabe said carefully. "You've got something to work out with Jacob, you do it with him, okay? I gave up being the go-between when I hit puberty."

Nick pulled up to the exit of the parking lot and watched the sweep of passing traffic. "Oh, I don't know. You made out pretty well being a go-between when we were kids. In fact, I remember a couple of summers you extorted candy bars from me just about every week to smooth things over."

"*Extorted* is an ugly word," Gabe said reprovingly. "I had a gift for working with people and you wanted to show your appreciation for my efforts. Who was I to say no?"

"Particularly when you had your hand out."

"When opportunity knocks…"

Nick punched the accelerator and whipped out onto the highway. "Exactly. Still like Baby Ruths?"

Walking down the white hallway to her lab at Exler, Sloane could hear the radio before she ever neared the door. The station promo segued into a song, accompanied by her lab intern, Dave Tomlinson, an MIT engineering student assigned to her for the year. Bright and efficient, he had a quirky sense of humor and a penchant for indie rock, preferably at high decibels. And invariably he sang along. Sloane fought a smile and reached out for the doorknob.

Dave's wobbly falsetto carried out into the hall, breaking off abruptly when Sloane opened the door. "Uh-oh." His hand was already on the dial, turning down the volume. "The warden returns."

"And none too soon. Do you know they can hear you down in manufacturing? You'd better watch out or the only place you'll be playing tunes will be your dorm room."

Dave sat at the computer workstation and grinned. "You say that, but I don't think it really bugs you. Deep down inside, I think you got a soft spot for me."

"Quite an imagination you've got. You should have gone to Berklee College to be a rock star instead of MIT," she said, flicking a glance at the list of chords and lyrics he'd scribbled on the lab white board.

"But then you'd have some boring goob of an intern instead of a talented, charismatic young guy you liked."

"What I like is interns who get their jobs done." Her tone would have carried more authority if humor hadn't hovered just beneath the surface.

"Yeah, that was what you said when you tutored me in thermo."

That had been when she'd known she was in trouble. Her ice look, the one that had always kept her assistants at a respectful distance, had never worked on Dave.

Now, he squinted unrepentantly at the computer and tapped the keys. "Hey, I get something done now and then. Did you notice these?" With a flourish he indicated the Orienteer modules and user manuals stacked neatly at one end of the lab bench. "All of them loaded up with software and calibrated, ready to go live. I'm running a simulation on the last one now."

"Very nice." Sloane admired them. "Fast work. How did you get all this done? You were only just starting when I left for my meeting."

He shrugged, clicking his mouse. "I kind of skipped lunch."

"What?" She frowned at him. "You're too skinny as it is, Dave." She didn't recognize herself playing the role of older sister because she'd never been one. "Go eat and I'll finish qualifying the last one. Go," she shooed as he hesitated. "Now."

Dave stood up and grabbed his sunglasses off his desk. "Okay, mem sahib, your wish is my command." He walked jauntily out into the hall. A moment later the door opened again and his head popped back inside. "Hey, boss?"

"Yes?"

"You really think I could be a rock star?"

Sloane tried to keep a straight face. "Truth?"

"Truth."

"Don't quit your day job," she advised.

The door to the lab clicked closed on his whistle and Sloane got to work monitoring the simulations. Her good humor slid into humming concentration as she ran the Orienteer module through scenario after scenario. When the phone rang, she picked it up absently. "Sloane Hillyard."

"Nick Trask, Ladder 67."

She would have recognized his voice even without the introduction. It was unsettling how clearly she could imagine the lines of his face. Still, no one was going to distract her from getting the gear qualified, no matter how good-looking he was. Too much was at stake.

She made herself speak coolly, impersonally. "Captain Trask. How are you?"

"Good enough. How about you?"

"Fine, thanks. I saw the fire at the tank farm on the news. It looked bad."

"For a while. We held onto it, though. Chief Douglass is a good firefighter." It was the highest praise a firefighter could give.

"I'm glad everything worked out all right." Sloane took a deep breath. "So what can I do for you, captain?"

"You could call me Nick, for starters. I only get called Captain Trask when I'm visiting schools or getting chewed out by the chief."

She blinked. "Why?"

"Why do I get chewed out?"

"Why should I call you Nick?"

"We're going to be working together, right? It might make things a little more friendly."

"You didn't seem too happy about the situation the other day. Why the sudden change of pace?"

"Call it an experiment. I know Ayre's an operator, but you were right the other day, I don't know you at all. I figure you deserve the benefit of the doubt."

Oh, nice wasn't fair, she thought with a little twist of alarm. Nice could be dangerous. Nice could be just the start of far more than she could handle. She paused. "So what can I do for you...Nick?"

"I thought it was the other way around. That was the gist of our conversation yesterday, wasn't it?"

"It was." Sloane drew a precise pattern of interlocking diamonds on her desk blotter, trying to ignore the quick flutter in her stomach. "You made it pretty clear you wanted nothing to do with pandering to the politicos." And she wanted nothing to do with any man who could make her stomach flutter. Especially if he was a firefighter.

"You hold a grudge?"

"No, but I need cooperation. Nick."

"Well, my opinion of the situation hasn't changed, but as you pointed out, it isn't up to me. So if I can help you out—safely—then I'll do it."

The stiff note in his voice let her relax a bit. "Start with an open mind."

"Done. If the equipment's good, you'll have my support. Just don't expect it to go any further than the testing. The day the department has the money to buy pricey electronics like you're peddling is the day I'll be driving to work in a Rolls."

Sloane took a deep breath. "I don't know what you drive, but I do know this equipment is going to be an important tool, as common in firehouses as thermal cameras."

"No doubt."

"No, there isn't," she said shortly. There couldn't be, not after all she'd been through. "Now is there something else, Captain Trask?"

"Nick. And yeah, there is. I need to know what you want to do about the testing. How many men you want, when, what kind of apparatus, all that. You might find an engine company better suited to your needs, by the way."

Sloane shook her head, forgetting that he couldn't see her. "No, it has to be a truck company. I've got five Orienteers to test, plus the master unit that I'll be using to monitor. I'd like to keep it to the same group of men."

"We can do that if you schedule carefully."

"Good. What I had in mind was a session or two at the training facility, where we'll have control. Once I'm sure the kinks are all out of it, you can start taking it onto fire grounds.

I need a minimum of three fire situations over and above the training facility sessions to get meaningful statistics."

"Okay. Let's set up some dates."

It didn't take long, when it came down to it, and she entered the dates in her computer with satisfaction. "We're all set, then. I'll see you at the Quincy facility on Saturday."

"All right." Nick paused. "You know, Bill Grant backed you when I talked to him. Despite his unfortunate tendency to cooperate with Ayre, he's a good man. Don't let him down."

Sloane hung up the telephone. *Don't let him down.* The words echoed in her mind as she stared at the computer screen. She wasn't seeing the data, though. She was seeing a red-headed boy hanging around the local firehouse, wiping down the engine and listening to the stories of courage and glory. *Don't let him down.* She saw him on the edge of manhood, wearing the blue of the Hartford fire service, his lieutenant's badge gleaming on his chest, pride gleaming in his eyes. She saw him at the altar, uncomfortable in his tuxedo and unmindful of the discomfort as he looked at the glowing woman who had just become his wife. *Don't let him down.* She saw his casket being lowered into the ground.

The fire had been in an abandoned warehouse honeycombed with cold-storage lockers, decrepit and way below code. Two of Mitch's guys had been searching a tangle of rooms for victims when the smoke had thickened and they'd gotten lost. Mitch had plunged in to find them. And had never come out.

How quickly had he passed out from the fumes after his air had run out? Sloane wondered for the thousandth time. Seconds? Heartbeats? Before or after he heard the voices of the firefighters on the other side of the wall, the firefighters who couldn't find him?

Before or after the whole room flashed over into merciless, killing flame?

Officially, the cause of death had been the smoke inhalation, but the real culprit had been the labyrinthine building and the lack of orientation equipment. It could happen to any firefighter at any time. It had been Mitch's bad luck it had happened to him. Even five years later, remembering made her tighten with the fury of senseless waste, struggle against the tearing loss.

Don't let him down.

She wouldn't let him down, Sloane thought now, staring around her lab, nor any of the people who staked their lives on the quality of their equipment. And she wouldn't let down their families. She remembered what it was like to lose someone. She remembered too well....

Chapter Three

It was visible as she drove in, an improbable, eccentric structure that looked as though a committee of quarrelsome architects had built it out of giant-sized Tinkertoys. The closer Sloane came, the more bizarre it looked, meticulously executed building segments arbitrarily slapped together into a four-story monstrosity, the whole considerably less than the sum of the parts. Depending on the side of approach, the structure looked like an apartment house, an industrial building, a parking structure or a tract house on stilts.

It was the showpiece of the Boston fire-training facility and every inch of it had been carefully planned. It would never win any beauty contests, Sloane conceded ruefully as she parked her car and got out, but its sheer quirkiness appealed to her.

Or perhaps it appealed to her because it was where she was going to get a chance to see what her gear could really do.

Anticipation sharpened her awareness of everything

around her, the early-morning tang in the air, the lines of the putty-colored tower silhouetted against the brilliant blue sky. Nerves knotted her stomach as they had since she'd awoken that morning. There was no need to worry, she told herself for the hundredth time as she got out of her car. Everything was going to go fine.

Ladder 67's truck was already parked on the wide concrete apron surrounding the tower, its aerial ladder stretched out to the top of the building. Nearby was a pumper, hoses trailing out toward the tower. From a distance, they looked like Tonka toys. In fact, the whole scene looked like nothing so much as a child's play area after its owner had gone for milk and cookies. A mind-boggling array of fireplugs poked out of the concrete at intervals. Sloane skirted one, heading toward where the ladder truck waited in the slanting shadow of the tower.

Why did it have to be Ladder 67? she wondered, glancing at the group gathered around the truck. Things would have been so much easier if Bill Grant had let her change to another company. She had enough to worry without having to contend with Nick Trask. Not that she was about to let a man distract her from her job, but she'd have far more peace of mind with a captain who was oh, say, pushing sixty, with the start of a paunch and a couple of grandkids on the way.

She wouldn't have felt so much at risk.

Still, Nick Trask was far from the first challenge she'd faced in bringing the Orienteer this far. She'd deal with him, just as she'd dealt with everything else. The important thing was to keep focused on what really mattered.

Making her brother's death mean something.

She recognized Nick immediately. He stood out from the other men, even though they were all dressed in their department T-shirts and dark trousers. Cockiness, Sloane thought immediately, but intrinsic honesty forced her to admit that it wasn't. Instead, it was confidence, complete confidence in his ability to deal with any fire that might arise and a man who could walk into an inferno without flinching wasn't daunted by much else. He turned to look at her from where he leaned against the side of the truck and against her will she felt the spurt of adrenaline in her veins. Oh, yes, the legions of women who probably fell at his feet had to have had something to do with that confidence, as well. Willfully ignoring the sardonic curve of his mouth, Sloane squared her shoulders and kept walking.

When she drew near, Nick pushed away from the side of the ladder truck. "What, is Councilman Ayre running late for his photo op?"

"No Councilman Ayre, sorry to disappoint you."

He studied her a moment. "Who said I was disappointed?"

No man should be allowed to have such long eyelashes, she thought. "Just a guess. It's good equipment. It can save lives, including yours." Pulling a neat pair of files out of the battered leather satchel at her feet, she stacked them on her clipboard. "After Hartford, I can't see any department giving up equipment like this."

"You're obviously new to Boston, or at least the politics."

"Hardly. I've been here three years."

He laughed. Sloane stared at him, her cheeks tinting. "What?"

"No wonder you're such an optimist." The high color that stained the edges of her cheekbones suited her, Nick thought. And it was definitely personal with her.

Sloane frowned. "If Boston's such a useless place and you hate it so much, why do you stay?"

"Loving the city doesn't mean I have to agree with the agenda of the people running it."

"I suppose, but why choose a job that's subject to the whims of the politicians?"

"I didn't. It chose me."

For a moment, she just stared back at him. She looked a little like a Hollywood femme fatale, Nick thought, in her black turtleneck and tan jacket, dark glasses hiding her eyes. Her hair caught the light like a shower of sparks. Her skin was milk-pale and flawless.

He wondered abruptly how it tasted.

Concentrate on the job, Trask. "So what's the plan?"

"First let's go over how the equipment works, then get some smoke going and let them take the Orienteer through its paces."

"You want smoke, we've got it. Come on, I'll show you."

A change came over her as she faced the burn tower, a tenseness he wouldn't have noticed if he hadn't been so aware of her. For a moment something in her stance suggested wariness, perhaps dread. It was there and gone in a flash. There was a story there, he thought again.

Sooner or later, he was going to find out what it was.

He led her into the cool of the burn tower's shadow. At close range, the cinder block walls were scarred by watermarks and black flares of soot.

"What do they use for the fire?" Sloane asked.

"Bales of hay, wood pallets. It depends on whether we want smoke or heat." Nick led her to stairs that threaded up the outside of the tower. He stood back to let her go first. He'd given the tour plenty of times. Funny, he'd never noticed the narrowness of the stairway before, even when it had been crowded with a dozen people.

They stopped at the first landing, in front of a discolored steel door that led to the interior of the building. Nick pulled it open. The metal groaned in complaint. Fire was never easy on anything. "Here's the first burn room, in through here."

Coming in from the bright sunlight, it took Sloane's eyes a moment to adjust to dimness as she shoved her sunglasses up onto her head. The air felt dank and close. In the mix of odors that assaulted her nose there was the stench of stale smoke, drowned char, of burned concrete and gasoline. Their footsteps echoed as though they were in a cave.

Nick stepped in behind her. The back of her neck prickled in sudden awareness. Then the room became shrouded in shadow as he closed the door. Sloane forced her attention to the space in front of her, away from the soft sound of his breath.

She blinked, then blinked again.

The scene in front of her was weirdly disorienting, like a surrealist painting or a scene from a psycho movie. There was much that was familiar, but the context bewildered. The space looked like an ordinary living room, if one discounted the fact that the walls and furniture were completely encrusted with soot. There were the familiar shapes of a couch and a coffee table, but instead of rugs, the center of the floor was piled high with gasoline-soaked wood. It was like something out of an arsonist's daydream—or a firefighter's nightmare.

"Well, the color scheme's simple enough," she said dryly. "Black on black."

Nick stood motionless by the door, watching her as she moved about the room. "The training people like to simulate a real-life situation as much as possible," he murmured. "The furniture's heavy-gauge sheet steel. Watch yourself, by the way. This stuff is coated with soot an inch thick."

The furniture was absolutely matte black, sucking up all the available light, baffling the eye. It looked both soft as velvet and absolutely solid. Sloane couldn't resist touching it with her fingertip. She gave a surprised laugh when her finger sank in to the second knuckle, sending soot cascading down in small avalanches.

"I warned you," Nick pointed out mildly.

"Empirical method." Sloane tried unobtrusively to shake the soot off her fingers. "I have to experiment and observe. I'm a scientist, it's part of my profession." She caught the quick gleam of teeth as he smiled.

Nick pulled a rag from his back pocket and tossed it to her. "Good thing you wore a black sweater. You ought to do a study sometime of the migration and breeding patterns of soot. You'd be amazed at how much of your clothing that little bit will cover."

Sloane gave a scrub or two to her hands and handed it back to him. "Maybe I'll turn into one of those people who write fan letters to the detergent companies."

"Maybe." He frowned and stepped forward with the cloth. Before she knew what he was about, he'd touched it to her cheekbone.

Sloane jerked back.

"Hold still for a minute. You've got soot on your face. You don't want to look like Tom Brady on game day, do you?"

She felt the touch of the fabric, the heat of his finger beneath. The heat of his body. He was too near, she thought, too solid, too hard to ignore. "Are you done yet?" She glanced up and locked eyes with him and the words caught in her throat. His gaze was intent, as if he were trying to see through her skin. His eyes looked hot and dark.

The silence stretched out. "Well, that's all we can do here. Come on," he said abruptly, moving to the far side of the room. "If you like interior design, there's more to see."

It was time to get out of this close, dark room. She didn't want to react to his presence so strongly, Sloane thought as they started down the interior stairs.

She didn't seem to be able to help it.

In the stairwell, sunlight spilled through an open door high above. Light and shadow, bright and dark. They climbed the stairs in sync, shoulder to shoulder in silence broken only by the hollow ring of footsteps echoing off the cinder block walls, the whisper of hands sliding on the railings, the almost imperceptible rhythm of breath.

"Is this the first time you've been in one of these?"

Sloane jumped at Nick's voice. "Yes. I didn't expect it to be like this."

"Are things usually the way you expect?"

You're not. "Often enough."

They came to a landing and stepped through a door into another burn room. Light streamed in through the empty window cutout and Sloane breathed a sigh of relief. There would be no repeat of the shadowed intimacy of the room downstairs, no repeat of the closeness of the stairwell. It should have helped.

It didn't, especially when she saw the furniture. "The master bedroom, of course." Her voice sounded stilted and strange in her own ears. Her mouth was dry. Silly.

"Not much sleeping goes on in here."

Sloane walked to the window to lean out of the open cutout, immensely conscious of every movement, every breath. "I didn't realize we were so high up," she murmured. "The tower doesn't look that big from the ground."

"It's a lot higher when you're hanging off it on a rope."

"No thanks. I hate heights." Sloane started to turn away from the window, then gasped and jerked backward, knocking into Nick. His hands caught her shoulders automatically; he released her a moment later.

But not before she absorbed the feel of his palms.

Deep in her belly something clenched like a fist.

Adrenaline, she told herself, that was all it was. Whether it was from Nick's touch or the thing she'd seen, she couldn't tell. Because she didn't want to find out, she stared instead at the figure wedged between the bed and the wall. "What in God's name is that?"

"That?" Nick grinned. "That's Harvey."

It lay flat on the concrete, dressed in turnouts and steel-toed boots, one arm stretched out plaintively toward her ankle. It was ridiculously thin and even in its reclining position was tall enough to have been instantly drafted by the NBA, had it only been alive. "Harvey?"

Nick seemed to relax. "Our search-and-rescue dummy. They stash him and his wife, Gladys, in here somewhere before they start the fires. When we send the crew in to search, they'd better come out with both of them. Harvey's set up to weigh about as much as the average man. Feel."

Nick reached past her to pick up the outstretched arm. He was near enough that she could catch the scent of male, near enough that she could see the play of muscle through his T-shirt as he bent over. She moved to step away but a stray piece of wood from the fire pile caught her heel and she stumbled backward, arms out to brace against the wall behind her.

And in a surge of terror felt only empty space.

There were moments of absolute clarity in life. One minute Nick was bending down over Harvey, glad of something to do, the next, Sloane's cry was ringing in his ears. There was no pause for thought, no time for horror. Operating only on reflex, he surged up toward the window cutout even as Sloane's feet left the floor. Pulling her back in to safety took a flicker of a second. For an instant there was only adrenaline. Then he swept her to him, holding her tightly.

"There was nothing there." Sloane's voice wavered. "I just backed up and there was nothing there."

Four stories. Four stories down. His mind repeated it like a litany of horror. And at the bottom, solid concrete. "It's all right," Nick whispered, as much to himself as her. "I caught you. You're safe now. You're safe."

He'd saved lives before. The amazement and rush were familiar, but no close call had ever shaken him this much. All the fragrant luxuries of her, the precious individuality, so fragile and so very nearly snuffed out. She was alive now, though, wondrously, completely alive.

He'd had no idea how right she would feel in his arms, close enough that he could feel her heart beating against his chest. For a moment, there was only the soft feathering of her breath over his neck, the silkiness of her hair against his cheek. He heard her sigh, then her body seemed to melt into his.

There was a shout and the sound of footsteps clattering up the stairs. Nick pulled away, staring at Sloane, who looked as shaken as he felt. Then O'Hanlan and Knapp burst into the room.

"My God, are you all right?" O'Hanlan turned to Nick. "Jesus, Trask, what happened? We turned around and there she was hanging half out the window."

Sloane sounded calm, looked calm unless you noticed how rigidly she'd clasped her hands together. "I tripped."

"Good thing Nick was here." O'Hanlan studied her with concerned eyes. "You're sure you're okay? You scared the life out of us."

"I nearly scared the life out of myself." Sloane glanced over at Nick, as though unable to help herself.

He knew how she felt. He hadn't caught up with what had just happened himself, knew only that it had started something, a drumbeat in his head that made the idea of professional detachment toward her a joke. "Let's get downstairs," he said brusquely.

It replayed in her mind over and over as they descended the tower. The whole thing had taken a matter of seconds. Shadow, then harsh sunlight, then a glimpse of blue sky as she'd rocked outside the building. And there had been terror, blinding terror. It had seemed like hours before her heart had begun beating again.

The solid ground under her feet came as a relief. Sloane couldn't understand why it was only then that she started to tremble, first her hands, then her whole body. The men milled about nearby, talking idly, staring over at her. She took a deep breath and willed the shakes away. If she just ignored it, she thought with a tinge of desperation, maybe she could manage.

Nick walked up and looked at her carefully. "Do you need some time to get calmed down?" he asked.

To her utter horror she felt tears threaten. For a ridiculous instant, she wanted only to be held by him again. Instead, she laced her fingers together to still their trembling and took a deep breath. "I'm fine." She attempted to smile. "Let's get started. The gear's in my trunk."

Nick studied her and shook his head decisively. "Give me your keys and go sit down for a couple of minutes," he instructed.

"Don't order me around," she returned. "I'm—"

"Look, don't argue," Nick said sharply. "I don't care how tough you are, anyone would need a couple of minutes to recover from a scare like that." His voice softened. "We've got plenty of time. I'll get a couple of the guys to bring the gear over and then we can go to it. Now sit." He paused. "Please?"

Sloane perched on the step of the ladder truck and gradually the wobbliness went out of her muscles. It was a relief to feel like herself again and ready to get started. Before she did, though, she had something to take care of.

She stood and dusted her hands off. "Hey, Trask?" Not Nick. Nick was far too personal now. "I'm ready to get rolling."

Nick turned inquiringly and crossed over to her. "You bounce back fast."

Time to get it over with. She cleared her throat. "Listen, I want to thank you for catching me in there. You saved my life. I'm sorry if I was rude just now." She fumbled for words. "I just…thank you."

He smiled then, clear and uncomplicated. "Relax. It's in my job description. Come on, let me introduce you to the guys."

He led her over to where the crew stood. "Sloane, meet the guys from Ladder 67. This is Todd Beaulieu, Tommy Knapp, George O'Hanlan, our chauffeur, and Jim Sorensen, our probationary firefighter." Nick pointed to each of them quickly. "This is Sloane Hillyard, from Exler. She designed the gear we're testing and she's running the program, so listen up."

Sloane picked up one of the Orienteer modules. "Nice to meet you all. You've gotten the briefing on the equipment. Basically, we use data from a couple of sources to track where you are in a building, so that your commanders and colleagues always know where to find you and you always know your way out." She paused. "The equipment is easy enough to use, but I'd like to demonstrate adjustments and operation first. Volunteers?"

There was silence while the men all looked at one another. O'Hanlan nudged Sorensen. "You should do it, Red. You're the probie."

Sorensen hesitated and with a sound of exasperation, Nick stepped forward. "I'll do it."

"Great." Sloane handed him a helmet and one of the breathing masks equipped with the sugar-cube-sized display module. Then she held up a flat black package about the size of a pack of cigarettes. "This is the Orienteer data module." She slipped the webbed belt around Nick's waist and pulled it around until her fingers snugged up against the flat, ribbed muscles of his stomach. Sudden awareness rolled over her and she fumbled with the clasp. *Shadow, then harsh sunlight... then the hard feel of his body pressed to hers.*

"I'll get it," Nick said abruptly, pulling the strap from her hands. With a snick, the clasp locked. He put on the helmet and breathing mask.

"The belt pack sends a signal to a head-up display embedded in your mask so that you get a blue schematic projected on your faceplate over the background," Sloane murmured, a catch in her breath. "The belt pack also communicates with the master unit at the outside command post so whoever's running the scene can monitor locations on an LCD. The belt pack's a wireless unit, so it can go under your turnouts or even in your pocket." She found herself aware of every slight shift, every scent, every inch of his body. "The switch on top triggers a distress alarm to all of the other units. It shows up on the display here."

As she tapped the clear plastic of his breathing mask, her fingers brushed Nick's cheek. She glanced up involuntarily to find his eyes leveled straight at her. Even with the clear shell of the mask between them, the intensity of his gaze, the desire that flared for an instant stopped her words in her throat.

If the pause was too long, she couldn't tell. For just that time, she was incapable of speaking. Sloane stepped back, too hastily. "I think that's all. If anyone has any trouble with the fit, just ask me."

Nick pulled off the mask. "All right, guys. We're going to run this as a standard timed drill. Keep your mind on the gear, but let's remember that this is also a search-and-rescue exercise. Treat it like the real thing. O'Hanlan, Knapp, you guys take the top two floors, Beaulieu, Sorensen, you guys take the bottom two. By the book, guys, and let's get Harvey and Gladys while you're at it, okay?"

It was the scent she noticed first, the odor of burning wood drifting across on the breeze. Faint tendrils of smoke trickled from the top window.

Knapp rubbed his hands together. "Smell that, guys? Break out the hot dogs and marshmallows, we're ready for a party now."

With casual efficiency, the men donned the masks and modules and walked to the tower. Sloane saw them give a quick thumbs-up to Nick, then they plunged into the thick pall of smoke.

Nick pulled on his turnouts, the thick yellow garments obscuring the lines of his body, to Sloane's relief—and a tiny, sneaky sense of unease that she didn't want to admit. "Are you going in, too?"

Nick slipped on his gloves. "Part of my job. I do it in all fires, unless there's no one else to supervise." He pulled on his gloves. "Besides, I want to see what your work is worth."

In full uniform he became anonymous, one of the ones who

walked into hell. She could almost forget how he'd looked at her. She wanted to, Sloane thought as he headed toward the tower. How very much she wanted to.

There was a gut-level dread of fire in her that skittered around her already nervous stomach. It was a controlled situation, Sloane told herself, there was no need to be apprehensive. Still, where fire was involved no situation was ever really controlled. There was always the freak accident, the unexpected. Firefighting was a profession predicated on risk. And if you took enough risks, it stood to reason that sooner or later you'd pay the price.

She'd won the state science fair in high school, had graduated with honors from both college and grad school. She'd won research grants to develop the Orienteer. None of it had meant as much to her as the fact that her first live test had gone flawlessly. The crew had a suggestion or two, but overall it had been a success.

Now she just needed more.

"Trask," Sloane called as O'Hanlan brought down the ladder. Nick headed toward her, his walk loose and athletic. He'd taken off his turnouts and wore only his gray sweat-darkened department T-shirt and blue pants. It wasn't fair that they looked so good on him.

He looked at her inquiringly. "What do you need? We should get back to the station."

"I wanted to talk with you about the upcoming schedule." She had to strain to be heard over the drone of the ladder motor.

"It's too noisy out here. Let's go into the observation tower." They climbed the steps of the squat tower that sat apart from the burn structure. Nick opened the door and let her go in ahead of him.

The small room appeared to be entirely made up of windows overlooking the training ground. Water had streamed over the concrete and the tangle of hoses from the fire engine. Harvey and Gladys sprawled over behind the ladder truck, amid a pile of helmets and turnout coats, Halligan tools and six-foot-long ceiling hooks. "It looks like a battleground from here," Sloane murmured. She didn't glance away as she spoke.

"It is a battleground. All fires are. It's a matter of winning before they claim any casualties."

Sloane shook her head at the idea and turned. She wasn't prepared to find Nick so close behind her. "You're all crazy, you know." She raised her eyes to meet his. "How can you walk into a burning building knowing you'll face fire, injury, maybe even death?"

Nick shrugged. "I'm a firefighter. It's what I do."

For a moment, Sloane was reminded of a statue of a Roman centurion she'd once seen, strong, proud and utterly fearless. A quick, primitive wave of response rippled through her.

She forced herself to breathe. "I want to do one more testing session in a controlled environment. We've gotten permission to burn down a condemned two-story unit in Roxbury in a week. I'd like to run the crew through there, through a floor plan they don't know to get them used to relying on the Orienteer."

"We can't afford any more time off the street."

His words were quick and final. Sloane's chin came up. "It's not your choice, Trask. I want to be sure about this."

"And I want to keep my men from walking into a burning building if they don't have to. Why not do the second round of testing here?"

"Because after one run through the burn tower, even I could navigate it through heavy smoke." She didn't bother to hide the sarcasm. And she didn't plan to take no for an answer. "I want a better approximation to a real fire ground. I'd think you'd want that, too."

"Look, you know my concerns."

"And you know mine," she countered. "We need to do the testing, period. One or two more days won't hurt."

"It won't hurt?" His eyes were turbulent as hell smoke. "Every minute we're out of the firehouse, people are potentially at risk. Ladder 67 had eighty-two calls last week alone. If an alarm comes in for our company while we're gone, they call in a truck from the next station over." He took a step closer and he was all she could see, all she was aware of. "The next station is two miles away, five minutes under the best of conditions. Do you have any idea what a fire can do in five minutes? Do you know how long even a second is to a person who's trapped, waiting for a ladder?"

The blood drained from Sloane's face. Her eyes were on Nick but her gaze was within as she remembered talking with Mitch's crew chief. "The flashover just took a second or two. If we could have found him, we could have saved him. We got there just after the flashover, but it was too late...."

With an effort, Sloane drew herself together. "I'm sorry about departmental policy, but we need to do this testing in the safest possible way. If everything goes well with the next round, I'll release the units to you to take on a fire ground. It's my decision, though," she warned him. "We've got to be sure everything's working flawlessly and the guys really understand what they're doing." And the conversation needed to be over with, now. She brushed past him toward the door.

"Wait."

"I've said everything I had to say." She was too close to the edge, Sloane thought desperately, way too close.

"Will you just hold on a minute?" Nick pushed his hand against the door. "Stop, dammit."

"What?" Her voice was tight with tension.

"You're right, okay? I'm sorry. I was wrong. It's a fair decision." He caught Sloane's shoulder and turned her to face him.

Because she hadn't had time to compose herself, she was still pale. Her eyes were huge. Nick looked at her slowly, carefully, feeling the pull begin again. "This really matters to you, doesn't it?"

She looked as if she was holding herself together with sheer nerve. "Of course. I want my design to work."

Nick shook his head. "There's more going on than that. You care about this project too much."

"I care about doing my job," Sloane answered stiffly.

"There's something going on here that doesn't have anything to do with the job."

He was right, this wasn't about the job. It was about what had started in the tower and was moving out of her control with frightening speed. "Perhaps you just have an overactive imagination," Sloane responded, fighting to keep her voice even.

"I don't know. Let's test it. Empirical method," he told her as he leaned in, sliding his fingers along her cheek. "Experiment and observe."

"You're out of your mind, Trask."

"Nick," he corrected softly, so close she could feel his mouth form the word.

"What?"

"Call me Nick." Then his lips brushed hers.

Sloane stilled at the contact. Warm, soft and unexpectedly gentle. The sensation didn't bowl her over but simply engulfed her like an ever-rising tide, deceptively calm, relentless in its power. For years, she'd kept herself separate from everyone, for years she'd shied away from a simple human touch. Now, her nerve endings hummed with forgotten sensations. A quick brush with the tip of his tongue, a nibble to tempt her, his exploration was unhurried and exquisite. She barely noticed as he slipped past her defenses and made her yearn.

The subtle sounds of intimacy filled the small space of the tower: the whisper of skin against skin, the soft, involuntary noises of breath, of arousal. And the scent of desire rose around them.

He knew she intrigued him. He hadn't expected the taste of her to trigger an immediate hunger for more. When she gave a soft sigh, he fought the sudden drive to go deeper, to find out if she carried the passionate urgency she brought to the project to all aspects of her life.

He forced himself to go slowly instead, his touch gentle. She was like a fire smoldering in a closed room. He could sense the heat and power but couldn't find its source. The taste of her skin was maddening, her scent powerful enough to make him reel. He journeyed from the soft side of her throat back to her lips and suddenly the fire blazed as her mouth came to life under his.

Sloane didn't know where the hunger came from, knew only that she was driven to taste, to savor, to revel in sensation. For too long, she'd denied herself any contact. Now she searched for more, driven by the feel of his mouth and light brush of his hands over her skin. Desire flashed through her, hot as flame, threatening to overwhelm her entirely.

A blast from the ladder truck's air horn made them jerk apart. Sloane returned to a rapid, flashing clarity. She stared at the scene outside, unable to tell whether any of the men were looking at the observation tower. "Very funny, Trask.

Was this some kind of a show for your men?" She attempted to brush past where he stood, unmoving.

"Hardly. This tower is designed so people can't tell if they're being watched. The windows are smoked so dark you can't see in with the lights on, much less off."

"You'd be the first to point out that designs don't always work as intended," Sloane said curtly. "Now listen to me very carefully, Trask."

"Nick," he corrected.

"Just listen," Sloane snapped. It was terrifying, how easily he'd slashed his way through the barriers she'd surrounded herself with. She had to push him out. She had to escape before he knew how much she was at risk. "I am here to do a job that is entirely dependent on the cooperation of your truck company. I will not have my credibility damaged in front of your men."

"It wasn't damaged."

Her eyes flashed. "It could have been. You're interfering with my work."

"The testing was done for the day," Nick countered.

"I'm on the job as long as I'm on fire department property."

Nick reached out to finger a stray curl of her hair. "Next time I'll make sure we're off department property, then." There was a hint of danger in his smile. It frightened her, because it made her want.

"There won't be a next time," Sloane flared, pushing past him. She paused, her hand on the doorknob. "After all, I'm just a tool for Ayre, right? Try to remind yourself of that every so often."

Chapter Four

The hands of the clock on the wall moved noiselessly, counting off minutes of quiet broken only by the faint tick of pencils, the rustle of paper. Ranks of men sat at the tables, bent over sheaves of paper. Some scribbled madly, some thoughtfully, some stared blankly into space as though answers might suddenly, magically appear in the air in front of them. The second hand made its inexorable sweep about the clock face. The precious minutes marched relentlessly by.

The proctor at the front of the room cleared his throat. "Time, gentlemen. Please stop writing and bring your papers up to the front."

Nick glanced up, feeling as though he had just broken to the surface after a long dive into a deep pool. Over the past months he had packed his brain with an enormous amount of detail about firefighting, fire management, personnel management, equipment, building codes, construction, hazardous materials and department regulations. He could recite the pump pressure of the fire engine and the weight of each size of hose, both empty and filled. Without thinking he could list the flashpoints of gasoline, methanol, dry cleaning fluid and a host of other chemicals. He knew as much about Boston building codes as any building inspector.

For nearly a year it had taken over his life. The hours of study had been worth it, though. The answers had been there when he'd needed them. Now that it was over, he felt light-headed, as though the facts that had poured out onto the paper had had weight. He set his paper down on the stack at the front of the room and walked gratefully out into the quiet of the hallway at fire department headquarters, rubbing his neck to loosen the tense muscles.

All done, he thought, and tried to take it in. For the first time in months he could relax without the voice of guilt reminding him he should be studying. Punching the elevator call button, he bounced a little on the balls of his feet, light with a growing sense of freedom. Maybe he could actually go out for a change, listen to some music, drink a few beers. A bell pinged and the elevator doors opened to allow him into the car.

"Hold the elevator." A voice from the hallway interrupted his thoughts, a voice he recognized with the impact of a fist in his solar plexus.

Sloane Hillyard.

He'd thought of her in the four days since the testing, oh, he'd thought of her. Waving the ladder truck back into quarters after an alarm, sitting down to dinner with the crew, over and over he'd found her on his mind. He'd remembered her scent as he'd pored over statistics about building codes and fire standards. The memory of holding her against him had derailed his review of chemical reactions. He'd studied and he knew a thousand and one facts about firefighting strategies. He thought of Sloane Hillyard and he knew only one thing.

That he wanted her.

Sloane hurried down the hall toward the elevator, her mind on the clock and the relentless calendar. She'd just been through a morning that could have won awards for lack of productivity. She could only hope the afternoon would be better. Ahead of her, the elevator doors opened back up. A sign, she thought. Something, at least, was going right.

And then she stepped into the elevator.

"Hey." Nick smiled at her lazily, leaning against one wall of an otherwise empty car that suddenly seemed very small. He wore a leather bomber jacket over a rough-weave blue shirt and khakis. She'd gotten familiar with the look of him in his departmental T-shirt and trousers. This was the first time she'd seen him in civvies.

She wasn't at all prepared for the impact. They made him look leaner, rangier and subversively sexy.

"Going to the lobby?" Nick's hand hovered over the lighted buttons of the control panel as the car started to move. "Better decide quick."

"The lobby, please." She stood next to him, immensely conscious of his eyes on her. After their last interlude, she'd resolved to put him out of her mind, which had worked about as well as the childhood game of not thinking of elephants. Still, just because she couldn't stop thinking of the kiss didn't mean she had anything to worry about. After all, how long had it been since she'd locked lips with a guy? Of course she'd overreacted. She probably would have with anyone. It was simply a physical response to an extremely attractive man, she'd told herself. Physical hunger was something she could recognize. Physical craving was something she could ignore.

But the feelings that assaulted her when she saw him weren't simple at all.

Nick studied her for a moment. "You look a little frazzled. What's up?"

She gave him the easy answer. "Too many meetings, not enough time." The numbers over the doors lit and extinguished as the elevator dropped. "I spent half the morning in a production meeting with our head of manufacturing and the other with OSHA over at Government Center. I blasted over to Quincy for an eleven o'clock with the National Fire Protection Agency regulator, who told me he had an unavoidable conflict and could I do it this afternoon? I came over here to try and switch my three o'clock meeting with Bill Grant and his gang in research to right after lunch, because of course today of all days I left my cell phone at home. And naturally they can't switch. So far the morning has been a complete write-off and I don't have a whole lot of faith in the afternoon," she finished in frustration.

"It's kind of early to be going to the NFPA and OSHA anyway, isn't it?"

"What do you mean?" She was in no mood to take grief from anyone, Sloane thought, as the elevator slowed. Particularly Nick Trask.

"NFPA certification. I thought that all happened after testing is completed."

"We've spent a lot on R & D for the Orienteer. Exler wants to go into production as soon as the testing is signed off. That means getting as much of the paperwork out of the way now as I can. Assuming that's okay with you." The doors opened and she exited into the lobby without saying goodbye.

She got a few steps outside the door of the building before Nick caught up with her.

"Sloane."

Reluctantly, she turned to face him, expecting mockery or suspicion. And finding neither.

His eyes were steady on hers. "How about if we call a truce? You're having a rotten day, I just got out of a two-hour exam. We both could use a break." He paused. "I'll buy you lunch, but only under certain conditions: no Exler, no gear, no fire department." He stuck his hands in his pockets and gave her a disarming smile. "What do you say?"

She should have refused. If he'd been in uniform, it would have been easy. But he wasn't. For the first time they were totally away from fire department territory, no reminders in sight. For the first time, she saw him as just Nick. Just a man.

And before she quite knew what she was doing, she nodded.

It was his favorite dive, a classic railroad-style diner sandwiched in a small lot between two buildings. Maybe the weather of countless winters had taken the shine off the brushed-steel front, but the windows gleamed and the steps that led up to the door at the end were swept clean. A cheerful neon sign spelled out Ray's in red script. Good Eats flashed above the name; Always Open flashed below.

The interior was just large enough to hold a counter and a row of narrow booths. The gold and white Formica tabletops were spotless, though they'd lost some of their gleam; red vinyl, cracked in places, covered the seats. Next to the cash register hung a photo of a grinning city-league softball team in their Ray's T-shirts; a Red Sox World Series pennant dangled from a thumbtack above it.

And Sloane looked absolutely transported. "I don't believe it," she exclaimed, following Nick to the only two empty seats at the counter. "This is exactly like a place we used to go to where I grew up, only the Blue Hen had pictures of the local bowling team and Little League instead of softball." She shrugged out of her silvery blue overcoat, sighing happily as the comfortable-looking redhead behind the counter laid paper placemats and cutlery before them. "My grandfather used to take us there sometimes for breakfast or after we'd gone sledding. They had the best hot chocolate."

"Where was this?" Nick hung their coats on the nearby wall and handed Sloane a menu from the oblong condiment rack.

"Rochester."

"Land of lake-effect snow?"

"Hey, it saves you money on alarm clocks. You don't need one in winter—the snowplows wake you up every morning."

"Now there's a recommendation."

Her quick, flashing smile stopped him for a moment. He couldn't recall seeing it before. He'd have remembered, he thought, savoring the jolt to his system.

"Sometimes you gotta take what you can get," Sloane said. "It's a good town. It knows where it came from. Like Boston."

The waitress stopped in front of them. "You folks ready to order?"

Sloane took a look at the menu. "Clam chowder for me."

The waitress nodded approvingly. "Made right here, every day. And to drink?"

"Hot tea, please."

"And you, hon?" the waitress asked Nick.

He scanned the menu. "How about the open-faced turkey sandwich and a coffee?" He wasn't interested in food, he was interested in Sloane, in finally having a chance to look his fill, in finally having a chance to peel away some of the camouflage and find out what lay beneath.

Nick shifted in his seat a little to watch her. She looked around the diner, still grinning. This was how he wanted to see her, he thought, happy and carefree for once. Then she glanced at him and he felt the punch of desire.

And in his bed. He wanted to see her in his bed. "Rochester, huh? So you're east-coast born and bred?"

"Not exactly. I'm originally from San Diego. How about you?"

"I've been a New Englander all my life," he said. "Lived in the same town until I was eighteen."

That raised her eyebrows. "Really. Whereabouts?"

"Eastmont, Vermont. It's just over the border from New Hampshire. You know, apple cider, maple leaves, all that stuff?"

"I've never been up that way."

"Too bad. You just missed the best time. Vermont's spectacular in the fall."

"In your unbiased opinion."

He grinned. "Everybody says so." He could see her there, he realized, that bright hair gleaming against the backdrop of blazing color. "When the leaves turn, you get entire hillsides just covered in red and gold. It's pretty spectacular."

"It sounds nice."

"Well, there's always next year to see it. So did you move to the East Coast when you were a kid or have you just been a latecomer to sledding and hot chocolate?"

She flashed him another grin. "Second grade. I thought snow was the greatest thing in the world. Couldn't get enough of it. Snowmen, snow angels."

"Snowball fights," he added. "Remember getting a couple dozen kids together for the monster snowball fight?"

She moved her shoulders. "I didn't know that many people."

She wouldn't have, he thought. He'd never met anyone so self-contained. "It must have been tough," he commented, reaching over to take the coffee the waitress set before him. "New town, new school, new friends. Everything changes."

In her eyes, a shadow flickered. "Everything did," she said softly, looked at the thick, white ceramic mug before her. "Hey." False brightness jangled in her voice. "These are just like the mugs they used to have at the Blue Hen."

Nick watched her unwrap her tea bag and drop it into the small metal pot of hot water to steep. She was an enigma, hard as steel, brittle as glass. There was vulnerability there and a fascination in the mystery. Only a putz fell for the puzzle instead of the woman, he reminded himself, but it didn't stop him from being drawn to her. "So is your family still in Rochester?"

She stiffened, so subtly he might have missed it if he hadn't been looking for it. "No. They're gone." Something in her tone of voice told him not to ask anything more. Fair enough. He'd stop with the family.

For now.

"San Diego, Rochester, Boston. You get around."

"Connecticut, too. I went to UConn."

"For engineering?"

She shook her head. "Biology. I was going to do DNA research, cure cancer, that kind of thing."

"What brought you to Boston?"

"Cambridge, actually." Sloane poured some tea into her mug. "Grad school at MIT. I built the Orienteer for my master's project."

"That seems like kind of a long way from biology and research."

And that quickly the wall was there again, hard and solid. "Things changed." She stirred her tea, even though she hadn't added any milk or sugar.

He studied her. Beautiful? Sure. Desirable? Without a doubt, but there was more to her than that and the more he saw, the more he found himself wanting.

Sloane took a sip of her tea. "Anyway, I seem to be doing all the talking. It's your turn. Tell me about growing up in Vermont. Is Eastmont town or country?"

"Pretty much everything in Vermont is country," he said dryly, "except maybe for Burlington. I grew up on a maple sugar farm."

"Seriously?"

"You bet. Sugar house, maple groves, the whole nine yards."

She gave him a bemused look. "I didn't think people did that kind of thing anymore. I figured it was all agribusiness, like cattle and wheat."

"Not hardly. There are a lot of small farms in Vermont, a lot with history. Trasks have been farming for five generations and we've been producing maple syrup the whole time."

A corner of her mouth tugged up. "With your own two hands?"

He waggled his finger at her. "Don't laugh. I grew up working the farm. Come the spring thaw, we'd be out in the groves before it was light, even, tapping trees, emptying buckets. As soon as we got home from school, same drill."

"I'm sure that violates some kind of child labor laws."

"I didn't mind it, really. I loved being out in the groves the morning after we had a fresh snow. And the smell of wood smoke and maple in the air when we had the sap cooker fired up in the sugar house, that was spring to me." The little surge of nostalgia took him by surprise. He gave his head a shake.

Sloane watched him over her mug. "It sounds like you miss it. Why aren't you up there on the family farm drawing sap or whatever it is you do?"

Now it was time for a few walls of his own to go up. "Just like you. Things changed. Or maybe I did." The waitress was coming by with their plates, he noticed with relief, welcoming the interruption.

"It must have been hard to go from being a small-town boy to living in a city like Boston," Sloane commented, unfolding her napkin in her lap.

"Not really. I don't know why but I just took to the city right off. I like it. It feels right, somehow."

"You don't miss the country?" She sampled her soup.

"Maybe sometimes. Hot apple cider after being out in the groves. All the green in high summer. And I miss skiing every day in the winter."

"Every day?"

He grinned. "When I wasn't cleaning sap buckets or whatever it was that had to be done. We lived maybe half an hour from three or four different ski lodges. We'd head over and do the double diamond runs."

"Why am I not surprised?" She could see him as a reckless sixteen-year-old. "What is it with you adrenaline junkies, anyway? What are you after?"

"Excitement, challenge." His eyes glimmered. "I guess I wanted to lead a reckless life."

"You do," Sloane said quietly, setting down her spoon, appetite suddenly gone.

"Not really. There are safeguards," Nick answered, both of them knowing skiing was no longer the topic.

"Not enough of them."

His expression sobered. "It's the nature of the job. If it's hazardous, it's only because it deals with potentially bigger hazards."

"You act like it's nothing, putting your life on the line." Sloane's voice tightened. It was all suddenly there, the danger, the fear. Today he was sitting next to her, chatting about childhood. Tomorrow he could be engulfed in flames. It was crazy to get to know him, crazy to let any of them get under her skin. It was everything about why she had to leave.

"Sloane." He reached out and turned her chin toward him. "We had an agreement, remember? No fire department."

His touch shimmered over her skin. "I have to go." The words held an edge of desperation. "It's close to time for my appointment." She set her napkin on the counter, refusing to meet his eyes.

Nick studied her. "All right." He rose to get her coat.

It felt cozy, too cozy to have him hold it for her, to feel his hands on her shoulders when he finished. He'd snuck up on her blind side with his talk of Vermont and falling leaves. Now, her only defense was escape. "You don't need to go also. You haven't finished your lunch."

"That's okay, I'm used to it." He picked up the bill and guided her past him with his fingertips in the small of her back.

And heat radiated through her.

She stiffened. This was not the way it was supposed to go. Nick Trask belonged with work and the fire department in the special "handle with care" compartment in her life. She couldn't let his sexy eyes and persuasive voice and pretty stories get to her. And that mouth that turned her mind to mush. She had to stop it and stop it now.

Leaving him at the cash register, she pushed open the door, hoping the October air would clear her head. Outside, the sky was the crystalline blue of a New England fall. The chill breeze whisked red and gold leaves along the avenue. *Entire hillsides covered in red and gold...* Sloane resisted the urge to pound her head against the cold steel pole of a streetlight. Behind her, the door opened.

"So, where to from here?" Nick walked up to lean against the light pole, looking like something out of a magazine ad.

Sloane gave herself a mental shake. "I should get back."

"You've got, what, an hour and a half until your meeting? There's time."

She jammed her hands in her pockets. "Look, it was nice of you to take me to lunch. I enjoyed it."

"So did I."

"But I don't think it should happen again. There's a job to do here, and in the interest of professionalism, I think we should keep away from any other involvement."

His gaze roamed to her mouth, lingered at her neckline. His hands ached to touch her. "What's unprofessional about spending time together?"

"I work for a vendor, you work for the fire department. You're involved in qualifying my equipment."

He couldn't prevent the corner of his mouth from twitching. "It's pretty fine equipment."

"Stop it." Face flaming, she stared at him. "I hardly think the fire department would want us involved. *I* don't want us involved."

"Are you sure about that?" He pushed off the lamppost and took a step toward her. The wind tugged at the collar of her blouse, exposing the long, liquid column of her throat. "What about the testing center?"

"The testing center was a mistake."

"It was pretty intense for a mistake." And it had kept him up at night more than once. "Answer me this. If you're not interested, then why is it you always start trembling when I get just a little bit too close?"

Her chin came up. "I don't tremble."

"Sure you do." He traced his fingertips down her cheek. "Just like you are right now."

Sloane blinked, then shook her head briskly. "You're imagining things." She glanced at her watch. "Look, I have to get back."

"That's a cheap out. You've got time. You can't keep ducking away from this, Sloane." Nick's eyes were smoke dark, snaring hers, not letting her look away.

Awareness rippled through every muscle of her body. Her breath caught in her throat. "Stick to business, Trask," she snapped, trying to mask the edge of desperation. Distance was evaporating. She couldn't continue this much longer. "Round two of testing is tomorrow and then we'll be ready to go live."

The wind caught at his hair, tossing it over his forehead. "Fine. Anything else?"

She should have recognized the dangerously tight tone in his voice. She was too preoccupied with trying to keep her own responses damped down to notice. "No, that's all."

"Good." He bit the word off and pulled her into his arms.

It was the suddenness that took her breath away. It was the unexpectedness that made her knees go weak. It wasn't desire, she thought in panic, it couldn't be.

She didn't have a choice.

There had been no warning, just complete sensory assault that broke through the diminishing distance that she'd surrounded herself with. If it had been quick, perhaps she could have waited him out, but it wasn't. His hands roved over her back, his mouth demanded a response. There was no gentleness this time. This time he took and she gave, oh, she gave.

He broke through to the wanting, released the desire she'd tried to shut away in a flush of heat that surprised them both. She met the challenge of lips and teeth and tongue, plunging deeper into the kiss and pulling him after.

Nick felt her quake as he held her. Her strength, her fragility, her secrets combined to draw him on and in. Nothing, no one had ever been like this for him. He couldn't pull back from it, couldn't pull away from her. Nothing in him wanted to.

She was intoxicating in her desire. It didn't matter that they were on a public street in broad daylight. The dominant thought in his head was *more*. He felt her hands in his hair, shuddered as she traced fingers down his back. He ran his lips down her jaw, tasting the silky skin, and heard her soft moan.

How could she defend against this, Sloane wondered dizzily. It was as though he'd taken her over. It seemed impossible that she'd existed without this feeling for so long. Now, like a starving woman confronted with a banquet, she was incapable of holding back. Get away, she thought, even as her arms pulled him closer. Then his mouth found hers again and for that instant of time she became incapable of coherent thought. There was only seduction and pleasure, the sharp nip of teeth tantalizing her, the taste and texture of his tongue arousing.

They were in public, Nick reminded himself. Some sane portion of his mind warned him to stop before he lost control entirely.

Before he took it too far.

He dragged himself back from the edge and gathered enough strength to press her away. They stared at each other, breathing hard. Sloane's eyes were hot with fury and desire.

"What the hell do you think you're doing?" she asked in a shaking voice.

"The same thing you were doing. Are you going to tell me you didn't enjoy it?"

"No, I'm not." Her gaze was unflinching. "But it doesn't matter. I keep telling you I don't want to get involved."

He reached out and traced a finger down her throat, watching her shiver. "I think it might be a little too late for that." He gave her a friendly smile. "Come on, I'll walk you back to the department."

Home was usually a sanctuary, but not that night. Sloane prowled her flat restlessly. Cambridge was never short of distractions, but she didn't really feel like being out among people. A workout might have let her burn off the nervous tension, but she'd already been to the gym that morning. She debated a glass of wine. To relax, she told herself, but she knew that it would be partly to banish thoughts of Nick and decided against it.

He was sadly confused if he thought that something was brewing between them. It wasn't going to happen. She couldn't afford to let it. And yet, somehow it felt as if it was slipping out of her control.

The sound of the front bell made her start a little. She crossed over to the intercom. "Hello?"

"Sloane, it's Candy."

It was the last voice she'd have expected. Candy, her brother's widow. Candy, who'd been as close a friend as she'd ever had.

Candy, whom she hadn't seen in over a year and a half. Once upon a time, they'd been almost like sisters. They'd done everything together. They'd been close enough to finish one another's sentences.

Once upon a time.

And the loss that never really went away came welling up again, made vivid by the reminder of Candy's voice.

The intercom buzzed again. "Hello? Is this thing working?"

Sloane bit down on her lower lip, hard. "Sorry, I missed the button. Come on up."

The minute it took Candy to come inside gave Sloane a chance to regain her composure. By the time she met her at the top of the stairs, Sloane could give her a hug and a genuine smile. For a minute, everything was all right.

Candy had lost weight since they'd seen each other last. Her hair was a brighter gold, there was a new assurance in her movements.

"What are you doing here?"

Candy's mouth quirked. "Gee, Sloane, it's nice to see you, too."

"No, it's great to see you. I meant what brings you up from Hartford?"

"I've got a two-day marketing seminar in town. I left a message on your answering machine about a week ago, asking about dinner." She glanced over to where the machine sat blinking. "Of course, you may not have gotten it."

Sloane shifted uncomfortably. "I don't check the machine here very often. Work's the best place to get me."

A mixture of reproach and resignation flickered over Candy's face. "Checking out from the world again?"

"Not at all," Sloane said briskly, shoving the guilt away down deep. "For example, tonight I'm going to take my sister-in-law out to dinner."

"Unless your sister-in-law takes you out first," Candy replied. "Expense account, remember? Dinner's on me, tonight." She grinned. "Get your coat and let's go somewhere nice. I'm starving."

* * *

They lingered over dinner at Icarus, bathed in the warm rosy glow of the tony South End restaurant's dark wood and blush-colored walls.

"So how are things?" Sloane asked. "You look good. I like the hair."

"Thanks. I was worried it was going to come out too blond, but it seems to work."

"Very polished. You look like a fast-tracker. Is the seminar going well?"

"Good. I'm learning a lot so time goes pretty fast. How's work going for you?"

"Great. I'm keeping busy."

"A good way to keep warm this time of year. I swear it's another four or five degrees colder up here than back home."

How had it come to this? Sloane wondered. There was a time when Candy would have been her first confidante about everything. Forget about hair and weather, they'd have poured some wine and started really dishing, sharing their lives. Now, they'd been reduced to small talk.

A wave of regret washed through her. She set down her fork.

"So, it's Pete's birthday in a couple of weeks," Candy was saying. "He's going to be thirteen. We're having a little party. I thought maybe you could come down for it. It would mean a lot to him."

Come down to the house where Sloane had lived with Mitch and his wife after their grandfather had died, while she was finishing high school, going to UConn. Sloane swallowed. "I don't see how I can." She remembered her last visit to the Hartford house, the memories crowding up around her until she couldn't breathe. The memories Candy brought with her. "It's just that I'm in a critical phase of this project right now."

"You've been in a critical phase for the past four years," Candy said quietly.

"We've started testing. Now's the time that really counts."

"Now's the time with Pete, too."

"Candy, I just need to get past this," Sloane said desperately, knowing as she said it that she wasn't talking about the Orienteer project.

"I know that you do." Candy's voice was soft as she looked down at the pale-rose tablecloth. Laughter erupted at a table across the room. The waiter leaned in to clear away their entrees.

"Dinner was wonderful. You're going to have to come here for marketing seminars more often," Sloane said, trying for a change in subject.

"Hartford's not that far away, you know," Candy told Sloane as she topped off their glasses. "You could come to dinner. We miss you," she added.

"I check in with you guys," Sloane protested.

"Sure. Birthday cards, holiday cards. Shoot, not a week goes by that Pete doesn't get a postcard or a letter from you. But I bet he could walk right past you on the street and you wouldn't recognize him. It's not the same, Sloane."

It felt as though she were sinking in quicksand and her chest tightened. "I've been pretty tied up with work."

"Sure. Work."

"I'm doing something important, Candy. When it's done, I'll have more time. Hey, how's Pete doing?" she asked, trying to ignore the flash of hurt in Candy's eyes. "He doesn't write back very often."

There was a pause. "Not great," Candy said finally. "He's a good kid but he's having trouble in school. He's not concentrating well. He hasn't, really, since we lost Mitch."

Sloane's stomach tightened. "Is he still seeing the therapist?"

"Some." Candy spun her wineglass slowly by the stem. "Do you mind if I ask you a personal question?" She hesitated. "Mitch never wanted to talk much about when you lost your parents. How was it for you?"

Like the world had spun off its axis and nothing would ever be safe again. And it was just the first time she would have that feeling. "God, Candy, it's hard to go back there. I was so young."

"Eight isn't that young, Sloane." Her eyes were bleak. "Talk to me. Help me understand. How do you get past it?"

How could Sloane tell her that sometimes maybe you didn't?

"The therapist says he has to work his way through it so that he doesn't get emotionally locked in. I don't think he's ever really grieved. How did you do it?"

"I don't know. I had Mitch. I had my grandparents." She paused. "For a while, anyway."

"Pete has my parents, he's got me. Maybe he's got to get used to the fact that that's all he's got."

"I do what I can," Sloane whispered.

Candy reached across the table and took her hand. "I know."

Chapter Five

The sounds of ringing shattered the silence in the dark room. Nick jerked awake. Reflexively, he reached for his turnouts, searching blindly with his hand. And came up with a remote control. Consciousness dawned even as the ring repeated.

It wasn't an alarm, he realized, it was his phone.

"Yeah," he mumbled into the receiver, swinging groggily upright on his living-room couch. He'd stumbled into his house after working a twenty-four-hour trick, dumped his kit and flopped down on the couch intending to relax for a few minutes before he did something about dinner.

That had been ten hours before.

"I'm sorry, honey, I didn't realize you'd be asleep. I'll call you later."

It was his mother. He scrubbed a hand through his hair. "Hey. Everything okay?"

"Of course. Everything's fine, I'll let you go."

"It's okay, I'm up now." He yawned. "Talk to me. I've got to stay on a normal schedule anyway. Billy's got a rush job to frame up a couple of houses." Billy Burnett was a local contractor who threw work Nick's way when he had time. "I'm going to work for him Thursday through Saturday."

"Those are your days off."

"I need the money. I didn't do a lick of work for him the last two months because of the exam. I've got a lot of catching up to do. Renovation of this place ain't cheap, you know," he added, looking around the living room of the Methuen fixer-upper he'd bought the year before.

"I think it's criminal that the fire department doesn't pay you men a living wage. What other job forces people to kill themselves working outside jobs to make ends meet?"

Nick rose and stretched. "Feel free to write the city of Boston, but I don't think it'll change any time soon. It is what it is, Ma. Besides, I like swinging a hammer."

His mother snorted, unconvinced. "How did your exam go?"

"I think I scored pretty high but that doesn't mean anything until the rankings come out. I'm hoping I'll wind up near the top of the list. Then it's just a matter of waiting for an opening."

"How long?"

"Hard to say. Could be months, could be a couple years." He rose and headed toward the kitchen, taking the cordless phone with him. "So how was your birthday?"

"Very nice. Jacob and I drove to Gabriel's hotel and we all had dinner. That's why we weren't home when you called."

"Champagne kisses and caviar dreams?" He rummaged in the cupboard for a new coffee filter.

"It's a beautiful place. A little too snitzy for me, but Gabriel loves it and you can tell the people who work for him like him a lot."

Now is was Nick's turn to snort. "It's all an act. They live in fear of him. He's broken their spirits."

"Oh, I expect he's a very fair boss, just like you are."

"And did you like your gift?" he asked, scooping coffee into the filter.

"It's lovely." Pleasure bloomed in her voice. "Such a sweet idea. I wish I could wear it all the time."

"Why can't you?"

She laughed. "Gathering eggs in the henhouse? With my luck I'd catch it on a nail or something and break it."

"Ma, if you want to wear it, wear it. That's why we got it for you. Put it under your shirt if you're worried."

"Do you think?"

"Yeah, I think. It'll be fine."

"Then I will," she said happily.

"Glad to see you've got some sense. So how's everything else going?"

"Oh, we're well. We got about six inches of snow last night, so Jacob's been up and down in the groves making sure everything is all right."

"It's good for him. Gives him something to do." Nick focused on the coffeemaker, willing it to brew.

"I think he's happiest when he's got a to-do list a mile long and most of it involves being outside," she agreed. "He's always been the best suited of the three of you to the farm."

God knew *he* hadn't been, Nick thought. Too much quiet, not enough action. Being in the ladder truck headed to a fire in Boston, that was where he was happiest. "Everything okay with Gabe? I haven't talked with him for a while."

"Oh he's fine. A little worried, maybe. The owner of his hotel passed away and they're making rumblings about changes."

"Gabe doesn't mind changes." That would be Jacob, who always wanted things to remain the same.

"Yes, but he wants to be the one to choose them. How did I raise three such stubborn men?"

Nick grinned as he poured coffee and took a blissful sip. "Surely we couldn't have gotten it from you?"

"You know who you got it from. There wasn't a more stubborn man born than your father."

"Lucky for us. Otherwise, he wouldn't have kept after you until you married him and we wouldn't be here."

"Well, I'm glad he stuck with it, too. Anyway, I should let you go. I was mostly calling to see if you survived."

"I did, thanks. Sorry I missed your birthday. I'll try to get up there soon. I've got a lot of work in the next couple months, but I should have a few days coming after that."

"We're going to see you at Thanksgiving, aren't we?"

Guilt pricked at him. "I wish. I'm booked for day shift the day before and then night shift on Thanksgiving."

"Oh." She paused. "That's a shame. The other kids are all going to be here and I've invited the other Trasks."

"The whole clan," he said slowly. "You haven't done that in years."

"I thought it would be nice to gather for something happy for a change."

Even all these months later, the whisper of grief still lurked in her voice. And it left him with the same helpless feeling it always did. "I don't see how I can do it, Ma. The best I could do would be drive up for breakfast and head out after."

"Of course not. You'd spend more time on the road than

you would with us. I don't want you to take the chance of being tired in a fire. Stay in Boston. We'll keep."

"I really will make it up there. I swear. Look, I've got a three-day break after the holiday. I've got some cabinets being delivered for the house, but I'll try to get up for a couple of days at the end."

"Are you ever going to finish that house?"

Nick looked around the living room with its stripped walls awaiting fresh paint. "One of these days."

"And then you'll sell it and turn around and buy another. You thrive on chaos, Nicholas," she said reprovingly.

"I thrive on hard work."

"Like your brothers. I thought now that your test was out of the way, we might see you a little more."

"I'll get up there the week after the holiday, I swear."

"And you'll spend the whole time itching to install those cabinets," she said in amused resignation.

Nick shrugged. "They'll keep."

"Put in your cabinets. Come up later if you can. Are you working Christmas?"

"Christmas Day. I'm off Christmas Eve, though."

"Then you can come up then."

"Or you can come down."

"Don't you want to see your brothers?"

Nick didn't want to go there. "Look, I'll make it up there," he promised. "Soon. Tell everyone I said hello and tell Jacob to give you a big kiss for me."

The last light from the setting sun was fading as Sloane pulled her car into the little parking lot next to the fire station. It was the worst part about fall, the gradual shortening of the days. Sloane turned off her engine and let out a long breath, tapping her fingers on the wheel. A week had passed since the scene in front of the diner. A week during which she'd been completely unable to work out any rational plan when it came to dealing with Nick Trask.

Not that she had a lot of experience when it came to dealing with men in general. Oh, she'd dated in high school a few times but little more. It had been college before she'd gotten serious about anyone. She'd met Greg Bentley in a lab class junior year. He'd made her laugh, talked her into study sessions that stretched into pizza and beer at the student center. Those sessions had morphed into dates, at first occasional and then regularly. Let me in, he'd said. He'd been patient and she'd finally trusted him enough, cared for him enough to give him her innocence in a night that she still didn't regret.

Then Mitch had been killed and it was as though everything had frozen up inside of her. She couldn't let anybody in, not Candy, not Greg, not anyone—not that anyone else was left. As the months had worn on, Greg had been first understanding, then impatient, then frustrated.

Then gone.

Because she'd never been able to tell him the truth, the fear, the lesson she'd learned over and over since she'd been a child—that everybody she loved, she lost.

After that, men hadn't mattered a whole lot. She'd been too preoccupied in grad school with building the Orienteer and finding a home for it. What physical needs she had, she could gratify herself. Then again, she'd never understood what physical needs really were until Nick Trask had come along.

With an impatient noise, Sloane got out of the car. All right, so five years of celibacy was enough to make any person a little itchy. There was nothing magical about Nick. He was just a man, she reminded herself, trying to ignore the little taunting voice in her head. The best thing to do was keep her distance.

The only problem was that she hadn't a clue how.

Popping the trunk, she reached in for a small plastic bin. They were taking the tests live, which meant the end was in sight. It had helped that Nick had skipped the testing session the previous week, called away as an emergency substitution for an absent officer at another company. She'd have suffered torture before admitting she'd felt even the tiniest hint of disappointment.

All that was left to do now was drop off the units for the live tests, supervise the fire incidents and log the data. She'd found herself more than a little tempted to drop the gear off during the day, before Nick and the rest of his crew arrived for their scheduled night shift. It was precisely because she'd been tempted that she made herself wait until dusk. She wasn't about to let the job suffer for her own personal qualms. All she had to do was stop in, drop off the gear and leave. Straightforward and quick, right?

Except Nick would be there and it wouldn't be straightforward at all. With a growl of frustration, Sloane looped her satchel over her shoulder and picked up the bin. The best thing to do was get it over with.

On the apron in front of the firehouse sat the pumper, its high red sides gleaming. Behind it, the apparatus floor was dark, lit only by lightning-quick flashes that dazzled the eye. Sloane frowned. Craning her neck to see around the vehicle, she skirted it and crossed under the overhead door. Cobwebs dangling from the door traced over her cheek. Unable to repress a shudder, she wiped at her face with her free hand.

And looked ahead at a bizarre scene.

Everything looked strange, disjointed in the flickering light of the strobe. She caught a glimpse of a limp figure in white swinging ominously from the rafters. Across the way, a zombielike form materialized out of the rack of turnouts and helmets and shambled toward her, blood spilling down the front of its shirt. In the stop action of the strobe, it seemed to vault forward in fits and starts. Even as she stared, another form leapt at her from the side, arms and legs waving and what looked like an eyeball dangling down its cheek.

Sloane jumped back reflexively, bumping up against something solid and human behind her. Quick arms came around her. She gave a muffled cry of surprise.

The zombies broke into laughter. "Gotcha," the one with the dangling eyeball said in O'Hanlan's voice.

The arms released her and she turned to see Nick. "Happy Halloween."

Adrenaline surged through her system. "Halloween," she said blankly. "I forgot all about it." Just another man? She'd been out of her mind even to think it.

"It's not Halloween," O'Hanlan said with a broad grin. "We had a rescue call, got a little messy."

Knapp cackled. "O'Hanlan lost his grip on a bag of O-positive. I think it's a good look for him. Whaddya think?"

Sloane grinned. "I think you're a bunch of sick puppies is what I think."

"We figured we'd reverse the trick or treat on the neighborhood kids, see if we can get them to give us candy for a peek inside."

"Yeah. Did you bring us candy?" O'Hanlan asked, looking with interest at her bin.

"Actually, I brought something better—the gear. It's time to go live. No more playing around."

"Hear that, Trask? No more playing around."

"Yeah," Nick said slowly. "I did."

Sloane cleared her throat. "If we could get away from the strobe light, I can hand this over and we'll be all set."

"Well, then, let's take it upstairs." He looked at the costumed firefighters. "All right guys, you know the rules. Only four kids at a time and Sorensen stays with them. Alarm comes, Red, what do you do?"

"Kids go out, I put on my turnouts in the truck," Sorensen returned snappily.

Sloane smiled at the probie's earnestness. "And what about the rest of you guys?" she asked the zombies.

"Hey, we take off the masks, close up our turnout coats, and who's to know the difference?" O'Hanlan asked.

Sloane grinned. "Let's just hope you don't get a medical aid call for a heart attack victim. You show up with that eyeball hanging down your face and they may never recover."

O'Hanlan batted at the plastic ball until it was swinging. "I kind of like it. I think—"

"Trick or treat," chorused a group of small voices behind them.

Nick gave a brisk nod. "Okay, guys, go to it but remember the rules. Sloane and I need to talk about what comes next." He took the bin from her. "My office?"

She took a deep breath and squared her shoulders. "Sure."

"So." Nick kicked the door shut with one foot to shut out the Halloween music from downstairs and set the bin on his desk. "Whatcha got?"

Sloane pulled off the lid. "Five Orienteers, all qualified and calibrated and ready to go." She set the transmitters out one by one. "The guys already know how to attach the display modules to their masks. I updated the software yesterday and calibrated the hardware. You're good to go. All you have to do is call me when you get to a fire so I can monitor."

Nick leaned on the edge of his desk, looking at her until she shifted in discomfort. "Are you aware that yesterday was Sunday?" He watched the color drift into her cheeks and fought the urge to brush his fingertips across them.

"Yes. What of it? Lots of people work on Sunday." She slapped the lid on the bin with unnecessary force.

"Nothing," he shrugged, amused at the defensiveness in her tone. "I just thought you might have forgotten that it was the weekend. All work and no play…"

"Is that a polite way of telling me to get a life?"

"Well, work isn't everything, you know."

"Did I ask for your opinion?"

Now he grinned. "My mistake. I thought I remembered us having a civil conversation a few days ago. Or was that just a cease-fire?"

"Détente." Today, she was in jeans and ankle boots, topped by a suede blazer the color of rust. In her throat, the pulse beat under her translucent redhead's skin.

Her hair, as always, was twisted up in a chignon, but this time there were little strands hanging loose around her cheeks from where she'd rubbed away the phantom cobwebs as she came into the firehouse. It made him think about what she'd look like in the morning, soft and heavy eyed with sleep.

After they'd spent the night making love.

"What are you looking at?"

"I'm trying to imagine what you'd look like with your hair down. Every time I've seen you, you've had it pinned up. It's long, though, isn't it?"

"Why do you care?" she asked suspiciously.

Because she was beginning to be all he could think about?

He reached out to touch one of the tendrils that hung along her cheeks. "I'd like to see it sometime."

Sloane stepped away from him and sat in the client chair. "Look, Nick, it was good of you to take me to lunch the other day. I enjoyed it."

"Are we going to have another one of these conversations?"

"If we need to." She gave him a green-eyed stare, chin raised mutinously.

Walking away wasn't an option. But perhaps there were others…. "Okay, maybe you've got a point about keeping personal and professional separate. I'd say this is a hardly an appropriate conversation for the station."

"I'm glad you've—"

"I think we should have it somewhere else. Preferably somewhere quiet with good bourbon. Any suggestions?"

Her brows lowered. "If that's a cute way of asking me out, the answer's no."

"Trust me, when I ask you out I'll be a lot more direct. It's simple. We've got an issue to resolve that I think you'll agree has nothing to do with the work we're both paid to do."

"Yes but—"

"I'm just suggesting we take it elsewhere."

"The issue doesn't need any resolving. We're colleagues, period. There *is* nothing else."

He took a swift step toward her chair and pinned her in place with his hands on the arms before she could rise. "I could demonstrate, if you like." Holding her gaze, he leaned in, close enough to smell her scent, close enough to hear her breath.

Close enough to see her eyes darken.

"Now do you think there's nothing to talk about?"

Sloane stared at him, every atom of her being focusing on his mouth hovering just an inch away from hers. She knew it was outrageous, she knew it was a chance they had no business taking but God, she wanted him.

And she knew she couldn't avoid what was between them anymore. "Fine," she said in acceptance. When he moved away to his desk, she wasn't sure whether to feel relief or disappointment. She rose. "You're right, we need to clear the air. You're off tomorrow, right?" He nodded. "Okay, then, tomorrow night at seven."

"Where do you live?"

"We're not meeting at my apartment," she replied firmly.

Nick smiled a little. "I didn't say we were. You picked the time, I get to pick the place. I want to make it convenient."

"Harvard Square."

"That's easy, then. Kendall's, on Brattle Street."

Sloane frowned. "Never heard of it."

"You wouldn't have. It's about a block down from Algiers, on the right, below the dry cleaner's. I'll meet you outside."

"Inside," she corrected. "This is not a date, Trask." She rose. "I don't know what this is."

Tucked away on a quiet corner blocks away from the university, Kendall's was discreet to the point of being practically hidden, with only a small sign advertising its location. Sloane descended the short flight of stairs to the doorway, holding her coat tightly around her for warmth.

"Couldn't find a parking place?"

She jumped to find Nick behind her.

"I thought I told you to meet me inside."

"I'm not very good at taking directions," he told her.

"Stubborn," she muttered.

"So I've been told." He opened the door and gestured her inside.

She wasn't sure what she'd expected. Considering it was the Harvard Square neighborhood, maybe an Irish pub, or a microbrewery, a student hangout of some kind. It was none of the above. Kendall's was a neighborhood bar, no faux nostalgia décor, no trendy signs, just quiet, clean and comfortably shabby. There were no drunken undergraduates teetering on the stools, just enough regulars to make the place feel homey without being crowded. A neatly bearded bartender in a white apron lined up glasses behind the bar.

"How did you find this place?" Sloane asked, following Nick to a pair of stools at the far end of the bar, where the polished wood met the wall. "It's got a good feel to it."

He slid onto a leather-covered seat. "I was working a job near here for a couple months. The guys liked to stop in for a drink on the way home."

"You worked for the Cambridge fire department?"

"Construction. Side job," he elaborated. "I frame houses, build decks, hang drywall. Firefighting's a great job but it doesn't pay. You do it for love, not wealth."

The bartender set a couple of napkins and a dish of peanuts on the bar in front of them. "What can I get you?"

Sloane considered. "Maker's Mark on the rocks, water back."

Nick looked at the bartender. "Two of those, please." He turned a little on his stool to look at Sloane. "Looks like we have something in common."

"Don't let it go to your head."

He gave a quick smile. "Oh, I don't think that's all we have in common."

With quick competence, the bartender delivered their drinks and retreated. Nick raised his glass. "To polite conversation." He touched his glass to hers.

Sloane tasted the bite of the bourbon and felt it spread tendrils of warmth through her veins.

"See now, isn't this better?" Nick asked.

"Than what?"

"Bickering, for one." He leaned against the wall, watching her over the top of his glass. "We're always fighting over something and I can't figure out why."

Sloane stared at the bottles on the back wall. "Bad chemistry?"

"You know better."

"Yes." She moved her glass in little circles on the polished wood of the bar. "I do." Her eyes were steady on his. "And I don't know what to do about it."

"Why do you have to do something about it?"

"Because, when I'm not around you, I can think of all sorts of good reasons why we shouldn't be involved." When he reached out to tangle his fingers with hers, heat zoomed up her arm. Sloane looked at him helplessly. "And then I get around you and you do something like that."

"It's supposed to be a good thing. I'm attracted to you, you're attracted to me. Normally, that's all people need to get together."

She felt as if she were standing on a sandbar that was slowly eroding out from under her. Sloane swallowed. "I don't get together."

"Ever?"

"Not often."

His eyes were very dark in the subdued light of the bar. "Then why are you here with me now?"

"I don't know."

"And that bothers you," he said quietly.

What bothered her was that he'd gotten under her skin with his persuasive voice and addictive mouth and relentless eyes. She didn't want to want him. She wanted her life to go back to being safe and normal and solitary.

The problem was, she wasn't sure that was possible.

Sloane cleared her throat. "Look, Nick, this project is really important to me. I've been working on it a long time. I can't lose track of it here at the end."

"You think I'd do anything to endanger that?"

"Not intentionally. Then again, you don't believe in it much."

"Uh-uh, you're talking about work again. This is about us."

"Work is part of it, don't you see?"

"No, I don't. Can't it just be as simple as you and me trying this out to see what happens? You know, the kinds of things normal people do, dinner, maybe, or a concert. We could have fun."

"Why are you so hung up on this?" Sloane demanded. "There have to be plenty of other women out there you could see."

"I don't want other women. I want you."

It snatched the breath from her lungs. The bar around them receded from her consciousness. All she saw, all she was aware of was the dark gaze holding her as though he wanted to delve into her soul.

"I'm stubborn, as you've already pointed out," he said. "And I'm not going away. You might as well start getting used to the idea."

"I can't do this yet, Nick," she said desperately. The shifting sand underfoot was gone and she was in over her head, struggling to stay afloat.

Nick gave her a long look. "Then I guess we'll have to wait a little while until you can."

Chapter Six

The bedroom smelled of musk and seduction, the sheets soft and tangled against their naked bodies. Nick's mouth moved over her neck and his hands, oh those broad, warm hands possessed her. She'd forgotten how exquisite the feel of skin on skin could be. It would almost be enough to have just this, the feel of his hard, sinewy body against hers, the freedom to run her greedy hands over his shoulders, the corrugated lines of his abs.

But there was more, she knew in giddy delight.

He stroked her breasts and she sighed, searching for his mouth with hers. "Take a chance, Sloane." His words were a tease, his lips a hairbreadth away, holding out the promise of a kiss to her like candy to a child.

Her answer was a moan.

His hands curved over her hips, tracing the tops of her thighs, lingering until she gasped. Like a gourmet, he sampled the flavor of her earlobe, her cheek. Sloane moved to capture his mouth, but he evaded her, continuing his slow, exquisite torture. "Take a chance," he whispered.

The bells of an alarm box interrupted his words and she realized that they were in the firehouse dormitory. The room erupted in motion, the crew racing for the fire pole. "Everybody goes," a voice crackled above the ear-bursting alarm. "Everybody goes." The cacophony merged into the shrilling of her clock radio as Sloane came fighting up out of sleep.

Groping blindly, she finally managed to shut it off and opened her eyes to the morning sun slanting across her bed. For a moment she just blinked at the light, waiting for the disorientation to fade. It had been too vivid. She was almost surprised not to see a dip in the pillow next to hers. Her body still buzzed a little with sensation. Even the sheets against her skin felt delicious, every movement an invitation. She was half-tempted to close her eyes and see if she could slip back into the dream, and it was that thought, finally, that got her out of bed.

The warm water of the shower slid over her skin, hypnotic as a lover's touch. Turning the tap to cold scarcely made a difference. Even the impatience she felt with herself was distant, unimportant. As though it really were the morning after, she moved in a cloud of fatuous pleasure.

Sloane dried her hair and slipped into lingerie, silk and lace whispering over her skin. Nothing in her closet matched her mood, she thought, staring at the ranks of discreet, tailored suits. They all looked too confining. The day demanded something different.

The knock at the front door was first a surprise, then, as she glanced at the clock, an annoyance. Visitors at seven-thirty were not the usual order of the day. She pressed the intercom button. "Who is it?"

"Nick Trask."

She blinked. Of all the people she might have expected at her door, he'd have been the last. Granted, he'd walked her home from Kendall's, so he knew where she lived, but still…

She pressed the intercom button. "Come on up. It's the door at the top of the stairs."

Ducking into the bathroom to grab her robe, she belted it on securely. Then she headed to the door.

And opened it to see Nick coming up her stairs.

Overnight stubble blued his jaw. He wore faded jeans and his leather jacket over a white T-shirt. If she ran her hands beneath the fabric, she knew exactly how the ridges of his abs would feel under her fingertips. Her first thought was not what he was doing there, but how natural he looked framed by her doorway. It was as though she'd expected him. In the aftermath of the dream, she wondered with a thread of disquiet if she had.

He stopped in front of her. "Good morning."

He'd come by on the spur of the moment, because he wanted, no, needed, to see her. If he'd known what the image of her standing at the door in her silky robe, her hair tumbling down over her shoulders would do to him, he might have driven on by. He'd give her time, he'd said. He wasn't sure how he was going to manage it. "I brought up your newspaper," he said, pushing the plastic-wrapped bundle at her.

"Thanks." She watched him, looking, he knew, at the mileage from a rough couple of days. "No offense, but you look like hell."

He ran a fist along his jaw. "That bad, huh?"

"When was the last time you got some sleep?"

Sleep? He couldn't remember. Yesterday seemed an endless time ago. "A couple of days. Things have been busy. Can I come in?"

"Of course." Sloane stepped back from the door, gesturing him in. "That way you can sit down before you pass out in my hall and give the classics professor upstairs something to sniff at on her way out the door."

"I'm not that far gone, don't worry."

"Are you sure?"

"Positive," he said, following her into the living room.

It was a spacious, high-ceilinged room with broad moldings and wide bay windows that brought in the morning sun. A milk-glass fixture hung from a rosette medallion on the ceiling. His builder's eye saw good structure, graceful lines. Unfortunately, it appeared to be furnished in Early American garage sale, with rugs courtesy of the remnant room at Carpets-R-Us. It was tidy verging on spartan, with little sense of warmth or indeed that anyone made a home there.

Sloane shifted uncomfortably. "I haven't had a chance to do it up yet," she said.

"Lived here long?" A couple of bookshelves lined one wall. She alternated between reading engineering texts and detective novels, as near as he could tell.

"A couple of years."

"Let me guess, you've been working." The couch, he discovered, was surprisingly comfortable and he leaned back with a sigh.

Sloane frowned at him, hands on her hips. "So how exactly did you get into this kind of shape?"

"Oh, a twenty-four-hour trick, the full moon, the four-way payday, a lot of things. We've been…busy." His voice was subdued.

"How about some coffee?"

"That'd be great."

The coffee was already brewed; she had only to go to the kitchen to get it. Walking back carefully to avoid spilling, she got to the threshold of the living room before she looked over at him. And then she simply stared.

Nick sprawled carelessly on her overstuffed couch, eyes closed, jacket off, long legs stretched out under the coffee table. How was it that he was completely relaxed in her home while she was suddenly awkward? "Here you go," Sloane said briskly. She set the mugs on coasters, then settled herself on the chair at his end of the couch, resisting the urge to clutch the robe to her throat like some vaporous Victorian maiden.

His charcoal eyes opened. For a moment, he simply watched her until she wondered if her ivory silk camisole was showing. With a low sound of effort he sat up. "Thanks. At least now I'll stay awake long enough to get home."

Sloane lifted her mug, the sides of the cup heating her hands. Empty seconds dragged by. She shifted on the chair. "So."

"So?" Nick took a grateful drink of coffee.

"Um, no offense, but what are you doing here?"

"I brought you a little present." He set something on the table and reached for the coffee again. "From one of your Orienteers."

"From one of…" Sloane leaned over and picked the object up. It was one of the helmet display modules, or had been at one time. Now it was mostly a warped clump of plastic. Comprehension dawned. And the beginnings of irritation. "You had a fire last night."

"A fire?" Nick shook his head, taking a drink and setting his coffee down. "No, I don't think you could call it a fire. Conflagration is a better word, or maybe inferno." He leaned his head back on the couch wearily and winced.

"You were supposed to call me so I could be there," Sloane reminded him.

Nick let out a long breath. "There wasn't time."

Sloane set the melted display back on the table. "Nick, this testing is important. The longer we take to qualify the gear, the longer it'll take to get deployed and the longer guys will be at risk."

"That's assuming it gets deployed at all. Look, we were fighting a fire. That takes priority over everything."

"How about the evaluation sheets? Tell me you at least managed to do that much."

"Sorry." He shook his head.

"Why not?"

"We barely got back to the station by the end of shift. The last thing I wanted to do was bother the guys for feedback. I'll get it next shift."

When they'd have forgotten most of the details. "So you didn't notify me, you didn't get evaluation sheets, you melted the equipment. You do remember you're supposed to be co-operating, right?"

Nick frowned. "It was almost three in the morning. I didn't have time to wait for you to wake up and answer the phone. We caught a three-alarm fire at one of the projects in Dorchester. People were going to die if we didn't get them out." He leaned his elbows on his knees and rubbed his eyes tiredly. "Your gear worked fine. The only problem is that the clips that hold the displays to the helmets aren't as solid as they could be. This one got knocked off Knapp's helmet by his ceiling hook."

Sloane picked up the display again. "If I'd been there, I might have been able to fix the clips."

"What do you think a fire scene's about?" Nick demanded, dropping his hands. "Do you think we'd be standing around waiting for you to MacGyver our helmets? We had everything we could do just to keep it from spreading to neighboring buildings and get people evacuated. There were people trying to jump from the fourth floor just to get out. There were..." he broke off, squeezing his eyes tightly shut as if closing off a vision.

Sloane became very still. There was a hollow ring to his voice, a soul sickness that ran deeper than exhaustion. She swallowed. "Nick, stop. Please. You don't have to explain. I'm sorry."

He stared at his hands. "I found a family in an apartment on the top floor," he said slowly, tonelessly. "We didn't get to them in time. The parents were by the children's room. They must have been hit by the smoke and the fire just...the fire just swept through." The words were colorless, but his eyes saw beyond her to a fiery orange room in a building that no longer existed except as ashes. He wasn't supposed to let it hurt.

It did nothing but.

"There were two little girls, not more than a year or two old, curled up together in their crib. They went to sleep last night and they'll never wake up." His voice cracked. "They never had a chance at life." His eyes came back to hers and he looked at her bleakly. "They never had a chance."

"Oh Nick." Sloane knelt before him, taking his hands in hers. They were cold, so cold. "Think of the ones you did get out, the ones who were trying to jump." He made no response. She pressed his hands to her cheeks, kissing his knuckles, noticing for the first time the tiny burn marks left by stray embers.

Slowly, Nick bent his head down and buried his face in her hair. For a long time he only inhaled, pressing his lips to the tumble of red. He hadn't known what he was after when he'd walked up to her door. It was only now that he was here, holding her, that he understood how much she'd become a part of his world. He drew her against him and held her, just held her, absorbing comfort, warmth, the reality of a living, breathing human being.

Then she shifted against him.

Sloane didn't know where it came from, the sudden hunger, the certainty of rightness. Pushing him away made no sense, only being with him did. *Take a chance.* For the moment, fear and common sense fled. She wanted only to hold, to heal, to feel his touch. Blindly she sought his lips, first tentatively, then with confidence. "Nick," she whispered softly. "Kiss me."

With a groan he tangled his fingers in her hair and gave in to growing need. Soft and pliant, fragrant and sweet, she was a refuge from the bleakness inside him. Her avid mouth tempted him with taste, touch and texture, combining them into heat. It might have been the first kiss he'd ever had. It was his return to the land of the living. Giving was unnoticed, taking was forgotten. There was only growing pleasure, drawing him deeper, always deeper.

Sloane traced the lines of his face, memorizing them with her fingertips as she had already memorized his mouth with hers. She felt the taut line of his cheek, the rough scrape of his stubble. And his mouth, so warm, so soft. With a sigh, she wrapped her arms around his neck and pressed herself to him, half lying across his lap. And feasted on him with abandon.

Nick raised his head to look at her. Her mouth was soft and swollen from his kisses. Arousal had turned her eyes heavy lidded and dark. The vivid blue of her robe gapped open to show pale silk and lace beneath that shifted with her every gasp, and under that…

Under that, only warm skin.

It dizzied him. He had wanted her until it had become a constant drumming in his head. Now, he had only to reach out and he could sweep her robe aside, have her against him. He bent his head to taste the fragile skin of her throat and her scent rose around him. And he touched her, because he had to.

When she felt his hands parting her robe, Sloane caught her breath in anticipation. Then his hands stroked over the thin silk of her camisole and she gasped at the soft seduction of the fragile fabric sliding along her skin.

His mouth roamed down into the shallow V between her breasts. For long moments, every nerve in her body was focused on the warmth of his lips, the teasing circles of his tongue. Desire tightened in her, impatience built for more than this teasing touch, for him to go further.

The slightly rough texture of his hands made her shiver as he pushed her robe off her shoulders, slipped down the thin straps of her camisole. Then his lips journeyed back up to capture hers with a power that made her go utterly still. More… this was more than any kiss had ever been, ripe with promise, decadent with pleasure. There was no thought of running or stopping now; she couldn't have borne it. Explorations and caresses blended into compulsion. Passion and need became inextricably tangled in a Gordian lovers' knot.

Everything a man could want, Nick held in his hands now. Everything he had burned for night after sleepless night was his. When he lowered his mouth to hers again, he had some thought of gentleness, but it was lost in her soft gasp as he slid one hand up under the thin cloth of her top.

It tore at his control, feeling the warm, smooth flatness of her belly, the curve of her waist and the slight swell where her breasts began. He took his time, testing them both with rhythmic strokes, fighting the urge to plunder. When he could wait no longer, he slipped his fingertips up higher to feel the hard points of her nipples.

And felt himself turn rock hard.

Arousal vaulted through her. It was exquisite, it was tantalizing, it was almost more than Sloane could bear. And there was more, she knew there was more.

Suddenly she couldn't bear it anymore, she had to feel Nick's flesh under her palms, his bare skin against hers, the muscles of his flat belly raised up in taut relief. With impatient fingers, she dragged the fabric up over his head. And when she ran her fingers over his chest, his nipples, to tear a moan from him, she gloried in her power.

Nick slipped both hands under her camisole. Sloane's breath caught as she realized his intent, then raised her arms to assist him. The scrap of silk slipped over her fingertips and wafted gently to the floor, forgotten. As easily as if she were weightless, he shifted her around to place her beneath him on the yielding cushions of the couch. A tension began to coil in her belly as she felt the weight of him against her.

Sloane ran her hands down from his shoulders to his wrists, feeling the rippling strength of the tendons, the curves of muscle under her fingers. "Touch me, Nick," she whispered, eyes heavy lidded and hot. "Touch me everywhere."

The words dragged him to the edge of control. With every passing moment, he swore it couldn't get any more intense. With every kiss they traveled further and further from the bounds of sanity. Her skin glowed, milk-pale in the morning light; her breasts were small and perfect. Around her shoulders her hair swirled in wild disarray, gleaming like flame. He leaned down to pleasure, to possess.

In a surge of mingled desire and delight, Sloane felt his

tongue trace a line down her neck to the taut peaks of her bare breasts. The slick caress of his tongue against first one, then the other sent her twisting against him. It was exquisite, maddening. He scraped his teeth lightly against her nipples and she gasped for air, clutched at him as he ran his hand down the line of her thigh where the silky nylons whispered under his palm.

"Oh man," he muttered as he reached the top of her nylons and found bare flesh and the lacy line of her garter belt. "I might just lose it right here."

"Not yet, cowboy." Sloane slid her fingers down, reaching for the buckle of his belt, but as his hands grazed the tops of her thighs, she went boneless and weak. For a whirling moment, she felt his touch on the silky triangle of fabric and the exquisitely sensitive nubbin beneath. With a moan she clutched his shoulders, her hands sliding urgently up to his neck. And felt broken skin under her fingers.

Nick jerked back, gasping in a sudden flare of pain that overshadowed even desire.

"What is it? What's wrong?"

He shook his head, blanking it out. "Nothing." He turned back to her, but the movement had him hissing.

"It's not nothing. Let me see it." Disregarding his hands, she sat up and examined the back of his neck. An ugly strip of burned, welted skin ran along the back of his neck. Sloane inhaled rapidly, trying to ignore a quick twist of queasiness. This was no time to get faint; she ordered herself. "God, Nick, what happened?"

"A falling stringer knocked my hat off and hit my neck. The medic put a bandage on it." He shifted, trying to ease the throbbing.

"Well, it's come loose." Sloane took another look. "You've got to get that taken care of," she said decisively, reaching for her robe. Her skin felt sensitized from his touch as she belted on the silk. The fabric felt strange, foreign now against her skin.

As though he'd read her mind, Nick reached out for her. "You don't need to be in such a hurry with that," he murmured.

"Nick, you need to go to the hospital," she persisted, batting his hands away. "Why didn't you?"

He gave up and simply wound his fingers through her hair. "During the fire, we needed every hand."

"You should have gone afterward, though."

Nick stroked her neck and brushed his thumb over her lips. "I wanted to see you."

For a moment, she lost herself in the smoky depths of his eyes. In the next heartbeat her mouth was on his, seeking, finding. Her hands slipped up to pull him closer and he flinched again.

"Nick."

"Forget it, it doesn't matter," he muttered, kissing his way down the neckline of her robe.

Sloane pushed back. "It does matter. Look, I'm sure I've got some bandages and stuff. I can clean it a bit and cover it for you, then you have to go get it taken care of." She stood up, not trusting herself to stay in physical contact with him, "Relax. I'll get the peroxide."

Of course, she hadn't actually seen the peroxide in a few months, she realized as she rummaged through the medicine cabinet over her bathroom sink. What had she done with it? More to the point, what in God's name was she doing? She tried to look sternly at herself in the bathroom mirror but only managed a rather foolish grin.

Yes, it was risky. But maybe, just maybe, it was worth it. She wouldn't fall all the way, but surely partway was all right, wasn't it? Taking a chance wouldn't destroy her, but turning away from a feeling like this just might. It had been so long….

Switching to the cabinet under the sink, she pulled out a nearly full bottle of store-label ibuprofen and peered at it. She didn't see an expiration date; then again, the label was so faded perhaps it had disappeared.

Illness generally made her impatient. Her method of treatment was to ignore everything and simply sleep until it was gone. It worked splendidly with colds and flu but was probably not going to be effective on lacerations and second-degree burns. "Ah-ha," she muttered as she unearthed a small first aid kit she'd gotten one time after she'd taken a fall running. At the back of the cupboard, she finally located the peroxide. Toting her prizes triumphantly, Sloane hurried back into the living room.

"I've got enough to…" she stopped. Nick had taken her order to relax seriously. He lay back on the couch, eyes closed, chest rising and falling in the steady rhythm of sleep. His lashes made dark, feathered crescents against his skin. Stripped of cares, he looked younger, almost vulnerable. Sloane shook her head.

"Damn you, Nick Trask," she said softly, looking down on him. "And damn the fire department, too."

Afternoon sun was slanting its way across the couch by the time Nick awoke to an empty room. He sat up stiffly, remembering too late not to touch his neck. He winced as he rose.

"Hello? Sloane?"

There was no answer in the silent flat. He was about to walk to the bathroom when he glanced down at the coffee table. Peroxide and gauze sat on top of a scribbled note. "There's food in the refrigerator if you want. Let yourself out the back door and don't forget to go to the doctor. I'll be in touch." No signature, just a capital *S* scribbled at the bottom.

Nick shook his head ruefully. Of all the idiot timing, his had to take the cake. He picked up his shirt from the table, where it sat neatly folded. Falling asleep on a lady was definitely bad form. Falling asleep on a woman like Sloane was criminal. Still, she hadn't booted him out on the street, however much she might have been tempted to. He'd have to categorize that as an improvement overall.

Pulling the shirt over his head with care, Nick began to whistle.

Yep, definitely an improvement.

Chapter Seven

"She's going to what?" Nick stared at the telephone.

"Sloane's going to ride along with your shift for a while," Bill Grant told him.

"You can't be serious." Nick loosened his jaw and tried for patience. Just thinking of Sloane conjured a mix of desire and frustration. He'd tried repeatedly to reach her over the weekend, only to get her answering machine. Getting close to her was like tracking some wild animal—every time he thought he was getting near, she dashed away again.

"Look," Bill said, "when I talked with Sloane last Friday she was concerned about missing the fire the previous night. She understands why it happened but she's got certain objectives to meet. To ensure she's on site for all fire incidents, she's asked to be there in the firehouse with your shift until the testing is concluded."

Perfect. Nick could just imagine working shift after shift,

Sloane around every minute as he did his best to keep from thinking about the feel of her nearly naked body against him. "It's going to cause an incredible disruption."

"For Christ's sake." Grant's voice rose. "You've been working with the woman for nearly three weeks. Deal with it. You've never complained about ride alongs before," he managed more reasonably. "What's different now?"

What was different? Most ride alongs hadn't turned into a constant grinding in his belly, for one.

"Nick, she's mostly interested in being at the fire scenes. Otherwise, I'm sure she'll stay out of the way," Grant continued. "She shouldn't interrupt your routines."

Interrupt his routines, hell, Nick thought. Be careful what you ask for, or you will surely get it. He'd wanted more time with her, more, period. He'd never in a million years wanted it to be at work. How was he supposed to concentrate on the job when all he wanted to do was tumble her into bed for about two weeks straight? He didn't care for endless days of frustration. And he particularly didn't care for having his decisions made for him. Nick scowled. "When's this going to start?"

"She should be there now. I told her your shift started at eight."

"Today?" Nick bit back a curse. "Why didn't you call and let me know this earlier?" he asked finally.

"I didn't want to bother you during your time off."

Yeah, right. Nick hung up the phone and stalked out of his office. No wonder she'd laid low over the weekend. He strode purposefully down the hall, hearing the noise rise as he turned the corner to the kitchen.

And stumbled into a mob scene.

"Hey, Nick," Knapp called out from the crowd around the kitchen table, "we got ourselves another rookie."

O'Hanlan thumped his coffee mug down on the painted wood. "Hell of a lot easier on the eyes than Red is, that's for sure."

"She's too smart to hang around with you truckies," said Ken Giancoli, chauffeur for the engine crew. "She wants work with the nozzle men, that's where the real excitement is. She should ride with us on the pumper."

"Nobody in their right mind wants to ride with you, Giancoli." O'Hanlan grinned, taking a swig of coffee.

Nick approached the table.

"Hello, Nick." Sloane looked up, surrounded by firefighters. "Looks like I'm on the crew for a while."

Every time he saw her again, he was surprised anew at the impact of those eyes, that mouth. That damned voice of hers. Maybe if he could stop her from talking the entire time, he'd be okay. Nick glanced down at the handful of department announcements he held. "Okay, let's get to it," he said curtly. "Night-shift guys, take up, you're relieved. Let's run through the announcements first and then the shift work." He sat down and began. Most days, friendly insults and jokes flew, but today he was in no mood for interruptions. Speeded by caffeine, the update went quickly.

When he'd finished, Nick looked at the crew. "Okay, work-detail assignments are on the bulletin board. Don't forget to sign up for next shift. Questions?"

Giancoli raised his hand. "Yeah. We gotta have O'Hanlan cooking today? He always uses too much garlic."

"I use just enough," O'Hanlan countered. "You sure you weren't fathered by the mailman, Giancoli?"

"Fa Chrissakes, O'Hanlan, I had to do mouth-to-mouth the other night after you cooked, this little old gray-haired granny.

I revived her and she turned around and passed out again from the garlic smell."

"We been meaning to talk to you, Giancoli," Beaulieu said. "There's this invention called a toothbrush you oughtta know about."

Nick raised a hand. "Okay, enough, time to get to it, guys. Maintenance first, then drills."

Reluctant to disperse, the firefighters milled about rinsing out coffee cups and joking.

"You can come help me out, Sloane," Knapp said, tucking her hand into his arm.

"No way," O'Hanlan argued. "You're going to vacuum the dorm. I'm going to check the ladder truck. She'll learn more with me."

"Ride alongs stay with me," Nick reminded them. "Sloane, let's go to my office."

As he led the way, all Nick was aware of was her scent. Okay, maybe he could concentrate if he could stop her from wearing it. He stood aside to let her walk into his office. The walk, though, the walk was still a problem. Maybe if he could stop her from moving. Or wrap her in a muumuu. Maybe if he could…ah hell, Nick thought as he closed the door. How the hell was he ever going to get anything done with her around?

She sat in his client chair, looking up at him, so cool, so composed, as though they'd shared nothing more important than a handshake. All he wanted to do was clamp his mouth on hers and bring that wild hunger into her eyes again, just to prove to himself and to her that he could. Instead, he leaned back against the edge of his desk and folded his arms across his chest. "You've been busy, I hear."

* * *

There wasn't enough oxygen in the room, Sloane thought uneasily. Nick's eyes smoldered at her, dark and dangerous. So maybe he felt as though he'd been blindsided. After all, she hadn't warned him of her idea. Then again, she hadn't thought of it until she'd been back at work, trying to put those hot, urgent minutes on the couch out of her mind.

It all made her want to run, and yet she was slipping closer and closer to the point at which running away wasn't possible. She was too honest with herself to pretend it wasn't what she wanted anymore. That he wasn't what she wanted. It didn't make things simple, though. Before, things had at least been clear. Now, nothing was.

So she focused on what was safe and all-important—qualifying the gear. "I assume you've talked to Bill Grant."

"About ten minutes ago. You, now," he said conversationally, "I tried to talk with you over the weekend but you didn't seem to be around." An edge underlay his words.

"I'm not very good about checking my home messages." Of course, if she'd picked up the phone when she'd heard his voice coming out of the machine, she wouldn't have had to. So close, she'd come so close, but she known where it would lead, and away from the heat of the moment, she just wasn't sure she was ready. If she'd ever be ready. In the end, she'd turned away, heart thumping.

"Grant says you called him Friday about missing the fire."

"I wasn't trying to get you in hot water," she said to forestall his anger. "I told him I understood why you didn't call me and that I was okay with it. It just can't happen again. This seems like a good solution."

"A good solution? More like a permanent problem in my firehouse."

She raised an eyebrow. "*Your* firehouse?"

"You saw how things went in the morning meeting," he said, ignoring her.

"It's a new situation. Of course it gave everyone something to talk about. Give it a little while and they won't notice me anymore."

"You've got to be kidding." He gazed at her and her face warmed. "Okay, so I didn't notify you of the fire the other night. It was a screw-up, I admit it. And I told you, it won't happen again."

"How do you know?" she demanded. "You were right, Nick. I thought a lot about what you said after I went to work on Friday. You were taking care of business, saving lives, and there is no way I want to interfere with that. We can't ignore the testing, though, because that can save lives, too. It'll be easier if I'm just here all the time."

"Easier? For you, maybe. But as far as my men are concerned, you're going to be a distraction."

"Really?" she tossed back at him. "Are you sure you're not just worked up because I'm trespassing on your turf?"

"I'm not worked up." He pushed off the desk with studied deliberation and strolled slowly toward her. "Or at least I'm not the only one. For example, why the big surprise? Why didn't you tell me about this before?"

"I didn't think of it before. I decided on it once I got to the office."

"You could have called me."

"How, by calling my house?" she shot back. "Besides, I was hoping you wouldn't be there."

"Was that why you walked away and left instead of waking me up? You're getting your stories mixed, Sloane."

"Don't start on me," she snapped as her temper heated.

"I'm not the one who fell asleep." And her eyes flew open in horror. Given a knife at that moment she would have cheerfully cut out her tongue.

The smile bloomed across Nick's face. "I'm sorry about that, more than you'll know. I usually have better manners."

"It didn't matter," she muttered, rising to walk past him.

"It did to me." He caught her arm and used it to pull her to him.

She warned herself not to get in too deep even as he lowered his mouth to hers. For a moment, she held herself away from him but then her control dissolved. When he was giving her one of those mind-bending kisses that turned her bones into taffy, anything seemed possible. Being with him seemed like the only thing. For long, hazy seconds the firehouse receded.

Footsteps sounded in the hall. Sloane broke contact and twisted away. "I don't think this is the place…"

"And that's exactly why you shouldn't be here."

She raised her chin. "We're not sixteen, Nick. I think we're both professional enough to deal with our hormones."

He stared at her maddeningly. "Is that what you think it is?"

"I don't…" she fumbled. "I don't think this is the time to get into this," she finished, her voice stronger.

"But we will."

Slowly, unwillingly, she nodded. "I know."

Hot triumph filled his eyes. He brushed his lips over hers. "I still think you should have called me."

"Would you have agreed?" Even just the quick contact had her head swimming.

He considered it. "No, probably not."

"Right. And I'd have gone to Bill and the same thing would have happened. This is important, Nick. I've got to get the gear qualified. I can't trust anyone else's opinion on this. I need to see with my own eyes."

Nick crossed back to sit behind his desk again. "Why does this mean so much to you?"

"It's important to me."

"Important." He tapped his fingers on his faux wood-grain desktop. "You're not always going to be able to shut me out like this, Sloane."

"Leave it, Nick." She stared at him and for once the snap and fire was replaced by a kind of pleading.

He let it pass, but the days when she could close herself off from him were waning. He needed more than that from her, he was discovering, much more. But now was not the time. "All right," he said abruptly. "If we're going to do this, let's do it right."

They stood on the apparatus floor by the racks of helmets and turnouts. O'Hanlan rummaged under the open hood of the ladder truck.

Nick plunked a helmet on her head. "See if this one fits." It slipped forward and the rest of the garage disappeared as it covered her eyes. "Oops. Okay, I guess you wear a different size."

Sloane pushed back the black leather brim until she could see again. "You think?"

The next wasn't any better, nor the next. One after another, they tried the spares without luck.

"Last chance," Nick told her.

This time, the helmet stayed in place reasonably well. Once Nick adjusted the inside, it held even when she shook her head. "Good," he said in satisfaction. "You'll probably never need it, but I'll feel better if you've got one on at a fire scene. Now let's get you some turnouts."

It was a longer, more difficult process. The coat wasn't a problem but the bunker pants were. Granted, Sloane was taller than a lot of guys. She was also more slender. Even the smallest of the spares hung from her shoulders by the suspenders, the waistband hovering at her waist like a clown suit at the circus. Nick's lips twitched as he looked at her. "I guess this'll have to do," he said finally.

"I'm not going in a fire. I don't see why I need them at all."

"During the day, you don't. When we get a call in the middle of the night, though—and we will, believe me—you'll see. You sleep in sweats and a T-shirt. All you have to do is step into the boots, pull the pants up and throw the suspenders over your shoulders and go. It's the fastest way. Now we just need to fit you for a vest and we're all set."

"A vest?"

"Body armor."

Sloane gaped at him. "You're joking."

"No. This isn't the best area in town, in case you haven't noticed. There's an area by the projects where someone's been taking potshots." He gave a humorless smile. "I guess they don't like the noise. One of the guys on A shift got grazed by one, so now we wear the vests any time we have a call in that area. Sloane—"

"Yes."

"I don't want you to get hurt. Why won't you give this up?"

Her shoulders squared. "I'd be at the same risk if I were driving to meet you at a fire." When he only looked at her in silence, she nodded slowly. "Unless you didn't call me. Nick, you can't block me. You take risks all the time. It doesn't stop you."

"It's my job."

"Right now, it's my job, too."

They stared at each other, neither backing down, bound

by that same swirling awareness. "All right," Nick said finally. "Come on."

The bulletproof vests were near the foot of the stairs. "The police department loaned us a dozen last week. Here." He selected one by eye. "Try this one."

Sloane slipped it on over her head, the fabric of her shirt tightening across her breasts as she tugged it down over her torso. "It needs adjusting, I think," she muttered, reaching awkwardly around her sides. "Damned things…why do they make them so you can't reach the…"

"I've got it," Nick said brusquely, pushing her hands out of the way. Sloane blinked at his tone of voice. His touch was impersonal, almost rough. His head bent toward hers as he concentrated on what he was doing, close enough that she could touch him and if he looked up, close enough to kiss.

She let out a breath. He was probably right, it was a bad idea to be there. She wasn't finding it any easier to be around him than he was to be around her. She thought of the feel of his mouth on her bare breast and her stomach did a lazy flip-flop.

"There." He pulled the bottom of the vest down, keeping his hands scrupulously away from her hips. "That should fit all right."

Though she wasn't sure exactly what fit entailed for a bulletproof vest, Sloane nodded. She needed to get away from him, somewhere she could get her equilibrium. The day seemed to stretch out unbearably. She'd take it, though. She had to. Stripping off the vest, she looked at Nick. "Where do I put this?"

"Over here." He led her to the ladder truck, where the boots and turnouts and hats were piled in careful, distinct stacks. Her jacket, he hung on the side of the ladder truck. "It goes back there in the same place every time the truck backs into quarters."

"Hey, cap?"

Nick glanced over his shoulder.

It was Sorensen, the probie, with a question about his house watchman duties. It was also a chance to escape, Sloane thought as she wandered over to where O'Hanlan was crouched down by the tire of the ladder truck.

"Is something wrong with it?" she asked.

"Nope." He squinted at the pressure gauge. "We just have to check the fluid levels and tires every day. These babies have to work right every time." He rose and walked a few steps to the next tire. "Anyway, doing this is a lot more interesting than the next item on my duty list."

"Which is?"

He gave her a mournful look. "Cleaning the bathroom."

"Come on, you guys don't really have to do that."

"Maid's year off," Nick said over her shoulder. "Besides, it keeps him out of trouble."

"We should conserve our energy," O'Hanlan countered. "How else can we save the lives and property of the good citizens of Bos—" The alarm bells began to ring. Instantly, the jokes ended. "Multi-car accident, intersection of Dudley and Columbia," Sorensen called out over the loudspeaker.

"Who goes, Sorensen?" Nick called over to the little house watch office at the front of the apparatus floor where the crew took turns logging calls in the station book and announcing alarms.

"Oh, uh, sorry, cap," Sorensen said, accidentally keeping the mike button depressed. He cleared his throat. "Um, Ladder 67 goes."

"All right, Red," shouted Knapp, clapping his hands as he headed to the ladder truck for his coat.

Nick pulled on his turnout pants and boots. "Sloane, you ride up front with us."

Thankful she didn't have to wear the clumsy boots and turnout pants in the daytime, Sloane climbed up into the cab and Nick swung in beside her.

"Everybody in place?" O'Hanlan asked, looking around from behind the wheel. "Okay, boys and girls, let's roll."

Flipping the switch for the siren, Nick gave a few blasts to the air horn and O'Hanlan pulled the truck onto the road.

Urgency. It permeated the air around them as O'Hanlan unerringly choose the most effective route to the incident. Too many of the drivers on the road, however, seemed cheerfully oblivious. On Columbia, a clot of traffic blocked their way. O'Hanlan laid on the horn. "You know, I keep telling the department, put a set of monster truck tires on this baby and I'll just ride right over all these civilians. Get to the scene faster and teach 'em a lesson or two." With surprising deftness, he threaded the truck around the worst of the snarl, forcing a few drivers up onto sidewalk. Finally, they were rolling forward again.

"There it is." Nick pointed. "Up ahead."

Sloane looked and felt sick. She'd never been the type to stare at accidents on the highway, preferring instead to keep her eyes on the road and be thankful it wasn't her. In this case, driving past wasn't an option. She was still immensely glad she wasn't one of the unlucky victims involved.

A one-ton pickup truck touted in TV ads for its size and toughness had gone head-on into a compact. The truck was indeed tough—it had turned the front end of the smaller car into a twisted crush of metal. O'Hanlan pulled to a stop.

"Okay, guys," Nick said, "let's get to it."

Sloane followed him as he approached the cop who crouched by the compact. "What's the situation?" Nick asked.

The cop rose and took a few steps away. "Four inside, two in front, a couple of kids in back. Got an ambulance on the way but we're gonna need your can opener to get them out." He lowered his voice. "The driver's pretty bad off."

Nick nodded and stepped away. "O'Hanlan, Sorensen, get the jaws and the torch. Knapp, Beaulieu, check out the passengers in the back. Get them stabilized. I'll handle the driver. We've got ambulances on the way." He pulled the bulky first aid kit out of a locker and went swiftly to the front of the car.

This was a Nick Sloane hadn't seen before, decisive and in command, and she was surprised at just how sexy that was. It wasn't just the offhand skill with which he applied pressure bandages and spinal stabilizers, it was the quietly capable way he dealt with the people in the car. If she were one of the victims, trapped and hurt, she'd want to hear a calm, reassuring voice like that telling her everything was going to be all right. He said it as though there was no possibility of anything but.

Metal screeched as the jaws peeled open the car as though it was made of tinfoil. Knapp and Beaulieu helped the pair in the back get out. Nick waited to remove the driver and front passenger until the ambulances had arrived with their stretchers. More quickly than she'd expected, the victims were spirited off to the hospital and the ladder-truck crew was heading back to the vehicle.

"This is my favorite part," O'Hanlan said. "Getting to go home when the interesting work's done. That poor schlep," he jabbed a thumb toward the cop, "has to wait for the tow truck and the cleanup crew. We'll be sitting down to lunch while he's still out here, I'm betting."

"Will they be all right?" Sloane asked as they drove back to the firehouse. The front seat was designed for two, not

three, and she was burningly conscious of the hard length of
Nick's leg pressed against hers.

"The kids in the backseat will be home tonight," Nick told
her. "The driver's going to spend time in the hospital, along
with the person riding shotgun."

"Don't you ever wonder what happens to them?"

"You kidding?" O'Hanlan asked. "This one calls the hospital and checks sometimes."

Nick shifted in his seat and looked out the window. "I just
want to make sure we're taking care of people."

"You are," Sloane said softly. "You are."

Chapter Eight

Nick stood in the courtyard of the fire station, watching Sorensen and the Engine 58 probie go through rope-tying drills. He'd left Sloane in the firehouse talking into her cell phone, computer open on her lap as she dialed into a meeting. She was out of sight. She should have been out of mind.

And he should have been a lottery winner. He knew she was there. He couldn't stop thinking about her.

He couldn't stop wanting her.

His cell phone rang. He flipped it open. "Yo."

"Nick, Jacob."

In a different era, Jacob would have been a trapper who lived in the wilderness and only came into a remote trading post every three or four months. Brusque and uncomfortable in conversation, he never seemed quite to know what to make of people, even his own family.

Which had never stopped him from trying to be the big

brother and telling Nick what he should do. And Nick had a pretty good idea that was what he was calling for right now.

"Hey, Jacob, what's going on?"

"I hear you're not coming to Thanksgiving," he said without preamble.

Other brothers who hadn't talked for months might have made small talk for a little while, Nick reflected. Jacob just got right to business. "Yeah. I'm working the night shift."

"You're an officer. Why can't you trade days and get it off?"

"What's your point, Jacob?"

"Look, you want to stay down in Boston it doesn't matter to me. I know you don't want to come back to the farm. It matters to Ma, though."

"She never mentioned it to me. It kind of sounds like I'm supposed to drop everything, haul in favors and get the day off because you think I should?" He knew it was surly; somehow Jacob always managed to bring it out of him.

"Is it really too damned much to ask, Nick? You know how hard these eight months have been for her? Or maybe you don't. It's not like you're ever around."

And here they were again, at the core issue that inevitably came up whenever they talked—Jacob's reminder, spoken and unspoken, that he was the only one living on the farm, that Nick should somehow find a way to do more. "Thanksgiving is two weeks away. How am I supposed to get anyone to trade their holiday?"

"You're off the day after, though."

"Sure, at 8:00 a.m. the day after, and I'm due back twenty-four hours later. I'd barely get up to the farm before I'd have to come back."

"So what you're saying is that you can't be bothered."

"No, I'm saying that it's not going to be a lot of quality time.

I'd rather wait and come up when I've got a three-day break, spend more time. Mom knows that. We've talked about it."

"Do you think she cares if it's a short visit? She just wants to see everyone here."

"Funny, she didn't seem to mind when I talked with her. It sounds like the only one who has a problem with it is you."

Jacob snorted. "Like she's going to say anything."

The guilt bit deep. "Cut with the big-brother stuff, Jacob," Nick snapped. "I'm not going to make it, okay?" He glanced up to see that Sorensen had finished his drill and was walking over, out of breath. "Look, I've gotta go."

"Funny how that works," Jacob said. "You always do."

Rescue calls, medical aid calls, inspections, even a false alarm; the day spun out in ongoing variety. And each time Sloane saw Nick walk up and quietly, capably take control of a scene, something scurried around in her stomach. She saw him lifting equipment and found herself remembering the feel of his hard hands on her body. She stared at his unsmiling, intent face and thought of the way he'd looked as she'd stroked her fingers down his belly. She watched him at work and she wanted him more than ever.

When they returned from their third medical aid call, O'Hanlan stopped the truck on the apron. "Hey, cap, I'm going to run up the ladder, give her a check." Outside, he stood at the control panel and pushed a switch to release the white supports that stabilized the truck when the ladder was extended.

Nick stood by, balanced and easy.

When Sloane had arranged the ride along, she'd never thought that being around him would be a challenge. The danger, she'd assumed, lay in his hands, in those persuasive kisses. Who'd have guessed that he'd have slid so easily under her skin without ever a touch?

He glanced over and caught her looking. He raised a questioning eyebrow.

Sloane cleared her throat. "So is this a typical day?"

Nick smiled faintly. "I'm not sure there is such a thing. You never know when you come in what's going to happen. Keeps life interesting."

"Is that what you like about it?"

"I like everything about it. The people, the variety, the fact that it's not something that everyone can do."

"You don't shy away from challenges."

His eyes locked on hers with the power of a punch. "Not when it's something I really want."

For just that instant, she couldn't breathe. Desire thudded through her. It seemed impossible to be this close and not have him.

Sloane swallowed. "And what you want is firefighting?"

"It's one thing. I like going up against a fire, head to head."

"Head to head?" she repeated, relaxing enough for amusement. "You make it sound as if it's alive."

"It seems it is when you're in the middle of it. It's fast, it's tricky and it keeps coming at you. I like beating it. And I like having a chance to make a difference," he added thoughtfully, watching O'Hanlan extend the ladder. "I like going to work knowing that maybe I'll have a chance to save someone's life today."

She remembered the awards in his office. "You already have, right?"

"I got lucky a couple of times." He shrugged. "Right place, right time."

He'd be uncomfortable with being called a hero, she

thought, even though he was. "It didn't sound as if it was just luck to me. It sounded as though you made it happen. What's it like?"

The corners of his mouth tugged and suddenly his smile was a mile wide. "It's the greatest feeling in the world. I was psyched for weeks, especially the last time, with the two kids."

"What happened?"

"It was a fire in a triple-decker about five blocks from here."

"Is that all you ever get around here, fires in triple-deckers?"

"Seems like it, doesn't it?" he agreed. "The same house, over and over and over, most of them in their second century, overcrowded, undermaintained. Wiring wears out, people start fires with space heaters, candles."

"Dangerous," Sloane commented.

He nodded. "It keeps us hopping. Anyway, this little girl was babysitting her brother on the top story. She was just a kid herself. Smart, though. She'd moved them both to the floor by a window. I got lucky."

"Sounds like she did, too."

"The fire came up the hall after me. The hose company hadn't gotten up that high yet and the far side of the room was starting to go up. They had the stick up outside but I figured if I opened the window to get to it, the oxygen would pull the fire that way. I wasn't sure I'd have enough time to get them out."

"What did you do?"

He shrugged. "Went for it. Handed the boy to the guy on the ladder, grabbed the girl and got on the windowsill. I figured I'd wait until they cleared the top of the ladder, but the fire was coming too fast. So I held the kid tight and got on the underside of the ladder. Surprised the hell out of the truckie who had the boy."

"But you saved the girl and yourself."

"Not by much. The fire chased after us pretty fast. We had O'Hanlan running the ladder. He was on his toes and got us out of there."

"I can't imagine what it's like to be that high up on a ladder."

Nick gave her a sidelong glance. "Want to find out?"

"You mean now?"

"Why not?" Before she could respond, he whistled to Beaulieu, who was standing house watch. "Hey, Todd, radio in an out-of-service for ten minutes. O'Hanlan, leave the outriggers deployed. Sloane's going to go up on the stick."

It was too good a show for the rest of the crew. In ones and twos they trailed out of the firehouse to watch. Perfect. Just what she needed—an audience. She'd never been particularly fond of heights, Sloane thought uneasily. "How high is the ladder, again?"

"Eighty feet," O'Hanlan said cheerfully. "Don't worry, she slides up smooth as silk."

"Okay, put on your helmet and turnouts," Nick directed.

"The pants don't fit."

"Put them on anyway. We need the belt clip. You can leave off the turnout coat if you want."

She felt a little like a clown in the oversized trousers and garish red suspenders. Knapp whistled. "Now you're styling."

"Lookin' like a firefighter," Beaulieu added.

"Fireman, fireman, save my child," O'Hanlan cried in a reedy falsetto, hands clasped in front of his chest.

In a few moves, Nick was on top of the ladder truck. "Okay, come on up," he directed, holding out a hand to grab her.

Atop the ladder truck, the ground was already far enough away for her, but no way was she going to back down. She'd get through it, Sloane told herself grimly. If they could do it, so could she.

The telescoped white ladder lay flat on the truck. "O'Hanlan, bring it up," Nick directed. Motors whirred as the layered bulk of the ladder tilted up to a seventy degree angle. The rungs for all of the telescoped sections were in line with one another, she saw. "Okay," Nick told her, "it's a piece of cake. I'm going to be right behind you the whole time, so you've got nothing to worry about. You're going to do great." He spoke in the same calm, reassuring tone she'd heard at the accident scene and bit by bit she began to relax. "Now climb up about five rungs up and stop. The ladder's going to unfold and take us the rest of the way up."

The metal vibrated against her palms as Nick stepped on, standing just below her. Holding onto a rung with one hand, he reached the other around in front of her to attach a carabiner from the waist of her turnouts to a rung of the ladder. "Safety line, just in case." He put both hands on the rungs, his body just behind hers, his breath feathering over her neck.

"Check your toes. Make sure you're stepping on just the rung for this section," Nick directed her and then raised his voice. "Okay, O'Hanlan, put 'er up slow."

The engines rumbled. "Going up," O'Hanlan called. "Top floor, ladies' hats, gloves and finer dresses." Smoothly, the white ladder began to rise into the air section by section. The movement didn't seem particularly fast, but the ground fell away all too rapidly.

Sloane gulped.

"Okay," Nick said, "you can move your feet more onto the rungs now, our section's untelescoped. Don't be tense. You're perfectly safe, trust me."

Trust me. Sloane concentrated on the calm words. Nick

would never put her, or anyone, at risk. She focused on the comforting feel of his chest against her back. She'd be okay, he was there.

"Take a good grip, now," he said in that same easy tone. "We're going to jerk a little when we hit the top."

The jolt had her looking down. Far below them, the truck was a small red square surrounded by tiny figures. Sloane closed her eyes and tried not to hyperventilate.

"Hey, you can look at the ground any time," Nick said. "Don't stare down. Look around you, at the city."

Sloane raised her head and clenching her hands on the rungs, opened her eyes. "Oh!"

She was, purely and simply, captivated.

"Prettier from up here, isn't it?"

She'd never realized there were so many trees in the city. Gold, red, glorious orange, everywhere she looked it blazed with autumn color. Boston had draped itself in its fall finery and it was all laid out for her enjoyment. To her left, she caught a glimpse of Boston Common and the Public Garden. The spires of the financial district appeared level with her eyes. A small blue slice of the Atlantic glittered far to the right. Dirt, crime, traffic, all the evils of city life were far away. "It's gorgeous," she breathed.

"Like magic, isn't it?" Nick murmured in her ear. Up this high, the engine was far away and Sloane could hear everything he said, even the rhythmic sound of his breath. His arms were around her, his body next to hers in what was almost a lovers' embrace, she realized abruptly.

"Look over there, you can see the Charles River." He reached over her shoulder to point.

Sloane searched the horizon, seeing only buildings.

"No." He gently turned her head. "Over there."

It was the first time they'd touched all day. His fingertips pressed little coins of heat against her jaw. A slow curl of desire awoke inside of her.

"I see it," she fibbed hastily. "What's back behind us?" She turned her head.

It put both of them at risk. It brought his mouth much too near. Dangling from a ladder, eighty feet above the ground was no time for her palms to get damp, no time for the want to start flowing through her. She took a shuddering breath.

"Seen enough?" Nick asked.

Not trusting her voice, Sloane nodded.

"Okay, hold on. The ladder might jump a little bit when it starts down." Nick made an arm motion and they headed back toward the ground. She felt a little twinge of disappointment as they dropped away from the view.

It was a bit like landing in a jetliner. At first the ground was unimaginably far away and exotic, then closer, then near enough to be mundane. Finally, the ladder stopped and they stepped down.

The crew broke out in applause and whistles. Sloane bowed to her audience from the top of the ladder truck, waving modestly. Behind them, a sedan pulled into the lot.

Laughing and breathless, she let herself be helped off the ladder truck. The men surrounded her, clapping her on the back, slapping the top of her helmet.

"Speech, speech," hooted Knapp.

"How'd ya like it?" O'Hanlan asked.

"Oh, it's gorgeous. I loved it."

"Well, you make it worth my while, I'll send you up again. I take brownies, ice cream sundaes or American Express," he told her.

Sloane tucked her tongue in her cheek. "I think you're an operator, O'Hanlan."

"To know me is to love me."

"Well, Sloane, you certainly seem to be diving into things," said a voice behind them.

And Sloane turned to see Councilman Ayre and his entourage.

It was a coincidence, Nick had to believe that. He saw the shock and dismay chase across Sloane's face. He wanted to believe she hadn't concocted the ride along as part of a cheap publicity stunt for Ayre, but one hand washed the other and the timing was eerily perfect.

Ayre walked up to her as though he owned the place, Nick thought furiously. As though he owned her. "Well, I see you've wasted no time getting to work. Glad we've got a go-getter like you on the job." Standing next to her, Ayre pasted on a toothy smile for the photographer who trailed him.

The photo op was everything, of course. It was the whole reason he was stopping by, to use them for a little campaign boost.

"I'm happy to see that you're so involved in monitoring the testing," he told Sloane, pumping her hand. "I'm even more impressed than I was before. We're really behind this equipment. I'm very excited about it."

"That's great," Nick heard himself saying. "Given the fact that you've voted for departmental budget cuts for each of the last seven years. Kind of hard to figure out how that's going to help us buy this fancy new equipment you're flogging."

For an instant, Ayre looked absolutely furious. Then his expression relaxed into an affable smile. "And you are?"

"Trask. Nick Trask, registered voter."

"Well, Firefighter Trask, I'm sure you realize developing

a budget is a matter of compromise," he said warmly, reaching out to clasp Nick's hand and give it a brisk shake.

"Captain Trask," Nick corrected. A flashbulb popped. Ayre held on. Another photo op, Nick realized in annoyance.

And when the camera was down, Ayre started to turn away.

"We'll be looking for that funding boost," Nick persisted.

Ayre swung back toward him, all of his caps showing. "I'm completely behind this project," he answered. "I'll be going to go to the mat for you guys, just like I always do." A young, slick-looking guy in hair gel and a fancy suit stepped up to murmur in Ayre's ear. The politician looked at his watch. "Well, looks like I've got to run to another appearance across town. It was a pleasure to meet you all," he said smoothly. "Don't forget to get out and vote tomorrow." He walked toward the waiting sedan.

Sloane stood frozen, staring at the car as it drove away. Just then, a red truck drove up and parked in the lot. The first of the night shift, coming in early. "Was that who I thought it was?" a burly, mustachioed firefighter asked incredulously.

"Sure was," O'Hanlan told him. "Nicky's never going to wash his hand again, are you?"

"As quickly as possible," Nick said shortly. "Todd, call us in as active again." He turned and walked back into the firehouse.

Chapter Nine

Sloane slipped out of the turnouts and helmet and hustled after him. "Nick, wait." She caught him on the stairs. "I wasn't a part of that."

He turned and flicked her a cynical glance. "Of course you're part of it. We're all part of it."

Anger whisked through her. "I didn't know they were coming."

"Oh no? I did. It's just that with everything else going on I kind of forgot." He turned to go the rest of the way up the stairs. "That was the payoff for the whole project, Sloane. He pushes your system, you give him the pre-election photo op."

"Did it ever occur to you that someone in the department might have tipped him off that I was here?" she demanded, on his heels. "They probably figured it was good for the department."

"No, it's good for Ayre. And it doesn't matter who tipped him off, it's the only reason you're here."

"I'm here to test the equipment and get it into the field."

Nick reached the top of the stairs and turned to Sloane as she joined him. "Look, I don't doubt your sincerity. I know this project means a lot to you, so it's probably more unfair to you than it is to us, but if you think that Ayre has considered buying your equipment for one minute…"

"I'm not working with him. I'm working for you," she returned hotly.

"Sloane, you're dreaming. Ayre's the one who controls the future of this thing. Why don't you just accept that this equipment is not going to make it in Boston no matter how good it is?"

Stung, she glared at him. "Aren't you sick of saying that, Nick? Because I'm sure as hell sick of hearing it. I'm going to get this equipment qualified, whether I've got your support or not."

"My support doesn't matter. It's not going to happen."

"It has to," she burst out passionately. "Firefighters can't keep dying. It has to *stop*."

A moment went by in silence. Nick looked at her. "Who was it, Sloane?" he asked softly. "Who did you lose?"

She couldn't swallow, couldn't breathe for the knot in her throat. "My brother," she whispered, fighting the urge to scream at the unbearable truth.

And downstairs, alarm bells began to ring.

The wind of the raw November night blew down Nick's collar as he stood on Sloane's front stoop and pressed the bell. He stepped back and squinted up at her windows. There was faint light there, but he couldn't tell if anyone was home. He jammed his hands into his pockets. All he could do was hope.

The alarm—a medical aid call—had stopped their conversation cold. By the time they'd returned, the night shift had arrived. One minute, he'd been talking with the night captain, watching Sloane hang up her turnouts. The next time he'd glanced over, she'd been gone without a word. Intentionally, he was sure.

That didn't mean he planned to let it end there. It was time to talk. He looked at the bell, considering giving it another push.

And then the door swung open and she was there, looking at him with wariness but no surprise. "Hello."

"You disappeared," he said, his breath making puffs of white condensation in the chill air.

She was barefoot, in a baggy green sweater and jeans, wrapping her arms around herself to keep warm. "I thought I'd get out of the way. You were busy and everything was finished."

"Not everything. Not our conversation, for one."

She shivered at little. "I thought we'd said everything that needed to be said."

"Not by half, but it's kind of cold to be going into it out here." He could hear the tension in her voice, see the shadows in her eyes. And he knew, because he knew her now, that she'd fight like hell to try to keep the barriers up. It wasn't going to happen this time, though. This time, she was going to let him in. "Do you want to go somewhere, get dinner or a drink?"

She hesitated and then let out a breath of acceptance and stepped back. "Why don't you come in?"

Upstairs, the flat was as tidy as it had been the first time he'd seen it, and as bare. No photographs of family sat around on any of the walls or surfaces, he noticed now. It was as though she existed in her own universe.

And maybe now he understood a little more why.

She stood at the living-room door, watching as he hung his jacket on the coat rack. "I'm having a drink. Can I get you something?"

He looked at her glass. "If that's bourbon, you can give me one of those, too."

"No ice," she told him. "Water? Straight up?"

"Straight up."

He walked over to the windows and looked out at the night. So it had come down to this, the whole possibility of anything happening with them came down to this conversation and what she'd been through. If he could get her to open up, lance the wound, then maybe they had a chance together.

He heard her come back into the room and turned to take his glass from her. When he saw the smudges under her eyes, he felt the tug of responsibility.

"So." She chose the isolation of the chair. "You wanted to talk?"

"Apologize, first, for getting you upset about Ayre." He took a swallow of the bourbon and sat on the couch. "I know you're not pandering to him. He just got to me. He always gets to me."

She nodded. "I'm trying to do something good here, Nick."

"I know. It's just that I don't believe you know what you're up against."

"And I don't believe in worrying about that. You just put your head down and get the job done."

"Kind of like the way you go through life?"

She gave him a sharp look. "You said apology, not five-minute analysis."

"Tell me about your brother," he said, his voice gentle.

She rose. "It's private."

He stood as well. "It's there in the room every time we're

together. It's here now." He reached out and closed his hand over hers. Trusting to the contact, he pulled her toward the couch. "Tell me."

She stared and moistened her lips. Finally, she sat in a corner of the sofa, her knees drawn up, her arms wrapped around them. "He was a firefighter." She swallowed. "In Hartford."

And he knew. It made the hairs on the back of his neck stand on end. "The packing-house fire."

She nodded.

It was infamous, a hellish conflagration in an almost entirely windowless building full of thick walls and sealed rooms. Firefighters searching the structure had gotten lost in the maze and the blinding, toxic smoke. And their would-be rescuers had been lost as well, in a hideous chain of events that left five men dead.

Among them, apparently, Sloane's brother.

"Mitch had always wanted to be a firefighter. When we were kids, he used to go down to the local station and hang around, wipe the truck, do whatever they'd let him. He was a lieutenant by the time of the fire, a veteran.

"They were in on the first alarm and the first pair of guys lost were from his company." She moved her head in blind misery. "Mitch went after them. It would never have occurred to him not to. I don't know if they ever even got close. The last thing they heard from him was over the radio, saying he was lost and running out of air." Her voice shook with the unbearable, imagining him moving in blind circles in the choking black smoke, methodically searching for escape.

She blinked back the quick sting of tears. "It haunts me, you know? You read about those pilots in falling airplanes who try all the different drills, right down to the point of impact. That was Mitch. He was a by-the-book guy. He'd have kept looking and when he found himself lost, he'd have kept trying to work his way out." Hoping for a miracle and trying to ignore the rising bubble of horror. "They said his voice at the end was perfectly calm," she whispered.

"So you built the Orienteer."

She swiped at her cheek. "I built the Orienteer because no one, no one should be in that spot ever again. No one's brother, no one's wife, no one's father or sister. And if I have to make nice with Ayre for that to happen, then I do it. It doesn't matter a hell of a lot to me, do you understand?" She gave him a searching gaze. "All I care about is the gear." She glanced down. "Anyway, now you know why I can't be involved with you."

"Because of your brother?"

"I can't do it, Nick."

He shook his head. "But Sloane, we *are* involved. You can't make it go away by pretending it's not there." And he had no intention of letting her.

Her eyes were hot and angry. "Don't push me into a corner."

"I'm not. I'm just sick of chasing after you."

"Then stop. It's easy enough."

He took her hand. "No, it's not, and you know that. Stop running, Sloane. You're too gutsy for it."

"I'm not running," she flared.

"Oh yeah? What would you call it?"

Self-preservation, but it was too late for that and she knew it. Rising, Sloane crossed to the windows and looked out at the bending trees in the street below as the wind stripped them of their leaves. "I don't know what to do about you, Nick," she said finally. She turned to find him behind her.

He smiled faintly. "I haven't known what to do about you from the beginning."

"Then why pursue it?"

"Because you don't turn away from things just because they're hard."

"You just don't know…"

"Yes I do. Take a chance with me, Sloane," he urged softly. "Take a chance and see where we go." And he slid her into his arms.

At first, all she felt was measureless comfort. For a moment, she curled against him, feeling his warmth, his solidity. And for that moment, he was a shield against all of her fears, that calm, quiet voice reassuring her that everything would be all right.

Nick pressed a kiss on her hair. Her breath eased out in a sigh as he lowered his mouth to hers. It was a gentle touch, so soft it was barely there. Intended to sooth rather than arouse, the exploration lulled her into trust, into comfort. He smoothed his hands down her back, over the curve of her hips.

And the slow pulse of the blood in her veins began to speed.

This time when her mouth met his, her lips parted to taste, to touch, to feel the tempting stroke of his tongue. For once, he wasn't dragging her into an embrace. She went willingly, eagerly, and the power of it shocked them both. Tomorrow, she would deal with the aftermath; tonight was for savoring, tonight was for taking chances.

It was like bringing a match to gasoline, comfort flaming into urgency. For too long he'd held back, for too long they'd waited. Now it was all released at once.

His hands raced over her, sliding down her hips, curving over her breasts, seeking the long, lean lines of her body under the bulky sweater. Impatient, he slipped his hands under the cotton weave to feel her, only her, springy and taut and fevered. Her skin was silky smooth and when he moved his hand up to feel the curve of her breast under his palm, Sloane gasped against him.

It wasn't enough, he thought as he tugged the sweater off over her head. It still wasn't enough. He wanted her, opening up to him physically as she'd opened up to him emotionally. He pulled off her sweater even as she tugged at his shirt with eager hands. Pulse hammering, he pulled her to him, body to body, skin to skin. And the feel of her half-naked against his chest dragged him into a hot arousal where nothing was certain except desire, silk and flesh in his hands.

Sloane couldn't hold back a moan, even with Nick's mouth covering hers. It was as though every nerve in her body were on edge, every fiber of her focused on the heat and pressure of his bare chest against hers. She felt his breath, his heartbeat. But she wanted to feel even more. And with eager hands, she tore at the waistband of his jeans.

Making a noise of impatience, he lifted her in his arms and walked to the doorway of the living room.

"Bedroom?" he rasped.

"Across the hall," she murmured, her lips against his throat.

Nick nudged the door open with his shoulder, stepping into her bedroom with a sort of exhilarated anticipation. The room was as spare as the rest of her home, the sole notes of femininity and indulgence injected by the pile of pillows at the head of the bed and the vivid turquoise of the silk robe hanging on the open closet door. The weak light cast by the lamp on the bureau made her skin gleam.

He laid her down on the bed, pressing her against the pillows. Seeing her breasts, pale and luminous, only made him want to see her fully naked, to feel her fully naked. She'd dropped the barriers earlier that night; he wanted the final barrier of clothing gone.

Sloane stared at him, watched his eyes darken to jet. Giddy expectation surged through her. She felt him unbutton her jeans. The air was cool on her skin as he slipped the denim down. She raised her hips to help him and felt the helpless surge of arousal at the motion. Molten desire burst through her. Then she was naked before him but for the scrap of silk and lace at her hips.

With a quick, impatient movement he stripped off his shoes and jeans. His body in the dim light was all lean lines and hard rises of muscle. She caught her breath as he stepped to the side of the bed, reached for him but he pressed her back against the pillows.

Gaze locked on hers, he reached out to touch her with his fingertip. Heat burst through her. Every fiber of her being focused on that burning spot. Then he slid his finger down, over her shoulder, into the dip above her collar bone, along the slight rise of her breast to the sensitive tip. She caught her breath there but he didn't linger, moving down the smooth flat of her belly to the point where the black silk blocked his way. He edged his finger under it until she moaned and moved against him.

His teeth gleamed. "Black lace, Sloane? I like that." And then he hooked his fingers in the sides and dragged it down her legs, tossing it aside. "I like it even better off."

He eased onto the bed beside her to press his body against her and she had to moan again because it had been so long and it felt so, so good. And because she knew there was more.

With a kind of delirious joy Nick ran his tongue down the slender column of her throat and then lower, to where her breasts began with their fragile skin and their exquisite sensitivity. Sloane moved against him but he took his time, sampling, tasting every inch until his lips were against the stiffened flesh of her nipples. He ran his tongue over each hardened nub in turn, feeling her body quake, hearing her shocked gasp as he bit gently.

The quick whisk of pain made the arousal more intense and she felt the tightness coiling in her body, at the apex of her legs where all sensation met. Each squeeze of her nipples had her catching her breath and arching toward him. It had never been like this for her. Never had she moved without volition, moaned without thought, ached to be filled. Her body, which she'd thought she'd known intimately, was his entirely and he was showing her just how much control he had.

He did things, bewitching things with his hands, stroking the dip of her sides, the long muscles of her thighs, coming closer to where she yearned, burned to be touched. He didn't, though, just kept stretching it out, tempting her until she couldn't hold back. The feel of his muscles under her fingers, the groans of his own arousal as she trailed her fingertips down his belly made her giddy with desire.

It wasn't enough to make love, Nick thought feverishly. The need inside him was a grinding ache. He didn't just want her to submit, he wanted her twisting against him in abandon. He wanted to take her to where no other man had brought her, a place where she couldn't regret, she couldn't second-guess, she couldn't hold back.

A place where she was his.

He stroked his hand up the inside of her thigh and she quivered against him. When he brought just two fingertips higher, he could feel the goose bumps on her skin. And then he went higher still, to find her already slick and hot.

It nearly undid him to know that she was so aroused. It took him even closer to hear her helpless moan, to feel her hips move against his hand. He wanted more, though, much more before he was going to let himself go. And when he went, they were going to go together.

He moved down between her legs, then, teasing her with

his tongue, first the flat of her belly, then the long lines of her inner thighs. Even here, she was exquisitely sensitive. He traveled lower to press a kiss on the fragile skin, to her mons and felt her twist feverishly against him.

"Please, Nick, please." She couldn't bear any more, Sloane thought as he took her to a higher pitch of excitement. The heat of his tongue slid down lower. His breath was warm on her skin, dragging a moan from her. And then his mouth was pressed against her there, finally, and all the waiting and arousal and temptation coalesced into that one shivering point.

Sloane flung her head back against the pillow in shock, trying to force air into her lungs. He drove her relentlessly, with pressure and liquid strokes, curving his hands around her thighs to pull her to him. She clutched at his shoulders, felt his hair beneath her fingers. Never, she'd never experienced anything like this, hadn't known it was possible for her body to be electrified, half-mad, shuddering with arousal. She was strung wire tight, everything in her drawing down to that one point under the heat of his mouth, the tension rising, drawing in, contracting until it exploded outward, rushing through her to the tips of her fingers, sending her writhing against him for endless minutes until she finally crested and drifted down.

But his hands were already driving her up again. This time, the path was known and she raced up it, straining at his touch, knowing she wanted more. "I need you in me," she whispered, dragging at his shoulders.

He moved up until she could reach down to find him shuddering and hard against her fingers. When she would have moved her hand, he stilled it, sliding his body over hers, his breath uneven, his face taut with the battle for control. She felt the velvety soft tip of him brush the entrance where she was already slick and ready. "Look at me," he murmured. "Look at me when I go inside you."

And with a thrust of his hips he buried himself in her.

It ripped a cry from her. He filled her utterly, pressed in to the hilt. For that moment, there were no evasions, there was no escape. And when he began to move, his back muscles flexing under her fingers, it was as though they were one being, the sensations that started in his body ending in hers.

Each stroke, each slick caress brought her to a new pitch of pleasure. If she'd thought she'd experienced what he had to offer before, she'd been mistaken. It was incomplete, gratification without substance. Now, with his body intimately connected with hers, everything tied together.

Deep inside her slick heat, Nick fought to hold on, to prolong the feeling. Sloane twisted beneath him like a wanton. Eyes fevered with excitement, silken legs wrapped around him, she cried out each time he drove himself into her. It dragged him to the edge, knowing he could bring her to this, knowing that at this moment she was utterly abandoned to it, to him.

To what they made together.

She stared at him, her eyes widening in sudden shock and then she was jolting under him, clenching around him, crying out her pleasure as the orgasm broke through.

And it was that, finally, that tore away his control so that he surged once, twice and spilled himself.

They lay motionless, still intimately twined together as their hearts gradually slowed. Nick kissed Sloane's shoulder, utterly overwhelmed. If he told her he'd never experienced anything like it would she believe him? Would she understand? She'd given herself to him, maybe with reservations at first, but wholly and completely by the end.

How was it he only wanted more?

Sloane made a move to pull up the sheet and he stilled her hand. "Hey, what do you think you're doing?"

She flushed. "Covering up."

"Don't. I like looking at you. When I see you in clothes again, it'll give me something to tide me over until the next time."

"The next time?"

He stroked a hand down her waist. "Yeah, the next time. I'm planning on a lot of them."

She did twist loose then to sit on the edge of the bed. "Nick, just because this happened doesn't mean…"

"Doesn't mean what?"

"It doesn't mean we're having an affair."

"You don't strike me as the one-night-stand type, Sloane."

"Yes, well—"

She yelped in surprise as he snaked out an arm and tumbled her back against him.

"So I guess we've got to be something," he said, gathering her to him.

She rolled on top of him, leaning on his chest. "I don't like somethings. Somethings make me nervous."

"Then don't think about it."

"We have to think about it," she protested. "We can't just barge into something—"

He kissed the tip of her nose. "There you go, worrying about somethings again. How about this—let's try it out, see where it goes. Maybe you can have some fun for a change, God forbid. There is life outside of work, you know."

"The project is important to me."

"I know. And I also know you'll do a better job at it if you give yourself a break once in a while." He stroked her back, enjoying the feel of the firm rise of muscle below. "You know, laugh a little, maybe see a movie or actually get out of Boston."

Sloane sighed. "You understand, Nick, I can't let this become too much. You can call it whatever you want—"

"Or not."

"Or not," she agreed. "But it has to stay contained."

It was the classic guys' dream—sex with a beautiful woman, no commitment. So why did it bug him? "Limits, Sloane?"

Vulnerability flickered in her eyes. "Only one. No promises. Let's enjoy what's here right now. Okay?"

It wasn't okay. It was very far from okay, just how far, he was tempted to tell her. But he knew already that it would take very little to make her take flight. It was still too soon. He'd known there was passion in her, had glimpsed it briefly, but nothing had prepared him for the fire, the generosity, the wantonness of her lovemaking.

And he had no intention of letting her walk away. He'd go along with her conditions. For now.

Nick kissed her lightly. "All right."

Sloane let out a sigh of relief, then she sighed again, in reaction. "Mmm, what are you doing?"

"Well, if this is only going to be a brief, meaningless non-something, we'd better get the most we can out of it, hadn't we?"

"You might be right," she said, pressing herself against him.

"Bet on it."

Chapter Ten

Nick sat at his kitchen table reading a *Globe* article on the latest Big Dig fiasco and savoring the morning quiet. Some people liked day shifts. He'd take a night tour anytime. So he got dragged out of bed a few times. Having a nice leisurely start to the day more than made up for it.

It would have been better if he'd been sharing coffee and orange juice with Sloane, but so far he hadn't been able to convince her to spend the night. It was early days, he reminded himself and tried to find patience.

His cell phone burbled. He checked the display and flipped open the phone with a grin. "Whadda you want?"

"Get up on the wrong side of the bed again today?" Gabe asked. "You'd never survive in the hospitality industry, bud."

"Who said I wanted to?" Nick asked.

"I figured you'd be tired of getting cats out of trees and vacuuming the firehouse floor."

"You're the vacuuming guy, with that antique you run."

"That national historic landmark, you mean."

"You hoteliers are so touchy." Nick went to the refrigerator to pull out the carton of orange juice.

"All I gotta say is don't expect the family discount next time you want to bring a woman up here to impress her," Gabe told him. "Not that any woman would be misguided enough to get involved with you, of course."

Nick picked up his orange juice glass. "Did you call to talk about my personal life?

"Not after I've just eaten. Actually, I just called to see what's happening over the holiday. You going to be up?"

"Not this year. I'm scheduled for a night shift on Thanksgiving."

"Yeah, I heard that."

He could just imagine. "Let me guess. You've been talking to Jacob. Did he tell you to give me a lecture, too?"

"There are other ways to deal with you. Did I tell you I've taken up tae kwon do?"

Nick grinned. "You think that will help?"

"Just keep it in mind. You're only a couple of hours away, you know," Gabe said mildly.

"Three."

"That's in range. Close enough for me to come down and kick your ass."

"On your day off, you mean?"

"On a workday, if it's important enough." Gabe's voice sounded amused.

"If I keep one arm tied behind my back, maybe." The grin on Nick's face faded. "So why are you doing Jacob's errands, Gabe?"

"I'm not. I was over at the farm for dinner last night and Thanksgiving came up."

"Gee, now there's a surprise." Nick leaned back in his chair. "What did Jacob have to say? Or do I have to ask?"

There was a pause. "Actually, it wasn't Jacob, it was Ma."

Nick blinked. "No kidding. What did she say?"

"It wasn't what she said."

"Are you trying to learn mind reading in your tae kwon do?"

"No," Gabe said quietly. "I'm just trying to make my mother stop hurting so much. Look, Nick, you got problems with Jacob, take them out on him, okay? Not Ma."

Gabe always had known how to deliver an effective sucker punch, Nick reflected. Especially when he was right. "Gabe, I've been through this with Jacob already. Even if I leave as soon as shift ends the day before Thanksgiving, I won't hit the farm until nine or ten at night. And I'd have to peel out by noon the day of to make it back in time for start of shift. There's no way to make it work. I'd hardly be there before I'd have to go."

"You've done it other years. Work isn't the reason you don't want to come."

"Really? What is the reason, Great Swami?"

"I don't know. I'd like to think you've got some babe that you can't tear yourself away from. Of course, you and Jacob always seem pissed off at each other these days, so it could be that you just don't want to deal with him." Gabe paused. "Or it could be that you don't want to come up because it'll make you miss Dad too much and feel guilty that you're never around."

Jacob bludgeoned and was no match for Nick's stubbornness. Quick, clever Gabe whipped in quickly to poke weak spots Nick didn't know he had.

The silence stretched out.

"Nick, you there?"

"Yeah." He shifted. "I'm here."

"Look, I'm not trying to play pop psychologist and I'm not playing Jacob's errand boy. I just thought you should know that it matters to Ma, even if she wouldn't tell you so. It's your call, bro. She's not going to blame you for not coming. She'll understand. But it might make it a little easier for her to get through the day with you there. Jacob and I are always around. You being there will make it special." He cleared his throat. "For her, anyway."

Nick blew out a breath and accepted the inevitable. "All right. I've taken a couple of shifts lately for a guy. I'll see if I can call in the favor, get the night off. Maybe even a couple of days."

"Don't go overboard," Gabe said. "There's only so much of you we can take."

"Hey, Gabe?"

"Yeah?"

"Practice that tae kwon do," Nick suggested. "Practice hard."

Half an hour later he hung up from his mother, the warm pleasure in her voice still resonating in his ears. Gabe had been right. Bitter as it was to admit, Jacob had been right. It was too easy, sometimes, far away from the farm, to forget what it had to be like for her to live with the daily reminders.

To go to sleep at night in an empty bed.

In the months after Adam Trask had died, family duty had whispered to Nick that he should take a leave of absence, return to the farm to help out. Yet that meant days under Jacob's thumb and nagging concern about the guys at the firehouse. Responsibility—loyalty—pulled him in two directions at once. The only easy answer was avoidance. Maybe Sloane wasn't the only one who hid behind a job.

Sloane... He'd held her less than eight hours before. He'd see her in another eight.

It seemed unimaginably distant. Tapping the phone, he punched the speed dial for her number and listened to it ring.

· Sloane sat in her office typing an e-mail to the production manager for the Orienteer project. She clicked Send just as a calendar reminder flashed up on the screen. Pete's birthday Saturday, buy present.

The party, she remembered. There was a time when she wouldn't have missed it. Not now, though. Because of work, she told herself and tried to ignore the fact that it felt like an excuse. A gift, though—she wanted to get him something he'd like, something to let him know she was thinking of him.

The phone rang and she picked it up absently. "Sloane Hillyard."

"A fine thing, as far as I'm concerned."

"Nick." It felt good to hear his voice, dangerously good. "How are you?"

"Not nearly as good as I'd be if you were around. How are you?"

"I'm fine. Trying to get some work done." Of course, she'd have had more success if she hadn't repeatedly found herself staring into space and thinking of him. Not good, she told herself. It was supposed to be a simple fling. It wasn't supposed to get in the way of what was important. It wasn't supposed to *be* important.

"So what are you doing at work? Don't forget, my crew's on night shift tonight."

She opened her Web browser and began searching for gift

ideas. "Business doesn't just shut down because I'm not here. I've missed two days this week while I was at the firehouse."

"But you've always got your laptop on."

"That's just to keep my head above water."

"A very fetching head, by the way."

She couldn't help the smile. "My, what a smooth talker."

"Aren't I, though? So, you have lunch plans? I thought I could come by and take you out. I don't have to be at the firehouse until five."

The little buzz of pleasure hit before she could block it. *Keep it contained, Hillyard.* "I can't make lunch."

"Meeting?"

"I've got to run an errand. My nephew's birthday is tomorrow and I completely forgot about it. I've got to go get him something and stick it in overnight delivery."

"Where does he live?"

"Hartford."

"It's not that far. You could drive it down."

No, she couldn't. Sloane hesitated. "It's complicated."

"Your brother's son?"

"Yeah. It's just too hard to get away right now."

Nick thought of his conversation with Gabe. "Yeah, that's a pretty easy thing to tell yourself."

She bristled. "I don't recall asking you to sort out my life."

The seconds stretched out in silence. "I guess I deserved that," Nick acknowledged finally.

"I'm sorry I jumped on you. I know you're only trying to help. It's just not the time. Anyway, I'm stressed out. I've got to get a present, get it packed and mailed and still make it to my two o'clock."

"So let me help. We can find your nephew—has he got a name, by the way?"

"Pete."

"We can find Pete a present and I'll take care of getting it boxed up and mailed."

"You don't have to do that. I'll see you tonight at the firehouse, okay?" Tonight, when she could keep her distance while she figured out just how she felt about the affair she'd blundered into. Because for all that they avoided labels, they were having an affair.

"Tonight is too far away," Nick responded. "I want to see you before then. Look at it as a time-management issue—if you don't have to take time to mail the package, you can spare a little while to have lunch with me."

Lunch. That had been when she'd started losing her footing with him and she'd been tumbling ever since.

"So do we have a deal?"

"Deal," Sloane sighed.

Voices and footsteps echoed off the tiled floors of the Prudential Center as they walked past the ranks of stores and kiosks. There was too much to go through. It left her feeling simultaneously harried and overwhelmed.

Nick caught her hand in his. "So what do you want to get him? A Red Sox jersey, maybe?"

"No way. He's a Mets fan."

Nick looked at her dumbfounded. "A Mets fan? He lives in Hartford. Close enough for all right-thinking people to be Sox fans."

"I see." She fought a grin. "Well, his daddy grew up in Rochester, so he was brainwashed from a young age."

"Tragedy. I suppose everyone has their story. So what are you going to get him?"

It was the question she'd been asking herself all day. "That's the problem. I haven't got a clue."

Nick looked at her a long moment. "Don't see them very much, huh?"

"Not anymore," she said, her voice barely audible. "Not for a long time. I used to live with them back when I was going to UConn. Since Mitch died, though…" She spread out her hands helplessly.

Nick reached out and brushed his fingertips across her hair. "It's okay. We'll find something. How old is he?"

"Thirteen. Maybe I can just get him a gift certificate he can use for music or video games or something. Kids like that, don't they?"

"Nothing says I couldn't be bothered to think about you like a gift certificate. There's got to be a better choice."

"Don't rub it in. I already feel bad enough as it is."

They stood near the end of the mall, staring back at all the stores. With all the possibilities, it seemed impossible. It would have to be the gift certificate, whatever Nick thought.

A woman walked past them toward the Prudential Center stop on the Boston subway. She opened the door to walk inside and the strains of a street musician floated out into the air.

Nick snapped his fingers and turned to Sloane. "Got it."

"What?"

"Do you have a price limit?" he asked quickly. "Could you go a hundred?"

She considered. "Maybe. It'd have to be a pretty great gift. What are you thinking?"

"It'd make you look goo-ood," he wheedled.

"Spill it, Trask," she ordered.

He pointed through the glass doors of the mall to the music store across the street. "A guitar."

* * *

"So you wound up ahead," Nick said, unwrapping his sub. "The ultimate cool present, the store takes care of shipping and you come off smelling like a rose."

"Maybe not a rose," Sloane said, wishing it were that easy. "It's a good present, though. I think he's going to like it. It sounds like he's been having trouble lately. A guitar will give him an outlet and a focus."

"Happy to be of help."

They sat at the food court, the only way to manage a quick lunch under the circumstances. Sloane had picked out an acoustic guitar in glossy golden wood that the clerk had assured her would take abuse and see Pete from novice to proficient player. The offer to ship was a pleasant surprise. She should have gone straight back to work. The fact that she couldn't make herself leave without a bit more time with Nick gave her pause.

"So how long's it been since you've seen Pete?" he asked casually.

Sloane toyed with her baked potato. "Do we have to talk about this?"

"Maybe I'm curious."

"What am I, your lab experiment?"

"No, you're someone I care about. I'd like to know about what's bothering you."

It stopped her for a moment. Slowly, she nodded. "What makes you so sure this is?"

"The fact that you don't want to talk about it?" He gave her a level stare. "Would it help if I said I might have some idea how it is for you?"

Hot protest bubbled to her lips but then she looked at his face and saw that he wasn't patting her on the head. "Tell me."

"Last March I lost my father. He had a heart attack in the groves during the spring sap run."

"I'm sorry."

He gave her a half smile. "So am I. I never thought it would be so hard to go home. I walk around the farm, the house, and I see him everywhere."

Sloane looked away.

"And I've been staying away, just like you have." Nick hesitated. "Sometimes the easy thing isn't the right thing. I've been staying down in Boston for all the good reasons—work, side job, fixing up my house. And I've been trying like hell to avoid thinking about what my mom's been going through."

The same way she'd been avoiding thinking about Candy and Pete. "So you think I should go down there?"

"I don't think it's for me to say. I'm still trying to figure out my own life. I will tell you that I was going to stay away for Thanksgiving this year. My brothers talked me into coming. I'm glad they did."

"You're going back to the farm."

"Yeah," he said, shifting a little. "I don't know what it's going to be like, but it feels like the right thing to do. So," he focused in on her, "got plans for the holiday?"

She gave him a suspicious look. "I'm working, at least part of it. You're on a night tour on Thanksgiving, remember?"

"Yeah, that was my excuse," he said. "Not anymore. I traded with the B-shift captain. I'm going to head up to the farm as soon as we get off the day before."

"Vermont, right?"

"Maple syrup." He finished his sandwich. "I don't suppose you'd want to go with me?"

Sloane blinked. "I can't go with you to Thanksgiving."

"Why not?"

Where did she begin? "It's a family holiday. It's where you bring someone that you've got a *thing* with."

"A thing sounds suspiciously like *something*. Off-limits, remember?"

"You know what I mean. Someone you're serious about."

"Not necessarily. I've brought friends along before and so have my brothers. My younger brother," he amended. "I'm not sure Jacob even *has* any friends. Anyway, back up. If we're not having a thing, then it shouldn't matter to you what my family thinks. After all, by that standard you won't be seeing them again."

"And in the meantime I get grilled as Nick's potential squeeze." She stared balefully at the Chick-fil-A stand. "Anyway, I don't need to be your charity invite."

"What's that supposed to mean?"

"I get it fairly regularly around the holidays. People ask what I'm doing, I say hanging, and there's this awkward silence and then presto, an invitation. People don't like the thought of me being alone. It makes them uncomfortable."

"Maybe they just want your company."

Her response was a snort.

Nick leaned forward. "You've been getting a lot of practice at pushing people away, Sloane. Why don't you try something different? Get out of town for a change. Meet some friendly people. Eat too much turkey and just kick back for a couple of days. Bathe in maple syrup."

"A couple of days?"

"A day and a half. Wednesday night to Friday afternoon.

You can tour the farm. Hell, you can hang out with Jacob. He'll be no threat to you. He's more antisocial than you are."

"And what are you going to say to them about your guest?"

He crumpled up his sandwich wrapper. "The truth. That we're seeing each other and I think you're good company."

She raised an eyebrow. "I'm good company?"

"Well, my usual rule is to invite people I don't like a lick, but I'm making an exception with you. Don't make a federal case out of it."

She scowled, tossing her napkin down on the tray. "I'm not making a federal case."

"You said you'd never been to Vermont. Come with me." He paused. "Unless the idea of meeting a few Trasks scares you."

"I'm not afraid to meet anyone," she retorted, knowing he was baiting her but powerless to keep from reacting.

"Well, then, it's easy. Come with me. Or am I going to have to mud wrestle with you over it?"

"You can get that idea right out of your head."

"Come with me, Sloane." He looked at her, the fun ebbing out of his eyes. "It'll be easier for me to get through it with you there."

And what could she do but say yes?

Chapter Eleven

Night shift on the apparatus floor and the air was filled with controlled urgency. The ladder crew hurried to don their breathing gear, slipping the harnesses on over their turnouts, pressing their masks against their faces. Breathing the compressed air, they stood ready to do battle with the flames.

Nick clicked his stopwatch and clapped. "Forty-five seconds, guys. Not bad. Okay, pop quiz. Sorensen, when your mask starts vibrating for your low-air warning, how much time do you have left?"

Sorensen took off his mask and considered. "Four or five minutes." He gave a quick grin. "Except for a blowhard like O'Hanlan. He might get thirty seconds if he's lucky."

There was a moment of surprised silence and then the group broke out into guffaws.

"I think that was the first time I've ever heard you make a joke, Sorensen," O'Hanlan said.

"Hard to get a word in edgewise with you around, O'Hanlan," Sorensen told him.

"You got that right, probie," Knapp said.

"Come December, he's not going to be a probie anymore," Nick said.

"Red as a grown-up firefighter?" O'Hanlan asked. "You know what that means, Knapp."

Knapp nodded vigorously. "He cooks us all a steak dinner. I like rib eye, Sorensen, in case you want to plan ahead."

"I'll be sure to stop at Burger King on my way to work that day."

"You hearing this, Nick?" O'Hanlan demanded. "He's getting mouthy now that he's almost earned his badge."

"Around you, O'Hanlan, it's self-defense," Nick said. He scanned his drill sheet and decided to have mercy on the crew. "Okay, we've pretty well done our hour. Let's call it good."

There was a general exodus. Nick was gathering together his notes when he realized that Sorensen was still hanging around.

He glanced up. "You need something, Sorensen?"

"I was hoping I could talk with you."

"Sure."

The probie looked at the corners of the room and cleared his throat. "I'm coming to the end of my probationary period, cap. Outside of overhauling and ventilating, I've only done searches in four fires. I want to work on one of the rescue squads eventually. When am I going to start really going on search detail?"

"When you've got a little more experience."

"How can I get more experience without going into fires?"

It was a logical question, Nick thought. He'd been slow to send Sorensen in for search and rescue, mostly because the kid looked so young. He wasn't a kid, though, he was a man.

Maybe it was time to start giving him the kinds of chances he was looking for.

Nick nodded. "No guarantees but I'll start trying to give you some more fire time. Keep working on your drills, do a good job inside and when it comes time I'll try to give you a recommendation for the rescue company."

"No kidding?"

"If you get it, it'll be because you've earned it. Fair enough?"

"Fair enough."

Nick glanced over Sorensen's shoulder to see Sloane walking up the stairs, her hips swaying. And that quickly, desire twisted through him.

Maybe she'd worked six shifts without seeing an honest-to-God fire but the ride alongs had given Sloane an appreciation for life in a firehouse. Including the experience of having yet another dinner interrupted by the bells. Not a medical aid call, this time, but a trash fire on a corner with a vacant lot. They'd put it out using the tank on the pumper and the ladder crew stumbled around on the heap to dig out the last sparks.

Now, they were back in the firehouse. Nick walked around the truck in his turnout pants, cleaning up. He'd shrugged off his red suspenders to dangle jauntily around his hips. His gray T-shirt stretched across his chest.

Was it any wonder that every woman she knew harbored a secret affection for firefighters? He looked her way and something twisted sweetly inside her. They didn't have a thing, she reminded herself. It was nothing serious, but, oh, it stretched a smile across her face.

Nick glanced over at her and stopped. For a long minute he just looked at her. Then, as though he couldn't help it, he walked straight over to her and brushed a hand over her hair.

She raised her brows. "Is that wise, Captain Trask?"

"What, you missed the general stampede for the kitchen? I can assure you, everyone's inside lining up at the microwave."

"What about you, aren't you hungry?"

His gaze was steady. "Oh, yeah."

"What do you suggest we do about it?"

He rested a hand against the ladder truck and leaned toward her. "I've got a few ideas we could try out. For example, we could—"

"Hey, you guys are missing out on warmed-over pork chops up here," Beaulieu's voice hollered down from the stairs. "Everything's all set."

Nick's eyes closed for a moment. "On our way," he called and gave Sloane a resigned shrug. "Life on the clock."

Sloane turned toward the stairs, tugging him after her. "Come on, I could use some dinner, anyway."

His lips twitched. "You are kind of skinny."

Sloane gave a sniff. "Junkyard dogs are skinny. I am not skinny. The term is *willowy*, Trask." They mounted the stairs.

He traced one finger down the center of her back, almost making her lose her footing. "Deliciously willowy, Hillyard," he murmured. "I'd be happy to show my appreciation at an appropriate time."

The warmed over pork chops, she had to admit, were not half-bad.

The dormitory was black as pitch. Nick rolled onto his back and stared up into the darkness at the invisible ceiling. He could hear Sloane's soft breathing in the darkness, felt the deep curl of need. She was only feet away, so close he could almost touch her.

Almost, but not quite.

Dinner had given way to a movie that he barely remembered. He'd sat in the darkened lounge, staring at the screen and conscious only of Sloane sitting in the chair next to him.

At this hour, it was as though the entire world were lost in slumber and only he lay awake. Wondering. Wondering if she slept, wondering if she dreamed, wondering if she lay awake staring into the darkness, wanting the way he wanted. If they'd been alone, he'd have gone to her. Nothing would have stopped him. He could imagine the feel of her sleek body, the silken spill of her hair against his cheek, the taste of her mouth, avid and hungry under his.

The seconds dragged by, stretched to minutes in the almost imperceptible march to morning.

There was a deep creak as someone rolled over and O'Hanlan's unmistakable grinding snore filled the air. Nick sighed. He reached beside his bed, feeling for the beanbag he kept there, as they all did. With unerring aim that spoke of night after night of practice, he lobbed it toward the source of the noise. There was a soft "oof" in the darkness and the snoring stopped.

And the seconds returned to dragging torturously by.

How long could a night last? Sloane wondered with a small stab of desperation. She shifted slightly on the mattress trying to find some position that would let her drift off. All around her there was only sleep. In her there was only awareness.

She wanted him. There was nothing to distract her from that knowledge. No battle, no sparring, only the thought that he lay so near and absolutely unreachable. She turned, but sleep remained stubbornly elusive.

Finally, she flipped back the covers and rose to pad noiselessly across the dormitory to the doorway. Maybe she couldn't sleep, she thought, easing the door shut behind her, but she shouldn't have to lie awake thirsty. A glass of water first and then maybe she'd distract herself with work or a book.

Her stockinged feet were quiet on the floor as she walked down the hall to the kitchen. She didn't need to switch on a light to see her way. Moonlight shone through the window across the floor, a broad swath of it, ghostly and serene. Sloane went to the window and looked out at the trees outside. The entire world had gone silent, hypnotic and washed clean in the pale light.

She thought afterward that she'd known he would come. The small sound didn't make her jump, but rather turn in expectation. His eyes were silver, his mouth intent. In silence, he came to her and in silence she flowed into his arms.

The moonlight spilled over her face, silvering her lashes, bringing her skin the pale translucence of marble. She looked, Nick thought, ethereal, fragile. In his arms she felt warm and alive. For a long time it was simply enough to hold her, browsing over her face with soft, nibbling kisses, feeling her heat.

"I want you," he murmured softly. Her response was to pull his face to hers. Her answer was on her lips. All heat and temptation, the kiss lured and aroused. For every desire it satisfied, it ignited a dozen more. Every touch made him want, every taste made him hunger. Desperation colored every move; there could never be enough.

Down the hall and behind the doors, a dozen men slumbered. Here, in this shadowy room, there were only the two of them.

The lights went up and the abrupt sound of the alarm bells shattered the stillness. They broke apart, breathing hard. Nick turned toward the dormitory. The others were just rising. Yawning, they stepped to the fire pole to slide down to the apparatus floor, taking no notice when Sloane trailed in after Nick.

Downstairs, the firefighters pulled on their turnouts. Sloane frowned at the stiff canvas. "They're the quickest way," Nick advised. "Step in and go."

Sloane dragged up the pants and threw the suspenders over her shoulders. The canvas was stiff, the boots awkward and heavy as she climbed up into the cab of the truck. So why was it she could still feel that wanton sense of arousal? Every inch of her was piercingly aware of Nick beside her. She didn't trust herself enough to look at him as the truck drove out of the lighted garage into the darkness of the streets.

"What I want to know is why these people always pick the middle of the night to have these fires," O'Hanlan groused. "I was having this great dream. I won the lottery and was sailing down the bay in Florida on this great big yacht. How people set their houses on fire at 2:00 a.m. is something I'll never figure."

"Nineteen-twenties' wiring and insulation, probably." Nick gestured at the dilapidated triple-decker ahead of them, smoke already seeping out of its second-floor windows. "Look at the place."

They pulled to the front of the building, by the knot of neighbors and the spectators who always seemed to have some sixth sense about fires. Ahead of them, the pumper had dropped hose by the hydrant ahead of the house and driven forward to give the ladder truck room. Already, the engine crew was stretching lines from the pumper to the hydrant.

Nick tapped Beaulieu on the shoulder. "See if you can find out anything about who might be inside." He turned to flag down Giancoli of Engine 58. "What's the word on occupants?" Nick asked as he tightened the harness on his breathing mask.

"Three apartments, one on each level."

Nick glanced over to Sloane. She stood staring at the fire like Joan of Arc facing the armies of France. He wished he could go to her. He didn't have that luxury. As ranking officer, he ran the scene until the district chief showed up.

Beaulieu hurried over. "Everybody's already out," he said, gesturing toward a small clutch of stunned-looking adults and crying children, shivering in the night cold.

That made it easier, though they still needed to run through the building just in case. "Let's get a one-and-a-half inch line in there," Nick directed. He turned to the ladder crew. "Beaulieu, Knapp, I want you on the roof ventilating. O'Hanlan, run the stick up over at the corner where the A wall meets the B wall, away from the smoke. Sorensen?" He looked at him. "You and I are on inside detail."

Excitement leapt in the probie's eyes. "I'm on it, cap."

It might have been nearly three in the morning, but people were straggling out of their houses, awakened by the noise. Unfortunately, the police hadn't shown up yet for crowd control, Nick thought in annoyance. Without the other companies on the alarm, who had yet to appear, he couldn't spare the time.

The sound of gasoline-powered saws sounded from the roof where Beaulieu and Knapp were cutting holes to let out hot gases and smoke. Once they'd ventilated the fire, the inside teams would have an easier time.

Suddenly, one of the children in the knot of occupants began to wail. A women crouched down to talk with him, but he shook her off and came pelting over to the firefighters.

"T.O.'s still up there," he burst out, even as a man who might have been his father hurried over to scoop him up.

"Don't bug the firemen, Jamal. They're busy." Behind them, a pair of enginemen hauled a hose line through the front door.

The boy twisted his in father's hands. "What's gonna happen to T.O.?"

Nick crouched down in front of him. "Is there someone still inside?"

"T.O.," the boy cried. "I want T.O."

"His hamster," the father said apologetically.

All of his problems should be so easily handled. "Okay. Where is it?"

"On the second floor, back bedroom, against the window."

Nick grinned. "Hey Sorensen, want to go rescue a hamster?"

The probie hefted his six-foot-long ceiling hook. "I got a nose for hamsters, cap."

"You mean a nose *like* a hamster," O'Hanlan heckled him as he headed toward the front door.

It wasn't much of a fire, Sloane reassured herself. White smoke streamed toward the sky from the hole the roof team had cut. White smoke was good. White smoke meant the fire was out, so why was she still riven with anxiety? To take her mind off it all, she turned toward the spectators. "Okay, every-one, move back," she said with the authority the turnouts gave her. "Let's leave the crews room to work." Repeatedly, she glanced over at the building, searching for an indicator of progress.

"Miss?" Sloane turned to see an older woman behind her. "Can you tell me how bad it is? I live on the top floor." Her face was worn, her eyes worried. Although she twisted her hands together in unconscious tension, her shoulders were squared and resolute beneath her shabby robe.

Anxiety was forgotten in a rush of sympathy. Sloane caught at the woman's hands. They were icy cold. "What's your name?"

"Latrice Winston."

"I'm Sloane. You're out safely, that's what matters."

"Everything I own is in there." Her voice wobbled for an instant, but she raised her chin. "I got to know what's happened."

It wrung her heart. "Here, sit." Sloane drew her down to the running board of the ladder truck. "I don't know the status, but I promise you I'll do everything I can to find out for you. Let me get you something to keep you warm first, though."

After she'd draped a red firehouse blanket around the woman's shoulders, Sloane turned to the house in time to see Sorenson and Nick emerge with a small cage.

"T.O.," a little boy shrieked and raced over to him. Grinning, Sorenson handed him the cage. Inside, a furry chestnut-colored ball stirred and unrolled to inspect them with beady black eyes.

"Here you go, one special-delivery hamster."

The boy clutched the cage to his chest. "T.O., you made it, buddy."

And Nick had made it, Sloane thought with a surge of relief. He was out of the house, away from the fire.

Safe.

She walked up behind him. "Hamster search and rescue?"

"I'm one of the best."

"I'm sure there's no one I'd trust more. How's the fire?"

"History. It wasn't much to begin with." He shook his head. "Looked like a candle tipped over in one of the second-floor units, caught the sofa and the curtains and a little bit of the wall. We'll spend an hour or so here overhauling to be sure there aren't any little pockets of embers, but the excitement's over."

And finally the iron clutch on her stomach could ease entirely. Then she remembered her mission. "How's the third floor? Any damage?"

"Clean. We're going to have to go into the walls to see if anything's involved up there, but unless we find that the fire's spread, we won't bring in water."

Sloane glanced over at Latrice and gave her the thumbs-up. "That's great. I have to go pass the message along."

"Who was doing crowd control?"

"I was."

"You?"

She shrugged. "It was a way I could help. Nothing's harder than watching."

"I know." He stared at her and she felt the buzz begin again. It wasn't what she'd choose, but choice had become irrelevant. He wasn't what she wanted but he was who she had to have. Silver-gray, his gaze delved into hers until it was inside her.

Nick took a step back and gave a brief smile. "Well, we've still got work to do here. Get comfortable, because we're going to be awhile. We've got business to finish."

And when the overhauling was done and they were back in quarters, she and Nick would finish the business between them.

Bright lights, loud thumps and voices. Dragged up from sleep, Sloane opened her eyes, staring groggily out into the dorm at men who rose slowly, stumbling to the bathroom in the hope that a splash of cold water might make them feel more human. She fumbled for her watch on the little bedside ledge. Six in the morning. They'd pulled back in to the station, she recalled, a whopping hour and a half before. An hour and a half of sleep.

It wasn't enough.

She rolled over, away from the light. And with her cheek to the pillow, she locked eyes with Nick.

He'd been awake for long moments watching her sleep, her hair like a pale cloud of fire against the white of the pillow-case. When she rolled over to face him, he quite simply lost his breath. Less than a yard of space stretched out between them but it was spanned by the heat that sprang up instantly, demanding satisfaction. Only the sounds of the fire crew stopped her from going to him. Only the knowledge that others were in the room prevented him from reaching for her.

They stirred and rose at the same time, keeping their distance from one another. Perhaps no one else would have noticed, but the certainty was there, in their eyes. When she rubbed her arms, he felt her skin. When he stretched, her hands knew the feeling of muscles flexing beneath them. The boundary between imagination and reality, awareness and experience thinned dangerously. They stared at each other, neither wanting to leave the room, to leave the other's sight.

The scent of coffee drifted into the dormitory, drawing the others. Sloane turned into the women's bathroom. Her reflection looked back at her from the mirror, eyes huge, mouth soft. She started to pull her hair back and then on second thought left it loose to tumble down over her shoulders. The soft cotton of her shirt feathered over her skin like a caress.

And when she stepped back into the hall, she saw Nick walking from his office to the kitchen.

It wasn't that she stopped, simply that her muscles no longer accepted the command to move. He was taut, lean in jeans and a fresh T-shirt. He hadn't taken time to shave away the dark overnight shadow on his jaw. His hair was damp, slicked back, but already loose strands hung down over his forehead.

Sexuality. It vibrated around him until she thought she could almost see the air wavering with it. Her heart slammed against her ribs in a violent tattoo.

To want this much was terrifying.

Nick saw the rise of Sloane's breasts as she caught her

breath. Desire wrapped around him until he wanted to groan with the need. It was like the moments before flashover, heat rising, coming closer to the instant when everything would spontaneously combust. She was so close. Just a few steps would take him to her. He watched.

She waited.

The edge of control sharpened.

"Hey, Trask, if you want any of this coffee you'd better finish up and get in here." The voice broke them free just as Nick approached the point where nothing mattered but touching her. He had to move away while he still could.

"We'd better…"

Sloane nodded, walking the few steps into the kitchen, trying to stay as far from Nick as possible. If they brushed against each other she didn't know what she would do.

Her every movement felt distinct, underlined with importance, with the certainty that he watched. She took the last empty seat at the table, dimly aware that the room had filled with the next crew, the hubbub of conversation filled with descriptions of the fire. Nick leaned against a cupboard. Their eyes locked.

Arousal hummed through her entire body, saturating the air between them. She wondered that it wasn't visible, like the rising, crackling sparks of a Jacob's ladder. The minutes ticked by unbearably. She waited for release.

O'Hanlan looked at his watch. "Well, boys," he said, clapping one of the day crew on the shoulder. "Looks like it's that time again. I can't think of better hands to leave the gig to. I'm outta here." He grabbed his shoulder bag and headed for the door. The rest of the shift began to trickle out.

In the parking lot, Sloane started her car. She pulled out to the driveway and paused. He would follow. She knew it.

The streets stirred with early-morning activity. Everything seemed unbearably vivid, unbearably clear. She didn't look for the red truck behind her.

She didn't have to.

The drive seemed endless, yet in a surprisingly short time she was parking in the small lot behind her house, turning off the ignition. Her feet made hollow thumps on the porch boards.

With a throbbing roar, Nick's car pulled in behind hers. At her back door, Sloane stopped and turned. His eyes were turbulent. Her satchel dropped from suddenly nerveless fingers. Swift, intent, he walked straight to her and wordlessly dragged her against him.

The kiss was explosive, as though a spring that had been coiled to the strain point, then coiled just a bit more had been suddenly, violently released. His mouth savaged hers and she gloried in it. Her fingers clawed at his back and desire pulsed in her. When they broke away they were both breathless, speechless, knowing only what they wanted from each other.

Sloane's fingers shook as she fit the key into the lock. It took an unbearably long time to get upstairs to her flat. And when she'd unlocked it, they fell inside, their mouths fused together, stoking up the heat, higher and higher.

Her lips moved hot and eager under his, her hands dragged at his shirt. He shrugged out of his jacket and pressed her toward the couch. The bedroom was way too far.

They'd made love night after night, but never like this. This time, desire owned them. They were swift and impatient to strip off every scrap of clothing. Naked, he would have slowed, but she drove him more quickly, her need egging him on. Tangled together, they fell to the couch, their mouths and hands frenzied.

Nick's mouth raced down her neck to feast on her breasts,

his tongue flicking over the nipples, the faint nip of his teeth making her cry out. The tug of desire started an answering throb lower down. Pleasure pressed itself to the point where it blurred into pain, intensity overwhelming the nerves' ability to discern the difference.

Never like this, all flame, possession and plunder. She discovered her power in a blaze of passion. The brush of her hands over his chest, his nipples, made his breath hiss out, made him jolt. When she followed the path of her fingers with her lips, she tore a groan from him. She ranged across his chest, dropping lower to nibble over his belly, then lower still.

And with her lips and her tongue she saw how far she could take him from civilized man.

His body arched, caught in a shudder of pleasure. He rode it almost to the point of no return, then reached down to pull her up to him again. When their mouths met, hers could have been made for him alone.

She surrounded him, the sleekness of her body, the softness of her skin. The dark taste of her threatened to overwhelm his senses. His hands ranged over her body, searching for hidden sensitivity, driving her, always driving her higher. When his fingers slid up the inside of her thighs she gasped. She arched as she felt his touch.

Then he took her up again, more intensely than she'd ever known, her body rising, rising to a crescendo. When he sensed she was teetering on the edge he shifted. Their cries melded as he plunged into her, then they drove each other to that final precipice and tumbled off, together.

Chapter Twelve

Sloane stared at the dark ribbon of pavement unrolling in the car's headlights. If it had been daylight, she could have been distracted by the Vermont countryside they were driving through. Instead, she could only focus on the visit that lay ahead. At least it was getting late. They'd left as soon as possible after the end of shift, but holiday traffic had conspired to delay them. Now, it was pushing ten-thirty.

The later the better, as far as she was concerned. With every minute that passed, her misgivings mounted. She'd been out of her mind to agree to come up for the holiday. Small talk wasn't her forte at the best of times, and certainly being grilled by family who saw her as a serious girlfriend—or threat—was far from the best of times. Maybe everyone would be in bed when they'd arrive and she'd get an overnight reprieve.

The headlights picked out a large sign painted in the vivid

colors of fall foliage. "Trask Family Farm and Sugar House" it read, with an arrow pointing toward a branch road.

"Almost there," Nick said.

Sloane felt the clutch of nerves in her stomach. "I don't belong here. Why don't you drop me off at that inn we passed a couple miles back and have your weekend with your family?"

The dash lights of the car showed the gleam of his smile. "Because I want you here with me."

Ahead, high-wattage arc lights created bright pools in the parking lot of what she assumed was the Trask farm. "If you really cared about me, you'd take me somewhere else," she said, only half joking as the car slowed.

"It's because I care about you that I'm not. Stop trying to get out of it. They're not going to bite." He turned in and headed to the far right of the lot, searching out a narrow lane that threaded its way past the sugar house and gift shop. Behind loomed the dark bulk of a farmhouse; a yellow light on the side porch gleamed in welcome.

Nick's family might not bite but she had a pretty good idea they were going to be very curious about Nick's friend. "What did you tell them about me?"

He flashed a grin as he stopped on the broad parking apron and turned off the ignition. "I told them you were in the witness protection program and they couldn't ask you any questions. Oh, and that you've already taught me a dozen new sexual positions."

Amused despite herself, Sloane gathered up her purse and opened the door. "A dozen, huh?"

He popped the trunk. "I didn't think they were ready for the real number."

Around them, the woods stretched out dark and silent. In

Cambridge and Boston, there was always light, always noise. Here, the chill night was its own presence. Sloane shivered.

"Come on, let's get inside," Nick said, grabbing the bags and leading her up the steps of the little porch. He opened the door without knocking and walked inside.

There was no place she could walk into like that, Sloane realized in an instant of painful clarity as she followed him into the mudroom. What was it Frost had said, "Home is the place that, when you have to go there, They have to take you in"? The only home she had was the one she paid for herself.

Nick walked through the mudroom and stopped at the door to the inside of the house. "Come on, what are you waiting for?"

Sloane shook back her hair and followed him.

The kitchen was warm, fragrant and welcoming after the raw November night. It probably looked just about the way it had a century before, with a broad planked floor and butter-colored wainscoting. On one wall, a granite fireplace big enough to stand in held an enormous copper kettle. Pots and pans dangled from an overhead beam. A swinging door led to what she assumed was a dining room; another empty threshold presumably led to the rest of the house.

In the center of the room sat a thick oak table with massive turned legs. On it, checkered dishtowels covered cooling pies. A half-dozen of them. Just how many people was Molly Trask expecting to feed? Sloane wondered a little desperately.

On the stove, onions and celery sizzled quietly. A spoon in the spoon rest and a pot holder tossed down on the counter gave clues that the cook was nearby.

"Hey, Ma," Nick called, walking over to turn off the burner. "You planning to burn the house down?"

"Nicholas?" Wiping her hands on her apron, a wiry-looking woman walked into the kitchen from the inside of the house.

Nick grinned and swept her into a bear hug.

"I can't believe your timing," she scolded when they were done. "I sit here all night waiting for you and the one minute I take to use the restroom you show up."

"We got a call a couple of weeks ago for a fire started by someone who'd left a pan on the stove unattended."

"I know, I know," she said with a flush. "I promise I won't do it again. Now introduce me to your friend."

"Sloane Hillyard, this is my mother. Ma, this is Sloane."

"Welcome." Blue eyes set like Nick's looked at Sloane in amusement. "My name's Molly, in case you want an actual name."

Sloane grinned. "Thanks."

She'd given Nick his good looks, but Molly Trask appeared to have other things to worry about than vanity. She wore an apron over jeans and a flannel shirt. Her iron-gray hair swung down to her jaw. Her skin might have shown signs of weathering, but it showed more signs of laughter. Crossing to the stove, she stirred the onions. "Can I get you coffee or tea or something?"

"Just some water for me, thanks," Sloane said. "No coffee at this hour or I'll never sleep."

"I'll take coffee, but I'll make it myself," Nick said.

"Like his father, this one," Molly said fondly as she scraped the cooked onions and celery into a bowl. "He'd drink coffee at midnight and still go out like a light. Same thing with Jacob," she added, nodding toward the sudden noise in the mudroom.

"Jacob what?" The kitchen door opened and a bear of a man walked in, all black beard and bulk in his parka, stamping the snow off his boots.

"Jacob's here to meet our guests," Molly filled in.

Vivid blue, his eyes flickered over Sloane before fastening on Nick. "You're parked in a soft patch."

"A soft patch?"

Jacob looked around. "Yeah. I need to get the whole apron rolled. They're predicting rain tonight and if it doesn't freeze, you're going to have a mess."

"I guess I'd better move it, then," Nick replied.

"Hello, Jacob. Oh, hello, Nick. Haven't seen you in a while. That's right, it's been since spring." Molly spread plastic wrap over the bowl and put it in the refrigerator. "Honestly, you could at least say hello, you two."

A corner of Nick's mouth twitched. "Hey, J.T."

Jacob stuck his hand out in resignation. "Nick."

No hugs, no shoulder pounding, Sloane noticed. An awkward current of tension ran through the room, something not quite comfortable.

"Jacob, this is Sloane Hillyard. Sloane, this is Jacob, my older brother."

She found her hand enveloped in Jacob's. She could see the resemblance now that she looked, but in contrast to Nick's ease, Jacob seemed awkward, too big for the kitchen. He belonged outdoors, she thought.

"Nice to meet you," he muttered. "Well, I just came in to tell you. The back door's open. I'll see you tomorrow."

Molly stifled a yawn as Jacob disappeared. "It's probably time for me to go to bed, too." She walked over to kiss Nick and squeezed Sloane's shoulder. "The guest room is made up."

The bedroom could have been in a B and B, with colonial blue walls and scatter rugs covering the wide-planked hardwood floor. She caught the scent of freesia from the vase of fresh flowers that sat on a maple bureau that had been polished until it glowed. The bed was a spindle-topped four-poster, with an intricate quilt laid over the top of the double-sized mattress.

Sloane cleared her throat. "We're not staying in here, are we?"

"You don't like it?"

"With your mother in the house? It doesn't quite seem right."

The corners of Nick's mouth turned up. "Old-school. I like that."

"I'm not a prude," she muttered, blushing furiously. "It just…well, it feels disrespectful."

Nick leaned in to kiss her. "God, I adore you. You didn't let me finish. You're staying in the guest room, alone. I'll be bunking in Jacob's house, out back."

"Well, you don't need to go to a whole 'nother building," she protested.

His eyes crinkled with humor. "I'm old-school, too. Relax. I'll come over in the morning and make you coffee."

She smelled it before she even opened her eyes. Sloane took a blissful sniff. Any man who would be up and making coffee for her at six-thirty in the morning was her hero.

Or heroine, she discovered a few minutes later as she walked into the kitchen to find Molly Trask wrestling with the turkey and cursing a blue streak.

Sloane stopped in the doorway. "Need some help?"

Molly glanced ruefully over her shoulder. "Yes, actually. If you could just hold the drumsticks together so I can get them tied, we'll be all set. They keep slipping out of the string."

It was about the biggest turkey she'd ever seen, Sloane thought as she washed her hands. "Just how many people are you expecting today?" She pulled the ends of the legs together so Molly could tie them securely.

"I think we're up to sixteen now, give or take a grandniece or -nephew," Molly said, snipping the ends of the string with kitchen shears. "The boys, you, my in-laws, their three kids and their families and a neighboring couple who have known us forever." She ticked them off on her fingers. "Now if you could just help me get the bird into the roaster, we'll be all set. I'll lift him up and you slide the roaster under," she directed. "Ready? One, two, *three*."

The turkey safely transferred, Molly wiped off her hands and leaned against the counter. "If you want coffee, there are mugs in that cabinet over there. Tea, too."

"Coffee's perfect," Sloane assured her.

"Well, how about if you pour us a couple of cups while I get old Tom in the oven?"

Sloane searched out a pair of pretty blue ceramic mugs. "These are nice."

"Nick got those for me one year for Christmas. He said they reminded him of my eyes. Always did have a romantic streak, that boy."

"Really?"

Molly picked up a dish of melted butter. "Well, he could hardly be a firefighter without it, could he? I mean, a lot of it is hard work, but a lot of it is making a difference, maybe saving a life. That takes being a romantic, doesn't it?"

And romantics didn't agree to relationships that had no future, Sloane thought uneasily.

Molly basted the turkey. "I hope butter doesn't alarm you. Nick's brother Gabriel brought home a girl one year who wouldn't eat a thing once she saw I was cooking with butter. Honestly, it's Thanksgiving, for heaven's sakes. Every now and then you throw out the rules." She shut the oven door briskly. "I'm a stickler for basting a turkey."

"My sister-in-law used to swear by cooking the turkey upside down until the last hour and then flipping it."

"Your sister-in-law?"

Sloane hesitated. "My brother's widow, I mean."

Molly's gaze softened. "Nick mentioned that you'd lost your brother. I'm sorry. It must be hard."

"It is," Sloane said simply. And to her surprise the sympathy was easy to accept for once, rather than embarrassing. Few people she knew were aware of her loss, a loss she kept fiercely private. Perhaps it was easier with Molly Trask because they had loss in common. Sloane looked at her. "Nick told me about your husband, too. I hope you're getting along all right."

"I keep thinking it will get easier. Does it?" For an instant, Molly's eyes held a glint of pleading.

She deserved frankness, Sloane thought. "Maybe. It's always there waiting for you when you least expect it. After a while, though, you stop getting ambushed so often."

"How long has it been since your brother passed away?"

She thought for a moment. "Five years." And it still seemed like yesterday.

"I can't believe it'll be a year in spring for us. It still takes me by surprise. Something will happen and I'll think, oh, I have to tell Adam and then I remember that I can't. When does that stop?"

"I don't know. For a long time I thought it never would. It's gotten easier lately, though." When had that happened, she wondered. Since she'd been so busy with the gear? Or since Nick? "I try to focus on other things, go on about life. Get past it." But who was she kidding? She hadn't gone forward at all.

Molly drew in a breath and gave an uneven laugh. "Well, now's not the time to talk about this, not with a house full of people coming."

"What can I do to help?" Sloane asked.

"Sit and drink your coffee. You're company. You don't need to do anything."

"I want to. I'll be more at home if you put me to work."

"Shy around strangers?" Molly's eyes were sympathetic. "Well, then, you can start by helping me fix breakfast."

Breakfast was a memory and the scent of roasting meat was beginning to perfume the house. Sloane stood slicing sweet potatoes, watching Jacob and Nick through the kitchen window as they repaired the soft spot in the parking apron. Being put to work was soothing; to her surprise, she was actually beginning to relax.

As she reached for the baking dish that Molly had set out she knocked over the box of brown sugar, sending it cascading onto the floor. "Oh hell," she murmured. The goal was to help, not make a sticky mess.

Sloane set aside the sweet potatoes and hurried over to the broom closet. Molly was out of the room ironing a tablecloth. With luck, Sloane could have everything cleaned up before she returned. Knowing how sugar migrated, she swept the better part of the floor before she finally had a small pile near the stove. All she needed was a dustpan and she'd be all set.

As she reached into the closet to pull the dustpan off its hanger, the hook flipped out of the wall to land in the back of the closet with a metallic tink. Perfect. Come for the holiday and tear the house apart. With a muttered curse, she groped in the corner for the hook, bending down to search with one hand.

And someone swatted her on the behind.

Halfway inside the closet, she jerked upright so quickly she thumped her head on the bottom shelf and came up cursing.

"Funny, Nick."

She reached back for help getting out of the closet. When she turned, though, she realized the hand wasn't Nick's. It belonged to a complete stranger.

"Oh hell," the man said, his wide grin dissolving into consternation, discomfiture and the beginnings of amusement. "I thought you were my cousin."

"You always greet your cousin that way?" she asked.

"When she deserves it, which is most of the time." The smile was back as he stuck out a hand. "I'm Gabe, Nick's brother. I take it you're his guest?"

"Gabriel!" Molly bustled into the room and gave him a quick hug. "You know Sloane?"

"We've met," he agreed, face straight.

"Hey, bro." Nick stood at the edge of the mudroom, stamping his feet. There was none of the uneasiness with Gabe that there'd been with Jacob, Sloane saw as the two men came together and thumped each other on the back.

Molly beamed at them. "Such good-looking boys."

It was true, Sloane saw. Gabe was perhaps more polished than Nick, his features and style more refined. Nick wore a chunky olive sweater and khakis. Gabe wore a black blazer over an untucked white tuxedo shirt and jeans, with loafers. She could see him wining and dining a lady at a five-star restaurant rather than taking her to a neighborhood tavern. And if Sloane found Nick's slightly rough-hewn, casual look more appealing, she was sure that Gabe had his choice of female companionship.

"You're the one who runs the hotel," Sloane said, thankful for Nick's briefing on the way up.

"Not just any hotel," Molly said, brushing his arm affectionately. "He manages the Hotel Mount Jefferson." The phone rang, adding to the cacophony. "You should see it." Molly walked over to answer the telephone. "It's gorgeous. Like the old hotel in that movie where Christopher Reeve goes back in time." She picked up the receiver.

"Or like *The Shining*," Nick added with a wicked smile. "Redrum, redddd rummmmm." He tattooed his fingers up Sloane's sides. "This isn't really Gabe, he's been taken over by the spirit of the hotel so that all he can do is walk around doing the white-glove test."

"You're just jealous of my organizational skills."

"We're going to need them," Molly said from across the room as she hung up the phone. "That was the Demmings. Their daughter Marta just showed up with a new fiancé in tow, so we're going to have two more for dinner."

"That'll be interesting," Nick observed. "Any ideas?"

Molly pushed open the swinging door to stare into the dining room at the crowded table, already stretching near to the French doors at the far end.

Gabe looked thoughtfully over her shoulder.

Molly frowned. "There's just no room, not with the French doors there. We can put a couple of the kids at the kitchen table, I suppose."

"Nope." Gabe stepped forward. "Now we come into my area of expertise. You've got a card table, right Ma?"

"Sure, but we can hardly fit another table."

"We'll take care of that. Jacob, do you still have those sheets of plywood left over from fixing up the sugar house?"

Jacob nodded.

"Perfect. Let's get one of them in here. And your toolbox."

"What do you have planned?" Molly demanded suspiciously.

Gabe grinned. "Trust me, you're going to love it."

Chapter Thirteen

The clink of serving spoons on china. The scent of roast turkey and stuffing perfuming the air. The murmur of conversation, the boisterous noises of children and above all, the sound of laughter. The place and faces might have been different, but the sights, sounds and scents of Thanksgiving never changed.

All things considered, Sloane thought, the table looked wonderful. Under Gabe's direction, Nick and Jacob had taken down the French doors between the dining room and living room and extended the dining-room table courtesy of the plywood and the card table. Molly and Sloane had done some last-minute juggling with place settings and table linens, and if everything wasn't a perfect match, the crowd around the table scarcely cared. What mattered was food and company.

And it felt way too good, she thought with a sudden twinge. Somewhere along the line, shyness had slipped away. There was no room in the Trask world for strangers, and the teasing, joking and sense of purpose had carried her along. This wasn't her family, though, she had to remember that. It wouldn't do to get used to the warmth and easiness. Sure, it looked great from the outside but everything ended.

She knew from firsthand experience.

Next to her, Nick reached out to squeeze her hand. "You okay?" he murmured.

Sloane glanced at him, startled that he'd known. "Sure, I'm fine." She gave him a smile. "Would you pass the turkey?"

Another thing that never changed about Thanksgiving was the dishes. Sloane set a stack of plates on the kitchen counter and looked around. They'd managed to convince Molly to take a break and let others handle the cleanup. Now they had to do it.

Jacob pushed through the swinging door that led to the dining room, his hands dwarfing the serving dishes he carried. Now that she saw him in his neat corduroys and pine-colored twill shirt, she realized that her impression of bulk the night before had been mostly a factor of his parka and unruly hair. True, he topped Nick by a couple of inches but he wasn't fat, not even remotely. Instead, he was solid with muscle built over years of manual labor.

She took the dishes from him and, with a nod, he left.

"Just set that over here," Lainie, Nick's cousin, directed. Sleeves pushed up and apron on, she was ready to work.

"Let me help," Sloane said. If she didn't wash dishes, she'd find herself facing the dreaded living-room conversation with the rest of the family. Better to pitch in.

Lainie grinned. "You want to work, you'll get no arguments here. You want to wash or dry?"

"I like washing."

"Hmm. I do, too." She considered. "Okay, rock, paper, scissors," she said briskly, making a fist.

Sloane considered. "All right. One, two, *three.*"

They both held out scissors. "Again," Lainie commanded, clenching her fingers together again.

This one took a bit more thought. Sloane bounced her fist three times and poked out two fingers in scissors.

And glanced over to see that Lainie had done the same thing. They locked eyes and burst into laughter. "Great minds," Lainie said.

"Two out of three?" Sloane suggested.

Lainie shook her head. "Nope, we think too much alike. We'd probably wind up in another tie. You're the guest. I'll sacrifice myself and dry."

Sloane slipped her hands into the warm wash water. "So your father is Nick's uncle?"

"Yep, more Trasks. We grew up just the other side of the ridge, but my parents live in Burlington now." She took the plate Sloane handed her and began to wipe it dry.

"Where are you?"

"Down in Salem, Mass."

Sloane set a stack of plates in the dishwater. "Oh, you're the witch cousin."

Lainie rolled her eyes. "Let me guess, Nick's been briefing you. I'm not actually a Wiccan, you know. I just run the museum." She took another clean plate from where they'd begun to stack up by Sloane.

"It sounds like a fun job."

"It has its perks. I got to meet Daniel Day-Lewis when they were filming *The Crucible* in town." She sighed.

"Nice?"

"Beautiful. *And* nice. If there's a reason I'm single, it's because he ruined me for mortal men."

Sloane gave her a dubious look before submerging the caramel-encrusted sweet-potato dish. "I don't know, do you have to have a reason at our age?"

Lainie snorted. "When you come from my family and all your other sibs are married off? You bet."

Sloane scrubbed at the baked-on caramel. "Looks like you're stuck, kiddo."

"Tell me about it." She lapsed into silence for a few seconds, then cheered up. "So have you known Nick long?" she asked casually.

Here it came, Sloane thought. "Not really. A month or so. I'm sort of working with him."

"You don't look like a firefighter."

"I'm not." She rinsed the sweet-potato dish and handed it to Lainie. "My company's built some fire equipment. Nick's testing it for us, seeing if it works."

"Seeing you, too, right? Is it serious?" Lainie's eyes were bright with speculation.

"Are you grilling me?"

"Hell, yeah." Lainie laughed. "I figure if everyone's worried about you and Nick, the heat's off me. Come on," she begged, "just one thing I can tell my mom."

Sloane raised a brow. "He knows how to handle his hose?"

Lainie just snickered.

Nick and Jacob carried the plywood sheet toward the work shed behind the house, the same way they'd carried loads together as kids. It was harder now to time their steps so that they were in sync, though. Each of them was so solidly set in his ways, maybe, that there was no longer room for compromise.

Around them gamboled Murphy, Jacob's big black hound who looked like a cross between a black Lab and a small horse. Dried leaves crunched underfoot. "The groves look good," Nick commented, looking out at the solemn silver ranks of trees.

"Thanks," Jacob said. "I'm trying to figure out whether to cull that stand over by the creek, plant some new stock. It's still producing but it's been falling off for three years running. We won't be able to tap them for thirty years but we've got to plan for the future."

Nick shrugged as best he could. "You're the expert."

"I guess it's not your problem anymore, is it?" Jacob fell silent and kept walking.

Nick felt the same stirring of irritation he always felt with Jacob. Only this time, he'd had enough. "Nobody made you stay here, Jacob. I thought you liked it. I thought it was what you wanted to do."

"It is."

"Then why do you always give me guff about leaving?"

Jacob stopped before the door to the shed, holding the plywood with one hand and opening the door with the other. "I don't."

"Yeah, you do. It's getting old." And it was time, long past time to have this out.

"Yeah, well it's getting old that you think you can just walk away and not have any responsibility to any of us." He set the wood down and turned to face Nick then. "You're still a part of this family."

"And you think I should come home and do my duty?"

Jacob frowned. "Here? To live? No way."

"Oh, come on." Nick rounded on him. "You hint at it every time we talk."

"I like working the property. It's a big job and I'm not quite sure what I'm going to do when the sap run starts in the spring, but that's my problem."

"When you talk about it, it becomes mine, too." And it made him feel like he should come up with an answer.

"For Chrissakes," Jacob snapped, "can't I ever talk with you about the stuff that's bugging me? Do I have to pretend that everything's perfect? Yeah, it's hard work and yeah, I'm a little concerned about the spring, but I'll figure out a way to make it work." He stalked over to the grimy window that looked out at the groves. "It's all of our property but guess who's responsible for it succeeding? Five generations, Nick, five, and it all comes down to how I manage it today." He swung back to face Nick. "Did you ever stop to think that maybe I just want you and Gabe to know what's going on? Did it ever occur to you that sometimes I just want to talk about it?"

"You never just want to talk about anything," Nick said, with a try for flippancy.

"And maybe you don't want to listen," Jacob retorted.

There was something in his voice, Nick realized, something he'd never heard before. A tiny, miniscule hint of self-doubt. Self-doubt? Jacob, the big brother? Jacob, the one who'd always known how it was supposed to be and rammed it down Nick's throat, whether he wanted it or not? Jacob, stubborn, opinionated Jacob, suddenly turning human?

Or Nick, maybe, finally opening his eyes.

And now he didn't know what to say. "Look, we never meant to throw everything on you. If you want to unload the property, we can—"

"Sell the farm? What are you, nuts? There's no way. You want out, fine, I'll buy you out, but this is what I do. It's what I am. I don't want out of the farm, but I'd like to be able to talk about it without you getting pissed or thinking that it's a jab at you. I'm not a big talker, you know that. So, God, cut me some slack when I do," he finished in disgust.

A second or two went by. "I think that's the longest speech I've ever heard you give," Nick said finally.

"Try me again sometime, if you can do it without getting pissed and stomping off. Nick, you're the only one who thinks you should come home, okay? You've got your life. I'm happy here alone. You moved back, we'd kill each other inside of a week."

He had a point, Nick had to agree. Still… "Look, you're right about it being a big job and I don't want Ma out there killing herself to pitch in. I could take a week or two of vacation during the sap run if it would help."

"If I need a hand, I'll tell you. But only if you don't hassle me about it."

"I won't hassle you about it." Nick held out his hand. Jacob stared at it a moment and then reached out and shook it. "Okay," Nick said briskly. "Now can we put this damned wood away? I'm freezing my tail off here."

A stealthy shake to Sloane's shoulder woke her the next morning before it was light. She opened her eyes to see Nick. He gave her a quick kiss. "Get up," he said softly. "We got new snow overnight. Come out and see."

They crept out of the house, their breath forming white plumes in the chill air. Above the ridge to the east, the sky was rosy with the light of the still-hidden sun. Nick caught at Sloane's hand. The path led around Jacob's house and to the trail that led into the maple groves.

It was magical, she thought as they walked out into the

frozen landscape. Soft, white and absolutely smooth, snow stretched out into the trees untouched in all directions. It was as though they were the first people to walk there, ever. The maples stood at regular intervals, silent sentinels in the pristine whiteness. The air was still and quiet.

"Wait a minute," Nick said, "Let me see something a minute." He stopped and looked around, then gave a brisk nod. "Yep, it definitely looks better with you in it."

She laughed and they resumed walking. "So how's it been, being back? Everything okay?"

"Yeah. Yeah, things are good. I got some things hashed out with Jacob." He scrubbed his free hand through his hair. "Things haven't been that great with us lately."

"I noticed when we got here." Sloane glanced at him. "Was that why you wanted me to come along? To dilute things?"

He considered. "I don't know, maybe at first. Mostly, I wanted you to meet my family because I thought you'd like them. I was pretty sure they'd like you. And they do."

"How do you know that? Have you guys been sneaking off and comparing notes?"

A corner of his mouth quirked. "Lainie and Gabe wanted to know why you're having anything to do with me. That's usually a good sign."

She grinned. "I'm glad I could measure—"

"Shh." He stopped and touched her shoulder. "Deer," he said, turning her a little.

It took her a moment but then she saw their soft reddish coats in the distance. "Oh," she breathed. Stiff-legged and graceful, they walked along in a line, threading their way through the maples in the hush of dawn. The sun just peeked over the nearby ridge then, sending a ray of warm gold light through the grove, gilding the deer from afar. Sloane caught her breath. "It's so perfect," she murmured and turned to Nick.

"You're perfect." And in the first glow of the rising sun, he kissed her gently.

Morning slipped into afternoon in a whirl of activity: snow-shoeing, exploring the sugar house, blind-tasting maple syrup. Getting on the road took longer than they expected. By the time they reached Nick's house north of Boston, it was push-ing eleven.

Yawning, Sloane stood on the sidewalk near her car. "This is where I wish I could just snap my fingers and go instantly across town to my bed."

"I can offer you the next best thing. Stay here tonight."

She gave him an amused look. "And get up at four to have time to get to my house before start of shift at the firehouse?"

"Not necessarily. You've got clothes with you, right? We can throw your clothes in the wash. Tomorrow, we just get up and drive straight to the firehouse."

It was tempting, especially after the numbing drive. She was more tired than she wanted to admit. Spending another forty-five minutes behind the wheel was the last thing she wanted.

"What do you say?" Nick watched her closely.

Sloane found herself yawning again.

"I'll take that as a yes," Nick said and picked up her overnight bag.

He was all efficiency, getting the bags inside, stopping in the laundry room, going upstairs. At the threshold of his bed-room, though, he stopped her with his hands on her shoulders.

"What?" Sloane asked.

Appreciation bloomed in his eyes. "This'll be the first time we've stayed together. I'm just savoring it."

It made her flush. "Yes, well, it's just the best way to get some sleep, that's all," she muttered.

Nick ran his hands up her spine, fusing the two of them together. "So tell me how I can miss you when I spent the last two days with you," he murmured and held her, just held her, for long moments.

"It's not the amount of time, it's the quality," Sloane returned.

"And it *is* quality," he murmured, tipping her face toward him with his fingertips. Softly, he kissed her so that pleasure dripped through her like warm honey. Without breaking apart, they moved into the bedroom and sank down on the bed.

His touch made her shiver. The heat of his body made her moan. When she would have quickened, Nick put his hand over hers. "Slow down," he whispered, kissing her eyelids closed. "We've got all night."

The gentle smoothing of a hand over bare skin. The soft exhalation of breath. She'd thought that passion meant flash and fire. It was a revelation that it could also be slow and sweet.

They undressed, but afterward she couldn't recall quite how. It wasn't the usual fever of tearing at each other's clothing but leisurely, deliberate, every inch of skin revealed all the more arousing. Naked, they came together in comfort and in quiet.

They touched, they tasted, they took each other up. Nerve endings that usually crackled with the flash and spark of a live fuse now radiated a deep, powerful heat. When he covered her body with his, she caught her breath softly. When he slid inside her, it was as though the barrier of skin no longer existed. Instead, they melded. The measured strokes, the bunch and flow of muscle sent desire flowing through them, one to the other. She felt suspended in pleasure, weightless and liquid.

And when they slipped over the edge they did it together, floating down softly and so, to sleep.

Sloane woke at first light nestled against Nick, his arm wrapped around her from behind. Her initial haze of bemusement morphed to consternation and then steadily increasing dismay. Resisting the urge to groan out loud, she slipped from under his arm and escaped to the bathroom.

She sat on the edge of the tub, her head in her hands. Trouble, big-time trouble. She'd made the rules. She'd set down the conditions. Lighthearted fun, no commitments. Nothing serious.

Yeah, right.

It would be easy to blame the night before on exhaustion but she knew it wasn't so. Just as she knew they hadn't had sex—they'd made love.

Panic lodged in her throat. How much of an idiot could a person be? The whole time she'd been going blithely along, telling herself she had it all under control, she'd been getting in deeper and deeper. She hadn't paid attention. She hadn't kept herself protected and now her heart was very much at risk. That was what happened when you let people into your life, she reminded herself, thinking of Nick, thinking of his family. You loved people and you lost them.

Not that she'd let herself fall in love with Nick, of course. She hadn't let it go that far. It was only a matter of time, though, if she kept on seeing him. Which was why she had to get out now.

Holding her breath, Sloane opened the door and slipped back out into the bedroom. Nick lay on his side, still out to the world, the depth of his sleep making up for the firehouse nights that consisted of little more than a series of catnaps.

For a moment, she stood helplessly and just watched him. Then she shook herself.

Escape first and deal with the fallout later. The fact that it was hard to walk away was exactly why she had to. He might be disappointed but he'd understand. It would be okay.

She bent to gather her clothes and tried desperately to believe it.

Chapter Fourteen

Nick was staring at the annual employee-evaluation paper-work in front of him, searching for the right mix of positive reinforcement and constructive criticism when a shout came from the direction of the kitchen. Impatiently he rose and strode down to the kitchen, only to stumble into a circle of noise and activity. It centered about the kitchen table, where O'Hanlan and Knapp arm wrestled while Beaulieu took the bets from the rest of the cheering crew.

"Why don't you give it up, Tommy, me lad?" O'Hanlan said between clenched teeth as Knapp pushed his knuckles back toward the table. "I'm just playin' with you."

"Looks more like work to me," Knapp replied, huffing a bit as he pushed O'Hanlan's hand down. "You're getting soft running the ladder, O'Hanlan."

"I'll show you soft," O'Hanlan gritted and thumped Knapp's hand over and down. He rose to cheers and slaps on the back. "There now, have I convinced you all or do I need to take on someone else?"

"You want to do anything else to impress me while I'm writing up your evals?" Nick snapped.

They gaped at him in sudden and surprised silence.

"If anyone wants me, I'll be in my office."

"Someone's in a bad mood," O'Hanlan observed as Nick walked out.

Someone was, Nick thought. He'd been out of sorts all day, from the moment after he'd opened his eyes.

And awakened in an empty bed.

Things happened, he knew that. Plans changed. It was just possible that Sloane had remembered something important she had to be home for. He had a harder time understanding why she'd sneaked out on him. That she hadn't wanted to wake him was the reason she'd given in her note. That she hadn't wanted to face questions was more likely.

She was hiding out, he was certain of it. Somehow, some way she'd gotten spooked and now she was backing out. And it surprised him just how much that stung. It didn't matter that they'd spent two solid days together at the farm, he missed her. It was hard to admit how disappointed he'd been to wake alone.

Only if they didn't get serious, she'd said, only then would she get involved with him. Only if they didn't let themselves care for each other. And that was bull, he thought in sudden fury. It was what made relationships work, the caring. Otherwise, it was just friction and hormones.

Frustration surged through him. He was allowed to get close, but not too close. He was supposed to keep his distance, pretend he didn't feel what he felt when he knew it, he'd known it for days.

He was in love with her.

* * *

Sloane sat in her living room, staring at the walls. She couldn't avoid Nick forever. He wouldn't let her, for one thing. More than that, he deserved better. She might not be able to give him her heart, but she could at least offer him honesty. Breaking it off like an adult was the only way to go. She owed it to him to be up front. And she would.

As soon as she could do it without falling apart.

It would be all right, she told herself. After all, he surely wasn't expecting happily ever after. A light fling, they'd said, nothing more. A light fling with an exit clause and she was invoking it.

So why was she sitting on the couch and shaking?

When her phone rang she jumped, heart hammering against her ribs. She couldn't talk to him yet, not yet. Another day and then she'd be able to go forward.

The machine clicked and the speaker buzzed a little. "Sloane?" said a voice.

The relief was only momentary. It wasn't Nick, it was Candy. Candy, whose life was the sum of all Sloane's fears. Candy, who'd lost the man she loved. Candy, who'd sat on the couch beside her in the nightmare hours after they'd heard the news that firefighters were missing, clutching Sloane's hand so tightly that her fingers went numb. And they'd waited with dread for the knock at the door.

The knock that had put the final blow to Sloane's world.

She reached out and picked up the phone. "Hi, Candy."

"Happy late Thanksgiving. How are you?"

Terrified. Desperate. Falling apart. "I'm okay."

"You don't sound so great. Something going on?"

She wanted so much to pour it all out, but how could she? To tell the woman who'd lost her husband that she was breaking up with a firefighter because she feared the same thing? Candy's face, her voice, conjured up the ghosts that haunted Sloane. Candy was a reminder of the worst that could happen. A reminder of why she had to walk away. "Nothing's going on," she said aloud. "Just working a lot."

"You didn't work over the holiday, did you?"

"No, I took a couple of days off. I'm paying for it now though." She was paying for it, all right. Sloane swallowed. "So how was your holiday?"

"It was nice. We went to my brother's house. I missed you, though."

And I miss you. "Maybe next year."

"Hey, Pete loves his guitar, by the way."

Sloane grabbed at the news like a drowning person snatching at a rope. "Does he really?"

"It's perfect. What made you think of it?"

Nick, she thought, and tried to push it away. "A friend suggested it."

"It's been like a miracle, Sloane. He's finally got an outlet. He's been pouring himself into it, playing nonstop. You'll have to get down here sometime and listen to him."

"I'd like that."

"Great," Candy said, "how about Christmas?"

"What?"

"Please come, Sloane. It would mean so much to have you here."

There, in the house where every turn reminded her of Mitch. Of what she could lose when she got involved, when she let herself care. "Oh, Candy, I don't—"

"Now don't worry that it's going to be a mob scene," Candy hurried on. "Mom and Dad will be coming, but that will be it. Dan and Rob are spending the holiday with their wives' families."

Sloane groped for a way out. "It's a lovely invitation."

"It'll be fun. We can hang out like we used to on the holiday, do jigsaw puzzles, maybe even ski if the snow holds out." Enthusiasm bubbled in her voice. "I've got a soup recipe I've been itching to try. It'll be like the old days."

Like the old days. "I'd like to but…"

"But you can't." Candy's voice went flat. "Of course. Do you have plans already?"

"No. I just…"

"You just don't want the reminder."

Sloane's throat tightened. "It's not you."

"I know." Candy gave a brittle laugh. "That makes it worse, doesn't it? God, you know it's been five years and not an hour goes by that I don't think of him. There's a hole there that's never going to be filled, but you go on." Her voice caught, shot through with pain. "You don't just keep your life empty, Sloane. You don't cut everyone off."

"I haven't cut you off."

"No. You just avoid us. Cards and presents don't do it. It's not about money and time, it's about you. That's all we want, the person we used to know."

"I've got responsibilities right now."

"Sure you do, and when that's done you'll find some other way to hide."

She felt backed into a corner. "What do you want from me, Candy?" she cried out.

"I want my friend back." The words shivered in the silence. "I didn't just lose Mitch that night. I lost you, too. God, Sloane, we were like sisters. It killed me to lose him, but then you were gone, too."

Sloane blinked back the sting of tears.

"We used to know every detail about each other's life. Now you're like a stranger. I know something's wrong and I can't help because you won't let me. There was a time you'd have told me instead of lying and saying everything's fine." She paused. "I loved him, too, Sloane, you know? We all did. But you've got to get past it and live your life. He'd have wanted that."

"It hurts too much, Candy," Sloane whispered.

"It hurt to lose Mitch, it hurts me every single day, but you know what? That's being alive. Try, Sloane," her voice caught on tears. "Just try. We need you."

"It's too hard."

"Hard? You want to talk to me about hard?" Sudden bright anger filled her words. "Tell me what I'm supposed to say to Pete when he asks about whether you're coming to Christmas, just like he asked about his birthday. You could help him, Sloane, you could help him figure this out. Maybe we could help each other. But instead you'd rather hide out in your little bunker."

"I can't!" It was as though for years she'd held herself together with string and packing tape and bare will, terrified to let loose for even a moment, terrified of what might happen. Suddenly, it was all threatening to fly apart.

And she didn't know how she'd survive if it did.

Seconds dragged by during which she didn't speak over the ache in her throat. She couldn't.

"All right, then," Candy said finally.

Sloane's hand tightened around the telephone receiver.

"You know, I keep thinking if I try one more time I'll get through to you, that you'll let it all out and go back to the person you used to be. I miss her so much. You have no idea."

Don't leave me.

Candy sighed. "Maybe it doesn't matter. Maybe you're happiest where you are. I hope so." Her voice was empty now of both anger and tears. "Happy holidays, Sloane."

Then the line clicked and she was gone.

And finally, finally the tears began to fall.

Sloane drove into the station parking lot the next evening, dreading the moment she'd have to turn off her key and go in. The night before she'd walked for hours, trying to clear her head, trying to make herself believe that things were okay. But they weren't okay and she knew it.

She just had to figure out a way to live with that.

Push it away. Don't think about it. That had been the way she'd always coped.

Somehow it didn't seem to be working anymore.

As for sleep, it had been nearly impossible. The only upside was that so far, at least, so far she'd managed to avoid Nick. She had to talk with him, she knew that. Just not now, not while she was holding on by a thread. She rested her forehead for a brief moment against the steering wheel.

Then she steeled herself and headed into the station.

The door to the apparatus floor was open and Ladder 67 was gone. A little surge of relief went through her. They were out on a call. Not a fire, she diagnosed rapidly by the presence of Engine 58. Just a rescue call. And if she hoped for it to be a nice, time-consuming rescue call, that didn't make her a coward, did it?

It was later, much later, when she heard the rumble of the approaching ladder truck. When it stopped on the apron, all the rest of the crew piled off.

"Hey, you missed out, Sloane," Knapp called as he waved. "We had a jumper all ready to go. Guy sittin' out on the ledge, threatening to take a header if we brought up a ladder. We had the nets out and everything."

"Did he go?"

Beaulieu snorted. "Do they ever? The ones who really want to off themselves do it quietly. Guys like this, they're not serious."

"Maybe he just wanted help and didn't know how to ask for it," Sorensen said. "It can happen, you know," he defended against the hoots and the eye rolls.

"Just as long as we're not sitting around for a time-waster like that when someone in a burning building really needs help," O'Hanlan said. "Guy like that needs to go to a crisis center."

Maybe that was what she needed, a crisis center. And then she glanced up and saw Nick.

He stood back, just watching her while the rest of the crew made their way inside. He took his time, waiting until O'Hanlan was backing the truck into quarters before he walked up.

"Hey." He tapped a fist lightly against her shoulder. "You're late."

"I was here at six. I must have just missed you. Something came up."

Something flickered in his eyes. "There's been a lot of that lately, hasn't there? I tried to reach you yesterday."

She should have known he'd brook no evasions. "I was—"

"And today," he continued, not allowing her any. "I left messages. I even dropped by. You weren't around."

"I've been busy."

"I guess. Look, we need to talk. Something's going on with you and I'd like to hear what it is." He locked eyes with her without blinking. "I don't want to walk away from this, Sloane."

"This isn't the place or the time, Nick."

"Then name the time and the place. Don't just disappear on me, Sloane. You've got more guts than that."

Once again, she found herself pushed into a corner. "You seem to think you know a lot about me."

"I want to know a whole lot more than you'll let me, that's for sure. I—" He broke off and raised his head.

"What?" Sloane stared at him.

"Smoke," he said slowly, walking out onto the apron and searching the sky. "There's a fire."

At the same moment she smelled it, the bells sounded. "Thirty-three Ramsey Street," Knapp, on house watch, read out over the PA system. "Abandoned building, fire showing. Everybody goes."

They didn't need to check the map. They didn't need help finding it as they pulled out of the station, siren blaring. They had only to drive toward the twisting column of black smoke that blocked the lights of downtown.

Streamers of smoke drifted past them as they turned toward it. Nick pulled on his gloves. He knew this building. He knew its history.

And it was trouble.

The four-story brick structure had started out more than a century before as a furniture factory that had been converted to a recording studio, then a gentlemen's club. Nick had inspected it a couple of times and knew that above the nightclub level on the ground floor was a warren of private rooms, and above that a maze of sound-baffled recording rooms, still coated with foams and plastics. When fire hit them, they'd create an inferno and release every toxic chemical under the sun.

As they drove up, flames shot around the edges of the plywood that covered the few windows on the third floor. It had blown the glass in places. At least it was partially vented, Nick thought, although all the airflow had done was strengthen the burn. Flame streamed fluidly up into roiling smoke, the crimson-streaked black churning like the fires of hell.

"First in." O'Hanlan pulled the ladder truck to a stop in front of the warehouse. "All the fun for us."

"Looks like there's going to be enough fire for everyone," Nick told him. "I'm calling in a second alarm. In the meantime, get the stick up."

O'Hanlan nodded and the rest of the crew hit the pavement. Gone were the jokes as they pulled equipment out of lockers. Now it was all about focus and efficiency. This was going to be a bad one and everyone knew it.

"Am I going to go inside, cap?" It was Sorensen, raising his voice over the sounds of the motors, the approaching sirens, the roar of the flames.

Nick looked at him. He wasn't doing the probie any good by protecting him. It was time for Nick to back off from being the big brother and let Sorensen take a few steps on his own. "Stand by for directions. You might get your chance."

With a whoop of sirens, Deputy Chief McMillan's red Expedition pulled up. They'd need the chief to coordinate something this big, Nick thought as he walked over. Seven engines, four ladder trucks, a rescue company and a tower company to drown the fire from on high. They had a crowd coming.

McMillan finished talking on his radio and got out of the truck, reaching in the backseat for his turnouts. "Trask, what's the situation?"

"It's abandoned and boarded up. Looks like it's fully involved. We've got some partial venting on the third story and one of my team reported flames showing in the back. Must be a mess inside. We're getting our stick up to vent it."

McMillan nodded. "I just called in another alarm. I don't like the looks of this building."

"It's one tricky mother inside. Used to have a strip club on the bottom two floors and a recording studio up above that. Floor two has all these private rooms with back hallways for the club people and floor three still has most of the sound-proofing materials in the sound studios. Lots of flammables and toxins in the walls there. We've inspected it a couple of times over the past five years." He hesitated. "It's a maze, sir. We've gotten turned around each time." Without the smoke, the heat, the pounding risk of a fire.

"You found your way out, though, right?"

"Yes."

"Then we need your company inside leading. You'll split the job with the rescue company. They should be here soon. Brief them before you go in."

Nick nodded and turned to go.

"Hey, Trask?" McMillan called.

"Yeah?"

"Watch your guys."

Sloane stared at the fire. This was nothing like the harmless blaze at the triple-decker. This was a ravenous beast, unleashed and ready to devour. Its red glow flickered over the faces of the men. Like gladiators, they girded up, snapping closed turn-out coats, pulling on air packs, picking up their tools.

Hands shaking, she pulled out her master Orienteer unit and turned it on, staring down at the LCD display. When she'd hoped for a chance to test the units, she'd never wanted the men to be put in harm's way, she'd never wanted a fire like this.

A fire like the one that had killed Mitch.

A sudden scream made her look up. A teenage girl fought to get past Beaulieu and Knapp, her beaded braids flying wildly as she struggled toward the building. "Dontrell!" she shrieked. "Dontrell's in there."

Sloane ran over to her. "What's going on?"

Hysteria had her gasping. "My man's in there. The Dudley Street Doggs pulled him in there and torched it. They going to burn him up." Her voice rose again in a shriek and she twisted to get out of their arms. *"Dontrell!"*

Sloane's eyes widened in alarm. "Nick," she cried.

"I heard." His face was grim as he turned to the deputy chief behind him.

McMillan raised his voice. "Okay, we can't wait for the rescue company. Trask, you get your men inside along with Ladder 61. I want three hose teams stretching two-and-a-half-inch lines, one to each of the three involved floors. All right, go!"

And with sudden horror, Sloane realized the obvious.

Nick was going inside.

She wanted to scream, she wanted to beg, do anything to keep him from stepping over that threshold into peril. But all she could do was stand frozen while he slipped on his breathing apparatus and hefted his ceiling hook and Halligan tool.

Engine 58 was already stretching a line into the front door of the building. She heard the whine of the aerial ladder as O'Hanlan sent truckies from other companies up to the roof to ventilate the blaze. It didn't matter. None of it mattered except that Nick was walking toward the building with his team.

And she couldn't do anything to stop it.

Chapter Fifteen

Nick stopped in front of the service doors on the front of the building. Smoke thickened the air around them and he could feel the hot breath of the blaze. He turned to his crew.

"The stairwell is just to the left, straight across the corridor," he told them, raising his voice over the growl of the fire and the roar of the power saws on the roof. "Okay, the place is supposed to be abandoned and empty but we've got one or more civilians inside. Floor one was a club, three main rooms plus bathrooms, production rooms and a line of offices to the left." He squinted through thickening smoke. "Floor two is honeycombed with a bunch of private rooms, orgy rooms, dance studios, who knows. Floor three is the worst. It was a recording studio for a few years. It's a maze of sound studios and the baffling's still up in a lot of places. Knapp, Beaulieu, we've been here before, so we'll take the upper floors. Sixty-one, you take the bottom floor. Sorensen, you stay with them."

"Cap, you said I could go with you."

Nick looked at him and hesitated. *Stop being the older brother, let him loose.*

"You take Beaulieu and I'll watch over the kid," Knapp offered.

Nick slid on his face mask. "If he's going in, he's coming with me. Come on, Sorensen. You want fire, you got it. And switch on your Orienteer. We're going to need it." He set his own unit, watching the blue display spring up on the right side of his face mask. One by one, blue spots labeled with each crew member's initials popped up in a tight tangle. "Okay, watch yourselves. Keep track of your direction, make sure you know where you came from. And keep track of the time."

Nick looked across to where Sloane stood, eyes enormous, face pale even in the growing light of the flames. He ached to go to her but there way no way to fix this, no way but to do the job that was his life. The job that could save a life. Instead, he raised a hand in salute.

Then he turned toward the inferno.

Smoke hazed the air as they climbed the stairs, stepping around the hoses that snaked their way to the upper levels. The rasp of Nick's breathing mask echoed in his ears as if he were Darth Vader. They could hear the fire growling and popping through the walls. Feet pounded on the metal stairs above them. Nick didn't waste his voice on shouting, just motioned Sorensen to follow him out the fire door to the third floor.

Hose stretched ahead of them down to the end of the wide hall where the team from Engine 58 knelt, knocking down the blaze that burned a dull orange through the smoke. Pinpoints of light showed on the wall to his left where the wash of arc

light from the fire equipment outside had searched its way
through holes and gaps in the thick plywood sheets covering
the windows. To his right rose the wall that hid the warren of
sound studios.

They crossed to the vestibule halfway down the hall. He
motioned to Sorensen and pressed their masks together.
"Okay, we've got the doors to the rooms here. Three on each
side. I'll take the doors on the left, you go to the right." To the
right, away from the fire. "Be careful going through the doors.
Make sure you keep track of your moves and don't get turned
around. If you find something, shout on the radio." His voice
sounded flat and muffled through the plastic of his mask.
Sorensen nodded and they plunged off into the smoke.

Nick started with the door closest to him, fumbling for the
handle with his thick gloves. The heat clenched him like a fist.
He ignored it, intent on his task. Keep to a search pattern, he
thought. Getting lost in the maze of doors and halls and smoke
would be deadly.

Setting his shoulder to the wall, he moved around the pe-
rimeter of the room, swinging his ceiling hook across the
floor in a broad arc to search for objects. To search for bodies. Amid the freight-train rumble of the flames, the creak and
groan of burning wood, softening beams, he strained to hear
a hint of a voice.

And on his display, the other blue dots moved in their own
restless circles.

Sloane stared at the fire, reduced to watching and waiting.
The LCD display on her master Orienteer gave her only the
illusion of control. She concentrated on the blue dots, knowing that the image before her showed just a fragment of the
picture. It might reveal the locations of the men in the bewil-

dering tangle of rooms. It didn't show the heat and smoke and power of the flames creeping closer and closer.

The blaze reflected out of the service doors on the ground floor. Two engine companies were inside, working it with two-and-a-half-inch lines, but the temperatures were too high to keep it knocked down.

Glass shattered as flames broke through a window on the third floor.

Where Nick was. She saw the dot with his initials pause and her heart hammered against her ribs. An agony of tension gripped her as she watched and waited. Had he found something? Had he been hurt? It was excruciating, not knowing what was happening to any of the men she'd come to know and care for.

Not knowing what was happening to Nick.

"Chief!" She heard O'Hanlan holler behind her from the controls of the ladder. "Where are the other companies?"

"A drunk driver missed the siren and T-boned Rescue 1. Engine 29 was right behind them, couldn't stop in time." He had to shout to be heard over the throbbing engines of the pumpers and the ladder truck.

"Anybody hurt?"

"A couple got banged up. The apparatus is out of commission. We got more help on the way. I called in another alarm."

More pumpers, more trucks. There would be more hands but would they get the water into the maze that was the inside of the building?

And would they help the men inside get out?

The building groaned. It might have been brick outside, but the skeleton was wood, massive timbers, long stringers. And as the fire progressed, the building suffered.

Nick hardly noticed the bulk of his protective clothing, the weight of his helmet and breathing apparatus. The smoke thickened, banked down toward the floor. Life, normally so complicated, was reduced to utter simplicity—enter right, exit right, shoulder to the wall. Sweep the ceiling hook, strain to hear, strain to see, strain to keep a sense of direction.

The door had led to a hallway with two more doors, each with studios and offices behind. *Through the door, straight, right, door to the left, search, door to the right, search, through the door, search, then door, right, door, left, straight, right, left, straight, through the door.* And pray he'd find the vestibule.

The inferno grew hotter still.

The smoke was down within a few inches of the floor now, He couldn't see, searched by contact. Enter right, shoulder to the wall, sweep with the hook, move forward, sweep with the hook, move forward, sweep—

The hook jolted in his hand. He'd touched something. Or someone. Adrenaline vaulted through him.

And then he was scrambling across the floor. It was a man, passed out facedown. Facedown was probably the only reason the guy was still alive, Nick thought as he tore off his helmet and mask to give the man a breath of oxygen. Now he just needed to get the guy out. He dragged him to the hall outside, slipping into the rhythm of buddy breathing. He turned and passed through another doorway, turned again.

And found himself in a dead end.

The building shook with the sound of something—a beam, maybe—crashing down. Nick focused on keeping his breathing calm. A man hyperventilating could go through a sixty-minute tank in ten, and he was already sharing it. He retraced his path in his mind. It was important to get back to the original room, figure out an escape before the man in his arms died.

His stomach tightened. He stared through the swirling smoke.

And blinked at the blue lines in front of his face. The Orienteer. The schematic. The way out. He'd gone through the wrong door, he realized, a door he hadn't seen when he'd entered the room. He was in a hall now that led directly back to the vestibule. It would be quicker than retracing his steps.

If it were right.

Did he believe it? Did he trust it? Did he trust Sloane?

And it was that thought that had him tossing the man over his shoulder and following the blue lines.

Sloane stared at her monitor where Nick's marker had stopped. The building gave a rending sound and a wall of flame roared up from the roof. Her hands clenched convulsively. She could hear the deputy chief on the radio.

"Ladder 68, roof team, are you hurt?"

The radio crackled. "Negative. We nee—off quick."

McMillan cursed as the transmission was interrupted by a call for the motor squad to the back exposure of the building. It was the chaos of a fire scene with dozens of radios, any one of which could be keyed on at any time. "Say again, 68?"

"We need off. This whole damned thing is going to go."

"Comin' to get ya, guys," O'Hanlan boomed as he guided the aerial ladder to pluck the roof team off.

The deputy chief keyed the radio mike again. "All hands inside, the roof is unstable. Get out now." The air horns from the pumpers blared out the high-low tones of a mayday signal.

The radio crackled. "Ladder 67."

Adrenaline spurted through Sloane as she heard Nick's voice.

"I found our guy. He's hurt—"

His fragmentary words were stepped on by another transmission and Sloane bit off a curse. "He needs air. I'm getting him out."

Knapp's voice broke in. "Ladder 67, we'll meet you on the stairwell."

The building was unstable, Sloane thought in anxiety. They had to hurry.

The radio crackled again and another voice came on, this time coughing and choking. "Ladder 67, need assis—" Another transmission broke in for a moment. "—lost. Did you copy, Command?"

"Say again."

"—run out of air. I'm lost—"

And Sloane stared at her monitor, where Sorensen's marker sat unmoving, deep in the building.

"Ladder 67, inside, did you get that? Ladder 67?" The chief shook his radio in frustration, but there was no answer. "Trask, get your man out of there."

The universe was fire and black smoke, raging heat and rumbling fury. The engine company had pulled out. Nick stepped into the stairwell. "Knapp?" he bellowed and began pounding his ceiling hook against the metal railing.

He watched the blue dots of Knapp and Beaulieu coming closer and suddenly they appeared through the smoke like apparitions.

"This the guy?"

"Get him out." Nick handed him over. "I've got to go get Sorensen." Suddenly, Nick caught a breath. "What the hell? What is he doing?" he demanded, watching the blue dot that represented Sorensen burrowing deeper into the building.

And closer to the fire.

He didn't bother to say goodbye, just turned around and plunged back into the hall.

The smoke had thickened, furling around him like black velvet, so heavy that he moved blindly along, staying low. He wore the standard high-wattage shoulder lamp. It didn't matter. He might as well have turned it off for all the good it did.

"Come on, come on," he muttered to himself. The building shuddered as Nick drew near the vestibule. Suddenly there was a ripping sound and the ceiling at the end of the hall collapsed.

Nick dove into the vestibule, feeling the wave of heat shoot over him as the fire roared in triumph. He stayed by the floor, scrambling toward the door that his display told him led to Sorensen. Somehow the kid had gotten disoriented, crossing the vestibule and going behind the far door on Nick's side rather than toward the exit. The blue dot was motionless. Sorensen's personal alert siren would be sounding but it was silenced by the walls of acoustic shielding.

The door opened into swirling blackness. Nick moved down a short hallway, tracking his location on the Orienteer. Right at the end, then through another door. More smoke inside this one, and heat eddying around him, but no flames. It was here somewhere, though, stalking him with the relentless cunning of a predator.

Heading blindly across the room, Nick stumbled over something, cursing. It wasn't Sorensen, but a heavy light fixture that had fallen from the ceiling. Ignoring the ache in his shin, Nick plowed forward. Then his boot hit something else. Not a piece of the ceiling, this time, he thought, shining his light on it. Through the oily black smoke, he saw Sorensen's black leather helmet.

And his stomach tightened. He fought the urge to sweep his ceiling hook, looking for Sorensen. He couldn't afford to waste the time. The display said he was further in. Nick had to trust it.

There was a rumble ahead of him. His radio crackled. "Ladder 67, the roof is going. Get out, repeat, get out."

"Negative, Command. I'm getting my man."

"Ladder 67—"

Nick turned it off.

He went through the next door more cautiously, watching for fallen debris. Another hallway, another turn. His mask began a thudding vibration against his face, warning him he had only a handful of minutes left on his tank. The mayday signal sounding faintly from the pumper told him to get out and get out now. Not a chance. Sorensen's marker said he was behind this door and that was where Nick was going.

He put his hand on the final door, feeling the heat as he touched it. Taking a breath, he turned the knob to open it.

And walked into hell.

Her eyes stung and watered from the smoke. Her head pounded from the fumes. The heat had grown so that even she could feel it now as it turned the November night balmy. And Sloane didn't care, all she cared about was the monitor in her hand. On the display, she watched Nick fight his way through the labyrinth, closer to Sorensen.

Further from safety.

Negative, Command. I'm getting my man. He would never consider doing anything else. No firefighter would. She knew that, she knew it.

And still she wanted to scream as she stared at the display, watching the little blue dot with Nick's initials creep away from the salvation of the stairwell, inch by torturous inch deeper into the maze.

The building rumbled and she looked up to see flame shooting out of the windows on the upper floors. The plywood had been consumed now, leaving openings for the hungry flames, showing the line of fire that would cut off Nick's retreat. The tower truck poured hundreds of gallons a minute of water through the openings, fighting back the flames, fighting to leave him with an escape, a chance.

There was a crunch and a whoosh of flame as another part of the roof fell in and she had to fight not to cry out. Nick, she thought in agony.

I never told you…

Fire and brimstone. Heat and fury. The far end of the room was bathed in flame that spat and popped and snarled. Black smoke wreathed the blaze, making it seem as though he were looking into the fires of hell themselves. Melting paint dripped down the walls. Even down low the temperature slammed into him, making it nearly impossible to think, to move.

And Sorensen lay on the floor, edging toward a door that would take him away from the exit. His mask dangled from his neck, straps broken, faceplate cracked. A trail of torn and blistered skin ran up into his hair where blood poured from a gash on his scalp. He'd been trying to breathe the cooler air down low, coughing and retching from the smoke.

Suddenly, the flames up by the ceiling brightened. The orange shaded to sunburst yellow, a yellow bright enough to burn through the shrouds of black, a yellow that shimmered and spread fluidly across the ceiling.

And Nick's stomach clenched in fear. He knew the signs, every firefighter knew the signs.

The room was about to explode.

"Come on," he roared, vaulting into the room to grab Sorensen, throwing him toward the door and not caring because they had to get out of that room and get out now.

Or die.

He slammed the door and dragged the probie down the hallway, watching the blue lines for the route to escape. There was a whoof of explosion behind them and a rush of heat that sent the smoke before him roiling.

Sorensen was half-conscious, weak and heavy. Maybe head injury, maybe smoke inhalation, it didn't matter. They needed to get out. Nick dragged off his mask and put it over Sorensen's face, giving him several seconds of the rapidly dwindling supply of air before taking it back. Only a handful of minutes left. Only a handful of minutes to escape.

Passing the mask back and forth, Nick hauled Sorensen through the maze in grim determination, knowing it was only a matter of time before the roof went, the floor went and it all came tumbling down. If they didn't run out of air first.

He keyed his radio mike. "Ladder 67 to Command, we're coming out into the third-floor hallway. Low on air, repeat, low on air." He handed the mask to Sorensen and reached for what should have been the door.

And his hands hit a blank wall.

The building groaned. Cold fear swept through Nick as he spread his arms blindly, searching to either side for the way out. He knew it was there, he'd seen it on the display seconds before. They were not going to die in this building. It was not going to happen. His fingers touched a doorjamb and he moved to it in relief.

Until Sorensen caught at his sleeve. "Wrong door!" he yelled, handing Nick the mask.

For an instant, Nick froze, shaken at how very nearly he'd taken them back deeper into the maze. The mask chattered against his face, galvanizing him into action. There was no time to waste. The blue lines. The blue lines would take them to safety.

One more set of doors and they'd be in the vestibule. He sipped a little air and passed the mask to Sorensen, feeling the warmth of the door up top. It was a risk they'd have to take. They edged to one side of the doorjamb and Nick reached for the handle. The building rumbled around them.

Swiftly, he opened the door.

The freight-train roar of the fire outside staggered him. They were walking into an inferno. It rolled along the ceiling and licked down the walls, fed by air from the now-open windows. The mask jittered in Nick's hand as he handed it to Sorensen. Maybe they were walking into an inferno but they had no choice. They were out of time.

They scrambled out into the vestibule. Ahead, water pounded in through the windows. The torrent gave way before the growling advance of the flames, though, neutralized as a hissing steam that boiled back toward them as they lurched around the corner to the main hallway.

Everything to their right was a seething mass of fire. To their left, Nick caught glimpses of the fire door to the stairwell behind a flickering wall of flames. There was no good escape. An ominous creaking sounded overhead. And throwing Sorensen's arm over his neck, Nick plunged through fire, hauling ass for the stairwell door.

Then they were through and in the stairwell. Stumbling down the steps, Nick shared the very last gasps of air with Sorensen. Almost there. They were almost there. They were going to get out. Adrenaline spiked in his veins as together they hit the crashbar of the fire door at the bottom of the stairs.

And the world came tumbling down.

* * *

Don't let anything happen to him, don't let anything happen to him, please don't let anything happen to him. The words ran together in Sloane's head like a witch's chant.

Except that she had no power to control or protect. All she could do was watch the display in her hand. Every fiber of her being was bent on it as she watched the markers creeping closer, ever closer to the door. She was desperate to help him, desperate to see him, desperate to get him out.

And in that moment, she knew that she loved him. She couldn't say when it had happened, couldn't say how, only that her life was bound to his in some irretrievable way. And his life was hanging by a thread.

With a snarling roar, the rest of the roof collapsed and flames shot toward the sky, smoke boiling upward.

Sloane turned to stare at the inferno, a horror deeper than torment coming over her. She stared at her display, at the motionless blue dot. Nick was still inside. "No," she whispered, trembling. *"No!"*

She sprinted over to the door. Knapp caught her around the waist, turning her half-around, stopping her. His face was tight and drawn.

"He's right there, at the bottom of the stairs," she shouted hysterically, fighting to get loose.

"We know he is. They're going after him." He pointed to where the engine companies had doused the flames by the entrance.

The smoke blew back in her face, making her dizzy. Knapp shook his head. "You can't help," he shouted. "You're going to wind up in the hospital if you don't watch it. Now go back to the ladder truck and sit down."

Numbly, she watched the rescue team step inside with

their tools and hooks. How could it have happened? How could he be gone, and now, when she'd only just realized she loved him? She wanted to rage to the heavens, rage at the fates for giving her this bitter pill to swallow yet again. How could she have lost another person she loved?

Suddenly a shout went up. "Over there." Knapp pointed to where the rescue company was stepping out of the wreckage of the warehouse. With them, still on his feet, was Nick.

Adrenaline surged through her system, making her shake. She blinked back the tears that slipped crazily from her burning eyes. He was safe, he was whole, he was coming back to her.

For now.

Sloane sat abruptly down on legs that would no longer hold her. Suddenly she saw it, the pattern of the future. Day after day, night after night of having Nick make it through one more shift, never knowing which fire would be the one he didn't escape, never knowing which night she'd open her door to see the deputy chief standing on her doorstep, white hat in his hands as he searched for the impossible words.

The knot of men around Nick slapped him on the back, laughing and whooping. Her stomach rolled with nausea.

She couldn't not love him, it was woven into the fabric of her self. She didn't have to wait around to watch him die, though. The decision was swift, the need to escape immediate.

She turned to O'Hanlan, at the ladder behind her. "I have to go. Can you tell Nick that I won't be going back to the firehouse?"

"Hold on, are you sick?" he demanded. "Did you get too much smoke? Go to the medics."

"I'm fine."

"But—"

"Tell Nick," she said briefly, then ran.

* * *

It wasn't until he'd seen Sorensen to the ambulance to be taken care of by the paramedics that Nick gave himself the luxury of thinking about Sloane. Flanked by Beaulieu and Knapp, he headed toward the ladder truck. His shoulder ached a bit where it had been pinned against a wall, but that same wall had supported a layer of fiery debris, keeping them from being crushed and burned. The brush with death had left him giddy and supercharged.

"You were lucky, Nick old boy," Knapp said, slapping him again on the back. "Someone up there likes you."

"I'd like to think a lot of people like me, Knapp," Nick returned, looking around for Sloane. "Where's Sloane?"

"I told her to go sit on the ladder truck," Knapp said. "She was pretty upset when we thought you were trapped. She's probably in the cab."

Behind them, O'Hanlan shook his head. "She took off. Said she wasn't going to go back to the firehouse."

Nick frowned. "Was she sick? How much smoke did you get out here?"

"Not too much. She said she was fine."

"Then why did she leave, dammit? She didn't have any way to get out of here." Cursing, he unsnapped his turnout coat swiftly. "You didn't let her walk, did you?"

"I was stuck on the ladder. I couldn't very well run after her. She headed out that way." O'Hanlan jabbed a thumb down the street.

And Nick looked away up the empty sidewalk.

Chapter Sixteen

She walked up Columbus to Mass Ave. without seeing a cab. By the time she made it to the Back Bay, she'd hit a rhythm. As long as she walked, she didn't have to think. And if she didn't think, she didn't have to miss Nick and if she didn't miss Nick, she didn't have to face what she was walking away from.

So she just kept moving, down Mass Ave., over the Charles, through Cambridge and home.

It took her two hours of walking but finally she let herself into her flat with her hidden key, her head pounding—with the effects of smoke inhalation, not with the efforts of fighting back the tears. There was nothing to weep about. Nick had survived and she'd learned her lesson.

That walking away was the best thing for her.

The hour might have been late, but sleep eluded her. When she drifted off momentarily, it was to restless nightmares of fire and loss, running in terror down endless hallways only to look down and find her hands empty of the treasure she'd been trying to preserve. When the sky began to lighten, she rose, exhausted, to start her day.

The hot, sluicing water of the shower let her find a certain oblivion. The trick was to avoid letting her mind wander, to avoid thinking about Nick.

To avoid thinking about what she was giving up.

From her closet, she took whatever was closest at hand. She didn't spend much time on her makeup—there was a haunted look to her eyes that she didn't want to face.

Sometime that day, sooner or later, she was going to have to talk to Nick. She was going to have to find the words to tell him that their relationship—and it was, she could now admit, a relationship—was over. Tell him she loved him? Not possible. Not now, not ever.

A breath of pain whisked through her. Ignore it, she told herself. She'd kept her feelings locked down for all these years. She needed to keep them locked down now.

Because if she let them loose for one moment, she might fly all to pieces.

She slipped on her coat and picked up her purse. Going into work early was good. Putting in a few extra hours would allow her to catch up the time she'd missed. It was a way to keep focused. She'd catch a cab to the firehouse to pick up her car then hit the office. Check in with Bill Grant at the fire office, let him know that she'd seen enough so that testing could proceed without her on site. Move on with her life.

It was a beautiful day outside, a day to be savored by lovers. Something twisted inside her and she pressed it fiercely down. She was locking her door when she heard a sound behind her. She turned to see Nick striding up the stairs, his boots thudding hollowly on the gray boards of the porch.

And the numbness dissipated like early-morning mist.

"Where the hell have you been?" He stopped before her, anger sparking in his eyes.

Hold it down. Don't feel it. Sloane stared at him. "What are you doing here?"

"Trying to keep from going nuts. One minute the roof is falling in and I'm getting my guy out, the next I look around and you're gone. No clue where and your car's still at the station when we get back. We were there overhauling until one in the morning and I spent the entire freaking time wondering if something had happened to you."

"I told O'Hanlan I was leaving."

"And walked off into Dorchester in the middle of the night. You know the statistics on violent crime in that neighborhood? I called when I got back to the station, over and over, and you never picked up." His voice rose.

"I had my phone unplugged."

"Like it was unplugged this weekend? What's going on, Sloane? Last night you said it wasn't the time or the place. Well, it's sure as hell the time now."

A look at his face, at the lines carved by worry and fear took the punch out of her sharp retort. She let out a breath. It had to happen, she knew that. It might as well be now. "All right," she said. "Let's go upstairs."

By the time they'd gotten into her flat, some of the tension had gone out of his shoulders.

"Coffee?"

"Sure." Nick followed her into the kitchen. He took a deep breath. "Look, I'm sorry I jumped all over you. I was just really worried. You shouldn't have left that way."

"I know. I'm sorry." Honesty. She owed him that much.

The coffee she'd made that morning was still hot and she

poured each of them a cup before sitting down at the kitchen table. "How's Sorensen?"

"He's fine." Nick pulled up a chair to sit next to her: "He needed a few stitches and they wanted to keep an eye on him overnight because of the head injury. A light fixture dropped on him. It knocked off his helmet and his mask, which put his Orienteer out of commission." Nick tapped his fingers restlessly on the table. "He made it through, though. Couple of weeks, he'll be back raring to go."

Back to dance on the edge of death. Sloane's stomach tightened. "You were lucky."

"If we were lucky, it was because of you." He looked at her soberly. "If it weren't for your units, we would have died in that building."

"I know."

"If nothing else, you should have stayed around so we could thank you."

She gave a halfhearted smile. "I didn't need to hear it to know you were grateful."

"No? Then how about you should have stayed around because you were the only one I wanted to see when I finally made it out? I was so damned worried when I didn't know where you were." He kissed the palm of her hand, then laid it against the side of his face. "I don't think I could handle it if anything happened to you," he said softly. "I love you." His gaze was gentle, unwavering. And sudden tears swamped her.

"What is it?" he asked, as they rolled down her cheeks.

"Nothing." At first she battled them, dashing them angrily away and then it all just broke over her like a wave, the fear, the tension, the fight with Candy, the déjà vu of the fire.

And the anguish of watching the roof fall in, certain that she'd just seen Nick die.

The sobs racked her body. He said nothing, seeming to understand words were not what she needed. He simply pulled her to him, cradling her head to his neck, letting the salt damp of tears soak into his shirt.

When at last Sloane raised her head, long moments had passed. Nick kissed her hair. "Talk to me."

Sloane rose and moved away from him. If she continued to touch him she'd never be able to say what had to be said. She walked to the bathroom to wash her face with icy water. When she came back, She didn't sit but leaned against the counter. "I'm sorry about getting upset."

"Don't be. I get the impression it was long overdue."

"Maybe." She wrapped her arms around herself. "Nick, I…" The words lodged in her throat. It took an effort to force them out. "I can't be involved with you anymore."

His expression didn't change, he just looked at her steadily. "I can't say I'm surprised to hear you say that. You've been working yourself up to this for a while now."

"I haven't been working myself up to anything. It's just what I need to do. I'm sorry if it hurts you." She cleared her throat. "We talked about it at the beginning, remember? No promises."

Nick stared into space for a moment, nodding his head as though to music only he could hear. When his eyes cut to hers, it was with the impact of a punch. "That's right, no promises. No one's allowed to care for you, nothing's allowed to matter. It must get lonely in that little box where you live."

Her eyes narrowed slightly. "I live the way I have to."

"You're going to have to do better than that. Something happened the other night when we were together. You can't look at me and tell me that it meant nothing to you."

She gave him a level stare. "I wouldn't even if I could."

"Then why are you walking away? Why won't you try to

make this work? I know the fire was bad and it probably spooked you, but it's like anything else. You get used to it, you get past it."

"No you don't," she burst out. "I don't. I can't sit back and watch what you do. I lived with Mitch and his wife. I saw what she went through every single time he went off to work, every shift, never knowing what would happen. The night he was killed I was over at their house. I was there when the battalion chief knocked on the door." Her voice died away and she bit her lip, staring fixedly at her hands. He wanted to go to her then, but something held him back. "You have no idea what it's like to sit there, knowing that they're coming. Hearing the knock, and you don't want to answer it because you think if you don't hear the words it won't be true, that you can just sit in the dark and close your eyes and make it all go away except you know that it won't, and you know that it's real and there's nothing you can do to change it."

And she looked fixedly ahead but he knew she didn't see him. In that moment and that time, all she could see was the nightmare inside her head.

"My God, Sloane," Nick said helplessly. "Why haven't you talked to anyone about this? You can't just let it sit there and eat you alive. You've got to deal with it. You either get a hold on it or it gets a hold on you."

"Been tuning into radio psychology shows lately?"

He ignored her, knowing she was striking out at him because of her vulnerability. "You lost your brother in the worst way, the worst way, but it's part of life. And I know it hurts like hell but we all go through it. I've lost friends. I lost my father."

"Funny, so did I," she said in a brittle voice. "Only it happened to me when I was eight and I lost my mother at the same time."

"What?" His eyes widened in shock. "How?"

"Car accident. Mitch and I went to live with my grandparents, then, only my grandmother got breast cancer three years later. My grandfather lasted a little longer. With him, I think it was just a broken heart." Tears began slipping down her cheeks again. "Mitch took me in, gave me a place to live while I finished high school. And then I lost him, too." She looked up at him. "Oh God, don't stare at me like I'm some kind of freak. There's all kinds of bad luck in the world. It happens, isn't that what you said?" She swiped furiously at her cheeks. "I'll get over it."

"But you haven't really, have you?" He was just barely beginning to understand the magnitude of the disaster and how deep it all went. "This isn't just about firefighting, is it? It's about getting close to anyone." It twisted viciously at something inside him, knowing what she'd been though, knowing there was no way for him to fix it but to love her.

And that was the thing she feared above all.

Her eyes burned at him. "Every time, every time I've cared for someone, really loved them, I've lost them. I can't do that again."

"So you stay detached from people for the rest of your life?"

"I don't know. Right now, I survive." She raised her chin. "You risk your life and maybe you have to, but I can't watch while you do it. I can't jump every time the phone rings while you're at work. I love you too much to wonder every shift, Will this be the day someone knocks on my door? Will this be the night I get the call from the hospital? Will this be the night…will this be the night your luck runs out on you?" She shook her head blindly. "I can't, Nick, I just can't."

"What if you don't have to?" Nick crossed to her. "I took the promotional exam last month to get moved up to district chief." *Believe me. Trust me.* "I'll find out the results next week. If I pass, I'll be on the street supervising more than I'll be actually in the fires."

"And you'll hate it. You'll want to be right up next to the burn in every fire you oversee. I know it, it's like an addiction with you guys." Unable to hold still, she paced across the room.

"I've been fighting fires for thirteen years. It's time to do something else." And if it took giving up firefighting to be with her, he'd do it. Even if it meant giving up part of himself.

She turned back to him. "How can you be sure this is what you want?"

"I can't, until I try it," he said simply. "But the chances are good that I *will* get to try it. We're going to be losing half our district chiefs to retirement and promotion in the next five years. I can't promise that I'll hit the top five percent in the exam, I can't promise how soon I'll be promoted, but I will do my damnedest to get out of the day-to-day fires."

"And what if you change your mind once you're there and want to go back?"

"Then we talk about it. Yeah, you're right, I can't guarantee how I'll feel in the future. Then again, I can't guarantee I won't drive down the street and get broadsided. I could walk past a building and have a wall collapse on me."

Her eyes sparked at him. "Don't give me that. There may not be any guarantees but there are statistics, Nick. The more often you risk yourself, the higher the likelihood that something will happen."

"You know how many career firefighters in the U.S. died on duty in 2004? Twenty-nine—out of almost three hundred thousand, and half of those were natural causes. Less than a hundredth of a percent. It sounds scary but the reality isn't so bad."

"Tell that to my brother's widow," she snapped.

"Sloane." His voice was quiet. "I took the test. I think I can make a difference further up the command chain and I want to try it. I'd be lying if I tried to guarantee anything more, except that I love you and I think we've got a chance to be happy." He held his breath, willing it to be enough.

Sloane stared at him, eyes haunted.

"Please tell me you'll try." And in the space of a heartbeat his world reduced to the two of them, outside of space, outside of time, suspended only in the moment of her decision.

The seconds passed.

Finally, Sloane moistened her lips. "I can't, Nick," she whispered. "I just can't do it."

He wanted to wipe the shadows away. He wanted to take away the power of the past to hurt. He wanted to help her accept what had happened, put it aside and move forward into the future.

Sometimes wanting wasn't enough.

Slowly, reluctantly, he released her hands and rose. "I guess that's it, then." He pulled his jacket off the chair and walked back over to her. For a second, his fingertips touched her cheek. "You might not want to hear it but I do love you," he said softly. "If you ever change your mind, I'll be here." He paused. "Be happy, Sloane. You of all people deserve it."

And he walked down the hall and out of her life.

Chapter Seventeen

A second. A minute. An hour. Sloane had no illusions things would get better quickly. She had too much experience with loss for such naiveté, so she sat at her desk and forced herself to work, grasping at it like a lifeline. Concentration wasn't possible; she focused on rote tasks that didn't require any and ignored the occasional concerned looks that Dave, her intern, flicked her way.

The phone rang. "Sloane Hillyard."

"Ms. Hillyard, this is Gil Snowden over at the *Chronicle.* I'm doing a follow-up story on the Dorchester fire. I hear that there were a couple of guys who almost died last night, who would have died without some new equipment that you built."

Sloane closed her eyes. "I'm not the right person for you to talk to. You should check with the fire department."

"I did. They pointed me to you."

Because her job description didn't include falling apart, she took a deep breath. "What do you want to know?"

"The basics, for starters. What does it do, how does it work, how common is it. You know, the whole spiel."

So she gave it to him, the essential rundown that she could give in her sleep, drowning him in details she'd memorized long before while his computer keys clacked madly in the background.

...there were a couple of guys who almost died last night....

"Okay, I think I got it," Snowden said after a final burst of typing. "So this is the gear that Councilman Ayre was talking about before his reelection, right? Do you think he's going to continue to push it now that the election's over?"

"I wouldn't know. Again, I'd check with the department."

"You must be aware of his record of voting for departmental budget cuts," he said, ignoring her. "Any comments?"

"You'll have to take that up with someone else." A typical reporter, Sloane thought. If he didn't get an answer to his question, he asked it another way, poking and prodding until he got something he could use.

"Of course, funding cuts would affect the chances of the city buying your equipment."

"I'm a resident of Cambridge," she said with an edge to her voice. "I don't really follow Boston politics."

"Well you should. The firefighters really want this equipment. I just interviewed one of them, a Nick Trask."

And an iron band tightened viciously around her chest. Dropping her head down in her hands, she waited it out. It would stop, eventually, she knew.

Just not any time soon.

She raised her head to see Dave staring at her. On the

phone, Snowden was still talking. "...a big outlay." He paused expectantly. "Ms. Hillyard?"

She gathered her wits. "Yes, well, I hope that the department will get the funding for the units. They ought to be standard equipment for every fire department in the country." A nice, positive, meaningless quote.

"Of course, you've got a vested interest in that."

"Pardon me?"

"Well, it's nice business for your company. Exler's a start-up in need of a cash cow. No wonder you're pushing it to fire departments. Makes you look good if you succeed. More stock options for when the company goes public."

"Stock options aren't my concern. The gear is."

"And the gear is good for business."

Sloane's eyes narrowed. "It's got nothing to do with my company or with business."

"But it would be great for your revenue numbers. I mean, you're not doing this for your health, right?"

In a flash, her patience evaporated. "You want to know why I'm pushing this equipment?" she demanded. "My brother was a firefighter, and he died in the Hartford meat-packing-plant fire trying to save the guys in his company." Dave snapped his head around to stare at her. "I'm pushing this equipment so that that doesn't happen again to anyone, anywhere. This is not about business, Mr. Snowden. It's personal."

Nick walked down the aisle of the home builders' warehouse, the beeps of the forklifts echoing through the air, orange metal shelves towering on either side. By this time, he could probably navigate the aisles with his eyes closed. He'd been there a lot lately.

His house was the better for it. First the cabinets, then

paint, then new tile in the bathroom. He'd spackled and plastered and grouted and sanded, wired in light fixtures and refinished doors. When he wasn't at the firehouse or his side job, he was working on his living room, his kitchen, his study.

Not the bedroom, though. Too many memories lurked there.

And now he had a problem. After almost two weeks of knocking himself out, he was running out of things to do. Just the thought made his palms sweat. If he ran out of things to do he'd have time to think and if he had time to think, he'd think about Sloane and if he thought about Sloane...

He refused to go there. He refused to wonder how she was doing. Okay, he couldn't help wondering how she was doing, but he refused to miss her. Except he couldn't help doing that, either, which was why he found himself running to the home builders' warehouse to pick out handles for his kitchen cabinets, of all ridiculous things, just so he'd have a way to keep his hands busy.

Glass or ceramic? Copper or bronze? Knobs or handles, hooks or rings? He scowled at the fixtures and tried to forget that he'd planned to bring Sloane to help him pick out hardware because they were the kinds of things that women cared about, and he'd wanted her to walk into his house and see something she'd chosen.

He'd wanted her to walk into his house and feel at home.

The omnipresent ache for her sharpened. And he grabbed a handful of plain white knobs because it just didn't matter.

An hour. A day. A week. Sloane drove herself relentlessly, working into the night until her neck ached and her vision blurred, driving herself pitilessly at the health club until her muscles refused to continue. Each morning, she set herself an impossible schedule in the hope that by night she'd be exhausted enough to fall into the oblivion of a dreamless sleep.

And each night she was disappointed.

Now, nearly two weeks after the fire, she stood in the hallway outside the city council chambers, waiting for Bill Grant.

"Sloane." Bill Grant strode up to her, beaming. "Glad you made it. You sounded kind of iffy when I called you last week."

"I'm still not sure what I'm doing here. What does the Ways and Means Committee need from me? They've got all my reports and all the specs. They've got the data from the rest of the fires. What happened in Dorchester should speak for itself."

"They don't just want to hear facts and figures, they want to hear about you. They want to hear about your brother."

She stiffened in outrage. "I'm not going to talk about that to a room full of strangers. It's personal."

"Sloane," Bill said in a low, urgent voice, "it's what it takes to get the message through. I know it must be hard and I'm sorry, but if you really want to be sure it doesn't happen again, then tell these guys what it's like. Make them understand the reality. Your buddy from the *Chronicle*'s out there. He'll make sure people hear about it."

She moved her head. "You don't understand."

"No, Sloane, *they* don't understand. And you're the only one who can make them. You of all people should know how much rides on this." The door to the chambers opened. Grant looked at her. "It's your chance to make a difference. Will you do it?"

A chance to make a difference. An appeal to let them paw over her soul. Could she live with herself if she did it?

Could she live with herself if she didn't?

Sloane took a deep breath and walked into the chambers.

* * *

Nick sat on his couch turning the envelope over and over in his hands, staring at the seal of the Boston Fire Department. A few weeks earlier, he'd have torn it open in anticipation and curiosity, waiting to see how he'd fared and what his future might look like. Now, he knew what his future looked like.

Without Sloane, pretty damned lousy.

It would get easier with time, of course. Everything did. Eventually, he wouldn't think of her every waking minute. He wouldn't seize up when he walked down a sidewalk past someone wearing her scent. Eventually, he knew, he'd get past her.

Sure. In a decade or two.

Ripping open the envelope impatiently, Nick pulled out the papers inside. The cover letter didn't matter; all he cared about was the list of results. And in a spurt of jubilation, he saw his name among those at the top. Not a perfect score but a ninety-nine percentile with a rank of second. Second out of more than two hundred. Not bad. The promotion would be coming as soon as a position became available.

And the one person he wanted most to call with the news was the one person who didn't want to hear from him.

The problem was, Sloane thought, there were too damned many ways for a person to be reached. Even when she slipped out for an hour-long meeting, she had to slog through a dozen messages when she returned. She clicked on her e-mail, reading text and deleting spam as she punched her way through voice-mail menus.

And sat bolt upright when she heard the first message.

"Sloane, George O'Hanlan of Ladder 67." The voice boomed out of the receiver into her ear. "Nicky got some good news about his exam so we're taking him out to celebrate Friday night. Thought you might want to come along. We'll be at Big John's in Southie about eight. Come on by if you get a chance."

Come on by if you get a chance.

And suddenly she found herself missing the men at the firehouse with a fierceness that surprised her. She missed their noisy good humor, the laughter, the ribbing, the warm crowded evenings in the firehouse kitchen. The unquestioned support. She'd only spent a few weeks around them. How had they gotten to matter to her?

Connections. They were suddenly all around, tripping her up everywhere she turned.

Sloane closed her eyes briefly and punched Delete.

The next voice mail was an interview request from the editor of *Fire Engineering*. He'd want to talk about the Orienteer. They all did. The *Chronicle* coverage of the Dorchester fire and the budgetary meetings had made Sloane the crusader of the month. There were the requests for demos, for test systems, for testimonials.

And the questions, always the questions. Her grief had gone from a very private thing to front-page news. In the first few days, walking into the Exler offices had made her want to cringe, colleagues gazing at her with eyes bright with sympathy, or worse, curiosity. She'd been through it back in Connecticut, in the aftermath of the fire, and had loathed it. The move to Cambridge had been a chance to get back her privacy—and her anonymity. And suddenly here it was, public all over again.

It was less difficult this time, though. Perhaps it was that time had passed. Perhaps it was because there was a purpose behind letting people know. Bill Grant had been right. If it was a way to bring attention to the Orienteer, a way to get people to look twice and to listen, it was worth it. And as the days went by, she found it hurt a little less.

If only losing Nick were that way.

She talked with the *Fire Engineering* editor briefly to schedule the interview. As she hung up, out of the corner of her eye she saw Dave watching her. "You need something?"

"No. I just, I uh…" He cleared his throat. "I just wanted to tell you that I'm sorry about your brother."

Since that day he'd heard her on the phone with Snowden, Dave had studiously avoided saying a word about her revelation. In the days after the news had been made public, days of questions and well-meant condolences from the other staffers, he'd respected her privacy, allowing Sloane to slip gratefully into the peace of the lab each day.

Until now. Oddly, it didn't make her uncomfortable. He was able to say it as if he meant it. Like Molly Trask.

Like Nick.

Her throat was suddenly tight. "Thank you. It was a long time ago," she said. And a longing for closeness hit her like a physical ache. She needed to be close to someone, she needed to be held, loved. To avoid thinking about it, she punched the next message up. Only to be buffeted again.

"Sloane, Candy. Sorry to bother you but I saw an article in the paper about you and your gear and Mitch. I just wanted to be sure you were okay."

Connections…

And abruptly she ached for them, for Candy, for Pete, for the people who'd been her family.

For Nick.

She was in her car and on the highway before she even knew what she was about.

* * *

The house looked different. Once slate blue, it had been repainted a cheerful yellow with white shutters. Flower boxes hung below the windows, empty now, but full of promise for spring. Seasons passed—chill autumn, barren winter—but sooner or later the ground quickened.

Sooner or later, everything was renewed.

Sloane rang the bell. She turned to look at the dogwood in the front yard, the one they'd planted together when she'd graduated high school. It had grown so much. They all had.

Behind her, the door opened and a rawboned teenager stood looking back at her, his eyes almost level with hers. Her jaw dropped. "Pete?" she breathed.

He studied her a moment, frowning. "Aunt Sloane?" he asked. His voice gave an adolescent squeak.

She nodded.

"What are you doing here?"

The suspicious note in his voice broke her heart. "I was in the neighborhood and…" She stopped. In the face of suspicion, honesty. "Actually, I wasn't in the neighborhood at all. I drove down because I missed you guys. I wanted to stop in and say hi."

He stared at her awhile and nodded finally. "That's cool," he said and stepped back from the door.

She wanted to hug him, but she wasn't sure how to handle this new, grown-up person. When she put out her hand to shake, he took it awkwardly, unused to the ritual. The hell with it, she thought and used his hand to pull him close. He was stiff against her for a moment, then yielded and hugged her back. "I've missed you, Pete," she murmured.

"Yeah," he agreed and gave her another squeeze before letting her go.

"So I hear you liked the guitar."

"Yeah. I was just upstairs practicing. You want to hear me play?" His tone was offhand but he watched her closely. His hair hung down into his eyes. The hems of his new-looking jeans ended around his ankle bones, as if he'd already grown out of them. He was no longer a little boy, he was a teenager on his way to being a man and she'd almost missed it.

"I want to hear everything," she said.

Pete had gone through his blink-182 and Green Day books and had moved on to U2 when they heard footsteps downstairs.

"Pete?" Candy called from the kitchen. "Whose car is that?" Sloane headed for the stairs just as Candy came up, only to watch her jaw drop open in shock. "Sloane?" She frowned. "What are you doing here?"

She'd made a mistake, Sloane thought with a sinking heart. *Home is the place where, when you have to go there, They have to take you in.* But too much time had passed and maybe this wasn't her home any longer. "I thought I'd drop by and say hi. It's Friday night, though. You probably have plans."

"Hey, Mom." Pete stuck his head out of his room. "Sloane's going to take me to see blink-182 next time they come to town."

"She's going to…" Candy held up her hand. "Hold on, let me catch up a little. Pete, you need to get the leaves up outside."

"Ah, Mom."

"You've got an hour before dusk. Get to it. Sloane, can you come downstairs a minute?"

Sloane bit her lip at Candy's tone and followed her down to the kitchen. "I'm sorry I stopped by without calling. I'll get out of your hair."

"Don't be crazy," Candy told her fiercely and pulled her in for a long hug. When they stepped apart, she was blinking a little. "I'm just surprised to see you. I didn't think I was going to for a long time, maybe never." She sat down at the kitchen table, rubbing her temples.

Sloane took a deep breath and sat across from her. "About the other day when we talked…"

"I was out of line," Candy said quickly. "I said a lot of stuff I shouldn't have. I'm sorry."

"No. I've been thinking a lot about it and you were right. It was a wake-up call. I was asking for it."

"No one asks for anything, Sloane. We're all just trying to get along."

"I haven't been, though." The words came out slowly. "I've been hiding out for way too long."

"It was a lesson you learned pretty young."

"I outgrew the clothes I wore as a kid," Sloane said. "I should also have outgrown that. I thought it would make things better. It didn't. I know that now."

"Good. I'm glad." Candy rose and opened a cabinet to remove a pot. "Are you staying for dinner?"

Sloane hesitated. "Sure, if I'm invited."

"Only if you chop the onions," Candy said, blinking again. "I always cry."

"So what's going on with you?" Candy stirred the marinara sauce she'd thrown together from diced tomatoes, garlic and spices.

"What do you mean?"

"There's something wrong. I could hear it when we talked the other week but it's worse now."

Sloane filled a pot with water to boil the pasta. "It's a man I was seeing. We broke up."

"That would have been my guess. Who is he?"

She should have known Candy would get right to the point. "A firefighter."

Candy snapped her head around to stare at Sloane. She shook her head. "You don't pick the easy ones, do you?"

"I didn't pick him at all." She set the pot on a burner and turned it up high.

"No. Sometimes the picking's done for you. So what happened? It just didn't work out?"

"Nothing had to happen." Sloane leaned against the counter. "You of all people should understand that. Look what you went through with Mitch."

"Yeah, let's look," Candy said slowly, covering the simmering pot of sauce. "Eleven years of thanking my lucky stars every morning when I woke up next to him. A wonderful son. The sister I never had by blood." She reached out to squeeze Sloane's hand.

"But God, Candy, what you went through every night when he was on the job. And now."

"Sloane, that was you." Candy's voice was gentle. "*I* decided not to think about it. I learned really early on to leave it to fate. One of the accountants at work died of a heart attack a couple of years back. Safest job you can imagine. He was sitting on the couch watching a football game when it happened." She gave a brief smile. "The clock's running on all of us. That doesn't mean you tuck yourself away and hide from life, that means you reach out for it while you can. Like I did with Mitch. After a while I wasn't scared every night when I watched him leave. I was proud. He was my own personal hero."

"I can't lose him, Candy," Sloane whispered. "I love him too much."

"But you've lost him as it is, haven't you?"

The words shivered through her. She missed Nick so much it ached. Automatically, she tried to push it down but it bubbled back up again, worse than before. Desperation choked her. After years of denying her emotions, of bottling up grief, loss, anxiety, she'd abruptly lost the ability.

She sank down at the table, face in her hands. "I can't do it, Candy, I can't do it."

"You can't do what?" Candy sat by her, rubbing her shoulders gently. "Love him or live without him? You're hurting right now and you have been for weeks. Gone is gone."

Sloane shook her head blindly. "No. I know he's out there."

"So you're choosing to hurt instead of having it forced on you. God, you talk about what it would be like to watch him go off to work every day, but how are you going to feel if you hear a report that something's happened to a firefighter? Do you think for one minute that you're not going to tear yourself apart imagining it's him? Imagining the worst?" Candy's gaze delved into her. "And what if the worst does happen? Are you going to feel any better reading about it in a newspaper than hearing the news face-to-face? Is it going to hurt any less?"

She'd thought she could avoid hurt by walking away. She'd never guessed how deep the loss would go. And for what? Sloane thought suddenly. She didn't have to be feeling this emptiness. She didn't have to be without him. All it would take was reaching out. "My God," she whispered, her eyes meeting Candy's. "I've been such an idiot. I've got to go find him. I've got—"

The lid began ticking on the boiling pot of water and she paused. Dinner. More than anything else she wanted to go to Nick, but how could she run off when she'd only just begun to repair the damage with Candy and Pete?

Candy rose to stir the marinara sauce. "You know, I don't think there's enough here for three of us," she said, peering into the pot.

"What are you talking about? You've got a ton of it."

"Pete's a big eater. You know how they are at his age. We'd better play it safe. How about if you go back to Boston tonight and we plan on a real dinner next weekend?"

Trust Candy to understand. She always had. The grin spread across Sloane's face until her jaws hurt. "Oh, I missed you so much." Sloane threw her arms around her. "I'll see you soon, I promise."

"We'll hold you to it." Candy kissed her on the cheek. "Good luck with your man. Call and tell me how it goes."

Sloane stopped at the door and gave her a brilliant smile. "Count on it."

Nick leaned out over the pool table and eyed his shot. He made one, two practice strokes and tapped the cue ball, which rolled across the table to nudge the eight ball into the corner pocket.

He straightened. "Looks like I win, O'Hanlan."

"Aye, that you do. That earns you the right to buy a couple more pitchers, Nicky, me boyo."

"O'Hanlan, how is it that the more beers you have, the more Irish you get?"

"The ale loosens me tongue, brings back the mother country."

A corner of Nick's mouth twitched. "Nice trick, considering your mother country is Southie."

"And if a man can't pick up a good Irish accent there, then where can he?"

"I don't know, but for the guest of honor, I seem to be running up to the bar an awful lot."

"Well, once you're promoted you won't be able to go drinking with us, so we'd better do it now."

Nick snorted. "Yeah, right. Hey Beaulieu, why don't you come along and help me carry?"

Set in the working-class neighborhood of South Boston, Big John's sat by the side of the railroad tracks in a beat-up wood frame building. Inside, a man could get good food, cheap beer and play pool at a few dozen of the sweetest carved oak tables Nick had ever seen.

And every time he'd been there, John Feeney had been behind the bar pulling beers, his wizened face never seeming to age from year to year.

Nick tossed down some money. "Three pitchers of Sam's."

"Coming up."

It was good to be out for a change. And if his heart wasn't entirely in it, it was still better than recaulking his shower, which was about the last thing left to do at his house.

"Hey." Beaulieu nudged him. "You've got a fan club."

A few feet away, a curvy blonde whispered into the ear of her girlfriend and gave Nick a playful look.

Nick frowned and rubbed the back of his neck. As far as he was concerned, the beer could come any time.

The blonde leaned his way. "Having fun tonight?"

"Good enough."

His terse reply set her back only for a minute. She stared at the gray T-shirt he wore, with its Ladder 67 shield. "So are you really a firefighter?"

"He really is," Beaulieu supplied.

"Thanks, Todd," Nick said under his breath.

"This is where you start offering to show her your hose," Beaulieu murmured.

"Funny."

She tossed her hair and moved toward him, managing to inject maximum hip sway in just a few steps. "Our table just got called. Want to play with us?"

Nick looked at her. Blond hair, clear eyes—and about as much character as a glass of water. "Not right now. Thanks for the offer, though." He shoved his change in his pocket and grabbed two of the pitchers John slid across to him. "Hey Beaulieu, you want to get the other one?"

"I can't believe you just did that," Beaulieu said aggrievedly when they were back at the pool tables.

"What?"

"They were complete babes, man, and her girlfriend was giving me the look."

"Maybe she had dust in her eyes." Nick refilled his glass.

"You don't just turn around and walk away on women like that. What's gotten into you?"

Nick took a brooding sip of his beer. It wasn't a question of what had gotten into him but who.

And her name was Sloane Hillyard.

Sloane stood at the doors of Big John's trying to calm her jitters. It had been nearly three weeks since she'd seen Nick. Perhaps he hadn't been out of her mind for more than a minute at a time, but he might have gotten past her a lot more quickly. Or he might still be furious with her.

If you ever change your mind, I'll be here. He'd said it, she reminded herself. Surely his feelings wouldn't have changed that quickly. He was a steadier man that that.

At least she hoped so. The only way to find out was to go through the door and do what she'd come there to do.

Inside, the room was noisy and clouded with smoke, the buzz of conversation punctuated by the clack of pool balls smacking together. Old George Thorogood played on the jukebox. A voice over the PA announced tables.

And Sloane stood inside the door, scanning the room for faces she knew.

Looking for the man she loved.

Glass in hand, Nick watched O'Hanlan set up a shot. The burly Irishman sighted the angles and stroked his cue decisively.

And the ball went well wide.

"Great partner you've got there, Nick." Sorensen hooted. "Way to go."

Nick winced. "For Chrissakes, O'Hanlan, we've got five bucks a piece riding on this game." He looked away in disgust, reaching out for his beer. And froze.

At the table, Beaulieu sank the five ball and scratched. Groans and cheers erupted around the table.

"Now who's the one to talk about partners, Sorensen?" O'Hanlan needled. "Your shot, Nicky." He turned. "Nicky?"

But he was talking to thin air because Nick was already moving purposefully toward the door.

Their eyes met with a snap of electricity. When she saw him, it was as though the rest of the room receded in some way, leaving only Nick. The longing for him was a physical thing crouched in her throat. It paralyzed her, so she could only stand, staring, as he walked up. Her pulse hammered.

"Hey," he said.

She couldn't stop the grin from spreading over her face. "Hi. Having a good time?"

"It's just improved immeasurably." He wore just jeans and a T-shirt, nothing special. And he looked perfect, absolutely perfect. "So what brings you here? Did you just happen to be in the neighborhood?"

"Maybe I was just out for a walk." She tried for a joke.

"All the way from Cambridge?"

Her heartbeat thudded in her ears. "If that's how far I have to go to find you."

"Well, you've found me."

Suddenly she couldn't find air. The whole drive from Hartford she'd thought about what to say to him. Now that the moment had come, she was tongue-tied. *Just do it.*

"Let's get some privacy." He reached out for her hand and tugged her to the door.

Outside, the air was frigid. "Nick, you can't be out here without a jacket," she protested. "You're going to freeze."

"I'm not worried about it. Talk to me." He reached out for her hand. "What's on your mind?"

Somehow, the dim light and the quiet released her. "I was an idiot the other day," she told him, the words tumbling out in a rush. "I've been an idiot the whole time and I'm sorry, sorry for everything."

The overhead streetlight set his eyes in shadow, carved deep hollows below his cheekbones. "Sorry for what?"

"For trying to walk away. I was so afraid of what might happen. I can't live my life that way, though. I know that now. You helped me understand." Her voice shook a little and she tried to steady it. "You told me if I changed my mind I could look you up. Well, I'm looking you up now. I want to try this out. I want to be with you."

For long, excruciating seconds he was quiet. "Are you sure about this?" he asked finally. "It isn't just because of all the stuff you went through with the papers, is it?"

She shook her head. "I'm sure, as sure as I can possibly be. I don't guarantee that I might not get scared sometimes but it doesn't matter. It's life. I don't want to be without you." She locked her eyes on his. Everything rested on this, everything. "I love you and I want to take a chance." She swallowed. "If you haven't changed your mind."

For answer, he swept her against him and held her close. Long minutes went by while they just absorbed the feeling of one another's bodies again, the closeness. "Being without you the past month has been hell," Nick murmured against Sloane's hair. "I love you so damn much."

Being in his arms again was everything she'd ever needed, Sloane thought dizzily, and she laughed that everything that had been so wrong could suddenly be so right. "I'm sorry it took so long. I just had to figure things out."

"Don't be. You're here now. That's what matters." He leaned back and frowned a little. "Just exactly how did you wind up coming here, anyway?"

"O'Hanlan told me you were going to be here."

Nick raised an eyebrow. "Oh, did he?"

"He said you had something to celebrate." She kissed him lightly on the lips. "He didn't say what."

"Ranking second on the exam. I'm in line now for promotion."

"Nick, that's wonderful. You must be thrilled about it."

"Not nearly as much as I am about this. Don't get too excited," he cautioned, "I still have to wait for an opening. It could be soon, it could be awhile, there's just no telling."

"It doesn't matter." She brushed the backs of her fingers

against his cheek. "It's not about whether you're promoted or not. This is about us. You, me, together."

And the kiss was like coming home.

"Ah, young love," said a voice nearby.

"Don't it just get you all choked up?"

They looked up to see O'Hanlan and Knapp leaning out the door, grinning at them.

"Now, didn't I tell you there was a reason Nick was so grumpy?" O'Hanlan said to Knapp.

"Now that we've fixed things up for him, he'll start being human again," Knapp agreed.

"Seems like that ought to be worth another pitcher of beer," O'Hanlan commented.

"You're an operator, O'Hanlan," Sloane told him, grinning.

Nick laughed and swung her around. "And I'm so glad of it."

DON'T MISS...

the books in this mini-series:

FAMILY FOUND

Adding To The Family
Gina Wilkins
November 2005

The Borrowed Ring
Gina Wilkins
December 2005

AVAILABLE FROM

Target • K-Mart • Big W
• selected supermarkets
• bookstores • newsagents

OR

Call Harlequin Mills & Boon
on 1300 659 500 to order now
for the cost of a local call.
NZ customers call (09) 837 1553.

Shop on-line at www.eHarlequin.com.au

Books only available from Harlequin Mills & Boon
for 3 months after the publishing date.
Release dates may be subject to change.

THE PRICE OF PRIVILEGE. THE POWER OF FAMILY.

The Fortunes of Texas are back with a long-awaited new 12 book collection!

Featuring all of your favourite authors including Ann Major, Marie Ferrarella and Laurie Paige.

TWO BOOKS EACH MONTH

BEGINS JANUARY 2006

AVAILABLE FROM BIG W, KMART, TARGET, BORDERS
NEWSAGENCIES AND SELECTED BOOKSTORES.

Shop online at www.eHarlequin.com.au
or call 1300 659 500 (AU), 09 837 1553 (NZ) for home delivery

FT1205

Available Next Month

Marriage, Interrupted
Karen Templeton

Where He Belongs
Gail Barrett

The Sheik And The Virgin Secretary
Susan Mallery

Under The Mistletoe
Kristin Hardy

Past Imperfect
Crystal Green

Her Special Charm
Marie Ferrarella

AVAILABLE FROM
Target • K-Mart • Big W • Borders • selected supermarkets
• bookstores • newsagents

OR

Call Harlequin Mills & Boon on 1300 659 500 to order
for the cost of a local call. NZ customers call (09) 837 1553.

Shop on-line at www.eHarlequin.com.au

explores the dramas of living and loving

Harlequin Mills & Boon

Special Edition

6 Brand New Stories Each Month

Get your favourite books delivered direct to your home!

There's so many benefits - here's why you should subscribe:

☑ **FREE Home Delivery** - no postage and handling charge.

☑ **No risk and no obligation** - no minimum number of books you have to buy and you can cancel or suspend your subscription at anytime!

☑ **Get your books earlier than the stores** - delivered direct to your home!

☑ **Our friendly customer service team really do care** - they are more than happy to answer any questions and help with your account.

☑ **You'll never need to search in the bookstores again** - the best books will be delivered to your home every month.

☑ **Choose from 13 different series of romance novels** - there really is something for everyone!

Save $$$

Save time

Call now!
Australia: 1300 659 500
New Zealand: (09) 837 1553

DTC01

Send in for a
FREE BOOK
today!

How would you like to escape into a world of romance and excitement? A world in which you can experience all the glamour and allure of romance and seduction?

No purchase necessary - now or ever!

To receive your FREE Harlequin Mills & Boon romance novel, simply fill in the coupon and send it to the address below, together with $1.00 worth of loose postage stamps (80 cents in NZ) to cover postage and handling (please do not send money orders or cheques). There is never any obligation to buy!

Send to: HARLEQUIN MILLS & BOON FREE BOOK OFFER
Aust: PO Box 693, Strawberry Hills, NSW, 2012
NZ: Private Bag 92122, Auckland, 1020

Harlequin
Mills & Boon
Direct to you

✂ —

Please send me my FREE Harlequin Mills & Boon Sexy romance valued at $6.15 (NZ$7.25). I have included $1.00 worth of loose postage stamps (80 cents in NZ). Please do not stick them to anything.

Name: Mrs / Ms / Miss / Mr: _____

Address: _____

_____P/Code _____

Daytime Tel. No.: (_____)_____

FBBP05/ZFBBP5

This offer is restricted to one free book per household. Only original coupons with $1.00 worth of loose postage stamps (80 cents in NZ) will be accepted. Your book may differ from those shown. Offer expires 31st December, 2005 or while stocks last. Offer only available to Australian and NZ residents over 18 years. You may also receive offers from other reputable companies as a result of this application. If you do not wish to share in this opportunity please tick the box. ☐